中国莎士比亚研究

（第 5 辑）

四川外国语大学莎士比亚研究所
中国外国文学学会莎士比亚研究分会　主　办

李伟民　主　编

西南交通大学出版社
·成　都·

图书在版编目（CIP）数据

中国莎士比亚研究. 第5辑 / 李伟民主编. —成都：西南交通大学出版社，2022.11

ISBN 978-7-5643-8976-5

Ⅰ. ①中… Ⅱ. ①李… Ⅲ. ①莎士比亚（Shakespeare，William 1564–1616）– 戏剧文学 – 文学研究 Ⅳ. ①I561.073

中国版本图书馆 CIP 数据核字（2022）第 197305 号

Zhongguo Shashibiya Yanjiu
(Di-5 Ji)

中国莎士比亚研究
（第 5 辑）

李伟民　主编

责任编辑	郭发仔
助理编辑	张地木
封面设计	原谋书装
出版发行	西南交通大学出版社 （四川省成都市金牛区二环路北一段 111 号 西南交通大学创新大厦 21 楼）
发行部电话	028-87600564　028-87600533
邮政编码	610031
网址	http://www.xnjdcbs.com
印刷	四川煤田地质制图印刷厂
成品尺寸	185 mm × 260 mm
印张	17.75
插页	4
字数	465 千
版次	2022 年 11 月第 1 版
印次	2022 年 11 月第 1 次
书号	ISBN 978-7-5643-8976-5
定价	98.00 元

中華药学

曹禺题

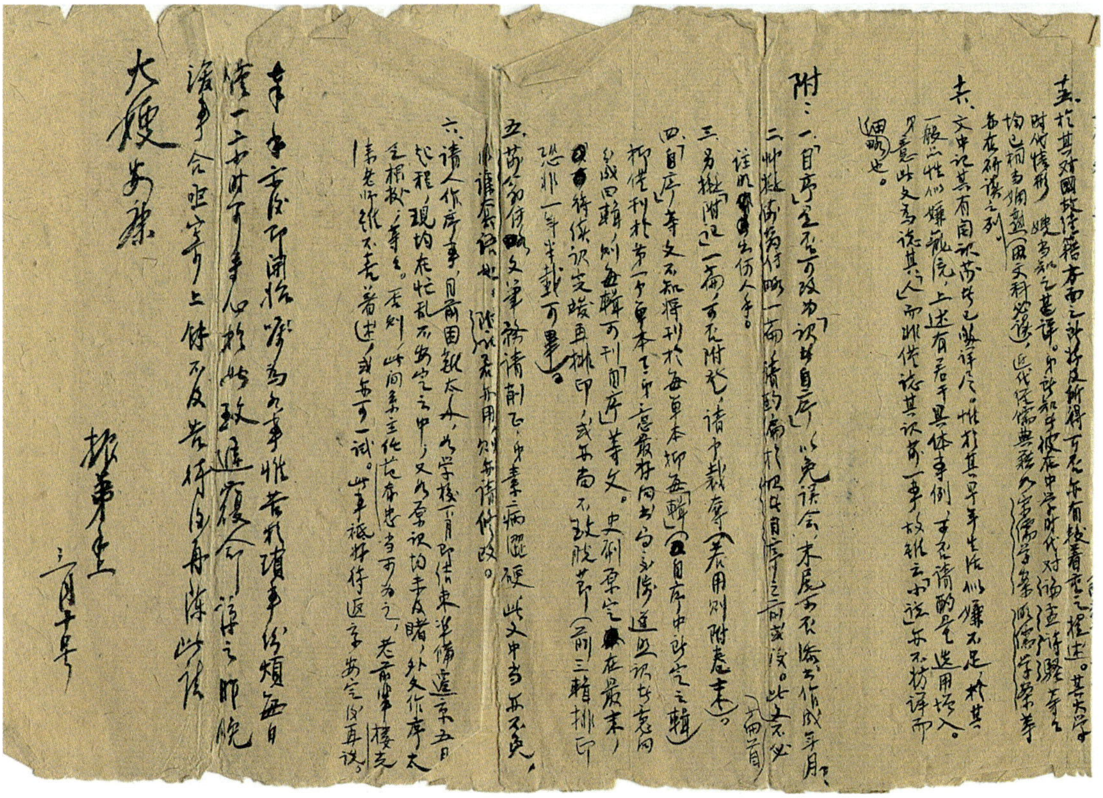

朱文振《对“译者小志”拟商数点》（2）*

* 学术原因，（1）暂不公开。

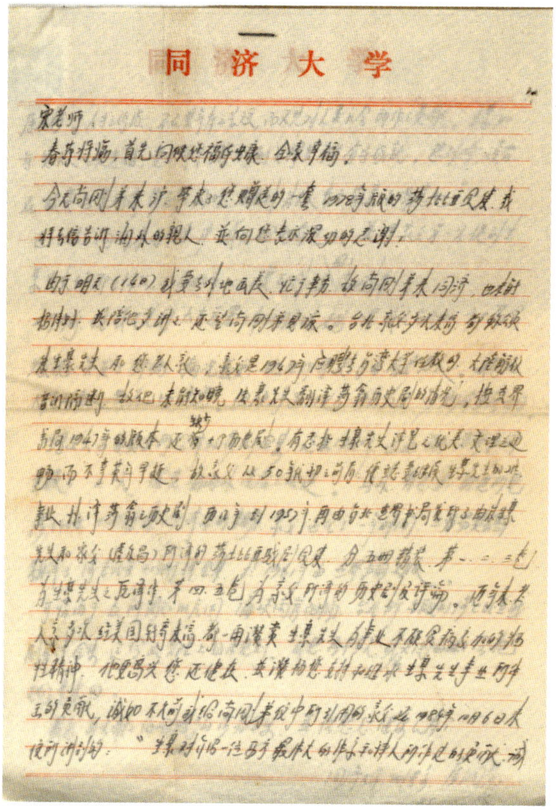

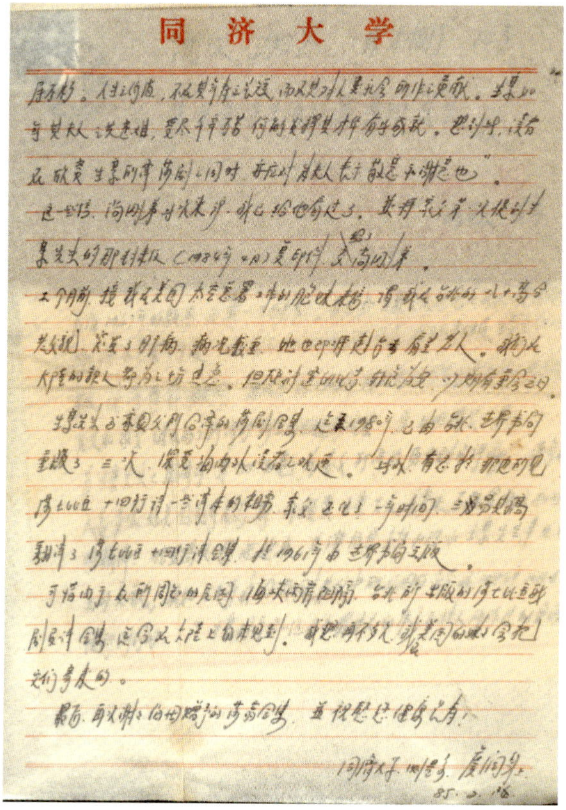

虞润身教授（虞尔昌之子）致宋清如（1985 年 2 月 13 日）信件

《中国莎士比亚研究》编委会

目　录

第一编　莎士比亚与世界

第二编　莎士比亚悲剧研究

第三编　莎士比亚与西方文学

第四编 续史贯珍

第五编 翻译研究

第六编 莎学书简（5）

第七编 莎学信息

第一编

莎士比亚与世界

George Eliot's and George Henry Lewes's Engagement with the Bard Shakespeare: Reflections on "mid"-Nineteenth-Century English Readings

William Baker

【**Abstract**】The great Victorian writer George Eliot (Mary Anne Evans, 1819-1880) and her partner, significant other George Henry Lewes (1817-1878), philosophical writer, literary critic, dramatist, actor, editor, loved Shakespeare. Eliot's engagement is clear from her novels where she cites the bard, 31 times in her chapter epigraphs, more than any other writer, apart from herself. In her letters, she mentions Shakespeare over one hundred times, and also in her notebooks and journals on innumerable occasions. Her partner's engagement with Shakespeare is evident too, in his early acting, in his literary criticism that had an impact upon subsequent English Shakespearian criticism (see Hirshberg: 183-184), and in his miscellaneous prose, letters and marginalia. In this paper, I will present the evidence of their love for Shakespeare, discuss what specifically in Shakespeare appealed to them, explore differences in their responses to Shakespeare, and what their Shakespearean engagements reveal about their work, themselves and, very briefly, the ways in which they reflect elements of the reception of Shakespeare at the time.

【**Key Words**】George Eliot; George Henry Lewes; Shakespeare

乔治·艾略特和乔治·亨利·路易斯与莎翁的际会：对 19 世纪中期英文阅读的思考

威廉·贝克

【**摘　要**】维多利亚时代的伟大作家乔治·艾略特（玛丽·安妮·埃文斯，1819—1880）和她的伴侣，杰出的乔治·亨利·路易斯（1817—1878），哲学作家、文学评论家、剧作家、演员、编辑，都热爱莎士比亚。艾略特与莎翁的际会从她的小说中清晰可见。她在小说中引用莎翁超过 31 次，远超其他作家，除此之外，在她的章节引言中、信件中引用也超过 100 次，在她的笔记本和日记中的引用更是不胜枚举。她的伴侣与莎翁的际会也是显而易见的，在他早期的表演中，在他奠定英国莎士比亚批评根基的文学批评中，在他的杂文、信件和旁注中。本文将展示他们热爱莎士比亚的证据，讨论莎士比亚作品中特别吸引他们的地方，探索他们对莎士比亚作品的不同反应，以及从他们与莎士比亚作品的接触对他们作品的影响，他们本身以及反映出来当时接受莎士比亚作品的方式。
【关键词】乔治·艾略特；乔治·亨利·路易斯；莎士比亚

Daniel Deronda (1876), George Eliot's final published novel begins with an epigraph or introductory motto: “Men can do nothing without the make-believe of a beginning”. Setting the gender issue aside, let me, begin this presentation at the end of George Eliot's career, with her last published novel *Daniel Deronda.* There is, in addition to this introductory motto, a quotation to the work as a whole beginning “let they chief terror of thine own soul.” To put it simply, watch yourself, your vanity, your ego, and drives because they may lead you into deep waters and trouble. Both these prefiguring guides to what is occur in the rest of the novel have obscured the lines the author wrote on the manuscript, now at the British Library. They were not lines of her own as the other two passages are, but inscribed “To My Dear Husband George Henry Lewes” followed by lines from Shakespeare's Sonnet XXIX beginning “When in disgrace with fortune and men's eyes”. To remind you:

When in disgrace with Fortune and men's eyes
I all alone beweep my outcast state,
And trouble deaf heaven with my bootless cries,
And look upon myself and curse my fate,
Wishing me like to one more rich in hope,
Featured like him, like him with friends possessed,
Desiring this man's art, and that man's scope,
With what I most enjoy contented least;
Yet in these thoughts myself almost despising,
Haply I think on thee, and then my state
(Like to the lark at break of day arising)
From sullen earth sings hymns at heaven's gate.
For thy sweet love remembered such wealth brings
That then I scorn to change my state with kings.

Of course, some of the sentiments expressed here, especially those of dependency upon the other gender, may well not appeal to current views of gender relationships. It must be remembered that George Eliot was writing in the 1870s about something which she deeply felt and found best expressed in Shakespeare's sonnet. It would indeed be tempting to spend the remainder of my presentation explicating what she meant and perceptions of what she meant.

I would like to draw attention to the fact that the “I” of the sonnet appears socially isolated with no means of comfort from fellow human beings or heaven. The speaker has nothing to look forward to in terms of material riches, lacks friends, is jealous of others and is unhappy — “With what I most enjoy contented least”. At the turn of the poem, line nine, the use of “Yet” implies that not all is lost. By thinking "on thee" — a word between "thou" and "you" implying close affection and relationship in late Elizabethan English usage (used frequently in the translation of the King James Bible, 1611, to convey the relationship of the human being with the Divine) the sonnet and its speaker take a turn. Wealth, prosperity, money, and social position all are subsumed. What becomes more important is "thy sweet love remembered."

Daniel Deronda and the quoted lines are dedicated to "To My Dear Husband George Henry Lewes". Now Lewes was not officially her husband: they had lived as man and wife since departing for Germany together in 1854. Eliot write this dedication twenty-two years later, in 1876, some_two years before Lewes's death. Major concerns of *Daniel Deronda* and much of her work are the need of human beings for another, the problems of_social isolation and its consequences, the difficulties of relationships based on power, and money, and the devastating consequences that such relationships can bring to the human beings involved.

I have begun with these allusions because they demonstrate the way in which Eliot used Shakespeare creatively and what Shakespeare meant to her personally. Quotes from Shakespeare are used 31 times in her final three novels when she began to use citations at the start of her chapters to indicate their essence. They are used on 14 occasions in *Felix Holt*: [DON'T READ OUT-SHOW: just give a number of times in each novel]

8 Ⅱ Henry Ⅳ, Ⅲ.i.97

9 King John, Ⅲ.i.15; Richard Ⅱ, Ⅱ.ii.9-12

13 Richard Ⅱ, Ⅳ.i.166-67

23 Ⅱ Henry Ⅳ, Ⅴ.i.5-7

24 Midsummer Night's Dream, Ⅳ.ii.5

26 Henry Ⅴ, Ⅰ.i.28-31

27 Sonnet xxiii.14; Coriolanus, Ⅱ.iii.124-28

28 Titus Andronicus, Ⅳ.iii.83-85

30 Coriolanus, Ⅲ.i.255-60

33 Julius Caesar, Ⅲ.ii.265

36 Ⅱ Henry Ⅳ, Ⅲ.i.92-93

40 Ⅰ Henry Ⅵ, Ⅴ.iii.78-79

Twelve times in *Middlemarch*:

24 Sonnet xxxiv. 1 1-12

26 Troilus and Cressida, Ⅱ.iii.3-5

32 The Tempest, Ⅱ.i.288

33 Ⅱ Henry Ⅵ, Ⅲ.iii.32-33

41 Twelfth Night, Ⅴ.i.408-09

42 Henry Ⅷ, Ⅲ.ii.297-98

58 Sonnet xciii.5-12

60 Ⅱ Henry Ⅳ, Ⅲ.ii.77-78

66 Measure for Measure, Ⅱ.i.17-18

71 Measure for Measure, Ⅱ.i.133-38

77 Henry Ⅴ, Ⅱ.ii.138-40

82 Sonnet 1.14

On five occasions in *Daniel Deronda*:

5 Much Ado About Nothing, Ⅲ.ii.52-54

12 I HenryⅣ, Ⅴ. ii.82-85

31 The Winter's Tale, Ⅳ.iv.576-77

53 Antony and Cleopatra, Ⅴ.ii.1-2

59 RichardⅡ, Ⅱ.iii.46-47

To repeat, she quotes the bard in her letters over one hundred times, and also in her notebooks and journals on innumerable occasions. The plays most frequently cited, from letters written over nearly forty years, are *As You Like It*, *Hamlet*, *Macbeth*, *Othello*, and, *The Winter's Tale*. The notebooks she used in the preparation of her novels are replete with Shakespearean citations, with extracts that appealed to her at the time and sometimes weave their way into her work through allusions or direct citations.

In her work, "by alluding to other texts, characters, or allegorical figures (Love, Mischief, Rumour), the epigraphs establish themes, identify the genesis of a character," flesh out that which appears abstract "create irony through discrepancies, or metaphorically sketch in ideas or characters subsequently fleshed out in chapters." Furthermore "the Shakespearean epigraphs work with other allusions to instruct, entertain, and build dramatic structures within the novels" (Van den Broek: 378: Higdon: 127-51). Unfortunately, a specific copy text of Shakespeare that she and Lewes frequently used hasn't been located. A reconstruction of her and George Henry Lewes's libraries and sales of their books indicate that they used various editions. There is the 9 volume *Works* ed. W.G. Clark, J. Glover and W. A. Wright published in Cambridge from 1863-1866, Clark and Wright's edition of *Hamlet,* Oxford 1872, Wright's edition of *King Lear*, Oxford 1875, their present whereabouts are unknown. She and Lewes did own a copy of what is known as the fourth Folio from 1685. This is now at the Folger Library in Washington DC but appears to lack marginalia. (Baker: *Libraries*, items 822-832, p.107).

Perhaps of more interest is the 12-volume second edition of Charles Knight's edited and published *The Comedies, Histories, Tragedies, and Poems of William Shakspere* (1842-1844). This is also_now at the Folger Library and contains Lewes's extensive annotations, marginalia and other indications of engaged reading. There are a few instances too of George Eliot's marginal linings. Lewes read with pen and pencil in hand, to mark passages that appealed to him for one reason or another. His markings are in the form of underscoring, perpendicular lines, marginal explanation marks, and detailed observations (also in the margins) placed next to printed words. Some of his notes extend from the margins of pages to the foot of the following page. Or they are distributed, scattered across the pages in between and other times overlapping with Knight's text, Knight's notes found at the foot of his page or his "Supplementary Notes" at the conclusion of each act.

Helpfully Lewes dated his reading, a characteristic of his annotative practices, found elsewhere and not only in his copy of Shakespeare. Thus, for instance, an August 1843 dating is found at the conclusion of *Hamlet* Act IV scene vii. Laertes worked up by the King decides to take revenge upon Hamlet. Lewes underscores "I will do't" and "I'll anoint my sword" and places two lines at the conclusion of the short speech: "It may be death." Lewes also underscores the Queen's "There is a willow grows aslant a brook, That shows his hoar leaves in the glassy stream" He underscores "hoar leaves" twice and other words and lines in Gertrude's powerful melancholy speech.

It is Laertes' lines that evoke Lewes's extensive marginalia. He writes:

> After long considerations I venture to assert that there is a double fault in this scene: an artistic & asthetic [sic] fault.
>
> I Artistically the whole plan is confused. If Laertes believes that Hamlet murdered Polonius why does he not insist on trial? Or if fearing the trial of a prince he resolves on assassination, why not set about it in a rational & consistent style, and set aside such questionable & uncertain means as he proposes?
>
> 11 Asthetically [sic] it is a violation of truth of character or else too unprepared a development, to make Laertes honorable, upright, & noble-and then suddenly to make him propose an unnecessary and treacherous villainy.
>
> For either fault a modern poet would get no mercy; nor would he deserve it. (Aug[t]1843)
>
> Note also that this very Laertes when he suspects the King has killed his Father meets him like an open foe in spite of the divinity that doth hedge a King, yet now he must poison his weapon for Hamlet!
>
> (Cf Baker: *Hamlet:* 64-65).

Germane to a consideration of Lewes's reading of *Hamlet* and other plays in the Knight edition (dated by Lewes between 1843 and 1844), is his lengthy review essay "Shakspere and his Editors" in the *Foreign Quarterly Review*, 43 (1845) 21-41. In this review, Lewes assesses at length Charles Knight's twelve-volume edition. Lewes's marginalia and his responses to individual plays can be viewed as preparations for his article. Lewes's essay may be perceived as a liturgy for the state of Shakespearean editing and commentary in the England of his time. For instance, Lewes observes:

> Except Pope and Johnson, no man of preeminent intelligence has under-taken the task demanding an immense intelligence: the task of restoring the text almost hopelessly corrupt. Perhaps the worst evil of this corruption is the maggots it has generated. Had Coleridge disliked the opium and possessed industry, he might have given the world an edition which would have endured.

Lewes adds that "the greatest of all poets has had no poets for an editor" (41, 40). There is some unfairness here in the comment relating to Coleridge's lack of industry, which Lewes cites throughout his article and draws approvingly upon Coleridge's observations in his marginalia.

Lewes's review takes up much space on the deficiency of English editing rather than to a consideration of individual plays. His marginalia represents his close reading of the time of Shakespeare's texts, and also demonstrates, as does his intertextuality, an awareness of editorial commentary and concern with metrics.

Lewes lambasted the editions he had access to. It is difficult to resist citing his contempt for the Malone-Boswell edition published in 1821. Here is Lewes:

> We can nowhere point to such an accumulated mass of industry, which is at the same time such a mass of rubbish. It is impossible to conceive a greater amount of stupidity, dribbling, pedantry, senseless learning, collected into one work. Note upon note, blunder upon blunder, conjecture upon conjecture, drivel upon drivel: without order, without method, wearisome, tantalizing, and profitless [cited Murphy: p.130]

Briefly, then, I turn to Lewes's intertextuality which emerges in both his marginalia and his article with references to Aeschylus' and other Greek texts' tragedies. Lewes also cites the works of the French historian Michelet, German commentators on Shakespeare such as Goethe, Gervinus, Schlegel, Schelling, and others. Amongst English commentators and editors, in addition to near-contemporaries such as Coleridge and Hazlitt, Lewesengages with for instance Pope, Warburton, George Steevens and Thomas Tyrwhitt amongst others.

Lewes's annotations in his copy of Knight's Shakespeare and in his 1845 article demonstrate "patterns in engagement with Shakespeare and European literary traditions. These included Aeschylus and Homer from the Greek tradition; two Italians from the pre-Renaissance period, Boiardo reworked by Berni and Boccaccio; Shakespeare's almost contemporary, the great Spanish dramatist Calderon; and Elizabethan and post-Elizabethan English voices such as Thomas Dekker and John Fletcher." They also reveal an engagement with, until the recently unfashionable area of investigation into how Shakespeare's verse was pronounced at the time he was writing, and his use of metrics and versification (see my "Shakespeare and Others" and "G. H. Lewes Reads *Cymbeline*").

What of Lewes's subsequent engagement with Shakespeare? Much of this is found in his role as a theatre critic and his reactions to contemporary performances found in journals such as *The Leader*, *The Pall Mall Gazette* and elsewhere. Some of his articles are collected together in his *On Actors and the Art of Acting* (1875) containing his strictures on individual performances and demonstrating his perception that Shakespeare should be considered primarily as a dramatist, as a working dramatist and then as a poet: this was a view in opposition to many of the critics of his day (see Hirshberg 179-80).

But what of George Eliot? Her engagement with Shakespeare, as suggested at the start of this presentation, was lifelong. In an early letter, to her friend Sarah Sophia Hennell from [26 November 1846], she "jokes...about the writer's double problem-the reluctance to write and the urge to write" (Hardy, 2006, p.154). "My letter writing pen is entirely at the mercy of a host of little sprites, more timely and ethereal than the train of Queen Mab, and it is only when they come tickling my forefingers and thumb, making them itch for the same pen, that the strong repulsion from it is overcome" (*L.*, I. 228). As Hardy astutely indicates "Shakespeare is not invoked as mere mock-solemnity but in creative recognition of Mercutio's brilliant comic demonstration of creative dreaming" (p.154: the reference is to *Romeo and Juliet*, I, iv).

Following her association with Lewes, both of them delighted in reading Shakespeare aloud to each other and, as I said earlier, her journals are replete with references to the Bard. In another [5 December 1859]letter to her old friend Sarah Sophia Hennell, she wrote following the publication of her first fiction, *Scenes of Clerical Life* [1858]:

in opposition to most people who love to *read* Shakspere I like to see his plays acted better than any others: his great tragedies thrill me, let them be acted how they may. I think it is something like what I used to experience in old days listening to uncultured preachers - the emotions lay hold of one too strongly for one to care about the medium (*L.*, 111: 228-29).

For her Shakespeare's dramatic power was important. There are Shakespearean_allusions in early fiction, to Shakespearean characters and the association with them to make the readers more understanding and sympathetic towards them. For instance, in her story "The Sad Fortunes of the Reverend Amos Barton" the central character of the title is mentioned in comparison with the antihero of the Scottish play and with_Hotspur in *Henry IV, Part One*, not because he has the same standing but to remind the readers that he has ideas, feelings, and beliefs too. These are confused and lack reason yet they are still deeply felt and held.

Clearly, as her fiction developed, and matured, the use of Shakespeare took on greater subtlety and suggestiveness._Many instances of Shakespearian echoes in her work can be given. For instance, in the depiction of disillusionment, lost love and its resurrection in *Silas Marner* (1861) there are echoes of *The Winter's Tale*. In *Middlemarch*, for instance, the epigraph to chapter 60 conjures up Justice Shallow's (2 *Henry IV*, 111.ii. 73) "Good phrases are surely, and ever were, very commendable" response to Bardolph's use of the seemingly impressive word "accommodated" a few lines earlier (l.66). This is both comic and on another level reveals the ways in which minor characters provide a commentary or parallel to the main action: here snobbery and deception.

In a notebook, dating from the period in which she was working on the composition of *Middlemarch*, Eliot writes passages from 24 of Shakespeare's sonnets that provide instances of Shakespeare's "Confidence in his poetic immortality":

Here are only 24, & some of these one lingers over rather for the music of a few verses in them than for their values as wholes. I am convinced that the greater number of the sonnets are artificial products, governed by the fashion of sentiment which had probably grown out of the imitation of the Italian poets. These "sugared sonnets among private friends" have owned much of their mysteriousness to the imaginations of writers who set out with the notion that Shakespeare was in all things exceptional, & so never think of comparison with contemporaries even when the occasion is thrust upon them.

The probable date for these remarks, as with others in this notebook, is 1869. Following this passage, the date "1872" is inserted, accompanied by the observation: "Nevertheless, I love the Sonnets better & better whenever I returned to them. They are tunes that for some undefinable reason suit my frame" (J.C.Pratt and V A Neufeldt p.213: cf. Van Den Broek p.379).

The later date coincides with the conclusion of *Middlemarch* and the gestation of *Daniel Deronda* which returns us to the beginning of this presentation, or to quote another Eliot "in my end is my beginning."

To sum up then, the evidence from Eliot's and Lewes's published works, their letters, journals and notebooks, demonstrates an abiding love for Shakespeare's drama and poetry. In this, they were in the company of many of their contemporaries, in a period that witnessed the mass production of Shakespeare in print and proliferation of scholarly attention [see Murphy].

参考文献

[1] WILLIAM B. 2021. G. H. Lewes reads Cymbeline: his annotations in Knight's Shakespeare[J]. Notes & Queries, September.

[2] WILLIAM B. 2017. George Henry Lewes's reading of Hamlet[J]. George Eliot—George Henry Lewes Studies (1): 53-67.

[3] WILLIAM B. 2020. George Henry Lewes's reading of Othello[J]. George Eliot—George Henry Lewes Studies (2): 103-153.

[4] WILLIAM B. 1981. The libraries of George Eliot and George Henry Lewes[M]. Univ of Victoria Dept of English.

[5] WILLIAM B. 2021. Shakespeare and Others: an intertextual miscellany[J]. Medieval and Renaissance Studies (5): 3-15.

[6] ELIOT G. 1876. Daniel Deronda[M]. Edinburgh and London: William Blackwood and Sons.

[7] ELIOT G. The George Eliot Letters[M]. G. S Haight eds. 9 vols. Yale University Press.

[8] ELIOT G. Middlemarch: A Study of Provincial Life[M]. Edinburgh and London: William Blackwood and Sons.

[9] ELIOT G. 1858. Scenes of Clerical Life[M]. 2 vols. Edinburgh and London: William Blackwood and Sons.

[10] ELIOT G. 1861. Silas Marner[M]. Edinburgh and London: William Blackwood and Sons.

[11] HARDY B. 2006. George Eliot: A critic's biography[M]. London: Continuum.

[12] HIRSHBERG E W. 1970. George Henry Lewes[M]. New York: Twayne.

[13] KNIGHT C. The Comedies, Histories, Tragedies and Poems of William Shakespeare[M]. 2nd ed. 12 vols. London: Charles Knight & Co.

[14] LEWES G H. 1875. On actors and the art of acting[M]. London: Smith Elder.

[15] LEWES G H. 1845. Shakespeare and his editors[J]. Foreign Quarterly Review, 43: 21-41.

[16] MALONE E, BOSWELL J. 1821. The plays and poems of William Shakespeare[M]. London: F. C. and J. Rivington.

[17] MURPHY A. 2021. Shakespeare in print: a history and chronology of Shakespeare[M]. Cambridge: Cambridge University Press 2021

[18] PRATT JC, NEUFELDT V A. 1979. George Eliot's "Middlemarch" notebooks: a transcription[M]. Berkeley, Los Angeles, London: University of California Press.

[19] Mr. William Shakespeare's comedies, histories, and tragedies [M]. 4th Ed.

[20] CLARK W G, WRIGHT W A. 1872. Hamlet[M]. Oxford: Clarendon Press.

[21] CLARK W G. 1875. King Lear[M]. Oxford: Clarendon Press.

[22] BROEK V D. 2000. "Shakespeare William" in Oxford Reader's Companion to George Eliot[M]. Oxford & New York: Oxford University Press.

作者简介：William Baker，北伊利诺伊大学教授，主要从事莎士比亚研究。

让他当恺撒吧[①]

迈克尔·道布森（著）　鲁跃峰（译）

【摘　要】本文参照心理学、社会文化历史学、跨文化和经典阐释学等方法，梳理了克里夫著《莎士比亚暴乱》[②]一书中的结论，勾画了美国平民演员福雷斯特和英国贵族演员麦克雷迪在莎剧演出中一系列冲突，以莎剧中诸多角色、场景、演员为背景，以纽约阿斯特广场暴乱为突破口，分析了 19 世纪英美两国莎剧文化的历史、现状、传播空间组合及生态景观分布、考证了莎剧最佳演员竞争暴乱背后是美国平民的反英、反精英及反富人情绪的爆发。最后得出了一个悖论式的结论：反对英国的美国的广袤大地需要英国的伟大的莎士比亚，英国的莎士比亚戏剧需要当年逃避英国莎士比亚戏剧的那些美国人的后代的狂放不羁的舞台。

【关键词】迈克尔·道布森；奈杰尔·克里夫；《莎士比亚暴乱：19 世纪美国的报复、戏剧和死亡》；福雷斯特；麦克雷迪；莎士比亚戏剧

Let Him Be Caesar

Michael Dobson

【Abstract】Adopting the methods such as psychology, socio-cultural history, cross-cultural and classical hermeneutics, this book review combs the conclusions of Cliff's *The Shakespeare Riots*. Employing a series of conflicts between American civilian actor

① 本文原载于《伦敦书评》，2007 年 8 月 2 日（*London Review of Books*, August 2nd 2007），经作者授权，由鲁跃峰先生译为中文并给予注释。

② 奈杰尔·克里夫（Nigel Cliff），历史学家、传记作家和评论家。曾就读于牛津大学，并在那里获得了贝丁顿英国文学奖，《伦敦时报》的戏剧和电影评论家，《经济学人》和其他出版物的撰稿人。他的第一本书《莎士比亚暴乱：19 世纪美国的报复、戏剧和死亡》（*The Shakespeare Riots: Revenge, Drama and Death in 19th-Century America*），是 1849 年纽约阿斯特广场歌剧院暴乱的社会研究和文化史研究，首次印刷 25000 册，入围国家艺术写作奖，并被《华盛顿邮报》评为 2007 年最佳非小说类书籍之一。书中描述了当时两位著名的莎剧演员威廉·查尔斯·麦克雷迪（William Charles Macready，1793—1873）和埃德温·福雷斯特（Edwin Forrest, 1806—1802）之间的小争执如何演变为 1849 年 5 月 10 日的那场暴力血腥的阿斯特广场公众暴乱，美国历史上最致命的一次，致 25 人死亡，100 人左右受伤，表面起因是美国本土平民演员埃德温·福雷斯和英国贵族演员威廉·查尔斯·麦克雷迪这两位莎士比亚演员各自的粉丝团对于谁是最好的莎士比亚演员的竞争。但其中有更深层次的因素在起作用：广大平民的反英、反精英以及反富人情绪的爆炸。据称，这两位演员象征着美国文化中贫富对立的两个阶层以及英美两个国家之间新旧制度的对立。有趣的是，阿斯特广场歌剧院此后从未再恢复演出，因此获得了“DisAstor Place”（演员被侮辱、驱赶的灾难之地）的名声（DisAstor 这个单词由 Disaster 灾难；Dis-actor 驱赶演员、侮辱演员这两个单词合成而来）和“Massacre Opera House（麦克雷迪福雷斯特大屠杀歌剧院）”的绰号（Massacre 意思为大屠杀，这个单词的发音中包含着这两个人名的部分发音：Macready 麦克雷迪，Forrest 福雷斯特）。该场所最终被出售，在骚乱发生 50 年后，它被拆除，取而代之的是一个名为克林顿堂（Clinton Hall）的图书馆，该图书馆至今仍在使用（尽管现在是星巴克）。

Forrestt and British noble actor Macready in Shakespeare's plays as the axis, with many characters, scenes and actors in Shakespeare's play as the background, taking the Riot in Astor Square in New York as a breakthrough, this paper humorously analyzes the history, current situation, the combination of communication space and ecological landscape distribution of Shakespeare's drama culture in Britain and America in the 19th century, and verifies that behind the riot of competition for the best actors of Shakespeare's drama is the outbreak of anti-British, anti-elitist and anti-upperclass society feelings of American civilians. Finally, this paper comes to a paradoxical conclusion: the United States, which opposes Britain, needs great British Shakespeare for her vast lands, and British Shakespeare's plays need the unrestrained stage of the descendants of those Americans who evaded British Shakespeare's plays.
【Key Words】 Michael Dobson; Nigel Cliff; *The Shakespeare Riots: Revenge, Drama and Death in 19th-Century America*; Forrest; Macready; Shakespeare's plays

2005 年，当奈杰尔·克里夫在写他关于阿斯特广场暴乱的精彩著作时，我也常去那几个他查阅过资料的档案馆，即纽约表演艺术公共图书馆和纽约历史学会，去做同样的事情。我对 1849 年 5 月 10 日的事件着迷已久，离开曼哈顿之前，我必须去阿斯特广场朝圣。但到了那儿却发现，根本就没有任何东西表示对纽约最血腥事件之一中的那 26 位遇难者的纪念；也没有在任何地方提到美国演员埃德温·福雷斯特和英国演员威廉·查尔斯·麦克雷迪这两个人，正是他们长期以来对谁是这个时代最伟大的麦克白扮演者的竞争，最终导致 15000 多人的暴徒和一支国民警卫队的分遣队发生冲突。如今，这个社区几乎不像纽约市阶级斗争的前线。这里已不再是高雅住宅区的社交名流和鲍厄里帮派成员的热闹的聚集地，而是挤满了纽约大学的学生和富有的购物者，如今他们最大的聚会地点不再是当年暴徒们寻衅滋事的那个歌剧院的周围，而是一家店名为凯伦的素食咖啡馆。

然而，又一个下午我没去图书馆查资料，相反，我去了纽约西 44 号大街贝拉斯科剧院观看了《尤利乌斯·恺撒》的日场，没想到，这更能说明培育福雷斯特和他的那群肌肉发达的粉丝的俱乐部的文化。是丹泽尔·华盛顿扮演的布鲁图斯，恺撒在共和政体的美国比在不列颠更受欢迎。就像在福雷斯特的时代一样，每当他们的心仪的明星没能出演时，许多观众都会毫不掩饰地大声说话，考虑到二队演员阵容的表演水平，这似乎并不算太不合适。然而，每当华盛顿出演时，他们都会表现出极大的热情，现场的火爆往往会淹没布鲁图斯的台词。意识到他的作品将会被视为这样一位伟大演员的载体，导演勇敢地处理了莎士比亚在第 1 幕第 2 景之前布鲁图斯还未在舞台上露面的问题，于是，在开场的街景中，在其他人说任何台词之前，导演为他和波西亚添加了一个没有台词的配角，在这样小小的一段表演过程中，即使只不过是一个微不足道的额外改动，这个无台词的配角也收到了那种狂喜的喝彩声。这种喝彩，对于一个英国舞台演员来说，即使用不着等待一辈子，也可能要等上一整夜才能等来。

华盛顿扮演的布鲁特斯非常出色，这是他在好莱坞扮演多年的又一位高贵谦逊的大众英雄—— 自从我在整理一本由著名演员撰写的关于在莎士比亚悲剧中扮演主角的随笔时，我想演出之后我应该去后台见他一面，看他是否有可能参与此事。但是我这样打算时却没有考虑到纽约大众的因素。在斯特拉特福德或伦敦，你通常只需走到舞台门口并提出请求，就可以与一位著名的莎士比亚演员安静地交谈，但在百老汇却完全不是这样，至少当丹泽尔·华盛顿出演时不是这样。尽管观众们根本就没有好好观看演出，但在不吝赞美之词的谢幕声终于结束的那一刻，大多数观众似乎都从剧院里来到了舞台门外的街道上，而在这里，他们希望能够多看一眼华盛顿，甚至有可能请他在节目单上亲笔签名，他们紧靠着金属警戒线，冲向路中间(已经形成交通阻塞了)，并试图与一支面目可憎的保安队谈判企图进入，但没有成功。如果让这支保安队来对付阿斯特广场暴徒，他们可能会比1849年的那支国民警卫队的分遣队军团做得更好。最后，我几乎被急切的人群挤得喘不过气来，我只能在华盛顿经过时往他手里塞了一张明信片，这是当时唯一可能的与他交流的方式，因为当时整个世界都像剧中那些绝望的请愿者一样群情汹涌，激动异常。正如一些莎士比亚笔下的罗马平民，因为欢迎布鲁图斯的平等主义言论，用“让他当恺撒吧！”的口号为他先发制人的暴政辩护一样，华盛顿的粉丝们，即使是在把他当成是一个普通人和生活中的大众明星为他欢呼时，也似乎不能不把他视为一个神。

美国观众的民主理想与明星体系中逐步形成的那种不怎么高尚的英雄崇拜之间的矛盾在莎剧的先驱演员埃德温·福雷斯特的生活中得到了最好的体现，他被崇拜他的现代传记作家理查德·穆迪（Richard Moody）描述为“第一个拒绝认同国家文化自卑情结的演员”。然而，正如莎士比亚暴乱所表明的那样，福雷斯特深受这种自卑情结的影响，他一生中的大部分时间都在告诉英国人他是多么坚决地拒绝接受这一观点。当没机会可以出演莎士比亚戏剧的主角去勇敢地展示那种自我声称是最好的莎士比亚演员时，他会故意选择那些可以强化他的自我塑造，使他成为一个桀骜不驯、粗壮的美国爱国主义化身的角色。他最喜欢的角色有罗伯特·蒙哥马利·伯德（Robert Montgomery Bird）的情节剧《角斗士》（*The Gladiator*，1831年）中斯巴达克斯，在该剧中，斯巴达克斯被塑造成一个善良的叛逆者，对抗一些看起来非常英伦的贵族；还有罗伯特·康拉德（Robert Conrad）的《杰克·凯德》（*Jack Cade*，1835年）中的那位反贵族英雄，一位殉道者，他临死前说道：“奴隶复仇了，我的国家自由了！”也许令人惊讶的是，福雷斯特没有出演自由主义者布鲁特斯，尽管这是出于美学而非意识形态的原因：按照他的标准，这不是一个有足够男子气概或重要的角色。在他出演《恺撒大帝》的少数几次演出中，福雷斯特扮演了那位不那么理智、却给人印象更深的马克·安东尼。但他更喜欢那些莎士比亚式的角色，让他可以在演出时大部分时间都主导舞台，然后以一场壮观的死亡告终：理查三世、哈姆雷特、奥赛罗、李尔王，尤其是麦克白。

考虑到他长期以来形成的仇英心理，以及与麦克雷迪之间那种似乎不可避免的冲突（这仍然是他职业生涯中最著名的事件），福雷斯特准备将自己的声誉如此之多地押在表演英格兰国宝剧作家作品的能力上，这似乎有些奇怪，但到1806年福雷斯特出生时，在这个年轻共和国，莎士比亚已经得到大家普遍认可。事实上，甚至在殖民地起义之前，就有人将莎士比亚戏剧的想象力与新大陆所特有的潜在的发展前景联系起来了。1757年，有人就在德鲁里巷①朗

① 德鲁里巷（Drury Lane）是德鲁里巷皇家剧院（Theatre Royal Drury Lane）的简称，地处伦敦西区科文特花园，是英国戏剧史的缩影。剧院面朝凯瑟琳街，背朝德鲁里巷。最早的建筑历史可追溯到1663年，若还存在就是伦敦最古老的剧院。历史上大部分时期，它是特许剧院，专门上演规定种类的戏剧。1660年代早期托马斯·基利格鲁下令建造这所剧院，雇佣了包括妮尔·格温在内的一批当时著名演员来定期出演剧目。1672年失火，于是基利格鲁又在其基础上重建了更大的一所剧院，1674年开张。这第二栋建筑伫立了将近120年，经任院长为柯莱·西伯、大卫·加里克、理查德·布林斯利·谢立丹。1791年谢立丹将旧建筑拆毁，再次扩大面积。新楼在1794年开张，但是15年后的1809年就再次失火焚毁，现在的建筑建造于1812年，由Benjamin Dean Wyatt设计。埃德蒙·基恩、丹·雷诺等演员曾在这里出演、居住。二战以后主要上演音乐剧。现剧院所有者是作曲家安德鲁·劳埃德·韦伯的公司真正好集团。

诵了一首威廉·哈佛（William Havard）的颂歌[①]，将莎士比亚确定为世界戏剧的哥伦布，并预计一个多世纪后，这位剧作家和这位探险家的雕像将作为原始的建国之父在中央公园（Central Park）面对面地树立起来。莎士比亚作品的价值在边疆地区得到了更加务实的认可，1764 年，探险家托马斯·莫里斯（Thomas Morris）冒险进入现在的伊利诺伊州，令他惊讶的是，他不仅不是第一个来到如此遥远西部的以英语为母语的人，而且当地人已经知道他文化中的皇冠上的宝石到底值多少钱了："一个印第安人……叫小酋长，送给我一本莎士比亚戏剧集作为礼物；一个野蛮人送的奇异礼物，他只是乞求一点火药作为回报，火药在当时是一种比钻石更珍贵的商品。"后来小酋长率领其部落成员屠杀了他探险队的所有其余成员，也许是为了收回这本书，以便能在他的同类再次踏入他们的土地时能够重复交易。但当时莫里斯在自己的独木舟里全神贯注地阅读安东尼和克利奥帕特拉，因而流连忘返，所以逃过了一劫。

独立战争结束了英帝国对这些充满愤怒、前景无法预测的领土的控制，但它并没有将莎士比亚逐出这些领土，尽管事实上那些清教徒的朝圣者祖先从英国移民出去要逃避的事情之一就是莎士比亚戏剧。尽管那些在敌对行动期间接管纽约约翰街剧院的英国军事当局一定想知道他们在 1777 年至 1783 年间在那里上演的《理查三世》《李尔王》《驯悍记》和《麦克白》等作品是否会是大西洋以西的任何其他地方最后的莎士比亚表演，或者是任何其他别的什么东西，他们当地的对手已经开始演出莎士比亚戏剧了。1778 年，义军在新罕布什尔州的朴次茅斯上演了《科里奥拉纳斯》，从而建立了美国军方表演莎士比亚戏剧的传统，并延续多年。1845 年，年轻的尤利西斯·S. 格兰特中尉[②]在得克萨斯州等待自己的部队对墨西哥军队采取行动时，在剧中扮演了苔丝狄蒙娜。

随着对英国的胜利，一场关于在可耻的等级森严的君主制下创作的戏剧是否适合作为真正的民主党人的娱乐的公开辩论开始了，1784 年《自由人杂志》发表的一封读者来信警告说，习惯于每天在舞台上看到国王、公爵和贵族的我们将会逐渐承认他们在我们中间的真实地位。但其他人，包括乔治·华盛顿和约翰·亚当斯[③]，却认为莎士比亚那种未经约束的灵魂应该属

---

① 威廉·哈佛（William Havard，1710?—1778），出生于爱尔兰的英国剧作家、演员。主要作品如下：《坎德培格》（*Skanderbeg*, 1733）基于同名主人公在 15 世纪领导了一场反抗奥斯曼帝国的叛乱的生活所写的悲剧。《查理一世》（*King Charles Ⅰ*，1737）这部剧模仿了莎士比亚历史剧的风格，主要讲述了查理一世在内战中战败后被监禁和被英国共和国处决的故事（本人参演）。《雷古鲁斯：悲剧一种》（*Regulus: A Tragedy*, 1744）马尔库斯·阿蒂利乌斯·雷古鲁斯（Marcus Atilius Regulus），（307 BC—250 BC），是罗马政治家和将军，担任过两届平民执政官（267 BC, 256 BC）。是一个传奇人物。雷古鲁斯于前 267 年第一次任执政官时，率兵征服了伊利里亚人的城市布伦迪西乌姆。前 256 年又率领部队粉碎了迦太基的强大舰队，并随后率领罗马军团在非洲登陆，威胁迦太基本土。之后不久，雷古鲁斯又在克鲁彼亚附近取得一次重大胜利。前 255 年罗马军队在突尼斯被彻底击败他及 500 名罗马士兵被迦太基俘获。关于雷古鲁斯此后的经历没有准确的记载。罗马帝国时代的大诗人贺拉西在他的《诗简》说：迦太基人在前 250 年的一次惨败之后释放了雷古鲁斯，企图通过他与罗马人议和并交换俘虏。但雷古鲁斯回到罗马后却在元老院发表演说，指出绝不能与迦太基人议和，然后自愿遵守了自己的诺言，坚决地跟着使团返回了迦太基，将罗马贵族的信用（fides）表现得淋漓尽致。返回迦太基后，被酷刑处死。这个使雷古鲁斯名垂千古的故事西塞罗也提到过。后世的诗人和演说家们为了增强悲剧效果，说迦太基人愤恨于列古鲁斯怂恿继续战争的做法，用非常残酷的手法将他处死，可能的处死方法是将他的眼皮割去后逼着他眼睛直视太阳；也可能是将他放进了一个装满尖钉的箱子里（本人参演）。《私奔》（*The Elopement*, 1763）（本人参演）。还在《温莎的风流娘儿们》等剧中担任过角色。他被引用最多的论述自由的名言是："一个自由出生的民族最大的荣耀就是把自由传递给他们的孩子。"（The greatest glory of a free-born people is to transmit that freedom to their children.）

② 尤利西斯·S. 格兰特（Ulysses S. Grant, 1822—1885），美国上将、政治人物，第 18 任美国总统。

③ 约翰·亚当斯（John Adams, 1735—1826），美国第一任副总统（1789—1797），其后接替乔治·华盛顿成为美国第二任总统（1797—1801）。

于自由之地，而不是他的出生地，这并没有什么不妥；还有，1795 年，第一部美国版的《莎士比亚全集》，对英文文本的盗版，在福雷斯特的家乡费城出版了，但是加了一篇前言，目的是让那些自命清高的共和党人放心，告诉他们"布道讲坛上对舞台戏剧的那种暴风雨般谴责并不适用任何莎士比亚的舞台，任何理由都不可以"。1786 年，另一位费城人彼得·马科（Peter Markoe）雄辩地总结了美国人对莎士比亚戏剧的民族适应性问题的普遍看法：

喜欢垄断的不列颠啊！不要再自夸
说你们的天才只限于自己的那个小国家啦；
莎士比亚的勇敢精神在寻找我们的西海岸，
这是在诚心赞美造物主的意愿，
并且，正不甘落后地打造一个崛起的时代，
最高贵的吟游诗人需要最高贵的舞台。

而最高贵的舞台倒过来也需要最高贵的演员，埃德温·福里斯特生来就是为了响应这个时代的呼唤—— 或者更确切地说，是通过自我造就响应了时代的这种呼唤。"早年，"他回忆道，"我进行了大量的锻炼，使自己成了现在的我，一个赫拉克勒斯般的大力神。"他从不知羞怯为何物，14 岁时就参加了一个展示笑气的效果的巡回展览，当那位主持人要求一名志愿者时，福雷斯特便大步走上前去，在受笑气影响的情况下，仍能背诵出《理查三世》中那些大段大段的台词，让观众大跌眼镜。他很快就签约在费城的胡桃街剧院演出，在西部巡回演出一段时间后，他在新奥尔良的人气暴涨，开始有了自己的"粉丝"。可是，在这里的学徒生涯中，他并没有专注于剧本阅读和台词朗诵，更多的时候看起来反倒是像一个真正的拓荒者：他在明轮蒸汽机船上喝酒、赌博和打架，挥舞着吉姆·鲍伊亲自送给他的鲍伊刀，向一位英国剧院经理发出决斗挑战；还有，在一个叫普石马塔哈（Push ma ta ha）的乔克托人的陪伴下，度过了一段荒野生活。由于看到埃德蒙·基恩[①]在他的一次美国巡演中的表演，他重新燃起了对莎士比亚的热情；1826 年，21 岁的福雷斯特在纽约首次以奥赛罗的角色亮相，给观众留下了深刻的印象，但搬回东部并没有减少他那种杰克逊式的平民爱国主义热情。他在海报上将自己列为"本土悲剧演员"，还有，1828 年，他从他刚开始赚到的那一笔大钱中拿出 500 美元，悬赏征求"最好的悲剧剧本，要有 5 幕，其中主人公，或是主角，必须是这个国家的原住民"。

最后约翰·奥古斯都·斯通[②]创作的《梅塔莫拉；或者，最后的万帕诺亚格印第安人》胜出，赢得了这个奖项。福雷斯特在接下来的四十年中在《梅塔莫拉》中的表演给人留下了一个这样的印象—— 特别是在边境观众中—— 在密歇根州、俄亥俄州、伊利诺伊州和印第安纳州仍然有被称为梅塔莫拉的城镇。该剧重复了波士顿茶党（Boston Tea Party）首创的修辞手法，美洲大陆殖民者以受害者的身份出现［伪装成莫霍克印第安人（Mohawk Indians）潜入商船，将英国东印度公司运来的一整船茶叶倾入波士顿湾］，福雷斯特就是扮演了这样一个高贵的美洲野蛮人（noble American savage），挺身反抗英国人，尤其是那位邪恶菲茨诺德勋爵。舞

① 埃德蒙·基恩（Edmund Kean），19 世纪早期最著名的莎士比亚演员，其舞台表现艺术被认为无与伦比。
② 约翰·奥古斯都·斯通（John Augustus Stone, 1800—1834），演员、剧作家，出生于马萨诸塞州康科德。他最出名的戏剧《梅塔莫拉；或者，最后的万帕诺亚格印第安人》（*Metamora; or, The Last of the Wampanoags*, 1829），赢得了演员埃德温·福雷斯特（Edwin Forrest）的比赛，该比赛的主角是"这个国家的原住民"。

台上的福雷斯特以其袒胸露背的表演绝技，既表现出了盖尔人传说中的奥西恩（Ossianic）那种夸张的风格神韵，又散发着那种以后会激发阿斯特广场暴徒活力的情感，给人留下了极为深刻的印象：

如果你喜欢亲人的骸骨安息之地的寂静，就唱起那吓破敌胆的战歌，跟我来吧！如果你喜欢初升的太阳火焰永远照亮大神给我们的明亮的湖泊，那就高叫着万帕诺亚格战歌，随我一起走向战场……召唤那些阵亡勇士快乐的灵魂，高呼："我们的土地！我们民族的自由！或者我们的坟墓！"

不幸的是，那唯一善良高贵的野蛮人只是一个死去的高贵的野蛮人，万帕诺亚格人，其中包括梅塔莫拉的幼子，惨遭屠杀。酋长亲自杀死了他的妻子纳米奥基，以防止她落入敌人手中。梅塔莫拉被英军士兵包围，近距离枪战中身受重伤，弥留之际，用尽全身最后的力气，发出对敌人的诅咒、对妻子的呼唤：

最后的万帕诺亚格战士诅咒你们……坟墓的灵魂，我来了！但是梅塔莫拉的诅咒将一直留在白人身上！我就要死了！我的妻子！我的王后！我的纳米奥基！

跌倒，死去；形成舞台造型。鼓声和号角声渐弱，舞台帷幕随之缓缓降下。

这是一种与众不同的表演风格，也是一种与众不同的存在方式，与威廉·查尔斯·麦克雷迪截然不同，麦克雷迪曾于 1827 年去纽约演出，并观看了福雷斯特的第一部《奥赛罗》。麦克雷迪病态地痴迷于那种他永远没有把握实现的尊严，虽然对自己的年轻同行的活力和浑然天成的表演表示极为钦佩，但他更喜欢福雷斯特在梅塔莫拉这样的情节剧中出演，而不是去主演莎士比亚剧中的角色，因为他早就认为那只能是属于他自己的角色，部分原因是他觉得福雷斯特的莎士比亚表演被那些无知的观众廉价的掌声轻松掌声给惯坏了，还有另一部分原因是他从未完全确信福雷斯特可以完全理解莎士比亚戏剧台词的内涵意义。克里夫尖锐地指出，尽管如此，福雷斯特和麦克雷迪还是有很多共同之处，第一次会面时（在福雷斯特 1836 年的英国巡演期间），他们就成为好朋友。但是，接下来的十年中，两人之间的友谊因为生活习惯截然不同不可避免地破裂了：除了那次告别演出之外，这位性格固执僵化的英国中年演员从来不让自己的孩子去看自己的演出；而那位本土悲剧演员则整天与乔克托人一起漫游闲逛。而这背后更深层次的原因还有不列颠和美国的关系日益恶化，但最主要的还是二人性情相似相克：专横霸道、抑郁易感的个性的演员很容易变成病态的自大狂，而且他们年龄越大，相互之间就越不容易相处。

对于特别讨厌的人和事，福雷斯特看似只有一种令人望而生畏的自负和冷漠，但富有同情心的克里夫却恰到好处地解释说，那是因为麦克雷迪总在寂苦中渴望体面的尊敬，并为此不顾一切后果。他的父亲是一位放荡的外省艺人经纪人，把他送进拉格比公学，希望他以后永远别为了生计被迫在剧院工作，而麦克雷迪直到生命结束都坚信这个职业不值得他去做，尽管因家庭破产他还是被迫进入戏剧界。（社交上他会避开大多数同行，并将新成立的加里克俱乐部[①]视为“一个下流肮脏之地”。）在摄政时代[②]剧院的日常生活中，天可怜见，类似于这种对戏剧界的攻击咒骂处处可见，并非没有自己的道理，那些脾气比麦克雷迪更柔顺的人遭受刁难的事情也处处可见。德鲁里巷皇家剧院的经理詹姆斯·温斯顿（James Winston）的日记中经常出现这样的条目：“在排练期间，埃利斯顿把玛格丽姆、艾利森、爱德华兹、托克利和飞利浦这些女演员带进了他的房间，并试着动手动脚，但被拒绝了”（1822 年 4 月 1 日），还有：“演出开始时，大家都在等基恩，等了好几分钟。他的回答是：‘戏剧开始前我总是要做个爱的。’”（1820 年 8 月 16 日）和福雷斯特一样，麦克雷迪也非常欣赏基恩赋予莎士比亚的主人公的那种心理本能行动。但是，在麦克雷迪的青春期，由于这位伟大的戏剧演员因酗酒身体变得太虚弱、又经常出痘，或者就是因为太固执，常常不能上台表演，这时总是由年轻的麦克雷迪随时顶上，这种情况发生得太多了，所以他就不再像福雷斯特那样崇拜基恩，从而失去了对于基恩那种狂放不羁的生活方式，或是对着顶楼楼座那些粗俗的观众大喊大叫表演风格的激情。对年轻的麦克雷迪而言，不列颠，尤其是不列颠戏剧界，还真的没有办法迅速彻底地跟上维多利亚时代的保守风尚。这真是一个遗憾。

克里夫讲述的故事具有极其可悲的讽刺意味，麦克雷迪对于将德鲁里巷和考文特花园皇家剧院视为妓院的贵族的憎恨，更甚于对于那帮将戏剧界视为罗马马戏团的乌合之众的憎恨，所以他怀有梦想逃离不列颠，来到开明的、民主的美国，并与全家定居于马萨诸塞州的剑桥，等待他心目中即将到来的良性英国革命。但在 19 世纪 40 年代的文化氛围中，他竟然被美国记者描绘成一个既傲慢又卑屈、既腐败不堪又奉行精英主义且充满威胁的君主政体的代表，而他与查尔斯·狄更斯的友谊——狄更斯的《美国纪行》（1842）和《马丁·瞿述伟》（1843—1844）曾激怒了美国的民族自豪感—— 也没在其中起到什么好作用。麦克雷迪在美国继续受欢迎的前景被福雷斯特之后全面爆发的宣传战进一步破坏掉了，福雷斯特确信他在 1845 年英国巡演期间收到的差评是麦克雷迪影响的结果，他去爱丁堡看了麦克雷迪主演的《哈姆雷特》，并在演出中发出嘘声，以抗议麦克雷迪对于哈姆雷特所做的那种女性化的演绎。“没有一个英国演员会做这么卑鄙的事！”麦克雷迪在日记里发泄了自己的愤怒。“在整个戏剧历史上从来没有发生过这样的事情！那个低鄙的恶棍！”最后他借用麦克白夫人的台词来嘲笑福雷斯特：“他虽然很想杀人，但却很没种！”哈德良长城内外的报纸，很快还有大西洋两岸的报纸，一连几个星期都在报道这件事。

三年后，当麦克雷迪开始了漫长的告别美国巡演之旅时，民众的情绪也没有平静多少。波士顿的观众很有礼貌，但在福雷斯特的家乡城市，麦克雷迪的麦克白既得到了欢呼，也遭到了嘘声，既有人往台上投掷花束，也有人往台上扔鸡蛋，两人的“粉丝”团体旗鼓相当，

---

① 加里克俱乐部（Garrick Club）位于伦敦西区，于 1831 年为纪念大卫·加里克而建造。大卫·加里克（1717—1779），英国演员、经理和剧作家，是英国舞台史上最多才多艺的人物之一，也是有史以来最著名的英国演员之一，在悲剧、喜剧和闹剧中都游刃有余，他将表演职业从流浪卖艺提高到了受人尊敬的演艺事业程度。在 29 年的经营管理中，他解放了舞台，在场景设计和舞台灯光方面进行了创新。作为一名剧作家，他创作原创作品并改编他人的作品。他主持了作为国家诗人和偶像的莎士比亚剧本创作的修复，但总是依据赞助人的口味来改动莎士比亚剧本，在其中添加了一些自己写的场、景和独白。

② 摄政时代即是由乔治四世 1811 年至 1820 年期间因为父王乔治三世精神失常而兼任摄政王的年代。然而，由于 1795 至 1835 年英国文化艺术领域都深受乔治四世影响，所以人们笼统地将这一时间段统称为摄政年代。摄政时代的英国社会快速发展，滑铁卢和其他欧陆战役的胜利更是振奋了全民的士气，为维多利亚时代的“日不落帝国”的繁盛做了铺垫。而说到摄政年代，不得不提的就是摄政王乔治四世。乔治四世是个矛盾的人物，他因奢靡挥霍、热衷于女人和美酒臭名昭著，却又因其文学艺术造诣与贡献流传于世。

势均力敌。当麦克雷迪在一次谢幕致辞中回应情绪激烈诘难者时，一些人为他欢呼，另一些人则为福雷斯特欢呼。福雷斯特本人对这篇谢幕致辞的报道内容持有异议，两天后便在《大众纪事报》上发表了对麦克雷迪几乎是一篇挑战的文章，嘲笑地把他在爱丁堡攻击对手的原因来了一次老调又重弹，突然间，英国“杰出悲剧演员”（或者用福雷斯特现在的话说，“淌口水说胡话的老朽”）和最后一个万帕诺亚格人的英雄模仿者之间的敌对情绪又一次占领了新闻界的头条位置。“现在有两派，美国人和英国人，我确信前者会胜利”，福雷斯特在给英国出生的妻子的信中写道：“英国人根本就是欠揍……我想，在这个国家，麦克的职业生涯已经遭到致命的打击。这里对他的不满情绪日渐高涨，很快就会蔓延到整个欧洲大陆。”几周后，这对夫妇在一场愈演愈烈的丑闻中分居，有人声称，正是这对夫妻在福雷斯特对麦克雷迪的态度上的分歧导致了这场婚姻的失败。

福雷斯特所说的那种感觉，如果说它从来没有完全覆盖整个大陆的话，也肯定蔓延到了许多剧院，最终蔓延到纽约的街道上。尽管麦克雷迪在新奥尔良受到热烈欢迎，但俄亥俄州的观众甚至比费城的观众更为动荡失控，起哄的花样也更多。麦克雷迪的传记作家威廉·阿切尔（William Archer）决心不让阿斯特广场暴乱掩盖其写作对象的成就（据他所述，这仅仅是“国际社会长期不满情绪的恶性爆发”），他试图淡化那里发生的一件意外事件，但对麦克雷迪来说，这几乎就是用来压垮他的那最后一根稻草了。用阿切尔的话说：“在辛辛那提，在《哈姆雷特》的演出中，一位喜欢开玩笑的绅士把半只羊的尸体扔到了舞台上：但这似乎只是一种充满友善的活泼天性的爆发，而不是一种意见的表达。”但是麦克雷迪还是禁不住注意到，这枚不同寻常的炮弹是专门为福雷斯特在观看其《哈姆雷特》演出发出嘘声的那一幕场景所准备的，他在日记中写道，“说到令人作呕的暴行、猥亵的暴行和恶意的野蛮行为”，将羊扔上舞台绝对会是“在任何文明社区的剧场中都从未发生过的”。

当麦克雷迪到达纽约时，福雷斯特正在等着他，早就计划好了要于 5 月 7 日晚在百老汇剧院主演麦克白，恰好就在麦克雷迪早已定好的在阿斯特广场歌剧院（Astor Place Opera House）主演麦克白这位大领主的同一时间。命中注定这两家演出中会有一家只能演到第 3 幕就没有机会再演下去了，但令人遗憾的是，克里夫在此时没有停下来进一步描述一下麦克雷迪和福雷斯特各自的扮演的麦克白是什么样的，或者说，为什么这两位演员都对这个角色如此着迷。对麦克雷迪来说，麦克白的独白可以为他提供足够的空间，供他在进行性格探索时可以模拟那种清醒的突然思维转折—— 经常要靠使用那种令人惊讶的停顿才能做到，这种技巧后来被称为“麦克白停顿”，而整部戏剧的进展轨迹仍然令人满意、道德立场依然明确，塑造出了一个自我意识极强的男人，他只有在杀气腾腾的情绪中，或是高贵的情绪中才能扮演并演好这个角色，最终不可避免地堕落到愤怒的自我厌恶中，这是麦克雷迪熟悉得不能再熟悉的性格情绪了。

然而，美国人通常更喜欢莎士比亚笔下的主人公表现得更加英勇和果断，而福雷斯特的麦克白与其说讲述了遭到公正惩罚的弑君者故事，不如说讲述了一个强大的白手起家的勇士在反抗命运的努力中惨败的情景，逃离过去，抵抗英国支持的入侵。考虑到他的父亲是一位以兜售格子呢为生的苏格兰移民，福雷斯特的麦克白中很有可能有一种《勇敢的心》中的元素：果不其然，1849 年 5 月 7 日，整个百老汇剧院为之长时间起立鼓掌的台词是：“什么样的大黄、山扁豆，什么样的泻药，才能一下子把这些英国佬都排泄掉，以后再也见不着？”

此时，麦克雷迪已经被嘘声和大炮轰鸣般的愤怒声轰下了阿斯特广场歌剧院的舞台，剧院里那些有预谋的帮派成员纷纷往舞台上扔硬币甚至是椅子，他还有别的演员都受到了轻伤。按照福雷斯特的支持者劳伦斯·巴雷特（Lawrence Barrett）的说法，如果麦克雷迪在第三幕结束时没有走下舞台，使劲儿瞪着那些闹事儿的观众，瞪得他们安静下来，也许一切都会好起来，但在目前已经被激起的那种气氛中，他所做的任何举动都会被视为一种民族性象征挑衅：“如果他当时能采取一种不同的做法—— 一种更符合我们的民族感情、更符合我们美国人民那种众所周知的善良本性的做法—— 我们怀疑，接下来的情景是否会发生。然而，从寓言的角度来说，这是狮子在挑战老鹰—— 实际上，确实是约翰牛藐视乔纳森大哥”。然而，由华盛顿·欧文为首的一个由知名公民组成的委员会说服麦克雷迪不要中断他定好的巡演行程：他们将采取措施确保不再发生类似这种令人不快的事件，必须不惜一切代价维护纽约市的荣誉和文明。麦克雷迪鞠躬致谢，答应了他们的要求，并同意在 5 月 10 日再次主演麦克白。这成了他在美国国土上的最后一次演出，最后的结局竟然是麦克雷迪伪装成观众，混入血迹斑斑的逐步散开的人群，然后乘火车逃往美国北部，再从那里返回英格兰。

5 月 10 日当晚，福雷斯特在百老汇剧院主演《角斗士》，但剧院里面观众只坐了一半：他的“铁杆粉丝”们都去别处忙着搞事情了。然而，这次阿斯特广场歌剧院 成功脱手的票数比以往要多得多，尽管有几伙人在麦克雷迪演出麦克白时一直在大喝倒彩，但演出还是一路进行到了第五幕的结尾，终于完成。但到那时，这座建筑已被一帮 15000 人左右的暴徒所包围。这是一个动荡不定的混杂群体，其中既有新近移民的爱尔兰人，他们对英国人对爱尔兰大饥荒的管理不善感到愤怒；也有顽固的美国本土主义者①，他们同样对英国人的管理不善感到愤怒，因为爱尔兰天主教移民正潮水般地涌入他们的城市；但无论他们的种族是什么，无论他们属于哪个帮派，他们似乎都认为，本周前些日子观众们对麦克雷迪流露出来的暴风雨般的愤怒已成定论，等于判了其死刑，而歌剧院的这些富有的庇护人却还邀请其再次演出，这简直是对人民意愿肆意愚弄，绝对不可接受。暴徒们一直都在用铺路石头攻击这座建筑，试图冲破那些匆忙设置了路障封锁起来的大门。当时，负责防御的部队被迫退却到墙根儿，根本没有空间可以组织起步枪刺刀冲锋，于是他们开火了。当晚至少有 25 人死亡，约 100 人受伤；第二天，在市政厅公园举行的抗议集会上，一名小男孩被挤压而死。

这场骚乱标志着那个美丽谎言的终结，即从炮台公园到十五区，所有纽约人都是自由出生的平等公民，而不是被分为富人和穷人；同样，这场骚乱也标志着作为跨阶级大众娱乐形式的莎士比亚现场演出在美国的终结。100 年后，最具福雷斯特风格的继任者会在大众媒体上播放他们的拓荒者情节剧和斯巴达克斯的朴素版，而莎士比亚对这些大众媒体肯定是一无所。

---

① 这些人指的是鲍厄里男孩儿（the b'hoys of the Bowery or the Bowery b'hoys）：是十九世纪上半叶活动于纽约曼哈顿波威里区的一个最大的帮派，或者说几个有着松散联系的、各方面比较类似的较小的帮派，因为其成员主要是健壮年轻、时髦性感、狂野不羁的纽约本地人，所以有很强的排外情绪，他们反天主教、反移民，主要是反爱尔兰移民，阻止他们占领附近地区。鲍厄里男孩儿帮派成员大部分是消防队员、机械师、商人和屠夫，他们工作时大都是遵纪守法的工人，在社区里是正直的公民，下班以后则身着奇装异服，呼朋唤友，去波威里剧院观看鲍厄里男孩儿风格的戏剧，或者是出没于附近的酒吧，在这些地方喝酒、抽烟、找女人，谈论艺术，以放荡不羁的艺术生活方式著称。他们还是新兴大众娱乐的忠实拥趸，包括体育比赛。政治上属于反叛的街角激进者，希望引起政府对贫困的工人阶级的注意。其帮派一旦与其对手帮派，爱尔兰人组成的“死兔子”起冲突，他们便会不顾一切地与对手开战，在这种街头混战骚乱中展示出他们好勇斗狠和暴力越轨行为的另一面。请注意，因为约定俗成的原因，Bowery 表示地方时大多翻译成“波威里”，表示人的时候大多翻译成“鲍厄里”。

有声电影《麦克白》中的主角儿将由当时的实验性演员奥森·威尔斯[①]扮演，而不是充满激情的约翰·韦恩[②]，而电影明星丹泽尔·华盛顿（Denzel Washington）[③]的布鲁图斯（Brutus）则只是一个例外情况而非常规。莎士比亚的美国化走了其他的路子：例如，以那个绝对是民族风格的阴谋理论为指导，迪莉亚·培根[④]写作《莎士比亚戏剧理念解密》（*The Philosophy of Shakespeare's Plays Unfolded*, 1857）背后的主要驱动力主要是决心将诗圣莎士比亚的著作的目的确定为致力于进步事业，此书认为莎士比亚的著作权属于一个由一些匿名的才华横溢的大师组成的秘密团体，他们以弗朗西斯·培根爵士为首，与其说是因为培根是一位贵族，还不如说是因为他被视为经验科学的创始人，从而成为美国工业现代性的先驱。

现在人们可能很难带着怀旧的心情回想起福雷斯特那种充满了爱国精神的狂热的莎士比亚崇拜[⑤]（他立下遗嘱，建立了一处退休演员之家，并规定他们每年必须在独立日和莎士比亚生日举行两次准宗教性的公共庆典活动仪式），也很难回想起迪莉娅·培根的那种几乎不堪卒读的伪学术著作。但值得一提的是，美国人曾经为了乌托邦式的未来而试图将莎士比亚从历史中解救出来，而不是像最近的学术研究中更常见的那样，将他的作品寄托于一个遥远的、半妖魔化的、半异国情调的业已逝去的旧体制。

克里夫对阿斯特广场暴乱的描述一它的起源、多重意义及其后果一既引人入胜又富有学术性。其稳妥的跨大西洋视角有助于使我们避免劳伦斯·莱文经典著作《高雅与低俗：美国文化等级制度的出现》（1988年）[⑥]当中所表现出的那种多愁善感——这种视角下，1809年伦敦的“不许涨价”暴乱事件[⑦]，特别精确地预示了纽约阿斯特广场暴乱的许多特征。遗憾的是，出版商不够慷慨，没能再多提供一些插图：书中的插图复制非常棒，但仍有一些极具福雷斯特和麦克雷迪神韵的幸存照片值得收录，如果再添上一张阿斯特广场地区的详细地图，克里

---

① 奥逊·威尔斯（Orson Welles，1915—1985）是集演员、导演、编剧、制片人等多种角色于一身的电影天才。作为演员，他参与了一百多部电影（包括配音）；作为编剧，他写了42个剧本；作为导演，他执导了近40部影片。1975年，AFI授予威尔斯终身成就奖。

② 约翰·韦恩（John Wayne），生于艾奥瓦州温特塞特，素有“公爵”之称的西部牛仔明星，1939年以《驿马车》稳定了自己的戏路，他塑造了美国西部开发时期纵马持枪、见义勇为的牛仔形象，刻画了他们剽悍好斗、勇敢坚毅的性格。在往后的二百多部电影中扮演了无数令人难忘的西部英雄。他在银幕上所表现的朴质敦厚与刚毅不屈也成为美国精神的代表。曾以《大地惊雷》获得奥斯卡最佳男主角金像奖。也是自30到70年代的十大卖座巨星之一。

③ 丹泽尔·华盛顿（Denzel Washington），1954年12月28日出生于美国纽约州弗农山，伟大的美国黑人演员、导演、制片人。多次获取各种顶尖电影奖项。

④ 迪莉亚·培根（Delia Bacon），与那位大名鼎鼎的集大作家、哲学家、科学家以及政客于一身的弗朗西斯·培根爵士并没有血缘关系，是一位美国戏剧和短篇小说作家，她最著名的作品是关于莎士比亚的作者问题。她提倡这样一种理论，即莎士比亚的戏剧是由一群人创作的，其中包括弗朗西斯·培根、沃尔特·罗利爵士和其他人，其中可能包括埃德蒙·斯宾塞、巴克赫斯特勋爵和牛津伯爵。后人称之为阴谋论。

⑤ 莎士比亚崇拜（Shakespeare worship）；诗圣偶像崇拜（bardolatry）：英国剧作家萧伯纳（全名乔治·伯纳德·萧，George Bernard Shaw）曾将莎士比亚戏剧描述为“舞台垃圾”。另一次，萧伯纳说他想把莎士比亚从坟墓里挖出来，再向他扔石头。萧伯纳对莎士比亚崇拜的粉丝也同样严厉。他称他们为“愚蠢的诗圣偶像崇拜者”（foolish Bardolaters），笔下会出现“诗圣偶像崇拜的无知者”（“Bardolatrous” ignoramuses）这种字眼，并称盲目的莎士比亚崇拜为“诗圣偶像崇拜”。奇怪的是，萧伯纳并不鄙视莎士比亚或他的作品（相反，他自己承认他是一个崇拜者），但他鄙视那种绝不允许对莎士比亚进行任何批评的人。萧伯纳将莎士比亚的另一个称谓“诗圣”（the Bard）与一个可以让人联想到“偶像崇拜者”（idolater）的词缀结合起来，创造了“诗圣偶像崇拜者”（bardolater）这个词，并且一直流传至今，但是它最初的一些讽刺批评意味现在已大大弱化了。

⑥ *Highbrow/ Lowbrow: The Emergence of Cultural Hierarchy in America*（1988）.

⑦ “不许涨价”暴乱事件始于1809年9月18日新建的考文特花园剧院的《麦克白》开幕之夜，观众因票价上涨而骚动，发起了“不许涨价”的消费者抗议运动，共要求恢复剧院座位的以前的老价格，成为英国历史上持续时间最长的剧院骚乱。抗议活动最终取得胜利，并于1809年12月15日结束，持续了67晚。

夫这本既生动又细致的莎士比亚暴乱研究编年史的用处就会更大一些。克里夫才华横溢，这有时会误导他加入一些不必要的脚注，这些脚注听起来像是他最喜欢的本科论文中的亮点（例如，关于哥特式的含义的，或关于《李尔王》中各个人物的真实动机的那些），这或许也是一种遗憾；我这一生中，总是会有人给我讲关于麦克白这出苏格兰戏剧的各种故事，听上去全都是傻傻的，绝不可信，可我却从未听到过任何一个故事说是莎士比亚不得不在首演时为麦克白夫人做替补，或者说詹姆斯一世憎恨这部戏剧，甚至于下令禁演这部戏。

克里夫还错过了一个花招儿，他没有听过 1922 年威廉·哈格里夫斯音乐厅那首经典歌曲背景中阿斯特广场的鬼魂的声音，这首歌绝对值得引用：

合唱：
我戏演得好悲惨，房顶儿像魔法升了天，
所有观众都大喊："你他妈的真会演!"
他们把街砖送给俺，一次朝俺扔一块砖。
有人还扔铁围栏，把俺打得只叫惨，
俺把白旗举老高，受不了啦想叛变。
他们都在奚落俺。他们都想弄死俺，
另一伙人在扔石头，那是想要砸死俺；
还扔坚果和葡萄干儿，还有香蕉跟煎蛋，
麦克白的戏太惨，这辈子再也不敢演。

尽管如此，《莎士比亚暴乱》仍然是一部精彩的处女作，与前两本同主题的书比起来，一本是理查德·穆迪的《阿斯特广场暴乱》①，另一本是理查德·纳尔逊的那本莫名其妙地欠缺了不少戏剧性描写的《两个莎士比亚演员》（1990）②本书内容更加丰富、观点更加敏锐。如果我们能有机会在纽约再次见面，凯伦家的胡萝卜蛋糕就轮到我请了。

作者简介：迈克尔·道布森（Michael Dobson），牛津大学学士、硕士、博士，本科时期获得过对硕士设立且极难获得的查尔斯·奥尔德姆莎士比亚奖（Charles Oldham Shakespeare Prize）。是欧盟莎士比亚咨询委员会联合主席（Co-chair of the EU Advisory Group on Shakespeare），《莎士比亚季刊》《莎士比亚研究》编委会成员（Member of the editorial boards of *Shakespeare: Shakespeare Quarterly* and *Shakespeare Survey*）。欧洲莎士比亚研究协会创办人和委员会成员（Founder member and board member, European Shakespeare Research Association），伦敦大学伯贝克学院莎士比亚研究教授。伯明翰大学莎士比亚研究所教授、所长。主要研究领域：莎士比亚研究。出版著作数十部，发表论文百余篇，参与修订《牛津莎士比亚指南》（牛津出版社，2015，获"信息服务技术奖"）；《莎士比亚和业余演出：一部文化历史》（剑桥出版社，2011，获乔治·弗里德里图书馆协会纪念奖）。

译者简介：鲁跃峰，河南师范大学外国语学院讲师，主要研究惠特曼、莎士比亚、英语戏剧翻译。

---

① *The Astor Place Riot* by Richard Moody, 1958.
② *Two Shakespearean Actors* by Richard Nelson, 1990.

The Performance Traditions of *Romeo and Juliet* and *Peony Pavilion*: Similarities and Departures

Wang Huimin

【Abstract】 Shakespeare's plays enjoy a great diversity of manifestation worldwide, while Tang Xianzu's (汤显祖) plays have seldom crossed over the boundary of *kunqu* (昆曲) in China. To account for the different receptions of the two dramatists' works, this article compares the performance traditions of Shakespeare's *Romeo and Juliet*and Tang's *Peony Pavilion* (《牡丹亭》) as both plays are featured the theme of forbidden love. There are similar patterns in David Garrick's production of *Romeo and Juliet* (1753) and the *Zhuibaiqiu* (《缀白裘》) (a cloak of white fur) edition of *Peony Pavilion* (1764), like taking liberty with the text and the crave for stage spectacles. But unlike the clinging to the *Zhuibaiqiu* tradition in later *Peony Pavilion* performances, great divergence from Garrick's *Romeo and Juliet* has been observed in later Henry Irving's and William Poel's productions. From an intercultural perspective, I argue that solutions for the current stagnation of *Peony Pavilion* performances can be found in Western theatre reformers' experience of producing *Romeo and Juliet*. Overall, I am seeking the freedom and diversity of performingclassical Chinese plays apart from the artistic form of traditional theatre.

【Key Words】 *Romeo and Juliet*; *Peony Pavilion*; David Garrick; *Zhuibaiqiu*

《罗密欧与朱丽叶》和《牡丹亭》的表演传统：相似与背离

王慧敏

【摘　要】 莎士比亚的戏剧在世界范围内形式多样，而汤显祖的戏剧在中国很少跨越昆曲的界限。为了阐释两位剧作家作品不同接受程度，本文比较了同为禁忌爱情主题的《罗密欧与朱丽叶》和《牡丹亭》的表演传统。大卫·加里克改编的《罗密欧与朱丽叶》（1753）和缀白裘版本的《牡丹亭》（1764 年）有着相似性，都追求行文自在。与倾向于缀白裘传统的《牡丹亭》不同，在亨利·欧文和威廉·坡的作品中，人们观察到了与加里克的《罗密欧与朱丽叶》的巨大差异。从跨文化剧场角度，本文认为，解决目前牡丹亭表演停滞的方法可以从西方戏剧改革者制作《罗密欧与朱丽叶》的经验中找到方法。总的来说，除了传统戏剧形式之外，我们正在寻求中国戏剧表演的自由和多样性。为了充分挖掘戏剧的潜力，我们呼吁进行跨文化解读和创新，以振兴中国戏剧的剧目。

【关键词】《罗密欧与朱丽叶》;《牡丹亭》; 大卫・加里克;《缀白裘》

A glance at Shakespeare's *Romeo and Juliet* and Tang Xianzu's *Peony Pavilion* (《牡丹亭》) will reveal that both plays are more than mere love stories. Both plays are set against a profound social background and their dramatic structures provoke the audience's critical reflection. Given the textual similarities of the two plays, like the theme of "forbidden love" and the dramaturgical juxtaposition, why is Shakespeare a global cultural icon while Tang's fame is mostly confined in China? Why has *Romeo and Juliet* been adapted into various artistic forms, but *Peony Pavilion* is invariably performed in the form of *kunqu*?① Is it possible to reinvigorate the performance traditions of *Peony Pavilion* by learning from the experience of adapting Shakespeare? Antony Tatlow provides a positive answer: "The impulse from another culture is sought and absorbed, because it enables an otherwise difficult, if not impossible, engagement with what has been repressed at home."② Tatlow's intercultural perspective can be promising in solving the current predicament of *Peony Pavilion* as an intercultural experiment of this play may help excavate the repressed elements that have never been performed in mainland China.

Following Tatlow's proposal, this article adopts an intercultural perspective and tries to explain the different receptions of the two dramatists by comparing the performance history of *Romeo and Juliet* and *Peony Pavilion*. Due to the lack of detailed and complete performance records in Shakespeare's and Tang Xianzu's times, I start from comparing David Garrick's production of *Romeo and Juliet* and *Zhuibaiqiu* (《缀白裘》) (a cloak of white fur) edition of *Peony Pavilion*in the mid-eighteenth century.③ The two productions share contemporaneity and great popularity. Historically, Garrick adapted *Romeo and Juliet* at least three times, ④ and there are five versions of *Zhuibaiqiu*.⑤ For the sake of direct parallels, this article is based on the well-received Qian Decang's (钱德苍) edition of *Zhuibaiqiu* published in 1764 which is closest to Garrick's third edition of *Romeo and Juliet* in 1753.

Garrick is the most representative Restoration actor, and his production of *Romeo and Juliet* sets the paradigm of performance for nearly one century.⑥ Garrick's adapting practice does not stand alone, rather, there are many adaptations of *Romeo and Juliet* during Garrick's lifetime, like that by Theophilus Cibber, and that by John Rich at Covent Garden. But the texts of productions

① *Kunqu* (昆曲) is one of the oldest traditional Chinese theatres with its origins dating back to the end of Yuan dynasty (1271-1368). It combines singing, speaking, acting, and martial fighting, and is featured with codified gestures and movement and the tune-type musical structure.

② Antony Tatlow, *Shakespeare, Brecht, and the Intercultural Sign* (Durham: Duke University Press, 2001), pp. 3-4.

③ *Zhuibaiqiu* (《缀白裘》), compiled by Qian Decang (钱德苍), ed. by Wang Xieru (汪协如) (Beijing: Zhonghua Shuju, 2005).

④ David Garrick, *The Plays of David Garrick,* edited with commentary and notes by Harry William Pedicord and Fredrick Louis Bergmann (Carbondale: Southern Illinois University Press, 1981), vol. 3, p. 78.

⑤ Mao Jie(毛劼), "The Study of Kunju zhezixi in *Zhuibaiqiu*"《〈缀白裘〉昆剧折子戏研究》(Nanjing University: Master thesis, 2014), pp. 6-8. Also see Liu Qing(刘庆), "The Different Performance Forms of *Peony Pavilion* in *Zhuibaiqiu* and *Shenyin jiangulu*"《〈审音鉴古录〉和〈缀白裘〉中〈牡丹亭〉演出形态的差异》, *Theatre Arts* 戏剧艺术, 6 (2012), 69-74 (p.69).

⑥ See George C. Branam, 'The Genesis of David Garrick's *Romeo and Juliet*', *Shakespeare Quarterly*, 35.2 (1984), 170-179(pp. 178-179).

prior to Garrick are not easily attainable, given the fact that most of them have not been passed down to this day.① Garrick has altered much of Shakespeare's text, still he is said to "put a stop to much of the degradation into which Shakespeare's plays had fallen" and his version actually paved the way for the complete restoration of Shakespeare's texts.② From this aspect we can see how unfaithful previous Restoration productions have been.

In contrast to Garrick's production, *Zhuibaiqiu* is still well-received, mostly among *kunqu* connoisseurs and performers ever since its publication in the mid-Qing dynasty and is in continuous demand for reprint. Different in form from Garrick's productions, *Zhuibaiqiu* is a collection of highlights or zhezi (折子) (scenes) extracted from different plays, thus *Zhuibaiqiu* is a literary miscellany of the playscript of zhezixi (折子戏) (performance of selected scenes).③ The practice of dian xi (点戏) (picking out a certain scene for performance) in various occasions like ritual ceremonies, festivals, weddings, birthdays, funerals, and many others accounts for the growing popularity of performing individual scenes instead of the full play, the latter is often too long to be performed within several hours.④*Zhuibaiqiu* includes twelves *zhezixi* from *Peony Pavilion*, namely *Ming pan* (《冥判》) (Infernal judgment), *Shi hua* (《拾画》) (The portrait recovered), *Jiao hua* (《叫画》) (Calling the lady in the portrait), *Xue tang* (《学堂》) (The schoolroom), *You yuan* (《游园》) (Wandering in the garden), *Jing meng* (《惊梦》) (The interrupted dream), *Xun meng* (《寻梦》) (Pursuing the dream), *Yuan jia* (《圆驾》) (Reunion at court), *Quan nong* (《劝农》) (Speed the Plough), *Li hun* (《离魂》) (The soul's departure), *Wen lu* (《问路》) (Asking the way), and *Diao da* (《吊打》) (Interrogation under the rod). This *Zhuibaiqiu* edition changes some of the original scene titles, for example, from the scene title of *Wan zhen* (《玩真》) (The portrait examined) to the zhezixi title of *Jiao hua* (《叫画》) (Calling the lady in the portrait), and from *Pu zhen* (《仆侦》) (The servant asking the way in search of the master) to *Wen lu* (《问路》) (Asking the way). The zhezixi titles are simplified, and sound more colloquial, which reflects the taste of the shifting audience — the elite audience of the late Ming dynasty is outnumbered by middle-class audiences in the mid-Qing dynasty.

Garrick is an actor, and *Zhuibaiqiu* is a collection of actors' performance texts. The two texts' shared popularity testifies to a similar historical trend in England and China where actors entered the realm of publication. The booming economy in the Georgian time and mid-Qing dynasty also

---

① Thomas Otway's production of *Romeo and Juliet* is readily attainable, but this production is so removed from Shakespeare's *Romeo and Juliet* that I do not include it in the discussion.

② Harry William Pedicord and Fredrick Louis Bergmann, 'Introduction' in David Garrick, *The Plays of David Garrick*. edited with commentary and notes byHarry William Pedicord and Fredrick Louis Bergmann (Carbondale: Southern Illinois University Press, 1981), vol. 3, pp. xiii-xiv.

③ Apart from *Zhuibaiqiu* and *Shenyin jiangulu*, other miscellanies include*Yuelu yin* (《月露音》), *Cilin yixiang* (《词林逸响》), *Wanhe qingyin* (《万壑清音》), *Yichun jin* (《怡春锦》), *Chantou bailian erji* (《缠头百练二集》), *Xuexue pu*(《玄雪谱》), *Zui yiqing* (《醉怡情》), mostly published in the late Ming and Qing dynasties. See Zhang Xueli(张雪莉), "A Study on Commentaries, Revisions and Miscellanies of *Peony Pavilion*" (《〈牡丹亭〉评点本、改本及选本研究》)(Fudan University: PhD thesis, 2010).

④ See Wang Ning (王宁), *A Study on Kunju Zhezixi* (《昆剧折子戏研究》) (Hefei: Huangshan shushe, 2012), pp. 11-20, and Li Xiao (李晓), "Qianjia tradition of the performance art of kunju and its inheritance" (《昆剧表演艺术的"乾嘉传统"及其传承》), *Hundreds Schools in Arts* (《艺术百家》), 4 (1997), 86-115 (p. 86). *Peony Pavilion* is consisted of 55 scenes, and the performance time for Chen Shizheng's 陈士争 full version of *Peony Pavilion*(1999) lasted more than 20 hours.

referred to as the high Qing era, created a high demand for entertainment.① It contributed to the prosperity of commercial playing troupes and the establishment of acting as a profession, which lead to actors' rising social positions. The literati no longer dominated the interpretation of a play, and thus performers gained the freedom to adapt a play based on the audience's taste. In Qing dynasty China, the strengthened state censorship like *wenziyu* (文字狱) (literary inquisition) limited literati writers' creations. As the declining number of new plays could not meet the high demand for performance, *kunqu* performers played a leading role in adapting previous plays. Publications of performers' variations of literati playwrights' plays, like *Zhuibaiqiu* and earlier miscellanies such as *Zuiyiqing* (《醉怡情》) (Drunken pleasure) marked a new era in the performance history of *kunqu*, revealing "a gradual shift from theatrical literature controlled by playwrights to one that registered the creative efforts of performers."② Similarly in England, Levenson reveals that Garrick's production of *Romeo and Juliet* allows other actors to add their views in his explication, which is part of eighteenth-century theatre conventions.③

In the hand of *kunqu* performers, the original plays are like malleable raw material apt for re-creation and adaptation. Performers take the initiative to translate the scripts in selected scenes into audio-visual appealing stage symbols in order to fully tap the stage potential of a particular scene. The expert on *kunqu zhezixi*, Wang Ning (王宁), acutely pinpoints the features of *zhezixi* that it raises the priority of displaying technical skills and downplays the importance of the story plot.④The complete story plot weighs less than the presentation of physical skills, and adapters sometimes even rewrite the play to create a new *zhezixi.* For example, the original scene 10 *Jing meng* (《惊梦》) "The interrupted dream" of *Peony Pavilion* is divided into two *zhezixi*, *You yuan* and *Jing meng*, separating the protagonist Liniang's sightseeing in the garden and having a dream in her boudoir. Adapters structurally alter Tang's garden scene, which obstructs the continuity of text, and disrupts the original musical structure. Similarly to Shakespeare, Nicholas Rowe (1674-1718) firstly divided Shakespeare's plays into acts and scenes in his edition of *The Works of Mr. William Shakespeare* (1709). The division of scenes and acts is carried on in Garrick's production.

Apart from artificial scene divisions, actor-adapters also simplify the plot, and severe cutting can be observed in both practices of Garrick and *Zhuibaiqiu*. The simplified plots centre around the title roles, accentuating the feeling of "love at first sight". Minor characters and sub-plots are sacrificed, which leads to the weakening of the social background and the social problems along with it. "To represent only the love episode is to make that episode far less tragic, and therefore less dramatic."⑤ Indeed the significance of the minor characters cannot be overestimated as they help to

---

① See John Styan, *The English Stage: A History of Drama and Performance* (Cambridge: Cambridge University Press, 1996), pp. 274-278, and Willard J. Peterson, 'Introduction: The Ch'ing Dynasty, the Ch'ing Empire, and the Great Ch'ing Integrated Domain', in *The Cambridge History of China*, vol. 9,ed. By Willard J. Peterson (Cambridge:Cambridge University Press,2016),pp.1-15.

② Catherine C. Swatek, *Peony Pavilion Onstage: Four Centuries in the Career of a Chinese Drama* (Ann Arbor: The University of Michigan, 2002), p. 101.

③ Jill L. Levenson, *Romeo and Juliet: Shakespeare in Performance* (Manchester: Manchester University Press: 1987), p. 25.

④ Wang Ning, *A Study on Kunju Zhezixi,* p. 59. His original word in Chinese is "戏曲故事的弱化和演员'玩意儿'的凸显". I do not distinguish *kunju* (昆剧) and *kunqu* (昆曲) in the article because in most cases they are used interchangeably. Literally, *kunju* emphasizes more on the story plot, while *kunqu* emphasizes more on the singing tune.

⑤ William Poel, *Shakespeare in the Theatre* (London and Toronto: Sidgwick and Jackson, Ltd., 1913), reprint by AMS Press in 1974, p. 156.

narrate the working of the social background for the title roles. The bustling liveliness of minor characters is indispensable because it prevents the love stories to be too ethereal to be real.

Both productions not only simplify the plot but also purify the characters, trying to set the protagonists as role models. Their practice inevitably has a didactic tone. John Styan notes that "the moralistic shift in taste governed everything on the stage" as in 1704 Queen Anne ordered her Lord Chamberlain "not to license anything that is not strictly agreeable to religion and good manners" which turns the stage into a pulpit.① Garrick purifies the characters, like deleting all references to Rosaline, Romeo's first lover, in his third edition of Romeo and Juliet in 1753. He constructs Romeo as an unequivocally loyal lover of Juliet in order to cater to the moral standards in the Georgian era. He also carefully adjusts Juliet's age, from fourteen to eighteen as Lord Capulet tells Paris that Juliet "hath not seen the change of eighteen years"②. Garrick changes this detail probably because he deems that marriage at the age of fourteen is rather indecent according to Georgian standards.

Zhuibaiqiu also purifies Liniang's characteristics because of the strict ideological control – Emperor Qianlong encourages the construction of moral examples for his citizens to follow. The morals become a guiding principle for *kunqu* adapters. Catering to the audience's taste and the state's political control, they re-wired the selected scenes to be the embodiment of traditional Confucian values imposed by the ruling class, like loyalty, filial piety, chastity, and righteousness.③ For example, adapters politicize "the spectacle of Liniang's death, which in the staged version becomes the occasion for an elaborate display of filial piety."④ They demonstrate Liniang's filial piety by adding the detail that Liniang insists to kowtow, the foremost etiquette, to her mother, to show her regret for failing to fulfill her filial duty due to her early death. This detail does not accord with the intention of the play - blind obedience of parents' order is what Tang Xianzu is criticizing, and what Liniang's ghost is later fighting against. This kowtow detail adds a didactic tone in *Peony Pavilion* at the sacrifice of the integrity of this play's spiritual value.

The emphasis on the love story of the "spotless" lovers leads to the accentuation of feelings in the performance. The third quarter of the eighteenth century notably marks the watershed towards "a more expressive emotionalism" in England.⑤ Sentimentalism is more than evident in Garrick's production where he makes Juliet revive before Romeo dies of poison, and gives the lovers a very limited amount of time alive together.⑥ According to theatre reviews, this added scene is remembered as "a moving closing to the story"⑦, that overwhelms the audience. Similarly in scene

---

① Styan, pp. 280-281.

② *Romeo and Juliet. A Tragedy Altered from Shakespeare*, by David Garrick, ESQ. Taken from the Manager's Book (London: printed for R. Butters, at the Theatre Royal in Covent-Garden, 1795), p. 6.

③ See Feng Wei 冯伟, *Intercultural Aesthetics in Traditional Chinese Theatre From 1978 to the Present* (London: Palgrave Macmillan, 2020), pp. 52-53, 'In a narrow and most recognized sense, morals in traditional Chinese literature and art denoted Confucian codes, that is loyalty, filial piety, chastity, and righteousness.'

④ Swatek, p. 113.

⑤ George WinchesterStone, '*Romeo and Juliet*: The Source of Its Modern Stage Career', *Shakespeare Quarterly*, 15.2 (1964), 191-206 (p. 191).

⑥ Even though it is Thomas Otway who initiated the practice of making Juliet revive before Romeo dies, Garrick's choice to adopt Otway's practice can also reflect his taste for sentimentalism. For a more detailed discussion on Garrick's rewriting of the tomb scene, see KatherineL.Wright, *Shakespeare's Romeo and Juliet in Performance: Traditions and Departures* (Lewiston: Mellen University Press, 1997), p. 58.

⑦ KatherineL.Wright, *Shakespeare's Romeo and Juliet in Performance: Traditions and Departures* (Lewiston: Mellen University Press, 1997), p. 133.

20 of *Peony Pavilion*, *kunqu* adapters leave no effort in accentuating the poignancy of Liniang's early death, especially the sorrow of seeing one's child die (白发人送黑发人). In *Zhuibaiqiu* edition, a great number of stage directions are added to show her parents' bereavement while cutting the hypocritical conversation between Liniang's father, Tutor Chen, and Sister Stone regarding the funeral arrangement. Liniang's parents' tears lead the audience to believe that they are, unequivocally, victims of fickle fate - an old pathetic couple whose only daughter is now dead. Avoiding the depiction of their hypocrisy not only in this scene but throughout the play does not provide the audience with a full picture of the complicated family relationship, and prevents the audience to realize the real reason behind Liniang's suspicious early death.

This "expressive emotionalism" in English theatre is enhanced with the aid of stage spectacles, and Garrick's *Romeo and Juliet* was the object of pictorial experiment. In order to satisfy the taste for scenic spectacle and surprising stage devices, David Garrick appointed Philip de Loutherbourg from Paris for the scenography design. De Loutherbourg's work went beyond painted scenery - apart from shutters and flats, he built ramps and levels, achieving a vertical dimension within the acting area.① Among all the spectacles, the grand funeral procession coupled with a choral dirge is a prominent feature of Garrick's *Romeo and Juliet*. Count Frederick Kielmansegge reported in 1761 that an entire funeral was beautifully and naturally represented, with bells tolling, and a choir singing. Juliet lay on a state bed with a splendid canopy over her, guarded by girls who strew flowers, and by torch-bearers with flaming torches. Amazingly, around fifty actors, including dancers and singers, to be seen on one night, "whilst there are probably as many absent", the sheer number of actors standing on the stage is a spectacle itself. Kielmansegge also noted that different decorations, machinery, and dresses were "provided regardless of cost and with thorough completeness"②. The high budget of stage and costume design is the signature of spectacle-oriented commercial productions. Though the funeral procession is irrelevant to the written play, George C. Branam argues that "spectacle was its own justification" as "Garrick rushed it [the funeral procession] into place in the struggle for box office supremacy"③. Commercial reasons lie behind Garrick's addition of irrelevant stage spectacles which, unfortunately, is at the cost of a play's continuity as changing the scenery takes much of performance time.

For the productions of *Peony Pavilion* in this period, a similar trend towards visual spectacle is suggested with the increase of flower spirits' number in the scene of "The interrupted dream", nicknamed "the garden scene". In the early seventeenth century, there was only one flower spirit dressed plainly "in red cloak strewn with petals and ornamental headdress on his piled-up hair" as in Tang Xianzu's stage direction.④ The aesthetic taste for colour and grandeur in eighteenth-century

---

① see Styan, p.278.

② *Diary of a Journey to England 1761-1762*, trans. Countess Kielmansegge (London, 1902), pp. 221-222. Quote in David Garrick, *The Plays of David Garrick*, edited with commentary and notes by Harry William Pedicord and Fredrick Louis Bergmann, 4 vols (Carbondale: Southern Illinois University Press, 1981), vol 3, p. 411.

③ See George C. Branam, 'The Genesis of David Garrick's *Romeo and Juliet*', *Shakespeare Quarterly*, 35.2 (1984), 170-179 (pp. 178-179) .

④ Tang Xianzu. *Peony Pavilion* 牡丹亭, trans. Cyril Birch, 2nd edn. (Bloomington and Indianapolis: Indiana University Press, 2002), p.48.

eighteenth-century China cried for a more realistic performance of the garden scene. With the absence of backdrops, the brilliant scenography of the garden scene was presented through the gorgeous costumes of a dozen flower spirits. Since the early Qing dynasty, the performance tradition of flower spirits has evolved to be more exquisite. The number of flower spirits increases from one to twelve to satisfy the audience's quest for visual spectacles. Even though *Zhuibaiqiu* only adds *shui mo shen* (睡魔神, dream spirit) holding mirrors in his hand without employing any flower spirit, an earlier miscellany, *Zuiyiqing* depicts twelve flower spirits representing the seasonal flowers. This added scene also gains its own name, *Duihua* 堆花 (Heaped blossoms).①*Duihua* does not relate with the plot, and it is presented simply to enhance visual beauty on the stage - the flower spirits' colourful dresses and various floral props are trying to turn the stage into a virtual garden.

Point of divergence: the performance traditions of *Romeo and Juliet* from Garrick to Irving and Poel and to the present, and the performance traditions of *Peony Pavilion* from *Zhuibaiqiu* to *Shenyin jiangulu* and to the present

As we have observed, both Garrick and *kunqu* adapters of *Zhuibaiqiu* are confined by their ideologies; they tend to restructure and sanitize the plays to conform with their social and cultural morality. As a result, Garrick's *Romeo and Juliet* and *Zhuibaiqiu*'s *Peony Pavilion* are simplified, didactic, over-emotional, and have obtrusive spectacles. Their productions fail to capture the internal complexities in the original plays as Shakespeare and Tang Xianzu carefully present through an organic, integral, and open structure that gives the audience freedom of interpretation.

Despite the similarities between Garrick and *Zhuibaiqiu*, today the performance of *Romeo and Juliet* gains much vigor and is creatively being manifested in different theatrical cultures, which stands in stark contrast to *Peony Pavilion*'s more or less frozen performance traditions. What has contributed to the different performances and receptions of both plays and both dramatists? Why does Shakespeare succeed to be transformed and gaining vitality of interpretation? What is the point of divergence? To find out the reasons, I trace the variations of *Romeo and Juliet* from Garrick to Henry Irving and William Poel and to the present, and the performance traditions of *Peony Pavilion* from *Zhuibaiqiu* to *Shenyin jiangulu* (《审音鉴古录》) (Examining ancient music) and to the present. *Shenyin jiangulu* is a miscellany of *zhezixi*; first published in 1834, it is regarded as the most comprehensive and detailed collection of *zhezixi*, and is thus often reprinted until today.② It includes nine *zhezixi* from *Peony Pavilion*, i.e. “Speed the plough”, “The schoolroom”, “Wandering in the garden”, “The interrupted dream”, “Pursuing the dream”, “The soul's departure”, “Infernal judgment”, “Interrogation under the rod” and “Reunion at court”. Again, the title of each *zhezixi* in *Shenyin jiangulu* is the same as that in *Zhuibaiqiu*, a colloquial version of the original scene titles.

The trend of text integrity can be observed in later adapters after Garrick. A detailed study of

① Catherine C. Swatek, *Peony Pavilion Onstage: Four Centuries in the Career of a Chinese Drama* (Ann Arbor: The University of Michigan, 2002), p. 106.

② Anonymous, *Shenyin jiangulu* (《审音鉴古录》), ed. Wang Jishan (王继善), first published in 1834 (Beijing: China Book Publishing, 2012), vol. 6, pp. 19-20.

prompt books leads Sylvia Alexa Berg to reach the conclusion that Samuel Phelps' (1804-1878) revival of *Romeo and Juliet* in 1846 is probably the most fully restored presentation of the text on the 19th-Century stage as he replaces the acting versions with Shakespeare's folio texts.① Even though Phelps' edition were quite different from Shakespeare's original text, Phelps had made conscious efforts in using the dramatist's word rather than that of the actors. He advocated "Shakespeare in his integrity", which paved the way to more textually integrated performances.② Henry Irving (1838-1905) has also realized the importance of textual fidelity and has identified the previous disrespect of Shakespeare's text. He condemned the past "improvers", i.e. adapters of Shakespeare's plays, and deplored Garrick's rewriting of Shakespeare, like Garrick's cutting of Rosaline. Irving restored the character of Rosaline in his 1882 production as "Shakespeare has carefully worked out this first baseless love of Romeo as a palpable evidence of the subjective nature of the man and his passion."③Compared with Garrick, Irving is much more faithful towards Shakespeare's texts. He adopts the strategy of cutting rather than rewriting, and cuts certain parts in order to present the play "within a reasonable limit of time".④ But Irving has not yet realized that cutting can be as powerful as rewriting. His severe cutting of the final scene, for example, also centralizes the protagonists' love, robs the uncertainty of play's ending, and downplays the importance of social riot in the background.

Moving on to William Poel (1852-1934), Poel has been acutely aware of the mutilation of text in Shakespeare's plays, and he attributes this reason to "the despotism of the actor on the English stage, and consequently to the star system"⑤. Actors' and stage-managers' dominance of text lends them the freedom of adaptation, which is against Poel's upholding of absolute textual fidelity, as he shouts, "To all stage-managers who wish to mend or improve Shakespeare, I say: 'Hands off! Produce this play as it is written or leave it alone. Don't take liberties with it; the man who does that does not understand his own limitations!'"⑥

Having said that, Poel's practice does not always accord with his words as sometimes he rewrites the play due to the influence of Puritanism.⑦ He cuts the last scene almost entirely out of his production of *Romeo and Juliet*.⑧Despite the discrepancy between adapters' words and practice, the importance of textual fidelity towards Shakespeare's text is gaining ground. In contrast, later adapters after *Zhuibaiqiu* have not realized this aspect. Actors still dominate the interpretation of plays and have great freedom of rewriting. *Shenyin jiangulu* keeps the rewriting in *Zhuibaiqiu*, and adds more, as recorded in the stage directions. Nowadays *Shenyin jiangulu* is the main reference

---

① Sylvia AlexaBerg, "The Interpretation of *Romeo and Juliet* from Garrick to Bridges-Adams: An Historical Study of Tradition and Innovation in English Shakespearean Production" (The University of Alberta, British Columbia: PhD diss, 1989), p. 4.

② See Sylvia AlexaBerg, ch.2.

③ Henry Irving, "Preface", in *Romeo and Juliet, A Tragedy in Five Acts, by William Shakespeare, as arranged for the stage by Henry Irving, and presented at the Lyceum Theatre, on Wednesday, March 8th, 1882* (London: Chiswick Press, 1882), pp.v-vi (p. v) .

④ Ibid., p. v.

⑤ Poel, *Shakespeare in the Theatre*, p. 154.

⑥ Poel, *Shakespeare in the Theatre*, pp. 180-181.

⑦ See Claris Glick, "William Poel: His Theories and Influence", *Shakespeare Quarterly*, 15.1 (1964), 15-25 (p.17). Glick recorded that William Poel rewrote characters in *Measure for Measure* to meet with Puritan ideals.

⑧ See Glick, pp. 17-19.

book for *kunqu Peony Pavilion* performances, and consequently, today the original playscript is still not much respected in *kunqu* theatres.

Until today, *Kunqu* performers emphasize more on the manifestation of professional skills rather than understanding the depth of thought and the complicated pictures in the whole play. This problem was mentioned by William Sun Huizhu early in 1999 that "the majority of traditional actors in the past did not take literature seriously enough but concentrated on superficial virtuosities which seemed to have autonomous value"[①]. And this problem is also contingent today. When I asked the female lead of *Peony Pavilion* from a renowned *kunqu* theatre how many scenes were there in the play, she replied "thirty something" while actually there were fifty-five scenes. Her mistake is understandable as her teacher might not have taught her the full text, and only around 20-30 scenes of *Peony pavilion* are consistently performed. But, as Li Yu (李渔) comments that only by understanding the plot and its meanings can an actor sing convincingly.[②] Thus, how can actors sing convincingly if they have not read the original play and lack a comprehensive picture of a plot? Particularly for the female lead, it is vital to know the full text in order to master the construction of the complicated character Liniang.

From page to stage, in terms of stage design, compared with Garrick, Irving is conscious that "above all, the resources of the picturesque must be wholly subordinate to the play. Mere pageant apart from the story has no place in Shakespeare"[③]. But his deeds did not necessarily accord with his words. His stage design for play reached the culmination of stage spectacles as contemporary critics commented. A great amount of time was needed for the carpentry to change the scenery. And the spectacles are a distraction for the audience to appreciate the actors' performance as William Poel complained that "those outward decorations and subordinate details" not only "divert a careful observance of the acting" but also "obliterate the main object of dramatic work"[④]. Thus Poel called for a return to Elizabethan stage management, one feature of which is scenic simplicity. Poel has cast a long shadow on later theatre directors, like Peter Brook, and this simple stage set can be observed in most modern theatre productions of *Romeo and Juliet*.

But the taste for spectacles grew in *Peony Pavilion* performances. One evidence is the growing number of flower spirits in the added scene of *Dui hua* (《堆花》). *Shenyin jiangulu* is a stage-based playscript, and its illustration reflects the contemporary staging. This illustration depicts thirteen flower spirits and one dream spirit overseeing the dream lovemaking between Liniang and Scholar Liu. The flower spirits are played by different role types as a way of showing a troupe's rich personal resources. In total there are fourteen deities in this scene, which outnumbers a combination of the twelve flower spirits in *Zuiyiqing* and one dream spirit in *Zhuibaiqiu*. Besides the growing number, the costume is probably more sophisticated. The costume of the fourteen deities is

① Sun Huizhu William, "The Paradox of Acting in the Traditional Chinese Theatre", *New Theatre Quarterly*, 15.1 (1999), 17–25 (p. 25) .

② His original word is "唱曲宜有曲情，曲情者，曲中之情节也。解明情节，知其意所在，则唱出口时，俨然此种神情". Li Yu (李渔), *Incidental Records of Passing Feelings*, ed. by Du Shuying 杜书瀛 (Beijing: Xueyuan, 1998), pp. 178-9.

③ Henry Irving, "Shakespeare as a playwright", in *The Henry Irving Shakespeare*, ed. by Frank A. Marshall (Cambridge University Press, 2010), vol.1, pp. xvii-xxiii (p. xxii) .

④ Poel, *Shakespeare in the Theatre*, pp. 7-8.

embroidered with elaborated patterns, and their diverse headdress indicates their different identities. Beautiful clothing is usually expensive. As recorded in Li Dou's (李斗) (1749-1817) *The Painted Pleasure Boat of Yangzhou* (《扬州画舫录》), the play troupe of the Zhang family spent ten thousand gold coins for the costume of flower spirits in *Peony Pavilion*.[1] Later, Kunju chuandai (昆剧穿戴) (*The Costume of Kunju*) [2] takes the labour to record the embellished details of each deity's costume and prop, for example, the dream spirit should be dressed in a green shirt, black pants, and should wear a fake black beard, [3] and the head of flower spirits is played by the role of lao sheng (老生) (old male) who should wear a crown, yellow shirt, red pants, high-platform shoes, and hold a peony flower in the left hand as well as a yun zhou (云帚) (fairy brush) in the right hand.[4] *The Costume of Kunju* sets specific and detailed directions of costume and props, and serves as a reference book for today's performances.[5] The early performance traditions of *kunqu* with a simple set of one table and two chairs are gradually enhanced with the addition of stage spectacles that may not necessarily bear any relation with the plot.

Illustration of thirteen flower spirits and one dream spirit in *Shenyin jiangulu*

In a brief summary, productions of Shakespeare's *Romeo and Juliet* progress towards textual

① Li Dou (李斗), *The Painted Pleasure Boat of Yangzhou* (《扬州画舫录》), ed. by Zhou Chundong (周春东), first published in 1795 (Jinan: Shandong Youyi Chubanshe, 2001), p. 159. The original Chinese word is "小张班十二月花神衣，价至万金".

② Zeng Changsheng (曾长生), *The Costume of Kunju* (昆剧穿戴), ed. by Xu Lingyun (徐凌云), Bei Jinmei (贝晋眉) (Suzhou: Suzhou *Xiqu* Research Office, 1963) .

③ The original Chinese word is "穿绿素褶子，黑彩裤，着镶鞋，戴知了巾，套梦神脸，挂黑吊搭".

④ The original Chinese word is "九龙冠、黑三、黄蟒、黄宫绦、红彩裤、高底靴、左手执牡丹、右手云帚".

⑤ For more details on the flower spirits' costume and function, see Wang Huimin (王慧敏), "Inclusion and Exclusion: Gender Politics in the Performance Traditions of the flower spirits in *Peony Pavilion*", *Emergence* 11 (2020), pp. 1-12.

fidelity and scenic simplicity, but *kunqu* productions of *Peony Pavilion* still lack the respect toward text - the productions emphasize external manifestations, like spectacles, costume, and professional skills rather than the internal value of the play, like the depth of thought. Early in 2002, Catherine Swatek pointed out the interpretive chasm between a play as performed and a play as written.① How does this chasm come into being? Can *kunqu* accommodate the internal complexities of *Peony Pavilion*? Does the aesthetic taste of *kunqu* accord with that of *Peony Pavilion*? The following discussion on the aesthetic standard of *kunqu* and the artistic standard of *Peony Pavilion* is trying to answer these questions.

The interpretive chasm: the aesthetic standard of *kunqu* and the artistic standard of *Peony Pavilion*

Elaborated and refined stage spectacles reflect *kunqu*'s emphasis on and aesthetic pursuit of beauty. Media coverage and scholarship in this field have all focused on the "beauty" aspect of *kunqu*. As Yang Ming (2019) observed, the word "beautiful" has been adopted by media coverage of *kunqu* productions, and it was the very word used in audience responses to new *kunqu* productions from 2001 to 2015.② When summarising the aesthetic characteristics of *kunqu*, current scholarship distinguishes *kunqu* by the beauty of every gesture and movement. Chen Duo's (陈多) theory of *meixing qusheng* (美形取胜), lit., "beautiful form takes victory" is highly influential. In his view, other elements of *kunqu*, like drama writing and musical composition, are supposed to concertedly achieve the ultimate goal of beauty in performance.③ Wang Ning similarly states that *kunqu zhezixi*'s final pursuit is *hao kan* (好看) "beauty".④ Pai Hsien-yung (白先勇) writes "beauty is the essence of *kunqu*"⑤. Influenced by the beauty-oriented aesthetic, nowadays *kunqu* productions of *Peony Pavilion* are judged by whether it is "beautiful" or not. Most, if not all, *kunqu* theatres in mainland China and elsewhere focus on the romantic love story of *Peony Pavilion*. The subplot of war is not "beautiful", so it is cut.⑥

Even if an artistic form should be beautiful, I do not think a good play equals to a "beautiful" play with beautiful language. The inner depth of thought and values are more important for a play than its physical "beauty". Denying the dark side in Tang Xianzu's writing renders the play into a

---

① Swatek, p. 256.

② Yang Ming (杨明), "Return of the Soul: Inheritance and Innovation in the Process of Artistic Creation in Major *Kunqu* Productions in the PRC, 2001-2015" (University of Hawai' I: PhD thesis, 2019), pp. 7-8.

③ Chen Duo, *Xiqu Aesthetics* (戏曲美学) (Chengdu: Sishuan renmin publishing house, 2001), p. 372. *Xiqu* (戏曲) is the umbrella term for classic Chinese theatre including *kunqu*. Apart from *meixing qusheng* (美形取胜), Chen Duo also proposes another three treaties*wurong gesheng* (舞容歌声) (lit., dance and song), *dongren yiqing* (动人以情) (lit., move people through emotions), and*yizhu xingcong* (意主形从) (lit., meaning dominates the form) .

④ Wang Ning, p. 136, "折子戏的终极追求是好看".

⑤ Pai Hsien-yung, "The New Aesthetics of *Kunqu* - From the Youth Edition of *Peony Pavilion* to the New Version of *The Jade Hairpin*" (《昆曲新美学—— 从青春版〈牡丹亭〉到新版〈玉簪记〉》), *Arts Criticism*, 3 (2010), 5-9 (p. 5), "昆曲本来就是精英文化、高雅文化，是文人雅士欣赏的艺术".

⑥ The emphasis of "beauty" in *kunqu* performance is an invented tradition, see Kim Hunter-Gordon, "Contesting Traditional *Luzi* ('Choreographic Paths'): A Performance-Based Study of *Kunqu*" (Royal Holloway, University of London: PhD thesis, 2016), pp. 8-10, 19-21.

sugar-coated love story that fails to excite modern spectators.

Another aesthetic standard intertwined with "beauty" is "elegance". Today *kunqu* is categorized as "fine art" and "high art" and is distinguished from the "grass-root art". At the turn of the 21st century, Pai Hsien-yung promoted the concept of *kunqu xin meixue* (昆曲新美学) (new aesthetics of *kunqu*), and in his view, "*kunqu* is originally an elite culture, it is elegant and is the art for the literati and the intellectuals."① I cannot agree with his word because it has the connotation that ordinary people without a college certificate is unqualified for appreciating *kunqu*. A quick glimpse of the history of *kunqu* will prove the fallacy in Pai's statement. Historically, *kunqu* appeals to both refined and popular tastes (雅俗共赏). It includes not only elegant verses (阳春白雪) written by knowledgeable scholars but also grass-root humour (下里巴人) in low-life character's dialect. During the reign of Emperors Kangxi and Qianlong (1681-1796), an exaggerated expression goes that every household could sing the opening lyrics of scenes from two popular plays, Li Yu's (李玉, 1610-1670) ② *Qian zhong lu* (《千忠戮》) (*The Killing of Thousands of Loyalties*) and Hong Sheng's (洪昇 1645-1704) *Changsheng dian* (《长生殿》) (The Palace of Eternity). Both plays gain popularity due to embedded genuine feelings, political undertones, and dramatic plot design. The two famous scenes depicted reflect dire situations caused by war rather than flimsy love stories. In *Fifteen Strings of Coins*, for another example, the anti-protagonist, Lou Ashu (娄阿鼠) "Rat", can hardly be deemed "elegant" judging by either his physical appearance or his inner mind. Still this play was hugely popular among audiences and successfully brought attention to the waning *kunqu* tradition in the 1950s.

Even though an artistic form like *kunqu* is supposed to be elegant, it is not always possible, neither it is desirable, for a play to use "elegant" language throughout. Being elegant is not believed to be the requirement for a play. But today's critics tend to merge the standard of a play with that of an artistic form. They criticize the "vulgar" part in *Peony Pavilion* and refer to it as "dross". They propose to cut it out because it does not meet the artistic standard of "elegant" *kunqu*, which is like trimming the foot to fit the shoe. For example, Xu Shuofang (徐朔方) deplores the Taoist nun's obscene and bawdy self-introduction in Scene 17 in his co-edition of *Peony Pavilion* with Yang Xiaomei (杨笑梅) (2005) ; Chen Fang's (陈芳) *The Performance and Inheritance of Kunqu* (《昆剧的表演与传承》, 2010) argues that scene 34 where Tutor Chen prescribed men's underwear for Liniang is ridiculous and superstitious according to today's standard. But she does not realise that even judging by the standard of Tang Xianzu's time, Tutor Chen's prescription is also ridiculous. Influenced by their opinion, modern productions almost always cut the "dross" in *Peony Pavilion* — the "vulgar" humour which actually liven the stage are excluded from the stage because they are not elegant. Opposing to current opinions, I think that the "dross" has profound dramaturgical meanings considering how the improbable "dross" is justified in the play world, and how the mixture of "dross" contributes to the audience's cognition of the play.

As an artistic form, *kunqu* is not only supposed to be beautiful and elegant, but also to be fixed.

① Pai Hsien-yung, ibid., p. 5, "昆曲本来就是精英文化、高雅文化，是文人雅士欣赏的艺术".

② Li Yu (李玉) is not the earlier mentioned drama theorist Li Yu (李渔) .

Renowned academics such as Pai Hsien-yung, Yu Qiuyu (余秋雨) and Yu Dan (于丹) [①] promote *kunqu* as the best embodiment of excellent Chinese cultural traditions that are stable, solid, and eternal. *Kunqu* has never failed to be figured as "a single, uncompromised lotus flower that resists all the temptations of hybridization and assimilation, symbolizing a perfect Chineseness"[②] even though the meaning of "Chineseness" is uncertain; in fact, the definition of so-called "-ness" like in "Chineseness" and "Englishness" should be called into question - who has the right and the capacity to define national identity? When *kunqu* becomes a symbol of "Chineseness", it has to be as unchangeable and fixed as the northern star that serves as the guiding axis.

As the impression of *kunqu* is fixed, performances repeat themselves in order to retain this impression. Carlson defines the physical theatre "a site of the continuing reinforcement of memory", [③] and the memory of past performances is haunting new performers who are consciously or unconsciously influenced by their predecessors. The haunting process reinforces the performance memory, and the process goes on without an end. Theatre becomes a repository of cultural memory that imitates itself. Compared with Western theatre, the "haunting" and the repetition of past practices is especially true for *kunqu* theatre. *Kunqu* tries to set a performance model for each play by regulating every aspect, like singing, gesture and movement.[④] Though there are changes by each new generations of *kunqu* performers, those changes are infinitesimal. New performers amend the performing style according to their individual conditions, and like to adjust the tone according to their voice. Their performance does not vary much and bears a strong mark of their masters. The audience often judges new performers based on how they acquired the essence of their master. Strict imitation of past practices leads to the impression that there is an unbroken line of performance tradition of *kunqu*.

Moreover, when *kunqu* was listed by UNESCO as one of the world intangible cultural heritage in 2001, *kunqu* actors are deemed responsible for reproducing the past performance styles correctly. A monumental effort has been made to archive the traditions by video-recording old maestro's performances. To be *yuan zhi yuan wei* (原汁原味) (original gravy, original flavour), new actors must follow the Qian-Jia tradition (乾嘉传统) (traditions formed during the reign of Emperors Qianlong and Jiaqing) and *Gusu fengfan* (姑苏风范) (style of the Gusu regions) as *kunqu* scholars like Chen Fang have effortlessly emphasized.[⑤]Chen Fang directly names *zhezixi* as *ding shi zhezi* (定式折子) (fixed *kunqu zhezi*) to announce the fixity of *kunqu.*[⑥]The clinging to and absolute

---

① See Pai Hsien-yung (白先勇), *Pai Hsien-yung on Kunqu* (《白先勇说昆曲》, Guilin: Guangxi Normal University Press, 2004), Yu Qiuyu (余秋雨), *The Extreme Beauty: Chinese Calligraphy, Kunqu and Pu'er Tea* (《极端之美——书法、昆曲、普洱茶》, Wuhan: Changjiang wenyi publishing house, 2013), and *The Sound of Dizi: About Kunqu* (《笛声何处——关于昆曲》, Suzhou: Guwu xuan publishing house, 2004), and Yu Dan (于丹), *A Startled Dream in the Garden: The Aesthetic Journey of Kunqu* (《游园惊梦——昆曲艺术审美之旅》, Beijing: Zhonghua shuju, 2007).

② Daphne Pi-Wei Lei, *Operatic China: Staging Chinese Identities Across the Pacific* (New York: Palgrave Macmillan, 2006), p. 255.

③ MarvinCarlson, *The Haunted Stage: Theatre as Memory Machine* (Michigan: University of Michigan Press, 2003), pp. 1-2.

④ Those regulations of performance have become distinct features of *kunqu*. Here I am not criticizing the regulations nor *kunqu*, but rather, with the discrepancy of *kunqu*'s aesthetic pursuit and the artistic standard of *Peony Pavilion*.

⑤ See Chen Fang (陈芳), *Performance and Inheritance of Kunju* (《昆剧的表演与传承》, Taipei: National Publishing House, 2010), pp. 78-79.

⑥ Chen Fang (陈芳), *Performance and Inheritance of Kunju* (《昆剧的表演与传承》, Taipei: National Publishing House, 2010), p. 88.

faithfulness towards traditions are encouraged in *kunqu* theatres. Each theatre advertises that their performance style as the most "authentic" by "sourcing lines of transmission"① from the Qian-jia tradition and trace the lineage of inheritance. Thus *kunqu* performances of *Peony Pavilion* become more and more fixed, trying to get closer to the airy ideal of Qian-jia tradition and Gusu style.②

But for a play, it is more desirable to leave the ground of interpretation open rather than fixing it or closing it up. Thus comes the key conflict between the written play of *Peony Pavilion* and the artistic form of *kunqu* — a play's meaning remains open, but fixed patterns of singing, gesture and movement in *kunqu* performance tend to eliminate the space of interpretation.

Another reason for the "interpretive chasm" between *kunqu* and *Peony Pavilion* is due to *kunqu*'s weakness in presenting a complicated psyche through the system of role categorization. There are five main role types in *kunqu*, *sheng* (生) (male), *dan* (旦) (female), *jing* (净) (painted face), *mo* (末) (middle-aged or old men), and *chou* (丑) (clown). Though each main role type has its own sub-types, the sub-types do not vary much from each other, or else they would not be categorized into the same type. Often the audience has a fixed impression of each role type (for example, all *dan* characters should be graceful), which is not conducive to form a new perspective on seeing a character's individual and idiosyncratic traits. Once the impression of characters is fixed, it is hard to excavate a play's "philosophical profundity"③. Thus Li Ruru once reminded us that "Shakespeare's philosophical speculations, psychological reflections and the inner conflicts of his characters"④ might posit a great challenge for Chinese *xiqu* adaptations of Shakespeare. This case is not only true for adapting Shakespeare's plays, but also for presenting the complicated characters in *Peony Pavilion* and other thought-provoking Chinese plays.

The aesthetic pursuit of *kunqu* does not closely equate with that of a play, and it is beyond *kunqu*'s capacity to present the structural complexities of *Peony Pavilion.* To seek the way out for modern manifestation of *Peony Pavilion*, I think it is helpful to adopt an intercultural perspective to see what can be learned from others as Antony Tatlow's words quoted in the beginning of the article promisingly predicts. In order to fully tap the play's potential and further, to reinvigorate the repertoire of classical Chinese plays, I call for an epistemological shift in theatre practitioners' perceptions and practices, which will be the topic for another article.

作者简介：王慧敏，英国南安普顿大学博士，主要从事文学与跨文化戏剧研究。

① Kim Hunter-Gordon, p. 119.

② The reason why I describe the Qian-jia tradition as "airy" is because that most of the performance traditions of *kunqu* were invented in the 1980s through the process of *nie xi* (捏戏) "kneading a play" [like a clay], that is to design new choreography and musical structure for old plays. For more details, see Hunter-Gordon, pp. 85-8.

③ Feng Wei, *Intercultural Aesthetics in Traditional Chinese Theatre From 1978 to the Present* (London: Palgrave Macmillan, 2020), p. 55.

④ Li Ruru, *Shashibiya: Staging Shakespeare in China* (Hong Kong: HKU Press, 2003), p. 117.

Shakespearean Allusions and National Identities in Elly Griffiths' Ruth Galloway Books

Lisa Hopkins

【Abstract】 In *Shakespearean Allusion in Detective Fiction*, I argued that in Golden Age detective fiction, "Sometimes DCI Shakespeare is assigned to border patrol… Above all, he is used to negotiating between the English and the Germans, and the question of what Shakespeare and Englishness mean to each other becomes particularly pressing when DCI Shakespeare enlists." In more recent years, however, Shakespeare has been used to insist on other ways of differentiating and demarcating Englishness. In this paper, I look specifically at how Shakespearean allusions have been mobilised in Elly Griffiths' Ruth Galloway books, a series of detective fiction which started in 2009 and is still ongoing. I argue that there are two kinds of intercultural engagement at work, one connected to the embedding of allusion to early modern plays within a twenty-first century novel and the other generated by the books' interest in migration, invasion, and encounters between different cultures. Elly Griffiths is in fact a pseudonym for Domenica di Rosa, who is, as the name suggests, of Italian origin but born and brought up in England, giving her a culturally liminal position on the edge of two different kinds of heritage, and the crimes featured in the books are often literally liminal in that they involve bodies buried on the edge between sea and land. They are also typically connected to stories of invasion and migration, and Shakespearean allusion is put into sustained and telling dialogue with concern about ethnicities, identities, and the weight of the past on the present. For Griffiths, Shakespearean allusion is a way of drawing out the resonances of her novels, but also of reminding her readers of how braided and hybridised national and cultural identities can be.

【Key Words】 Shakespearean Allusions; national identities; Elly Griffiths; Ruth Galloway books

艾莉·格里菲斯的侦探小说系列中的莎士比亚典故与国家身份

丽莎·霍普金斯

【摘　要】 在《侦探小说中的莎士比亚式暗示》一文中，笔者认为在黄金时代的侦探小说中，"有时 DCI 莎士比亚被分配到边境巡逻……最重要的是，他被用来在英国人和德国人之间进行谈判；当 DCI 莎士比亚入伍时，莎士比亚以及英国性对彼此意味着什么的问题变得尤为紧迫”。然而，近年来，莎士比亚已经常被用来作为其他方式来区分和划分什么是英国性。本文中，笔者特别关注莎士比亚的典故是如何在 Elly Griffiths 的 *Ruth Galloway* 系列书中被运用的。*Ruth Galloway* 是始于 2009 年的一系列侦探小说，至今仍在持续更新，有两种跨文化因素在起作用。一种是与 21 世纪小说中嵌入的对早期现代戏剧的暗示有关，另一种是由书中对移民、入侵和不同文化间遭遇的兴趣产生的。Elly Griffiths 实际上是 Domenica di Rosa 的笔名，顾名思义，Domenica di Rosa 有着意大利血统，但在英国出生和长大，这使她处在两种不同文化传统的边缘。她书中所描述的犯罪也通常是文学性的边缘地带，因为它们涉及埋在海陆边缘的尸体。它们通常也与入侵和移民的故事有关，并且莎士比亚式的暗示被投入到持续的、有说服力的对话中来呈现对种族、身份和过去对现在的影响的关注。对 Griffiths 来说，莎士比亚式的暗示是一种勾勒出她小说引起共鸣的方式，同时也提醒她的读者，民族和文化身份是多么错综复杂。

【关键词】莎士比亚典故；国家身份；艾莉·格里菲斯；侦探小说

In *Shakespearean Allusion in Detective Fiction*, I argued that in Golden Age detective fiction, “Sometimes DCI Shakespeare is assigned to border patrol... Above all, he is used to negotiate between the English and the Germans, and the question of what Shakespeare and Englishness mean to each other becomes particularly pressing when DCI Shakespeare enlists.” In more recent years, however, Shakespeare has been used to insist on other ways of differentiating and demarcating Englishness. I want to look specifically at how Shakespearean allusions have been mobilised in Elly Griffiths' Ruth Galloway books, which focus on a university lecturer in forensic archaeology who lives in Norfolk and has a complicated on-off relationship with a married detective chief inspector called Harry Nelson. I'll argue that there are two kinds of intercultural engagement at work, one connected to the embedding of allusion to early modern plays within a twenty-first century novel and the other generated by the books' interest in migration, invasion, and encounters between different cultures.

Elly Griffiths is in fact a pseudonym for Domenica di Rosa, who is, as the name suggests, of Italian origin but born and brought up in England, giving her a culturally liminal position on the edge of two different kinds of heritage, and the crimes which Ruth and Nelson investigate are often literally liminal in that they involve bodies buried on the edge between sea and land. They are also typically connected to invasions (by the Beaker Folk, the Romans, the Anglo-Saxons, the Vikings, and by a small party of German soldiers during the Second World War) and also to stories of refugees and migrants, and in all these cases the author's attitude is notably liberal. The events of *The Lantern Men* unfold in the shadow of Brexit - Ruth thinks that if she turns on Radio Four she may hear “*The News*, perhaps, Corrie Corfield making even the Brexit negotiations sound comforting” (334-335) — and perhaps because of that broadens its range of interest, introducing Detective Sergeant Tony Zhang and having Ruth reflect that “In China dying is called ‘going west’” (329). The next book, *The Night Hawks*, was published in February 2021, when the UK was in its third coronavirus lockdown, and includes two deaths caused by a vaccine and David Brown's theory that “just a few hundred years after the arrival of the Beakers, only ten percent of the native population remained. Neolithic Britons were wiped out. It's my theory that it was a plague. A new virus brought by the Beakers from Central Europe" (21) ; however any suggestion of blaming China is deflected by the fact that strontium isotope analysis of the bones of the potential Beaker person points to him being from Poland (255), and in the same book Ruth's father remarries "a woman of colour" (82).

As well as having a liberal sensibility, the books are often comic in tone, with Ruth and Nelson supported by a cast of likable regulars including a part-time druid, Ruth's annoying head of department (who once played Juliet at his all-boys school), and a ravishingly beautiful English Literature lecturer called Shona who is Ruth's best friend. It is Shona who first smuggles Shakespeare into the stories. In the first book in the series, *The Crossing Places*, Nelson shows Ruth some anonymous letters he has received over the years in connection with the disappearance of a child. One contains the sentence "A man may see how the world goes with no eyes" (59-60) and the fourth, addressed "Dear Harry" for the first time rather than "Nelson", begins "'A little touch of Harry in the night.' How wise Shakespeare was, a shaman for all time" (60) ; finally the letter dated Hallowe'en begins "Now is the time when the dead walk. Graves have yawned and yielded up their dead" (64). Ruth "recognises the Bible and Shakespeare, of course" (66) ; she makes a list headed "Literary" and topped by *King Lear*, *Henry V* and *Julius Caesar* (68). She wishes she had Shona for some of the other references'(66), but this wish backfires, for later "When she looks at Shona's bookshelves and sees T. S. Eliot nestling next to Shakespeare she thinks of the Lucy Downey letters" (188) and realises that Shona must have been involved in helping the anonymous writer. In a much later book, *The Night Hawks*, David Brown says "'The good is oft interred with their bones' ... We did Julius Caesar at school. I was Mark Anthony" and the narrator tells us that Ruth "distrusts people who quote Shakespeare. Shona's always doing it" (167).

Shona is not, however, the only person who quotes Shakespeare; indeed the narrator's own voice occasionally does so. In the second book in the series, *The Janus Stone*, "The diver appears a minute later, carrying a skull carefully on the flat of his hand. He looks like an actor playing Hamlet in an experimental production (Shakespeare meets Beckett perhaps?). Ruth takes the small skull in both her hands" (111). Later in *The Janus Stone* there is a diary entry for 20 June (these are nameless and dateless; only at the close do we discover that they are by Roderick Spens and date back to the 1950s):

> I am tired. Sometimes I just want to lie down and sleep and forget everything. By a sleep to say we end the heartache...
>
> *Hamlet* Act 3, scene 1. To die, to sleep; To sleep, perchance to dream: Ay, there's the rub. (163)

Finally Ruth, in danger from Roderick Spens, tells Nelson that he is the real ringslinger: "Ruth knows it's a long shot but maybe Nelson would be sufficiently intrigued to Google Ringslinger and find the Danish king, the grandfather, according to Erik, of Hamlet" (298). She is creatively using her knowledge of Viking mythology to counter Roderick Spens's familiarity with the classics, but the allusion also implicitly invites the reader to frame other events in the book in terms provided by

Hamlet. When we read that "Roderick looks quite hurt. 'I'm not mad, ' he says. 'I've got a first in classics from Cambridge'" (287) we may condemn his ludicrous egotism, but we may also start to think about what actually constitutes madness. Similarly we might think about the prince of Denmark when Nelson hears the gunshot and jumps in the river even though "He has no idea where he is going, he just knows that he can't stand to wait for one second longer, a useless bystander, hearing sounds of gunfire and doing nothing" (314). He fears to find Ruth in the water like Ophelia, a scene which Griffiths repeatedly evokes: in *The Ghost Fields* "Alice is silent for a moment, looking into the distance. There's a poster over her desk showing a girl floating in water, flowers all around her" (277), and in *The Stone Circle*, Judy notes that in Shona's office "There are pictures too, a poster of woman drowning in flowers (Ophelia?) " (42). Equally, though, we might notice that Nelson himself is the opposite of Hamlet, never introspective and always in action, and we might also connect the allusion with the book's interest in parents and children:

"Ah, fathers and sons."Reginald Wilson glances at his son, working industriously on the marble, its sides shining in the light from the fire. "That"s what it's all about, isn't it? Passing the business on to your son. That's the only reason why any of us do it. (240)

For Nelson, though, there is a different priority:

Fathers and daughters, that is the phrase that keeps running through Nelson's head (320).

The uses to which Griffiths puts these Shakespearean allusions are fundamentally connected to the series' interest in the relationship between the present and the past. Nelson and Judy are both Catholics, a confessional identity which *The Woman in Blue* reminds us was once universal in England (in *The House at Sea's End*, "The notice board proclaims the church as Anglican but, as Judy's Irish Catholic father would say, 'It was ours once'" [175]) ; Cathbad is a Druid, aligning him with pre-Roman Britain. In addition, Ruth, Nelson, Cathbad and Frank are all immigrants to Norfolk, and questions of immigration and indigenous identities are hotly contested in the books. In *The Janus Stone* Trace, who is later revealed to be Roderick Spens's granddaughter, says "The Romans brought law and order and infrastructure. We were nothing but a band of disparate warring tribes until they came along" (198-199), but there is a much more negative view of colonialism and empire-building when Nelson almost immediately afterwards explains that "Walter Spens built the house on Woolmarket Road. He was, by all accounts, rather an eccentric. Had a collection of stuffed animals and liked to dress as an African chieftain" (200). (Matters are not improved when we discover that Walter Spens's grandson had a school on Waterloo Road and made his children speak in Latin at mealtimes.) In *The House at Sea's End*, which like *The Janus Stone* has a son who must decide whether to cover up the sin of his father, Nelson thinks "Never trust a man who flies the Union Jack" (43), the plot directly centres on invasion. This is presaged when Ruth looks at the skeletons buried on the beach and imagines one as "A tall man (the long bones show that), blond-haired with a jutting chin. A Viking, she thinks, though she knows this is historically unlikely" (49). Later Archie Whitcliffe explains that the Home Guard went out at night "looking for invaders"

(105), and on one occasion they found some and shot them in what Dieter Eckhart identifies as "a British war crime" (129). Dieter himself almost immediately becomes the victim of another crime when he is shot by Craig, partly because of his investigation of events during the war — Craig says "I had to protect my grandfather's memory" (356) — and partly because he is dating Clara Hastings, whose surname suggests the last time Britain was invaded. Craig says "Can't have a Hastings marrying a German, destroying that fine English bloodline" (360), but when Irene Hastings says "My job was to shoot the children and shoot myself" (201) and Nelson points out the parallel with Frau Goebbels, the distinction between the Germans and "the English" collapses. A further perspective is introduced by Tatjana, Ruth's Bosnian friend whose child and parents were massacred by Serbs, who says "I'm sure the Celts were pragmatists too. When your land is invaded, you tend to be" (171). And once again the narrative is pointed by references to fathers:

Nelson thinks "Christ, why are people always talking about fathers?" (189) and later "has his own suspicions. Could Superintendent Whitcliffe be the father of Maria's little boy?" (384). The idea continues into *A Room Full of Bones*, where Nelson says "It's always the dad's fault" (322), and where changing circumstances and sensibilities are once again registered: *Gone with the Wind* is the favourite film of Nelson's mother Maureen (73), but "Over the last few years, a great number of refugees from Eastern Europe have come to settle in King's Lynn. It's customary for the press, and some police officers, to blame every crime on the new arrivals. Nelson knows it's his job to stamp on such talk" (76).

It is in *Dying Fall* that Shakespearean allusion is first put into sustained and telling dialogue with concern about ethnicities, identities, and the weight of the past on the present. The liberal Cathbad may maintain that "There's no such thing as pure-blood English" (188), but Ruth "remembers Dan's diaries and the letters calling him an 'upstart Jew'" (284) and Clayton Henry says of the White Hand's attitude to King Arthur, "They call him the White King, the High King. They wouldn't want him associated with the Romans. They see the Romans as foreigners, invaders" (173). Comically, the DNA of the bones which the members of the White Hand believe to be those of King Arthur identify him as having a parent born in North Africa, and the book also introduces the black detective sergeant Tim Heathfield, who towards the end "thinks about Pendragon and about Dan Golding and Clayton Henry. None of these men were fathers, unless you count Henry's stepdaughter" (379). This prefigures Tim's own story arc, which culminates in the uncertainty over whether Michelle's baby will prove to be his or Nelson's, but it is also connected to allusions to three Shakespearean tragedies which deal with fatherhood: "'The raven himself is hoarse that croaks the fatal entrance of Duncan under my battlements, ' says Lady Macbeth. And, of course, that visit went spectacularly well" (53) ; "Ruth finds herself looking at one picture in particular. Dan is examining the skull, which is lying on a tarpaulin by the trench. There is something Hamlet-like about the pose and certainly, in retrospect, something almost tragic about Dan's bowed head" (294) ; and "So many stories involve the appearance of an unknown 'other', the stranger whom nobody recognises. Who is the third who walks beside you? Christ on the road to Emmaus. Poor Tom on the blasted heath" (315). The first of these is obviously about *Macbeth*, a play in which the hero's own childlessness prompts him to murder the children of his rivals; the second is about *Hamlet*, where the hero must avenge his father's murder; and the third is about *King Lear*, where both the king and Gloucester make mistakes about their children but are forgiven by them.

Shakespeare is also a presence in *The Outcast Dead*. After Michael has been found Frank asks "All's well that ends well?" (394), the restaurant to which Phil invites everyone to celebrate Ruth's birthday is called Iagos (172), and when they have dinner there "Shona is laughing and flicking her hair around. Ruth knows that Shona too thinks she's wasted on the University of North Norfolk. How long before she's making a cutting-edge series on Shakespeare, striding around Stratford-on-Avon in a lace top and leather trousers" (191). *Hamlet* is remembered when Frank says "I'm just a historian who pops up on the cable channel now and again" and "Ruth, remembering Rebecca's reaction on meeting Frank, thinks that he protests a little too much" (192). Most significant, though, are a number of allusions to *Macbeth*. Corinna, presenter of *Women Who Kill*, says "I'm a serious actress ... I've played Hedda and Lady Macbeth. This is just a sideline" (188) ; on the Saltmarsh Ruth "thinks that she sees some little lights far out towards the shore ... 'The west yet glimmers with some streaks of day.' Where's that from? *Macbeth*, she thinks, a play too full of bloody babes and murdered children for her liking" (294) ; and finally when Cathbad visits "Ruth tells him about Mother Hook, how she was convicted of killing the children in her care. She tells him that Frank thinks she was innocent and the tension on set between Corinna's 'black as midnight hag' and Dani's wronged childminder" (406). A play with some similarities to *Macbeth* is also remembered: "Ruth looks up at the cameraman. His face is in shadow and, just for a second, the camera on his shoulder gives him a monstrous misshapen look. Richard the Third, the bottled spider" (351).

The Ghost Fields too is concerned with an inheritance: George Blackstock senior killed one of his older brothers and drove the other away, and his illegitimate son, the druid Hazel, has similar plans, so it is no surprise that Blake Goodheart refers to Ruth's appearance when the family is at dinner as "Banquo's ghost" (140). *The Woman in Blue* continues the interest in *Macbeth*: the letter to Freya says "You strut and fret your hour upon the stage, but then you will be heard no more" (279-280) ; when Ruth says she'll show the letter to the police Freya objects, "It's not worth it ... It's like the *Macbeth* quotation. 'Full of sound and fury, signifying nothing'" (282) ; "But *Macbeth*, thinks Ruth after Freya has left, is not the best omen. Not only is the play notoriously unlucky, but she seems to remember that quite a few people get murdered in it" (283). A little later Ruth thinks of "the threat wrapped up in the quotation from *Macbeth*: 'then you will be heard no more'" (295).

The Dark Angel introduces a new play. The book opens with Angelo Morelli telling the camera that "This countryside has been the scene of invasion and battle from the Neolithic times until the Second World War, when the German troops fought Italian partisans in the Liri Valley" (1) ; later he tells Ruth that "Some people still see the Romans as invaders" (222). Ruth says "I don't think we British can imagine what it must have been like to have your country occupied" (61), but her trip to Monte Cassino with Nelson is another reminder that the British too can be guilty of war crimes. Elsa says "I want people to remember Papa as hero" (295). This is a book about outsiders and insiders. Angelo says "the body was buried a little outside the main town. That, and the fact that he was buried face down, makes us think that Toni was an outsider" (101), which makes Ruth remember the graffiti which had greeted them when they first arrived at their borrowed apartment: "*Stranieri andate a casa*, thinks Ruth. She remembers Angelo saying that, here, even people from the next village are foreigners" (101). The book is set in Lazio, and Ruth explains that some people think Angelo Morelli "should be concentrating on the Italic tribes, like the Volsci" (82), to which Shona replies "The Volsci... Don't they come into *Coriolanus*? He became famous by fighting the Volsci, then, when he was exiled, he joined the Volsci to besiege Rome" (82). "Ruth has only the vaguest idea of the plot of *Coriolanus*. She did *Macbeth* for O level and *King Lear* for A level. Both tragic, doom-laden plays. *The sleeping and the dead are but as pictures ... Nothing will come of nothing*" (83). Later two more Shakespeare plays are remembered: "Cathbad ... is on his best form, keeping the children entertained with stories about statues coming to life" (282), suggesting *The Winter's Tale*, and "It's as if she had looked down at Angelo's feet and seen, instead of handmade Italian loafers, cloven hooves" (322), echoing the end of *Othello*. This is particularly appropriate because the events in Italy are counterpointed by Tim's affair with Michelle, which echoes the story of Othello and Desdemona in that Tim is black and Michelle is white, and there is an inherent ambiguity about whether the title *The Dark Angel* refers to Angelo, who is white but wicked, or Tim, who is black but noble: at the end of the book he dies to save Michelle and her daughter Laura, and Laura actually sees his soul fly out of his body in the shape of a bright and beautiful bird. For Griffiths, then, Shakespearean allusion is a way of drawing out the resonances of her novels, but also of reminding her readers of how braided and hybridised national and cultural identities can be.

参考文献

[1] GRIFFITHS E. 2016. The Crossing Places [2009] [M]. London: Quercus.

[2] GRIFFITHS E. 2016. The Janus Stone [2010][M]. London: Quercus.

[3] GRIFFITHS E. 2016. The House at Sea's End [2011][M]. London: Quercus.

[4] GRIFFITHS E. 2016. Dying Fall [2013][M]. London: Quercus.

[5] GRIFFITHS E. 2016. The Outcast Dead [2014][M]. London: Quercus.

[6] GRIFFITHS E. 2016. The Ghost Fields [2015][M]. London: Quercus.

[7] GRIFFITHS E. 2016. The Woman in Blue[M]. London: Quercus.

[8] GRIFFITHS E. 2018. The Dark Angel[M]. London: Quercus.

[9] GRIFFITHS E. 2019. The Stone Circle[M]. London: Quercus.

[10] GRIFFITHS E. 2020. The Lantern Men[M]. London: Quercus.

[11] GRIFFITHS E. 2021. The Night Hawks[M]. London: Quercus.

[12] GRIFFITHS E. 2016. A Room Full of Bones [2012][M]. London: Quercus.

作者简介：Lisa Hopkins，英国谢菲尔德哈勒姆大学教授，主要从事文学戏剧与莎士比亚研究。

Brazilian Tradapatations of *Romeo and Juliet*

Maria-Clara V. Galery

【Abstract】 The presentation proposes a discussion of whether tradaptation, a term coined by the Quebecois writer Michel Garneau, may be applied to the analysis of two Brazilian productions of *Romeo and Juliet* staged in the 1990s. Garneau used neologism specifically to designate his translations of *The Tempest, Macbeth* and *Coriolanus*, created in the latter half of the twentieth century. These Quebecois iterations of Shakespeare reflect a postcolonial context where the translator's choice of privileging the French spoken in Quebec, along with other local cultural references, highlight autonomy from the cultural dominance of France and rebel against the political and economic power of English Canada. Since then, tradaptation has been used in other contexts to address strategies of translation, especially ones committed to intercultural encounters where traces of alterity are obliterated in favor of local markers. Such is the case with the two Brazilian renditions of *Romeo and Juliet* I intend to discuss here: as hybrid creations, they fuse and bring into contact diverse fields of cultural memory, popular and canonic. Grupo Galpão's *Romeu e Julieta*, first produced in 1992, provides an intercultural vision of Shakespeare totally immersed in the folklore of the Brazilian state of Minas Gerais. It makes use of traditional songs and incorporates the language of *Grande Sertão Veredas*, one Brazil's most important and original novels. The other production to be examined is Ariano Suassuna's 1996 play, *A história de amor de Romeu e Julieta* [*The Love Story of Romeo and Juliet*]. This work is grounded in the tradition of *literatura de cordel*, the chapbook ballads produced in the arid Northeast of Brazil, where Suassuna remains an important playwright and cultural reference. The name *cordel* (thin rope or string), comes from the Iberian Peninsula, and refers to the practice of hanging booklets from a string for display in open-air fairs and markets. In my presentation, I intend to interrogate to what extent viewing these plays as tradaptions is relevant, bearing in mind that self-conscious awareness of imported European culture is a fundamental issue in Latin American critical reflection. *Tradaptation*, as a concept, offers a strategy for minority cultures to affirm identity and creatively appropriate the canon.

【Key Words】 *Romeo and Juliet*; Brazilian tradaptation; Shakespeare; Brazilian literature

巴西对《罗密欧与朱丽叶》的改编

玛丽亚-克拉拉·加勒里

【摘　要】本文讨论魁北克作家 Michel Garneau 创造的术语 Tradapatation 是否可以用于分析 20 世纪 90 年代在巴西上演的两部《罗密欧与朱丽叶》。加诺用这个新名词，专门用来指代他对《暴风雨》《麦克白》和《科利奥兰纳斯》的翻译，译作完成于 20 世纪后半叶。这些莎士比亚的魁北克版翻译反映了一种后殖民主义的背景，在这种背景下，翻译过程中，会选择将魁北克的法语和其他本土文化参照物放在首位，突出了法国文化主导地位的自主性，并对英属加拿大的政治和经济力量进行了反抗。继而，Tradapatations 就被用于其他背景下的翻译策略中，特别是那些应用于跨文化交锋的策略，在这种交锋中，他异性的痕迹为了满足呈现本土标记的需求而删除被抹去。笔者在这里打算讨论的《罗密欧与朱丽叶》的两个巴西版本就是如此：作为混合创作，它们使不同的文化记忆领域，流行的也好，典型的也好，开始融合并开始相互接触。加尔博（Grupo Galpão）的《罗密欧与朱丽叶》于 1992 年首次上演，提供了一个有关于莎士比亚的跨文化视角，完全沉浸在巴西米纳斯吉拉斯州的民间传说中。它使用了传统歌曲，并融入了一部巴西最重要的原创小说的语言。另一部要研究的作品是苏阿苏纳（Ariano Suassuna）1996 年的戏剧《罗密欧与朱丽叶的爱情史》。这部作品的根基是巴西民间文学传统，即在巴西干旱的东北部产生的民谣。在那里，苏阿苏纳仍然是一个重要的剧作家以及文化指称。cordel（细绳或绳子）这个名字来自伊比利亚半岛，指的是将小册子挂在绳子上以便在露天集市上展示的做法。在本文中，笔者打算探讨一下在多大程度上，这些戏剧是能够与 Tradapatations 有关联，同时也会考虑到外来欧洲文化的自觉意识是拉丁美洲批评反思的一个基本因素。Tradapatations 作为一个概念，为少数群体文化提供了一种身份认同并创造性地使用这种方法的思路。

【关键词】《罗密欧与朱丽叶》；巴西本土化改编；莎士比亚；巴西文学传统

I will start this discussion of Brazilian translations/adaptations of Shakespeare by pointing out that self-conscious awareness of imported European culture is a fundamental issue in Latin American critical reflection, where anguish over European influence has assumed various guises. Aesthetic movements as diverse as romanticism, naturalism, and modernism (derived, ironically from their European counterparts) have made national identity their centerpiece.① Latin American cultural specificity is contingent upon the construction of a "space in-between", where a rift is made between model and copy. What this means is that rather than copying the works that Europeans exported to the New World, artists and intellectuals must divert from these models and inscribe their difference.② In this manner, it becomes possible to move beyond the predicament of the

① Roberto Schwarz, "Nacional por subtração", in *As ideias fora do lugar: Ensaios selecionados* (São Paulo: Companhia das Letras, 2014), 81-102.

② Silviano Santiago, *The Space In-Between: Essays on Latin American Culture.* Ed. Ana Lúcia Gazzola (Durham and London: Duke University Press, 2001) .

center-periphery binary.

This is an important point to keep in mind while examining the various issues involved in the translation of Shakespeare and the fashioning of Brazilian Shakespearean identities. My aim in this paper is the discussion whether *tradaptation*, a neologism coined by the Québécois writer Michel Garneau, may be applied to the analysis of Brazilian production of *Romeo and Juliet* staged in the 1990s by Grupo Galpão. While it may seem ironic that yet another foreign concept is elected in a discussion involving Brazilian cultural identity, it is important to understand that, in a manner somewhat similar to Brazil, Québécois society also struggles to assert its cultural distinctiveness.

Tradaptation fuses the problematic distinction between two processes, translation and adaptation, viewed as distinct from one another. However, the difference between them is problematic and difficult to pinpoint. There are questions of value involved in the binary which oppose translation from adaptation. Among other points, the need to distinguish one from the other is tied in with the fallacy of authenticity and faithfulness, a perspective that considers translation as being superior to adaptation, for it views the former as closer or more faithful to the source text than the latter, achieving a higher degree of equivalence. Adaptation, following the same line of reasoning, is seen as deviant and domesticating. But, as Katja Krebs illustrates, appraising the value of translation over adaptation depends on the eye of the beholder, who might consider issues such as "creative freedom versus linguistic confinement, or piracy versus trustworthiness and faithfulness, depending on which side of the fence [the judge is] sitting on".[①] Furthermore, works considered to be translations in a certain historical moment and context may be viewed as adaptations in another. An interesting paradigm of this phenomenon is the rewritings of Shakespeare by Jean-François Ducis in France, during the eighteenth century. Ducis's rendition of plays such as *Hamlet* or *Othello* in French is seen as the first complete translations of the English poet in French, although the term translation is problematic here not only because Ducis spoke no French, but also because of the numerous alterations he imposed upon Shakespeare's text, making the plays conform to the conventions of the French neoclassical stage. Such domestication of Shakespeare, radically aligning it to the requirements of the target culture, approximates Ducis's work to the practice of adaptation.

In the theatre, the dramaturgical process for the rendition of the foreign text often blurs the line between translation and adaptation. This in itself would be a justification for the use of tradaptation when speaking of translation for the stage. But the term bears a specificity that should not be overlooked. Garneau coined it to describe his three iterations of Shakespeare in the 1970s and 1980s: *The Tempest/ La tempête* (written in 1973 and revised in 1982), *Macbeth* (1978), and *Coriolanus/ Coriolan* (1989).[②] The historical context in which these plays were done is all-important, for they took place during Québec's *Révolution Tranquille* or quiet revolution, where the Canadian province asserted its national identity, independent from French European culture, and

① Kbrebs, Katja "Translation and Adaptation — Two Sides of an Ideological Coin", in Ton Hoenselaars (ed) *Shakespeare and the Language of Translation* (London: Arden Shakespeare, 2012), 42-53, 43.

② Lieblein, Leanor "'Cette belle langue': the tradaptation of Shakespeare in Quebec", in Ton Hoenselaars (ed) *Shakespeare and the Language of Translation* (London: Arden Shakespeare, 2012), 240-254.

American influence. While discussing the relevance of tradaptation, Susan Knutson addresses two important characteristics: firstly, the visibility of cultural exchange; secondly, the immediacy of the occasion in which it appears. She quotes Denis Salter, who points out that "tradaptations should be exercises in radical contingency, responsible only for the particular historical moment in which they attempt to decolonize and reinterrogate the Shakespearean text". Akin to the ephemeral nature of performance, tradaptations should "vanish once their particular historical moment has passed and new tradaptations should take place".① A tradaptation does not seek, by any means, to be a definitive rendition of the play, but one that bears relevance to a particular place and time. Another important aspect is the linguistic texture used in the dialogue between source and target cultures, where the choice of language is crucial, in order to evoke memories and affections, as well as capture cultural specificity.

As mentioned before, one of the aims of this presentation is to examine whether the concept of tradaptation enlightens the analysis of two different renditions of *Romeo and Juliet* that took place in Brazil, a culturally diverse country. Both productions provided a dialogue between the regional context where they emerged and the wider tradition of Shakespearean dramaturgy.

In 1992, Grupo Galpão, a company dedicated to street theatre, presented a version of *Romeo and Juliet* totally immersed in the folklore of the Brazilian state of Minas Gerais. Away from the traditional cultural centres of Rio and São Paulo, the path blazed by Galpão is truly unique in the history of Brazilian theatre. Yet the origins of a group whose work is so intrinsically related to the popular roots of Brazilian culture are unexpectedly tied to foreign incentives: the company was first formed when a group of young Brazilian actors worked on a production of Brecht's *The Good Woman of Setzuan*, which came forth after a series of workshops with the Munich Free Theatre, promoted by the *Goethe Institut* in Brazil. The contact with German theatre practitioners provided a cosmopolitan perspective which was a key element for the development of the aesthetics of the company, enabling it to explore elements of Brazilian popular culture while warding off provincialism and parochialism.②

As the group became more firmly established, they decided to invest their focus on physical training, especially acrobatics, stilts and dance. They also underwent extensive training in the use of masks in *commedia dell'arte* with the Italian actress Ariel Genovezzi. Galpão then started experimenting with its own way of using masks, arriving at a distinctive style that combines and alternates the wearing of masks with colourful make-up.

Their production of *Romeo and Juliet*, under the direction of Gabriel Villela, was originally conceived as an open-air performance, but has also been performed inside theatres. It was shown at various international venues, and played twice at Shakespeare's Globe Theatre in London, first in 2000 and later, as part of the Cultural Olympiad, in 2012. For Villela, who comes from Minas Gerais but lives and works in São Paulo, directing Shakespeare's text was an opportunity to

① Denis Salter qtd in Knutson, Susan "'Tradaptation' *Dans le Sens Québécois:* A Word for the Future", in Laurence Raw (ed.) *Translation, Adaptation and Transformation* (London: Bloomsbury, 2013), 112-122, 13.

② Galery, Maria-Clara V. *Identifying Strategies for the Production and Reception of Shakespeare in Brazil and Argentina* (PhD Thesis, University of Toronto, 2000) .

experiment with the fusion of erudite and popular forms. While mounting *Romeo and Juliet*, Villela took the opportunity to become familiarized with the interior of Brazil, the "primitive" country distinct from metropolitan centres. In order to be consistent with their commitment of making art democratically accessible, Galpão anchored the staging of the play in open rehearsals conducted in Morro Vermelho, a small village in the interior of Minas Gerais, where the group interacted with the local inhabitants. Several of the props and also costumes of the play were inspired by the colours of the houses and the overall atmosphere of the village.

Making use of elements derived both from popular and erudite culture, Villela's rendition of Shakespeare evoked the image of clowns from a decadent circus troupe trying to perform a tragedy of love. This was a way of paying tribute to the *mambembe* or amateur travelling companies one might still find in the interior of Brazil. Galpão's declaration of intent as a theatre group, posted on their internet page, stated: "We belong to that class of wandering artists who have perambulated since the beginnings of History, like an epidemic surge, and without which the world would have lost its capacity to re-invent life through dreams, art and poetry [...]."① This statement relates the group to the medieval itinerant troupes of mountebanks in Europe performing in fairs and open-air markets, and that, as Patrice Pavis indicates, "always led an existence on the fringes of official theatre".②

To evoke the image of strolling players, the main scenic element was an old station wagon. Although an automobile might initially appear dissonant and intrusive, bearing no immediate relation to the play, the actors made creative use of the resources offered by the vehicle. Two balance beams were placed above it for the lovers to walk on, insinuating the balancing act of tightrope walkers, a stunt which acquired the metaphoric connotation of love's uncertainty and risk.

The dramatic text used by the group departed from a translation of *Romeo and Juliet* published in the 1940s by Onestaldo de Pennafort.③ This early Brazilian translation of the play has many characteristics of a scholarly endeavor, with several pages of annotations and explicative comments. It was praised for its easy and natural dialogue, which does not obscure the bawdy images, for, according to Antônio Candido, one of Brazil's most important literary critics, "nothing would sadden more the popular Shakespeare than thinking that his work had been transformed into an erudite project inaccessible to the audience."④ Yet Antônio Carlos Brandão, the dramaturg who worked on the production, not only made various cuts on this text, but also established a dialogue between the early translation of Romeo *and Juliet* and *Grande Sertão Veredas*, one of Brazil's most important and original novels, the magnum opus of João Guimarães Rosa.⑤ The language of Rosa's novel is celebrated for its poetic reworking of the speech of the backlands of Minas Gerais, exploring its sonority and archaisms, thus provoking a trance-like state, where the reader is

---

① The link to the page (http: //www.metalink.com.br/cultura/GrupoGalpao/espetaculos.html) is no longer available. It was viewed on 1998.

② Pavis, Patrice *Dictionary of the Theatre: Terms, Concepts and Analysis*. Trans. Christine Shantz (Toronto: University of Toronto Press, 1998), 40.

③ Shakespeare, William. *Romeu e Julieta,* trans. Pennafort (Rio de Janeiro: Civilização Brasileira, 1968) .

④ The comments by Antônio Cândido and Mário de Andrade appear on the book jacket of Pennafort's translation of Shakespeare's play.

⑤ João Guimarães Rosa, *Grande Sertão: Veredas* (São Paulo: Nova Fronteira, 2005) .

absorbed by the logic of a new linguistic universe.① Furthermore, the incisions to Pennafort's translation were supplemented with folkloric music, including traditional children's ballads and *serestas*, romantic songs used in courting serenades.

Vilella had asked the dramaturg to introduce the figure of a narrator, who would follow the characters on stage, comment and provide a pace for the action. The narrator is present throughout the performance, dressed in a mock-Elizabethan fashion reminiscent of a Brazilian backcountry Shakespeare. The language he speaks recalls that used by Rosa in his great novel. Galpão's rendition of *Romeo and Juliet* thus fuses an authoritative Brazilian translation with other linguistic textures derived from popular and literary sources, emphasizing the regional context. In this manner, the play may be viewed as a tradaptation, for it makes cultural exchange visible. It is not a definitive rendition of Shakespeare; it is, rather, the result of a specific moment in the history of the company, a moment when it chose to embrace Shakespeare and work with Gabriel Vilella, inscribing in *Romeo and Juliet* the difference and specificity of Brazilian culture.

Before concluding, I would like to turn to the words of Barbara Heliodora (1923-2015), an important Brazilian Shakespeare translator and specialist. She attended a performance of the play in Rio de Janeiro in 1993 and wrote a review for the daily paper *O Globo*, where she praised the production, defending the cross-cultural approach to the text. She was able to convey a good impression of the concept behind the production when she indicated that it was as if *Romeo and Juliet* were being performed by the rustic "mechanicals" of *A Midsummer Night's Dream*. According to the critic, with his "competence and talent, " Villela was capable of making Grupo Galpão "suggest exactly what Shakespeare hoped his actors would portray with the tragicomedy of 'Pyramus and Thisby': [...] the image of an inexperienced and not very talented group, struggling heroically to give their best." Galpão's talent is not in question here, but the image of Shakespeare's rustic "mechanicals" performing a tragedy of love is very apt for this down-to-earth Brazilian rendition of *Romeo and Juliet*, where the company translates, adapts and appropriates the play, imprinting their identity on the Shakespearean text.

作者简介：Maria-Clara V. Galery，巴西欧鲁普雷图联邦大学教授，主要从事文学戏剧与莎士比亚研究。

① For a discussion of Brandão's references to the work of Guimarães Rosa, please see Aline Miriane Guerios, *A atualidade de Shakespeare: um estudo sobre* Romeu e Julieta *do Grupo Galpão* (MA thesis, Universidade Estadual de Maringá, 2017) .

第二编

莎士比亚悲剧研究

悲剧再生的个体经历与反思：论《李尔王》与《邓巴尔》

张　琼

【摘　要】本文从重写策略及当代经典重写意义出发，探究圣奥宾的《邓巴尔》对莎士比亚《李尔王》的小说重写。作者在细致分析小说中悲剧人物、场景和事件后指出，莎剧批评给予《李尔王》丰富多重的诠释，也带来诸多开放的问题，而重写最有启发性的揭示在于：文学作品和现实世界产生各种纷繁复杂的联系，后者在被前者书写和重构的过程中，并不能由此得以闭合、有序、稳固地安排，而是随着人们的阅读和接受，作品不断被重新语境化，而在性别、社会、心理、历史等的研究探索中，作品内外的现实也在不断变化，因而我们对待经典改写的态度也不断变得更为包容和开放，并不断发现其无论显在还是潜在的可能性。

【关键词】《邓巴尔》；《李尔王》；莎剧小说重写

Individual Experience & Reflection on Tragedy Reborn: St. Aubyn's *Dunbar* versus Shakespeare's *King Lear*

Zhang Qiong

【Abstract】This paper is a study of St. Aubyn's 2017 novel *Dunbar*, an attempt at novelizing Shakespeare's *King Lear*. The author starts with careful comparison and analysis of the tragic characters, settings and events in both works, and proceeds to point out that criticisms on *King Lear* offers many open-ended possibilities for rewriting and re-constructing this canonical tragedy, when the re-contextualization of Lear and *King Lear* bring new insight into the issues of gender, society, psychology and history of the original in the contemporary world.

【Key Words】*Dunbar*; *King Lear*; Shakespeare novelization

英国当代著名作家爱德华·圣奥宾（Edward St. Aubyn）2017 年出版小说《邓巴尔》（*Dunbar*），是霍加斯出版社莎士比亚重写系列之一，也是将经典悲剧《李尔王》重塑的又一尝试。对经典的再创作、重新语境化，从来不是新现象，莎士比亚自身也经常借用、借鉴、整合前人的作品和故事素材。因故事的场景、时间赋予的意义变奏，不同读者、观众、学者的新诠释，演绎者的不同等，原作始终处于不断拓展和变化的过程中，变化才是持久不变的常态。在近几十年，甚至百年的历史中，重塑经典早已是普遍现象，而分析、解读、洞察经典和重写背后错综复杂、丰富的意义，动机，异同，启发，成了当下批评的一个重要关注。

在莎剧的重写创作上，无论是体裁、素材、人物、场景、历史语境的差异，还是新的文化争议的介入，让原作焕发生命力的土壤似乎从未贫瘠。《邓巴尔》在小说现实主义化的努力中，进一步渲染了《李尔王》中恒久的人性探秘和亲情质询，尤其将作家本人的情感经历和反思放入了悲剧净化心灵，甚而升华感情的体验中。这种不无个性原创的重写，无论对熟稔原作的读者，还是对与经典生疏陌生的读者，有着程度不一的新鲜感。

因尼斯在分析经典重写时指出，重写“光谱的一端是原作被解构或混杂拼凑……另一端是尽可能在语调、情感、角色上忠诚于原作……”(Innes),《邓巴尔》则处于光谱两端偏于解构的位置，它从截然不同于戏剧的小说体裁，彻底改变了情节产生的时空背景，聚焦于关于权利金钱欲望和亲情探索,通过让主人公亨利·邓巴尔从原作的一国之君变为当代跨国传媒大亨，让数字时代新的媒介成为全新的权力话语支点，引发当下媒体革命时期读者在作品内外的独特反思,让经典重写涉及作家往往谨慎回避的媒介焦虑和隐患,甚至触发当下正面临的信息汲取、创作载体、传播渠道等颠覆性变革。邓巴尔的传媒帝国覆盖了金融股市、广告宣传、跨国经营、行业并购等领域，也是一个源发、传递、扭曲、操控信息的庞大机构，李尔王曾经的失语、压抑、疯癫在这个媒体机构的系统中更加戏剧化和荒诞化，而他最后领悟并希望珍存的东西，也是我们普通人在信息革命中或许已然疏忽和抛却的东西。因此，企业帝国的维持，权力欲望的满足，亲情人性的养护和珍惜，也更具有不可控的变数和更戏剧化的张力。

圣奥宾擅长刻画家庭功能与心理机制的复杂关系,他让年迈的加拿大传媒大亨邓巴尔陷入类似于李尔王的人生绝境:他在生理上不可逆转地衰老,进入耄耋之年,日益偏执和暴躁;白手起家的媒体帝国在资本市场上动荡起伏;三个女儿中利欲熏心的两人觊觎并企图真正取代父亲的掌控权,两个女儿艾比盖尔和梅根与邓巴尔的私人医生鲍勃早已密谋要夺权控制邓巴尔帝国;充满文艺和理想主义色彩的小女儿弗洛伦斯与两个姐姐同父异母,因为性情直率,忤逆父亲的期待，早早离开家族，置身事外地追求着自己的梦想，让老父亲愤懑甚至暴怒。小说中，两个女儿秘密地将老父邓巴尔送至僻静的湖区疗养院，企图趁机彻底掌控董事会大权，将邓巴尔信托私有化，以此谋取最大利益。邓巴尔认识了同住疗养院的过气喜剧演员彼得(《李尔王》中傻子角色的衍生)，酗酒成瘾的后者协助邓巴尔逃出了疗养院。此后，邓巴尔经历了李尔王式的荒野绝望和愤怒疯癫,在暴风雪袭击的汉普斯特德荒野中爆发出一次次天问式的呐喊。弗洛伦斯赶来寻找到了父亲，两人达成了真正的理解和彼此接纳。然而，弗洛伦斯最后因为被姐姐们下毒而不治身亡，这不啻给走到人生尽头的邓巴尔以最绝望、致命的打击。

《邓巴尔》和《李尔王》有着诸多差异，但两者最戏剧、鲜明的特征是极具张力的心理崩坍和冲突的刻画，人性深处的矛盾挖掘，在两者跨越时空的揭示和启发中，折射着亘古的魅力。这部当代小说的莎剧重写，更像是作家在莎翁经典悲剧中，艺术而隐喻地经历和重塑着自己的个体情感和心理体验。李尔王癫狂的呐喊依然以人性在大自然中的真正袒露（无论是修辞意义还是身体意义上的）方式达成；而莎剧中隐含不露的女性性爱冲动在小说中得到了释放和揭示，读者能明显看到作家在人物刻画上有着聚焦和着力的变化，莎剧中人物主次的差异被弱化，而女性人物塑造也是一些书评者对重写予以批评的重要原因。例如，《卫报》有评论就提出圣奥宾在对女儿们的渲染上，“她们作为性欲强烈的女性，被刻画为必然令人不快，缺乏母性的形象，与圣奥宾其他小说中更微妙的女性人物不同。”（Bookmarks，2018）

一、重写《邓巴尔》的当下意义

将《李尔王》改写为《邓巴尔》，呈现了经典对当下生活和文学创作的影响，必然产生积极的启发。小说中老朽昏庸在李尔王和邓巴尔身上有深度揭示，而人类面对苍老和岁月流逝，其反应和反思的差异本来就是文学创作的丰富资源和灵感启发。在治国和管理公司的权利移交上，人物关系和感情的相应变化，立场和态度的转变等，都会产生巨大的诠释潜力。圣奥宾之前的系列创作以展现和剖析家庭生活的错综矛盾为长，他选择《李尔王》一剧，很大程度上也因为该剧是莎翁笔下家庭分崩离析和悲剧性毁灭的最重要作品，其中涵盖的权力、财富、仁慈、悔恨等母题，有着巨大的戏剧张力。

与李尔王保留君主头衔、放弃执行权的隐退类似，邓巴尔决定仅担任庞大公司董事会的非执行主席，“保留私人飞机、随从、资产、相应的特权等，但是卸下日常的信托管理重担”（2）。这样的决定，正如莎剧带给人们的领悟，连疗养院里精神不时错乱的过气演员彼得都会评述为“失却权力本身，就必然失去权力的表象”（3）。李尔王和邓巴尔都错误地以为头衔、姿态、名号等权力的表象即权力本身，沦为了无法真正看清人本质的悲剧主角。老迈的体能和现实让他们都明白“无法信任自己那忤逆背叛的身体”，却没意识到，除了衰老的身体，有很多表象之下的虚假，不少隐藏的、与表象背道而驰的欲望和情感，也随着衰老而渐渐露出真相。

在《李尔王》的真相不断被揭示的过程中，人们普遍认可柯蒂利亚、埃德加、肯特等角色的善良，鄙夷并贬低高纳里尔、里根、埃德蒙等的邪恶、贪欲和无耻。李尔王和大臣格洛斯特类似平行双线的悲剧命运，更是进一步激发了人们对于善恶的强烈反应。然而，《邓巴尔》中的副线直接被删去，基本的道德评判立场甚至不再如戏剧原作那样鲜明，人物潜在的动机和心路历程在文字叙述中有了更多的展现。弄臣傻子的明确角色和诙谐深刻的语言表达隐匿在前喜剧演员彼得身上，而彼得最终在两个女儿和鲍勃的逼迫下自尽的结局，也将原本不时以话语点破甚至警醒观众的角色，转化为更适于小说读者自行领悟的角色退场。

充满戏剧表演和语言表达的示爱测试在小说中当然不再如舞台上那样鲜明张扬，因而人们的关注会从强烈示爱的反转，从泾渭分明的善恶评判中转移，从《李尔王》近几十年来多重的批评视角中得到诸多启示。尤其是学者曾以“马克思主义，或文化唯物主义，女性主义，以及新历史主义三大重要流派”（Levin）的莎剧批评，对《李尔王》的悲剧动因从社会经济的时代转型和政体变革，女性对父权统治的颠覆企图，理性对感性的批判性审视，女性性爱需求的压抑等予以分析。此外，还有新历史主义视角下关于中心价值体系的历史维度的分析，仪式功能等。莎剧批评给予《李尔王》足够丰富多重的诠释和批评，也带给人们诸多开放性的问题。就小说重写的意义，其中最有启发的揭示在于：文学作品和现实世界产生各种纷繁复杂的联系，后者在被前者书写和重构的过程中，并不能由此得以闭合、有序、稳固地安排，而是随着人们的阅读和接受，作品不断被重新语境化，而在性别、社会、心理、历史等的研究探索中，作品内外的现实也在不断变化，因而我们对待经典改写的态度也不断变得更为包容和开放，对其无论显在还是潜在的可能性心存感念。

圣奥宾将至高的王权转换到了媒体巨头邓巴尔手中，让金钱、新闻、市场成为当下权力角逐的主要因素，更符合当下全球化和都市文化语境。邓巴尔周围的人属于都市圈中的上流阶层，涉及传媒界、航空业、金融圈、文化界等，其中的道德观和政治运作与莎剧《李尔王》中公元前 8 世纪的英格兰权力阶层形成了跨时空的对位。

父权与财力下的尊卑关系，精神尊严和物质肉体的拉锯平衡，家族亲情的信赖和背叛，个体理想和现实的冲突，依然是这场多元力量绞杀的重心。若说莎士比亚笔下的李尔王揭示了某个恒久的人性矛盾，即权力个体对自我尊严和荣誉的关注甚于公众的福祉安危，对自我情感满足甚于体察和理解他人，最终在傲慢的盲目之下，步入绝望；那么小说中邓巴尔类似的痛苦和癫狂，同样在权力光环褪下的过程中，为读者开启了一段悲剧性的灵魂洗涤之旅。

莎剧所给予的柏拉图式的质询，如公平正义、权力意志等，在邓巴尔的故事中依然不断变奏着，不过父女关系中，两个女儿的个性和权力欲望的继承和沿袭，弗洛伦斯对父亲的叛逆和挣脱，又多了几层作家个体经历和体验的内容。戏剧中相对的善恶分明被淡化，共情点相对散发与复杂。例如，弗洛伦斯在自我完善与个性追求的驱动下，忤逆并离开父亲，这与柯蒂利亚坚持忠于自我，反对谄媚有着异曲同工之妙，但是邓巴尔的暴君个性最终得到弗洛伦斯源于亲情的谅解甚至尊重，获得老友威尔森的崇敬，他在商业上的无所畏惧、受利欲驱动、耽于竞争、工作狂般的创业精神，其本质的善良与否本身是值得深思的，而在身心的痛苦煎熬中，精神的升华与否也提供了开放的诠释空间。

这种开放源于作家投诸其中的自身困惑和反思，实质上也是文学创作过程中的认知重塑。邓巴尔在雪夜中的感悟，是他在狂怒疯癫下的自由抉择，“也许在某个时刻，无序将成为新的秩序，或者至少是一种新的视角，就像飞行员在乌云密布的天空中挣扎，从雾霾中出来，进入上层大气宁静的光线里，俯瞰机翼下的云海，完全看清了方才朦胧的一切。”（106）衰老的颓势，退位的决定让他在亲情和尊卑关系的颠覆中回归到深层和本质的自我中，这是《李尔王》和《邓巴尔》带给人们的深刻启示，也是重新审视自我的警示。邓巴尔在荒野的呐喊“请别让我发疯啊”，与李尔王的“哦，傻子，我要疯了！”（2.4.283）几乎是一致的，前者在荒野和暴风雪中的领悟更为孤独，而李尔的流离失所始终有人陪伴，莎剧中的傻子和忠臣肯特在小说中几乎消失。邓巴尔的反省是没有同伴和规劝的，这个暴怒、绝望、疯狂、冷静、理性回归的过程更加孤独，有评论指出：“也许，在某种程度上，它映射了圣奥宾自己走出毒瘾和自杀企图的孤独旅程。他在各种访谈中都诉说过自己依靠某个期许从最糟糕的抑郁境地里挣脱出来的经历，这个期许就是一个执着的信念，即写作，没有写作他必将死去。”（Olmstead）由此看，圣奥宾向霍加斯出版社主动提出重写《李尔王》，也同样是他对自己一段不断挣脱低落和绝望的心路历程的体验和重现，这种自我警醒般的“往前走”的推动，是走出困境的决心和反省。圣奥宾让莎剧中傻子、忠臣肯特、弃儿埃德加、老臣格洛斯特的陪伴缺席，让邓巴尔饱尝孤独，也注定孤独，从而让自己更完整、共情地体验这份必然经历的冷寂。

二、个体感受与经典悲剧交织

《李尔王》跨文类重写的前后都贯穿着小说家圣奥宾通过莎剧对生活和文学创作的审视与反思。更有学者直言，霍加斯出版社的当代莎士比亚戏剧的改写式创作，就是对经典的“再度想象”过程，也是“转化式的模仿”（Ozick）。这种被很多莎剧迷和研究者奚落为“吃力不讨好”的尝试，常常会在各种书评中被认为保留了故事，失却了意义，放弃了原创，难有新意。在这些早已存在的创作障碍和挑战下，圣奥宾的执拗和坚持自有他早已认定的尝试意义。从一定程度看，他要达成的并非人们对小说重写的赞誉，而是他由此经历所获得的情感释放和生命启示。当邓巴尔神志恍惚地独自游荡在肯布里尔荒野中，当暴雪肆虐回应着他内心的狂澜时，小说中的独白既是邓巴尔自己的心灵呐喊，灵与肉的对话，也是作家自身的一次思想和灵魂的洗礼。场景中各种意象的叠加，氛围的渲染，与《李尔王》中的形成了一定的交响：

> 那棕色、紫色的层云零落塞布于昏黄天际，让他不由想起母亲的玳瑁梳子，他过去常常眯缝着一只眼睛，将梳子对着台灯，久久凝视，直到斑驳的光影和黑色块状充满整个视域……那些被暴雨浸湿的山脉在午后日光中隐隐闪现，水滴淌落。他是如此的笨拙，执意要拖着沉重的身体进入这美好、清澈、流动的景致中，就为了让水泥袋似的肉体倾倒于此，被雨水劈开，变得坚硬，落在这片原本不会遭受污染的山坡上。（130）

随即，邓巴尔感受到“一种轻盈和饥饿感，那样的一种与其他人类生活陈旧的关联感”（130）。这样的描述，较之李尔王在荒野的绝望呐喊，异曲同工地让人们生发强烈共情，这种重写和重述在文学创作特有的情感激发机制下就是一种感同身受的重新经历。当邓巴尔落下疲惫不堪的身体，任愤怒绝望在雨雪中被洗刷，那种“陈旧的关联感”因为在漫长历史中被重复了无数回而确实“陈旧”（threadbare），被磨损得失去了原形和新鲜的质地。

作家通过邓巴尔的感受探寻着大家共同的质问：“为何要活着承受这样的痛苦煎熬？”并以邓巴尔自己的回答“因为自己已经在承受”，给出了某种无奈而令人深省的沉思。有评论指出这个时刻和场景是小说挣脱经典悲剧束缚的一跃，达成了“一种人类悲悯的升华”（Ozick），这位评论者甚至认为，缺失了这样的共情和升华，“余下的，以一部普通的惊悚小说创作方式看，只是木偶戏和情节。”（Ozick）

如此批评的公允与否可以商榷，不过《邓巴尔》中的情感揭示和个体经历的创作重塑，确实值得关注，尤其是莎剧对于个人认知和体验的重塑和启示性，具有丰富的解读和挖掘潜力。尽管当代的经典重写必然淡化了莎剧文字的精湛隽永，邓巴尔和故事中各个人物的语言表达要符合当下话语风格，权力场从国家政权换转移至信托和股市的翻云覆雨，被商界集团的竞争和经济谋略取代。

然而，即便是面对莎剧《李尔王》，我们也明白，“正是通过弄臣一角，人们清楚地意识到，为何情节，无论在重组上如何巧妙绝伦，实质上是最次要的。”（Ozick）《李尔王》中宫廷弄臣傻子的角色，与其他剧作中的傻子有明显差异，类似于古希腊戏剧中合唱角色，承担着场景铺陈、旁观评论，推动剧情的作用，他不时地让观众从故事的沉浸中游离，戏谑幽默甚至跳脱地诠释着情节线索之外的深意，在一定程度上替剧作家巧妙地道出令人深省的道理。这个角色很难运用于小说的当代语境中，不过圣奥宾以彼得这个昔日喜剧演员的身份，让他以独特的视角参与了情节的发展，实质上是作家在对个体情感和矛盾体验中，巧妙地设置了一个审视点。彼得曾经是喜剧演员，滑稽古怪，有模仿名人的表演天赋，性情率真，毫无城府，酗酒成性。他在小说中的自杀结局，符合敏感、易信之人的性格走向。他陪伴邓巴尔逃出了疗养院的森严和压抑秩序，却在半途与邓巴尔分开，落入了两姐妹手中，并在鲍勃医生的逼迫和恐吓下，上吊自尽。他没有像原作的弄臣那样陪伴和见证所有的痛苦，而是成了入戏太深、无法自拔的牺牲者。彼得在生命尽头并未达成或给予他人深刻的领悟，他代表着某种程度的生活洞察，在模仿名人的表演中频频返回现实，以酒精麻木和钝化自己的现实感受，拒绝在身份的真假和转换中保持平静和抽离，而一旦经受苦痛和威胁，他的理智防线也最容易崩溃瓦解。

彼得身上体现的是人生如戏却难以自拔的障碍，他的各种喜剧角色的变换并未让他触及深层的真实；邓巴尔的身份认知相对稳定，他对于权力物欲的奋力企及，从童年经历的个性影响和塑造中能得到可信的解释，这是《李尔王》中略去的部分。但是，李尔在身份认知上的困境在邓巴尔身上得以呼应和渲染，李尔始终不明白王权是表象的附着，而非真正的自我，更重要的是，日趋衰老的必然会逐渐将华丽的附着层层剥落。在《李尔王》的一幕一景中，大女儿高纳里尔在一番甜言蜜语的孝敬表达后，目睹老父因为小妹柯蒂利亚的坦诚而暴怒，对二妹里根说："他年纪老了，脾气可就真叫人摸不准哪。"（1.1.291）里根更是一针见血地指出了"这就是他年老懵懂的地方—— 其实他做人一向都是不太清楚的。"（1.1.293）于是我们听到了高纳里尔其实很中肯的一句评论："就算他（李尔王）一生中最好、最明白的时候，也是暴躁的。"（1.1.295）若是搁置女儿对父亲的不敬和夺取权力的野心，这段对话中对李尔王的评断恰恰是李尔王自身的一个认知盲点，更普遍意义上，也是人们难以自知的典型表现。试问，当个人被各种身份附加时，谁能真正撇去诸多头衔，拨开层层华丽的装饰，诸如财富、地位、盛年光景等，直面褪下一切光环后真实本质的自我？邓巴尔独自一人在荒野里跋涉，质问"为何在自己最无助的时刻，没有人来恭维和支持呢？"（83）他明知自己曾经被"空洞赞美的光环围绕"（83），却依然难以自省洞明。

与原剧善于权谋、野心勃勃的埃德蒙对位的鲍勃医生，在小说中是邓巴尔的私人医生，出于自身利益的考虑，他与邓巴尔的两个女儿不仅有着性爱关系，还串通谋划了要掌控整个信托组织，甚至更秘密地联系了集团外的竞争者，成了双重背叛下的小人。鲍勃坚信可以通过自身的睿智、机敏、非凡的魅力，摆脱被动和奴役，他既联手邓巴尔家族的两姐妹，又暗地里勾结他人背叛她们，却决不"让自己的命运超出个人控制当下局势的能力范围"（73）。在他的马基雅维利主义思想下，达成目的，获得更大的人生和财富自由并不丑陋可耻，他甚至在出卖两姐妹的盘算中，泰然地思忖着自己实际上是在"保护信托公司不再继续衰落，不让它落入德不配位的继承人手中"（75）。更甚者，他觉得从长远来看，自己是邓巴尔信托的拯救者。读者不时会在鲍勃内心的自辩中看到圣奥宾小说中强烈的自省时刻，感受到作家在人物塑造上从原剧埃德蒙一角偏离的独特意义。鲍勃在作品中的笔墨并不多，但他对莎剧人物既破又立，不断希望冲破现实的和隐喻性的双重桎梏的努力，其行为的心理成因，与作家的个体经历和体会不无关系。

正因为此，邓巴尔王国缔造的历史在叙述中补充提及，三个女儿的抉择和个性也有心理和性爱层面的铺垫和诠释。以主角邓巴尔为例，他在现实中的衰老、偏执、崩溃，对应着他曾经白手建造辉煌的过往，他敏锐果敢地将业务拓展到世界各大洲，运用新的科学技术，只要能嗅到新兴意味，他必然乐于尝试，也正是这种绝对自信和坚持，促成了邓巴尔在商界的巨大成功，同时也引发了固执己见和过于强势必然导致的危机和悲剧。雪夜荒野中的邓巴尔依然不改猖狂的脾气，即便在筋疲力尽之际，“他想双膝落地，像跪拜祈祷的人那样，以谦卑抵消耻辱，可是他却有一种更强烈的渴望要往前走，挣脱这萦绕在四周的悲伤思绪。”（82）

读者会相信作家在刻画邓巴尔时是不断产生共情，放入自己的个体感受的。邓巴尔在最无助绝望时，深知两个女儿和医生密谋背叛了他，可他在愤怒的同时，多了一层与李尔王不同的自我谴责和批判，他明确意识到自己是因为“自身的背信弃义而被惩罚”（84），这种惩罚类似于天谴，他痛苦地反思自己“是那样的伪善”（84），曾经在感情上背叛了妻子，风流成性，薄情寡义，纯粹出于一己的报复心，将小女儿拒之门外。即便在荒野的困境和愤怒中，邓巴尔依然明白“他的罪恶甚于梅根和艾比盖尔，更别提鲍勃医生”（85）。这种觉悟令读者震惊，也是作家的认知投射，他通过邓巴尔道出了这样一个观点：在憎恶和对他人愤愤不平时，试着从不同的视角反观自己。邓巴尔意识到“女儿们想必有恨他的道德优势”（85）。

圣奥宾在改写经典的过程中，让濒于绝境的邓巴尔在面对一切不公和折磨时，感喟和深刻领悟到自己最理解“背叛的扭曲本质”（85），明白一切咎由自取，并在罪疚和自省的悲痛中几近疯癫。这与李尔王的悲情天问和呐喊有了较为明显的差异，弄臣的戏谑警示在小说中被邓巴尔的自我反省取代，同样是被观众接受的意义交付，从旁观者清的弄臣和肯特，换成孤身一人的邓巴尔的追悔式绝望，作家的个体情感代入强烈，与其说他在重塑人物，毋宁说是在重塑、想象和体会自身在痛苦境地里的经历，喟叹个中的命运差异。

所以，邓巴尔的荒野跋涉，他视为活该倒霉的身心折磨，作家让他独自一人在苍茫冰冷中体验。邓巴尔对此时不被人撞见反而是“心怀感恩”。他被孤独逼到了发疯的地步，没有人陪伴和见证，他也庆幸独自陷入这落魄。“或许从某一点来说，无序混乱会变成一种新的秩序，或至少是一种新的视角……”（106）这种冷静的审慎，显然与疯癫相悖，细究之下应该是作家的迫切介入与自我警醒。他让邓巴尔重新意识到自己有着“惊人的原始体能。只需要三个小时的睡眠就能完美运作一整天”。关键在于，在如此恶劣的状态下，八旬老人 “在自己的优秀体能和好强的激发下想探寻内在力量的真正所在”（110），更多应该是作家进入角色的情感反应。

小说创作中，作家通过邓巴尔这一角色不时反观自己的挫败和奋斗经历，也从邓巴尔的女儿们和其他相关人物身上重新审视、观察和理解他人与自我的关系。小女儿弗洛伦斯从少年时期开始就是坚定的劳工权利、环境保护、新闻媒体高度诚信的捍卫者，她和父亲的矛盾起因不限于柯蒂利亚对坦率诚实的执着。她与父亲老友威尔森之子克里斯（克里斯应该是埃德加的对位，但两者的相关性微乎其微，几乎是一个不同的角色）相爱却没有相守的结局，因为“太年轻、太任性而难以形成明确意图，太鲁莽、太感情用事而必然导致不测。”（121）这种彼此因为父辈的关系而多一层类似于手足关系的爱情，圣奥宾在他的系列小说创作和个人经历中已有强烈深入的刻画和体验，尤其是弗洛伦斯在面对和克里斯这种高于亲情和肉欲的关系时，怪异到会认为“其实她的婚姻才是不贞行为”（122），这种常规出逸的描写必然有深层的、源于作家生命体验的心理机制。

同样，大女儿艾比和丈夫马克的关系，与《李尔王》中高纳里尔和丈夫奥本尼公爵因为道德观的差异而导致的罅隙和矛盾，又有很大的不同。经典悲剧中奥本尼忠于良心和道德标准，而高纳里尔对他的平庸和无趣心生厌倦，移情至野心勃勃、年轻的埃德蒙。艾比和马克的婚姻匮乏新鲜和热情，这似乎是婚姻的常态，艾比的颐指气使态度和不孕不育成了最后一根压垮骆驼的稻草，于是两人开启了开放婚姻的模式。二女儿梅根在小说中被塑造成丧偶女性。梅根贪恋肉欲，利用金钱和地位让年轻强壮的保安吉姆死心塌地，而她却不为所动，甚至心狠手辣地不惜以他人的性命换取自己的利益。父亲对母亲的背叛让梅根和姐姐从少女时期就丧失了合乎道德和正义的伦理观，在受害和施害上的平衡维系着两人相对同盟的关系。缺失父爱，成长过程的情感冷漠，以及不断被强权、偏执的父亲影响，个性和价值观的扭曲并非一蹴而就。

从这对姐妹身上，我们既看到与《李尔王》中两个女儿的呼应和关照，又洞察到其中的质疑和颠覆。正如有学者指出的，“根据新古典主义的观点，重写是强调、支持、增殖既有的作品。与之相反的是，后现代的重写则建立了一种反写（conterwriting）的距离，一种自身与重写之间的撕裂，也是一种对此时和重写氛围下各种支配力量和自我之间的断裂。”（Lindhe）这种断裂确切意思上是对当下的自我和文化的某种重新审视和探寻，也是一种与原文本（host-text）在认知论层面的积极对话。换言之，艾比和梅根将邓巴尔信托重新私有化的企图，她们对弗洛伦斯刻骨的仇恨，对邓巴尔权力的消解企图，以及在情爱上的乖僻宣泄和操控等，充分地揭示了经典悲剧反派人物在传统诠释上的反叛和撕裂。如果说《一千英亩》对《李尔王》的重写凸显女性主义视角的解构，那么《邓巴尔》更着力于家庭和人际关系的个性塑造。试想，当邓巴尔这样一个始终要活在中心、居高临下位置的人出现在诸多其他人的生活中，压抑、挫败、愤懑、逃避等情绪自然会出现。两个女儿的忤逆和复仇式反叛，弗洛伦斯为了自由和尊严而出走，老友威尔森从愤愤不平到此后的同情，以及他在几方利益权衡下的矛盾，鲍勃对服从和卑微的反抗，以及压抑许久之后的权利觊觎，甚而彼得在恐吓威胁下的绝望自尽等等，所有的错综纠葛都源于邓巴尔的强势僭越。

在故事的最后，当弗洛伦斯中毒身亡前，医生给了邓巴尔一个痛苦的选择：濒临死亡的老父亲悲恸地看着女儿在自己眼前离世，或是奄奄一息的女儿目睹老父亲先告别人世，邓巴尔最终接受注射剂，愿意暂时推延自己的死亡，让弗洛伦斯在父爱的陪伴下抵达人生终点。他最终口述的遗嘱是彻底剥夺艾比和梅根对信托的权利，而且决绝地帮助竞争对手彻底胜利，掌控一切。这种大彻大悟的决断，与之前作家个体经历的代入读来不无矛盾，倒是与莎剧中李尔王崩溃前的呐喊异曲同工：“不，我不愿哭泣。/ 我虽然有充分的哭泣的理由，/ 可是我宁愿让这颗心碎成万片，/ 也不愿流下一滴泪来。”（2.4.280-3）

在个人成长中同样遭遇精神僭越和挫败的圣奥宾，他在邓巴尔和李尔王的悲剧离世中，又如何审视不断出现的愤懑、压抑、宣泄和不幸，并从中重建精神秩序，并传达领悟和见解呢？就小说重写的处理，我们并未找到明确的答案，作家对这一经典悲剧的变奏重写，仿佛是他对于个人经历中的各种无奈的回应，借由威尔森在小说最后的叹息："我们所有人都将化为尘土，但是这种理解不会被毁灭，也不可能被毁灭，只要还有人愿意说出真相。"（244）身为以文学创作为生的作家，只要"说出真相"的愿望和努力依然能在，那么对人生和世界的理解就不会被毁灭。当然，这个理解原文中用了动名词，更突出其不断形成的动态过程。这应该也是作家在莎翁悲剧的个人经历和诠释的重塑中，交付给读者的某种态度和答复吧。

三、权力欲望与家庭个体

邓巴尔在雪夜独行本质是一次自发的内省之旅，或许也是他人生中绝无仅有的反观时刻。"他从事实、数据、法律条文的世界进入了象征、洞察、各种潜在联系的世界。他并非自永不再返的战场飞离，而是依然身处无法挣脱的迷局，除非他穿越困境的核心。"（218）那个时刻在邓巴尔看来就是接近核心，找到出口的契机。他越发清晰地意识到自己就是引发各种风暴的暴风眼。在和弗洛伦斯相聚后，邓巴尔"似乎没有了愤怒和野心，只有爱"（225），他甚至从之前缔造世间最伟大的传媒帝国的宏图大志，转向了对无知天真的修复，这个"圆形旅程"在书中被表述为"爬过第二个童年"，朝着"第二次诞生"的方向，那个"似乎圆形循环的模式在最后时刻指向了一个新的境地，那里的一切仿佛完美无缺"（230）。

小说在改写经典悲剧的过程中，素材的增删处理自不必赘言。然而文本中人物心理成因的分析和诸如上述"第二个童年"和"第二次诞生"等的措辞，明显具有心理学视角的临床诊断的特征。邓巴尔的童年经历是他成年后权力欲望和自私武断的促发因素，小说对此不吝笔墨。艾比、梅根、鲍勃的恶从来不是毫无踪迹的神秘，个人心理动机常常与童年的伤害和恐惧不无关系，圣奥宾一直致力这方面的挖掘。尽管有评论指出"精神诊疗式的诠释弱化了莎士比亚戏剧带给人的惊骇和悲剧性。"（Olmstead）由于作品创作的语境存在巨大差异，当代经典重写中必然会有当下的文化和心理关注。例如，莎士比亚同时代的人对高纳里尔和里根无情残忍的态度，与当下的读者对两姐妹忤逆背叛邓巴尔的反应，必然因文化语境的变化而有所不同。成长过程中的压抑，长期的诉求不满，家庭父母关系的紧张，以及遗传学角度的个性影响等，当代社会的人们在遵守孝道和尊卑依从上也有了不同的观念。道德、伦理的关注比重在不同历史和文化中自有差异。举例来看，《李尔王》中埃德蒙为陷害同父异母的哥哥埃德加捏造了一封"大逆不道"的信，其中有一句"我开始觉得老年人的专制，实在是一种荒谬愚蠢的束缚；他们没有权力压迫我们，是我们自己容忍他们的压迫。"（1.2.51-52）放到当下的语境中，即便在不同的国家和文化背景下，都会在一定程度上引发年轻人的共鸣，与莎剧时代的观众或读者反应有很大不同。

因此《邓巴尔》中成年人的精神问题，有了现代心理学关于童年创伤的诠释语境。小说情节的发展与往昔追溯同步进行，产生一对逆向的组合，即当下步入将来和当下回溯过往同时进行。这种个体心理和动机的呈现，不同于相对同步的心理状态自觉意识，如李尔王在遭遇里根夫妇拒之门外的冷遇之后，暴怒之中还为对方留了余地："我们身体上有了病痛，精神上总是连带觉得烦躁郁闷。我且忍耐一下，不要太鲁莽了，对一个有病的人作过分求全的责备。”（2.4.104-9）李尔从未对两个女儿的态度有过溯源式的分析和反省。

《邓巴尔》中的父亲在对女儿的感情上就会有更复杂的心理成因。邓巴尔内心最喜爱弗洛伦斯，除了后者的诸多优点，“他爱她还单纯因为她是凯瑟琳的女儿，而凯瑟琳是他一生的至爱，这种爱，或者至少是爱的意象，因为死亡而不朽，不会因庸常凡俗而衰败或倦怠，让爱慕演变为忍受，再由忍受变成烦躁。”（37）这一心理回溯，让读者理解父亲对小女儿的爱在一定程度上是对逝去爱人的代偿。所以当弗洛伦斯追求独立和自由，不愿意承担家族事业和接受父亲的期待时，她的离去等同于邓巴尔情感上的第二次巨大失落。

即便是卸下了邓巴尔信托的执行重任，邓巴尔依然坚信“历史并不是仅仅被人们见证，也是被他的传媒帝国创造着”（42）。当下的信息流和媒体革命在对人际关系、观念认知的影响上发生着翻天覆地的变化。信息发布、接受操控着人们对现实的认知，从事传媒事业的邓巴尔和他身边的很多人都清楚意识到这一点。历史的缔造，换言之，或许也含有信息的捏造，成为《邓巴尔》所揭示的重要反思。这一点上看，《李尔王》不再是简单的创作模板，而是成为作家进一步探索现实和意识的起点，邓巴尔甚至被书评人隐射为传媒大亨默多克，或者是另一个重要的商界和政界人物，他充分利用了数字时代的媒介影响，与信息形成了操控和被操控关系，此人即特朗普。

受众在面对无论是戏剧舞台的《李尔王》，还是小说体裁的《邓巴尔》，这种由文字或舞台演出载体而传达的信息，对于现实的历史缔造或思想启示，应该成为我们当下的独特关注。在接受显在和潜在信息的同时，试问，被遮蔽和压抑的信息何在？这种质询也导向了诸多关于莎剧研究的不同批评视角。无论是女性主义对于母亲缺失和父权政治的深入分析，还是文学病理学研究关于老年失忆症影响与李尔王暴怒癫狂的关系的联系等，都让经典的当下重写与诠释有了丰富的潜力。阅读和比照的启示超越了单纯的共情，我们不会止于埃德加看到李尔王痛苦遭遇时的感喟“做君王的不免如此下场，使我忘却了自己的忧伤”（3.7.100-101），而是在戏剧落幕的终曲中，在李尔王的悲惨离世中，对忠臣肯特的那句“他只是篡夺了自己的生命”（5.3.318）感到震撼般的警醒，这一“篡夺”自己生命的过程，有多少人依然在执迷不悟？《邓巴尔》中的各个人物重演着这个篡夺过程，让过往的心理缺失“篡夺”当下，甚至未来，篡夺他人的权利，也篡夺了自己的安宁。这个反思，无论莎剧，还是当代小说，都在各自的历史文化语境中进行着，圣奥宾在小说的字里行间，都在推演着他从《李尔王》中汲取并运用于创作和自我认知的深刻意义。他让追悔不已的邓巴尔在与女儿弗洛伦斯重聚时，说出了“有时候，当我即将抵达愿望的终点时，却发现自己早已忘了是从哪个起点出发的。”（180）

小说应该就是圣奥宾从《李尔王》这个可以明确界定的方位，不断追溯各个人物，甚至包括他本人曾经出发的起点，去探寻个性、欲望、行为、人际的起承转合。弗洛伦斯始终明白放弃的意义，她深知邓巴尔需要的是“更深程度的权力放弃，而非权力复辟”（195）同样，柯蒂利亚与父亲重聚后的那句“存心良善的反而得到恶报，这样的前例是很多的”（4.1.1），与弗洛伦斯最终中毒身亡的结局，会激发人们深度的共情。父女相互和解之后，结局并未遂人所愿，其中有命运的无常，也有个性的必然。悲情的延宕能深化和激发人们的反思。就像爱而不得更令人刻骨铭心。小说增添了克里斯和弗洛伦斯的情感纠葛，克里斯虽然认定他对弗洛伦斯的爱毫无保留，但内心也明白“一部分的我觉得最近的这波爱潮汹涌与她的触不可及相关，当我们真正生活在一起时，我们每隔几个月就会分手”（199）。其中的反讽和无奈，是爱之失落的主题上的偏离和变奏。

四、结　语

重述和重写在文学创作的历史中不断进行着，无数知名或无名的作者必然或多或少地自经典的叙述中汲取素材，谱写自己的篇章。“这或许前所未有，对经典文本的再创作已经成为重要的文学事业……”（Schiff）同时，有学者提出，这种重述和重写在当代的盛行有两个重要的原因：其一，“文学经典和文化的变迁，尤其是我们在经典作品中对性别、阶级、种族等问题观念的改变。”（Schiff）其二是时尚的影响，诸如“视觉媒体”的重要作用等。

不过，在经典的高度和价值的焦虑影响之下，新作品被质疑、批评的压力也更大。相形见绌的观感也自然难以摆脱。互文比照下，各种问题纷至沓来。如，重述若是让读者对经典产生更深入、多元的解读，那它自身是否有不断被弱化忽略的趋势？经典和当下的重述的轻重主次究竟如何？读者对于经典悲剧的了解程度的差异对重述作品的阅读影响又如何？能否抛开前在影响完全将小说视为全新作品？

毋庸置疑，莎剧随着时间的演变不断被叠加着一层又一层的意义，自身就是人类共享的宝贵文化遗产，同时渗透并参与着当下的生活。或许，在数字时代的快节奏之下，个体在信息的疯狂轰炸和变异中，在代际和阶层的尊卑关系的认识变化中，已经不再像往昔的人们那样能深入理解《李尔王》，尤其对其悲剧力量产生强烈的共鸣。

从这个角度看，《邓巴尔》的重述，与诸多优秀的经典重写一样，从各个角度调适经典与我们的关系，从而让悲剧的心灵净化功能更有效地深入读者。无论是因为熟悉《李尔王》而对《邓巴尔》有了多重视角的解读，还是出于阅读乐趣将其视为全新的创作，通过阅读所形成的认知丰富，以及对个人经历的反思，心弦被拨动的每一个刹那，都应该是文学经典和创新的价值体现。

参考文献

[1] BLOOM H. 1992. King Lear[M]. New York: Chelsea House.

[2] Dunbar [EB/OL]. (2021-01-16). link.gale.com/apps/doc/A556230221/LitRC?u= fudanu&sid= LitRC&xid=f8942a49.

[3] GODDARD H. 1951. The Meaning of Shakespeare (Volume 2) [M]. Chicago: University of Chicago Press.

[4] HAYMAN S. 2017. Twice-told Tales[J]. Library Journal, 142 (18).

[5] INNES C. 2020. Introduction: remaking modern classics[J]. Modern Drama, 43 (2).

[6] LEVIN R. 1997. King Lear defamiliarized[M]// "Lear" from Study to Stage: Essays in Criticism. OGDEN J, ed. Associated University Presses: pp. 146-171.

[7] LINDHE A. 2005. Interpersonal complications and intertextual relations: a thousand acres and King Lear[J]. Nordic Journal of English Studies, 4 (1).
[8] OLMSTEAD G. 2018. Less than he seems[J]. Modern Age, 60 (1).
[9] OZICK C. 2017. An old, mad, blind, despised and dying king[J]. The New York Times Book Review (29).
[10] SCHIFF J A. 1998. Contemporary retellings: A Thousand Acres as the latest Lear[J]. Critique: Studies in Contemporary Fiction, 38 (4).
[11] SEAMAN D. 2017. Dunbar[J]. Booklist, 114 (2): 23.
[12] ST AUBYN E. 2017. Dunbar[J]. Hogarth: Crown.
[13] ST AUBYN E. 2017. Dunbar[J]. Kirkus Reviews.

基金项目：本文为教育部人文社科一般项目“当代莎士比亚小说重写研究”（19YJA752024）的阶段性成果。

作者简介：张琼，复旦大学外文系教授、博士生导师，主要从事莎士比亚及改编、英美诗歌与小说研究。

哈姆莱特：未践职的开明君主与哲学家王

—— 再读莎剧《哈姆莱特》

王化学

【摘　要】哈姆莱特复仇行为过程中的"延宕"是莎学研究的一个经典问题，直接关系对悲剧英雄的理解，可谓众说纷纭、莫衷一是。本文认为根本原因在于主人公纯良的精神气质排斥原始复仇方式而又未能找到符合文明价值观的法制方式；剧作家赋之以深厚的治国理政理论基础，这就是联系着王子本性的开明君主意识与哲学家王理念。
【关键词】哈姆莱特；延宕难题；开明君主；哲学家王

Hamlet: Enlightened Monarch and Philosopher King Who Does Not Take Office

—Re-reading Shakespeare's *Hamlet*

Wang Huaxue

【Abstract】The "delay" in Hamlet's act of revenge is a classic issue in Shakespearean studies, as it directly affects the understanding of the tragic hero. Opinions vary on this issue, and no decision has been reached. This paper argues that the fundamental reason for Hamlet's delay is that the pure goodness of his spiritual temperament rejects the primitive way of revenge, yet he fails to find a legal way in line with civilized values. Shakespeare the playwright assigns to it a deep theoretical foundation of governance, which is the consciousness of an enlightened monarch and concept of a philosopher-king linked to the nature of the prince.
【Key Words】Hamlet; the problem of delay; enlightened monarch; philosopher-king

一

莎士比亚的经典剧目《哈姆莱特》（1601）似乎已被评论得差不多了，然而正如歌德所言"说不尽的莎士比亚"，那么这出标志莎氏悲剧巅峰的戏当然更是如此。的确，每每读过总觉得有话要说，这是此剧的光荣！

然而毕竟，通过文本、移译、剧演、影视、画本等各种传播媒介，《哈姆莱特》誉满全球；

即使在我中华读书界（包括普通读书人），百多年来对它的了解和喜爱亦与日俱增，耳熟能详几成常势，真知灼见的至评亦非凤毛麟角！那么再谈是否还有必要？不过，有感于这个故事常读常新，以至为各种动机驱使所演绎，本事、情节、主题翻新迭出者不计其数，偶也碰见与自己感觉不相吻合的（改编或评论），还是不免生出非吐一得之见不可的冲动。兹爱“钻牛角尖”的思维方式或许是为文之人一个习惯性小疵也未可知。

正如读者或观众已熟悉，悲剧描写丹麦王子哈姆莱特为父复仇的故事。王子于德国留学期间，父王为其弟克劳狄斯弑杀，凶手掩盖真相，窃居王位，迎娶王嫂；哈姆莱特费尽周折，得以弄清真相，与奸王斗智斗勇，一波三折、惊心动魄，终于诛杀元凶，同时亦中对手毒计，复仇的同时以身殉难。

该剧规模巨大，人物众多、情节曲折、结构复杂，故其内涵甚为丰富。它似乎有意囊括一切，文艺复兴的时代元素，诸如才智、雄图、野心、铺张、艺术、阴谋甚至罪恶的气氛咄咄逼人，性格、矛盾冲突及动作进展复杂急促；崇高与卑下、伟大与渺小、善与恶、光明与黑暗奇妙地纠缠，芸芸众生被命运魔杖点拨而身不由己扮演着可悲角色。阿尼克斯特将其主题概括为“对于‘时代动荡不安’的认识”[1]122，确也！幕启即渲染出不祥预感：由于老王暴死，致宿敌挪威蠢蠢欲动，福丁布拉斯王子将兵压境，借军官马西勒斯之口描绘出紧张气氛：“为什么我们要有这样森严的戒备，使全国的军民每夜不得安息；为什么每天都在制造铜炮，还要向国外购买战具；为什么征集大批造船匠，连星期日也不停止工作；这样夜以继日地辛苦忙碌，究竟为了什么？”[2]7-8 而朝纲混乱，“殡葬的挽歌和结婚的笙乐同时并奏”[2]11，哈姆莱特心情郁闷像要爆炸，天空出现异象，老王鬼魂屡于夜半出现……活脱一个多事之秋的到来。处于该乱世王国权力中心的即那个弑君、篡位、淫嫂的奸贼克劳狄斯，他狡诈阴险、两面三刀，在其统治下，丹麦宫廷荒淫无度、阴谋成风，全国处于风雨飘摇之中。

二

然而最为研究者关注的，还是给人太多叹息的悲剧英雄（主人公）哈姆莱特的形象问题。

四个多世纪来，如何理解该王子令许多专家流连驻足却困惑不已的艺术形象成了一个学术难点。的确，哈姆莱特算得上世界文学中最著名也最具争议的艺术形象，所谓“有一千个读者就有一千个哈姆莱特”，便概括了他的复杂性。18 世纪以降，一些著名人物包括歌德在内，认为他虽天性美好，然而优柔寡断、缺乏意志力，在无力承受、又不能放弃的重负下毁灭了。19 世纪的浪漫派莎评，也大都承认王子缺乏决断，并认为根源于难以从思想中自拔的性格。如弗·史雷格尔说由于奇特遭遇使他“集中在不停思虑的理智上，他行动的能力却完全破坏了”[3]312。柯勒律治也说：“精力全花费在做决定上，反而失却了行动的力量。”[4]147 赫士列特则说“他是哲学冥想之王”，“周密推敲复仇的计划比立刻去实行更合他的口味”[5]214-215。实证派批评的大师泰纳说得更明确：“一个善于幻想而不善于行动的人，他沉醉在自己心造幻影的冥想里面，他把想象的世界看得太清晰了，以至无法在现实的世界中担负起自己的使命。”[6]86 而俄国大作家屠格涅夫，干脆将其视为意志消沉、抱怨不已、无所作为的利己主义者，一个与堂吉诃德的高尚志趣截然相反的人[7]。20 世纪的讨论更为广泛，最让人吃惊的也许应首推精神分析学家弗洛伊德的观点，他试图以“俄狄浦斯情结”理论对王子的优柔寡断进行精神分析，认为由性心理所造成：王子自幼恋爱母后，仇视父王；克劳狄斯谋杀国王篡位娶嫂，从这一罪行觉察到自己有同样心理动机；如果杀奸王而复仇，无异于杀死了灵魂中的自我，故一再迟疑下不了手[8]，等等，不一而足。可见这种犹豫不决，成为讨论哈姆莱特性格的关键点，见仁见智、莫衷一是。“西方莎学家们把这个情况称为‘延宕难题’(the problem of delay)，为托马斯·汉麦尔（Thomas Hanmer）于1736年首先提出的。”[9]6 围绕该问题从不同角度和层面的讨论，会发现许多启人思考的灼见，辜正坤教授就此概括归纳出20种说法[10]。所有这些对深入理解主人公的复杂个性及其悲剧无疑具有重要意义，而辜教授本人的研究可能最全面，因为是综合性的，故其称之“哈姆莱特延宕原因系统论”。在从主客观各方面的精彩分析中，笔者格外欣赏如下一个原因，即延宕其实也是剧作家所处时代的社会风气，是从伊丽莎白女王到其宠臣艾塞克斯伯爵（认为哈姆莱特对之构成影射关系）乃至整个朝廷上下普遍存在的拖拉作风的反映，可谓特定时期的民族习气或惰性。进而学者们发现，兹似乎为人的通病，存在于特定阶层，乃“人类相当大一部分的特征，具有某种普遍性。”[9]10 这几乎可说是哲学的洞见了。

悲剧是塑造英雄的，以哈姆莱特命名该剧①，余以为首先应该从“英雄”的应有内涵去定义王子；换言之，必须时刻牢记哈姆莱特的英雄本质，并由此理解、把握其性格的复杂性乃至矛盾性。

英雄有各种类型，勇往直前喋血沙场如阿喀琉斯是英雄，足智多谋出奇制胜如奥德修斯是英雄；罗曼·罗兰把“受苦、奋斗而必战胜”者如艺术中的约翰·克里斯多夫和现实中的贝多芬、米开朗琪罗视为最有力的英雄。莎剧中各色非等闲之辈如行事果断的罗马人恺撒、安东尼是英雄，思虑再三导致瞻前顾后举棋不定的丹麦王子哈姆莱特是英雄—— 显而易见，就特征表现的主要方面而言，前者为行动型，后者乃思想型。或可说问题的本质在此，作为“哲学冥想之王”，哈姆莱特是最合标准的“思想的英雄”，古往今来多少文学名著，未见写出如此深刻的思想家，一个学者型王子的复杂性与深刻性。

三

由克劳狄斯的一句台词可知，哈姆莱特原本在威登堡大学读书；直到回国奔丧、且尴尬地经历王后婚礼，对老王驾崩真相并不知情，尽管已有预感（老王被害）。然父死母嫁刺激太甚—— 后者的强度应该远超前者—— 其善思特点便明白无误地露出端倪。王子首次亮相是在第一幕第二场，一段长长的独白：“啊，但愿这一个太坚实的肉体会融解、消散，化成一堆露水！……”[2]14 表明所受打击之大，以至连世界观也改变了：人世不再美好，相反原来是个长满恶毒莠草的荒芜花园。当然，这还主要由“母嫁”所引起，不过却也不自觉地思索人性问题了。及见过父王鬼魂并从之得到宫廷谋杀的骇人信息，他的思考陡然间进入深邃、自觉之境，这是冷彻与痛苦的，但又不以人的意志为转移。他对知心好友霍拉旭说：“天地之间有许多事情，是你们的哲学里所没有梦想到的呢。”[2]31 其实这又何尝不是自我言说呢？不啻如霹雳的信息把他对人和世界的固有观念彻底打翻了，那本如天使、天神一般，有着高贵的理性、

① 本剧全称为《丹麦王子哈姆莱特之悲剧》（*The Tragedy of Hamlet, Prince of Denmark*）。

伟大的力量、优美的仪表、文雅的举动之“人”，那“了不得的杰作”，“宇宙的精华！万物的灵长！”，突然之间降低若尘埃，“这一个泥土塑成的生命算得了什么？”[2]46

鉴于事前王子正于德国深造，而所在的威登堡大学又是当时一个人文主义思想的传播中心，故一些莎学家将其定义为人文主义者。这当然没有错，而哈姆莱特的言语及待人处事风格也的确多带人文主义色彩，兹可视为剧作家思想情怀与理想倾向的折射。不过这势必会削弱该复杂个性的深度而导致理解的简单乃至平面化。他无可奈何地然而也是清醒地说出如下的话：

这是一个颠倒混乱的时代，唉，倒霉的我却要负起重整乾坤的责任！（第一幕第五场）[2]31

兹非但表明王子作为思想家的敏锐，更透露了他潜意识里强烈的责任感，那是本能的自然流露。哈姆莱特乃法定的王位继承人，尽管捷足先登的篡窃者花言巧语地要他把自己作为“父亲”，假惺惺地表示让其继承王位（第一幕第二场）。真是滑天下之大稽，抢了人家的饭碗还打扮成恩赐者！为什么克劳狄斯油盐不进、非认定侄儿没疯而必欲置之死地而后快不可，根本原因在此；同时也是王子所有郁闷、恼怒、愤激的纽结所在。哈姆莱特比任何人都更加禀赋救国安邦素质，乃其出身与成长环境所使然；但他发现已处于一个非常不利的环境，客观上其心绪也必难平静，其装疯又何尝不具备真疯的条件或机制呢？

然而作为思想的英雄，其非凡素质使他超越了所有恶劣的“物理与心理”项，首先是保持了清醒，其次是言语行动合于逻辑（“疯癫”之度把握精准，连奸王也无可挑剔）。单就前者说，其敏于观察和长于分析的特点表现得淋漓尽致，从个人不幸想到普遍苦难，由宫廷阴谋看到时代混乱，而把复个人之仇提到重整乾坤的高度。值得注意的是，哈姆莱特的多思也与多疑相纠缠，应该承认怀疑往往是思考的前提，没有怀疑、设问怎么能有推理、判断？王子完全确信其父王鬼魂之言吗？其实并未百分之百，相反还是存些微疑惑的；何以安排“戏中戏”？不过为了释疑而已。第二幕第二场最后，伶人甲表演一段戏文并为之感动落泪，激起王子兴叹超长独白，自责不能断然采取行动，但也道出了内心的秘密：“我所看见的幽灵也许是魔鬼的化身，借着一个美好的形状出现，魔鬼是有这一种本领的；……”[2]56 原来他要借此得到“更切实的证据”。思考和意识到的责任使其倍感力不能支，难道不引发绝望吗？悲剧主人公被孤独、自谴、矛盾所困扰，几近于炸裂状态，所以苦思也臻于极致，从现实黑暗、命运无情，到生死、斗争、责任，指涉皆人生观宇宙观的大问题：

生存还是毁灭，这是一个值得考虑的问题；默默忍受命运的暴虐的毒箭，或是挺身反抗人世的无涯的苦难，通过斗争把它们扫清，这两种行为，哪一种更高贵？……死了；睡着了；睡着了也许还会做梦；嗯，阻碍就在这儿：因为当我们摆脱了这一具朽腐的皮囊以后，在那死的睡眠里，究竟将要做些什么梦，那不能不使我们踌躇顾虑。……重重的顾虑使我们全变成了懦夫……（第三幕第一场）[2]60

这段经典台词，把哈姆莱特——思想的英雄——个性之特点与思考之广深揭示无遗，向被视为理解把握该文学典型的一个关键点。

四

然而几乎一刻不停地进行着紧张思考的王子在其复仇行动中并未得心应手，甚至相反，却显得很被动；那么对悲剧英雄而言，思想与行动是什么关系呢？这同样是理解该典型形象不可回避的问题。

在哈姆莱特，显然思想迟滞了行动，二者未能取得理想的那种对立统一效果，是颇为遗憾的。造成该结果的原因很多，因此导致莎学家们众说纷纭，亦即莫衷一是的所谓"延宕"问题的各种观点。王子的学者身份（求学期）给他太多思考和太重理想的性格加了码，以至做不到像亚历山大大帝那样让思想决断行动。通过观察与思索愈来愈认识到现实的黑暗，故心情沉重失去欢颜而成"忧郁王子"，他在为不得不面对的情境而焦虑！其实归根结底，是没能清晰地理出头绪，明确究竟该怎么做；或者换言之，关于报仇的事尚无胜算之把握。这也许说明思考或者思想的局限性，纯粹地思考现象包括究索本质还不是最高境界，如果不指向目标和手段，那么再深沉的思考也是肤浅的。尽管王子思想深邃，又天禀政治家素质，深知自己肩负的责任重大！但他还不是个成熟的政治家，没有从事政治斗争的经验，尚不懂得政治权谋之玄妙，这决定了其思考的局限性。假如情况刚好相反，那么他一定会利用忠诚于其父王和爱戴他本人的丹麦臣民及军队（这些人绝不在少数），要知道古往今来，不知多少善弄权者甚至利用还是襁褓中的小王子或仅仅一个王号就能号令军民、导致改朝换代。在这点上，好追根究底的哈姆莱特不如动辄拔刀相向的雷欧提斯，第四幕第五场写后者因其父亲暴毙急从法国归来，尚未弄清真相的情况下（误以为父死乃奸王所为）轻易纠集一帮"弟兄"冲击王宫，居然一度压倒禁卫军，"比大洋中的怒潮冲决堤岸、席卷平原还要汹汹其势……"[2]100。这非但证明变革世界的力量全靠掌握民众，亦可见在克劳狄斯统治下早已民怨沸腾。以王子的身份和威望（奸王深知国民对王子的忠诚与爱："他是为糊涂的群众所喜爱的。"[2]93），要拉起一彪正义之师匡正朝纲，当不是十分困难的事，但王子坐失良机了。

如果说王子的个性气质就是属于耽于沉思而不善行动的类型，那未免委屈了他。实际上，哈姆莱特从怀疑到鬼魂说知被害实情，即已抱定了复仇的决心；尽管还有一丝疑惑，所以安排"戏中戏"确证之—— 这既符合其以思想见长的性格特点也说明他不屈枉无辜者的纯良天性。但如此做必带来诸多麻烦，最大的麻烦是警觉了克劳狄斯，这就不得不使其以疯癫周旋之，不必说又把单纯的恋人奥菲利娅牵入其中，还导致误杀波洛涅斯，同时要对付遵奸王之命而刺探之的幼时学伴。如此地被动，为何？无良策也！黑格尔说："他所犹疑的不是应该做什么，而是应该怎样去做。"[11]311 怎样去做？天命论地穷于应付，积极的主体性缺位，可见黑格尔的概括相当准确！当然事实上王子并非无所行动，装疯就是应对策略的行为之一。这一过程漫长而极具悲剧性，最受伤害的即天真纯洁的奥菲利娅，不明就里的丫头片子怎能受得了心上偶像轰然崩塌？加之老父又为恋人误杀，她之真疯乃至死亡就是必然的了；其次是母后乔特鲁德，王子癫狂但又似充满无可辩驳逻辑的斥责使之看到自甘堕落的可怕程度，恐怕惨痛结局的自我意识就此觉醒。悲剧英雄之"疯"某种意义上乃作品的眼睛，光彩闪亮，佳妙在癫与不癫之间：癫，满口村言胡说八道；不癫，鞭辟入里入木三分。可进可退、可攻可守，老于世故的御前大臣备遭奚落，罗森格兰兹者流则屡被难堪，吃王子反唇相讥："你以为玩弄我比玩弄一支笛子容易吗？"[2]77 更有甚者，是令克劳狄斯如坐针毡、寝食难安—— 他丝毫不敢怠慢，立刻以命王子赴英催讨贡赋之名实施借刀杀人之计。虽然王子察觉阴谋中途矫诏智让监押者前往当替死鬼，而自己借海盗船助折回丹麦，但不幸又中奸王挑拨雷欧提斯毒设比剑局，置其罹谋杀之祸……

由此可见，哈姆莱特的行动不足以完成复仇大业，就是说在整个事件中并不具备有效的决定性，否则他就不会因伶人被戏文感动而触发自责，因挪威与波兰争夺弹丸不毛之地视死如归而大受刺激，因连续无实绩的蹉跎贻误而痛心疾首了！如此看来，他紧张的思考探索反而成了一种阻碍，成了其性格的一个弱点甚至是导致悲剧的落败原因，那么悲剧英雄的最本质要素究竟何在？这或许是揭开哈姆莱特悲剧的最核心处。

五

如果把该剧主要定义为性格悲剧，而主人公性格弱点乃导致悲剧之主因，那么这弱点或许在于太过纯洁。问题就出在这里，哈姆莱特非常光明磊落（正是这害了他！），他洁白无瑕的青年王子形象堪为完美无缺："朝臣的眼睛、学者的辩舌、军人的利剑、国家所瞩望的一朵娇花；时流的明镜、人伦的雅范、举世注目的中心……"[2]62 于他，高贵的天性容不得半点道德污秽，任何非公开的行动都可能被视为卑鄙，威登堡大学的教育更使高尚志趣锦上添花，文明种子已深植纯洁之心田。说穿了，复仇—— 避开法律以完全个人的方式，像原始时代野蛮人那样—— 太不符合哈姆莱特的教养和个性！必须指出，其潜意识中是厌恶这件复仇任务的，至少当把它作为个人行为时。与其说不能胜任，毋宁说本能地厌恶；之所以迟迟不肯动手，除了诸多客观不便外，根本原因或许在此。第三幕第三场的一个细节不可忽略：偶遇克劳狄斯独处一隅秘密忏悔的王子，却收起佩剑放弃了该实施复仇的天赐良机，理由是，在罪人心灵相对纯洁的忏悔时刻诛杀之会把他的灵魂送上天堂。其实不过是用以解脱厌恶亲手杀人心理的"遁词"而已，虽然是无意识的①。不妨说，这是哲学—思想家气质在起作用：十足骑士风度的王子是有思想、学问和修养的仁人君子，而非动辄拔刀相向、粗鲁野蛮的赳赳武夫，或如雷欧提斯者流的狭隘复仇主义者，更不是刽子手。以王子的性格，类似谋杀的复仇方式正是在其意识深处鄙视的，那与克劳狄斯的行为有何不同？假如真的瞅准时机从背后给了奸王痛快的一刀，试想他的悲剧气质还能留下多少？

请注意"骑士风度"的丰富内涵！它是中世纪骑士道的重要表现形态，只要想想堂吉诃德为冒牌的"白月骑士"打落马下便乖乖地认输卸甲即可理解其义。武有武道，属于贵族文化范畴的骑士制度是拒绝流氓无赖行为的。雨果的千古绝章滑铁卢战役描写中，怒不可遏地斥责奥地利元帅"老布吕歇尔玷污了自己"[12]35—— 因为他居然下令屠杀包括缴械的敌人！我国春秋时代以仁义著称的宋襄公故事亦具同质性："泓水之战"的窝囊结局令此公备受诟病，其实他是如哈姆莱特一样伟大的仁人志士，是恪遵上古军礼（兵家礼道）仅存的硕果！前春秋时代或春秋之初的战事乃贵族属性，其源远流长的礼信原则如空气般弥漫于中原诸侯的观念中。周礼的信条及权威成为无意识，这是今人难以想象的。不过礼信原则遭颠覆亦由此始，

① 其实潜意识里王子一直备受困扰，因为放不下与法治观念相悖的"子报父仇天经地义"的宗法观念，第五幕第二场他对霍拉旭坦言："我是不是应该—— 他杀死了我的父王，奸污了我的母亲，篡夺了我的嗣位的权利，用这种诡计谋害我的生命，凭良心说我是不是应该亲手向他复仇雪恨？"

楚成王的霸业之路足以说明，还有晋文公作辅证且比前者更高明（成语“退避三舍”的来源城濮之战概述备矣）。于是“谋”取代“则”，功利主义为圭臬的时代来临了，所以《孙子兵法》、“合纵”、“连横”渐成主流……周礼是什么？是对心的约束，是价值观，导向规范和秩序！礼崩乐坏何以让孔子痛心疾首？不言自明耳！从不受礼约束的楚成王最终被儿子所杀，也许是种轮回罢。

或许有问：但王子把波洛涅斯误为克劳狄斯而杀之时并未有刹那犹豫呀？辨析：情境不同导致行为区别。偷听一旦被发现王子必出剑无疑，意外猝发不容多想！何况哈姆莱特正处愤怒之巅，这愤怒正是为呵责母后与奸王之不耻行为而引起。莎翁乃心理分析的大师，兹安排之合情理足可以击节叹赏！

然而因厌恶而放弃承担或逃避复仇责任吗？否！王子无时无刻不渴望把弑君窃国者送进地狱。他深知肩负着为父申冤的道德责任和拯救国家的政治重任，其全部思想和行动都雄辩地证明他在分秒必争地为解决双重负荷而战斗，只是未能找到正确途径而已。他还不甚清楚，其实要找的，是如何光明正大地把罪犯送上绞架，用人类理性与正义原则的体现——法律利剑，惩罚罪恶、申诉冤屈、整饬纲纪。他苦苦探索的不过如是，虽然未形成自觉意识。所谓优柔寡断、忧郁踌躇，一应“延宕”问题的争议种种，症结就在于此。

王子光明磊落的君子品格乃出自天性也成于教养。这是种理想人格，凤毛麟角，现实中是很难找到的。从剧情的缜密安排和悲剧英雄内心世界的波澜起伏矛盾变化，可以确信剧作家塑造该性格经过了反复、充分琢磨，是极其自觉的。剧中哈姆莱特不仅经常鞭辟时世与人性的黑暗，而且不时剖析灵魂自我，谴责其中深潜的暗昧，“我的罪恶是那么多，连我的思想也容纳不下……像我这样的家伙，匍匐于天地之间，有什么用处呢？”[2]62 兹为以哲目洞悉普在，从“类”溯“属”，所以连自己也不放过。它的深刻处在于戳穿存在的盲目和无意义，虽为一时之念，杀伤力却很强，照此推论，那么不要说匡扶正义与重振朝纲，就是诛杀奸王其实根本没有必要，因为即使达到了目的也难保证结果会更好。迷惘带来虚无，思想家经常面临的困境！好在哈姆莱特天性美好绝非“逻辑”所可俘虏，故总能校正偏狭坚定信心，这就是英雄的本色！王子淳朴守正的天性于细微处也多所表现，如奥菲利娅下葬时，猝然的极度悲痛使与雷欧提斯墓穴内扭打（那是哈姆莱特唯一一次真正丧失理智），过后为自己的失礼真诚道歉：“原谅我，雷欧提斯；我得罪了你，可是你是个堂堂男子，请你原谅我吧。这儿在场的众人都知道，……”[2]130 可谓感人至深！相比之，后者居然以宵小手段行卑鄙勾当，就黯然失色了。

六

莎士比亚塑造了许多帝王形象，雄才大略与阴险狡诈者俱全，但未曾见哈姆莱特这样深邃的思想与高拔的品质。无可否认，他寄托了作家最美好的政治与道德理想，被赋予极丰富的性格内涵。如果说“思想的英雄”最接近该千古不朽之典型形象的本质，那么王子的悲剧，便是因思想而贻误了复仇时机从而也贻误了重整社稷乾坤机会的开明君主和“哲学家王”的悲剧。

作为卓越的戏剧大师，莎翁对人之政治存在的兴趣甚至超过艺术追求，这或许由于其本质上更是位热切关注现实的思想家。在莎士比亚的时代，引领潮流的人文主义进步思想于国制问题上通常持明君论，打击封建豪强寄望于强有力、敢作为的国王，唯其，成长的资产者才可能受到保护、得以发展。莎翁英伦史剧，或批判昏庸的、残暴的君主如亨利六世、理查二世、理查三世，或赞美雄才大略的英明君主如亨利四世、亨利五世，无不印证了剧作家以王道经略国家的思想；其罗马悲剧尤其是《裘力斯·恺撒》，则塑造了内涵极其深刻的政治人物恺撒、勃鲁托斯和安东尼，表现了关于统治者必备政治哲学素质的理想人格诉求，最具悲剧性的勃鲁托斯仿佛哈姆莱特类典型的预演，悲剧式地演绎了英雄失败的必然结局，振聋发聩、点铁成金！

不难发现，哈姆莱特王子具有理想的开明君主的整体素质，至少是剧作家所理想的素质。当然，如果说英伦史剧及罗马悲剧的这类形象优先突出面临严重政治事件时的果断判断与行动能力，即运筹帷幄决胜千里的盖世气概的话，那么在丹麦王子身上，则如前述—— 更突出其深邃思考的思想家气质，还有裁正大方、礼贤下士的君王风度。我们发现，类如骄横跋扈、颐指气使、放纵任性的做派完全与之绝缘，上引奥菲利娅认定王子“疯癫”后痛断肝肠之言（“朝臣的眼睛……”）概括备矣！她坚信世间不会再有第二个如此杰出的人物，而且那不光是她的爱，也是国家的未来！何以精神崩溃，因为那是她的命！

睿智、宽厚、爱人不唯明君更是仁君的个性标志，这在哈姆莱特也有很多生动表现，虽然作品基调不太容许过多渲染。对知己何等坦诚，可看他之于霍拉旭的态度；对臣下多么爱见，可看他以朋友的平等对待向其效忠的军官；即使受奸王指派前来探其心秘的老同学罗森格兰兹和吉尔登斯吞都能引发旧情，他三言两语揭破访者“鬼胎”，从中可以感知对故交变质的惋惜；他甚至和掘墓人“插科打诨”，谈论人生悲凉的哲理……王子心目中，被害父王就是理想君主的典范，“一个堂堂男子”，“真像每一个天神都曾在那上面打下印记，向世间证明这是一个男子的典型。”[2]83 他像战神威风凛凛，乃国家和人民的保护者；他忠于爱情，细腻到甚至怕风吹痛了王后的脸。在王子的眼里，君王不独是权力正义的化身，而且必须是道德伦序的典范！

洞悉社会人情世态、谙熟朝代迭替轨迹的剧作家，透彻理解国家治理乃人类社会的头等大事，所以莎剧的政治书写十分自觉。肇始并得以充分发展的古希腊罗马法政体系，为西方文明一道亮丽的风景线，虽然中世纪千余年小国寡民、分崩离析，天主教统治与封建割据导致近代欧洲民族国家形成较晚（文艺复兴前后），但希腊罗马古典的基础决定了其邦政文化不绝如缕，从未中断。该传统之于不列颠更是根深蒂固，英格兰早在约翰王时代就有了“大宪章”这样的不俗表现。一种柏拉图式地探讨社会由何人治理才可能成为理想之国的理念或为知识界与博闻者的责任意识，也成为贯穿莎士比亚戏剧尤其史剧与悲剧创作的一条重要思想线索，就这个意义而言，《哈姆莱特》乃一出最典型、最深刻地表达剧作家治国理念理想的政治大戏。如英伦史剧主要探讨开明君主观念，该剧则更重视“哲学家王”观念。哈姆莱特的悲剧形象，既是打开莎翁关于国家政治蓝图设想的钥匙，也是如是理想悲剧式地幻灭于严酷现实的哲学哀思，兹与人文主义密切相连，如若排除其消极成分，则是可以启发君主立宪政体观的思想源泉之一。

“哲学家王”理念来自古希腊哲学家柏拉图，他颠沛半生，遍游意大利、西西里、居勒尼、埃及等地，考察思索城邦政治的最佳形式即寻求知识破解国家治理之道，终于在《理想国》

提出这一概念—— 或为西方最著名的理国论之一。①他说："除非哲学家成为我们这些国家的国王，或者我们目前称之为国王和统治者的那些人物，能严肃认真地追求智慧，使政治权力与聪明才智合二为一。"[13]214 显而易见，哲学家除了服膺正义，尤其是智慧的爱好者。古希腊人把哲学家解释为爱智者，罗素指出："在柏拉图，哲学乃是一种洞见，乃是'对真理的洞见'。它不纯粹是理智的；它不仅仅是智慧而且是爱智慧。"[14]165 爱智者必然擅长思考，按现代人的理解，思考避免盲目，因此政治家也必然是思想家，一个厌恶或不善于思考的君王是不可想象的。无论柏拉图还是莎士比亚，或许最担心的是白痴一类的人成为统治者！

所以，好的政体是正义的必要前提，好的执政者则是实施正义的保证。王为什么是哲学家？因为只有哲学家才足够爱智慧且拥有智慧并通晓各门科学，唯有哲学家才真正懂得自觉承担正义从而为城邦而不是个人着想。黑格尔分析说："于是就应该使得现实与概念相一致，也就是使理念成为存在。"[15]173 他认为柏拉图所理解的哲学的含义，"是对自在自为的真理和正义的意识，是对国家的普遍目的的意识和对这种普遍目的的有效性的意识。"[15]174 柏拉图对于叙拉古并西西里的僭主狄奥尼修二世，一度认定（一厢情愿地）其即这样理想的统治者却终归破灭；历史上或许亚历山大、恺撒、马克·奥勒留、腓特烈二世、拿破仑符合条件，然而他们却往往做不到黑格尔所谓的"根据普遍原则来决定整个情况"[15]175。说穿了只是无节制的征服者而已。所谓哲学王者，现实中是不可能存在的。

但哲学家王成了贤良统治的最佳象征，莎翁无疑钟情于此，其对历史的看法可定义为英雄史观，莎剧毫不含糊地揭示出民族命运的决定者是王公贵族，纵横捭阖、握有统治权力的政治精英—— 主控国家命运乃至历史进程。

因此可以肯定，莎士比亚贤明政治理想的实现者即开明君主；某种意义上，这与柏拉图的"哲学家王"理念本质是一致的。此为古往今来不知多少仁人志士乃至思想家所梦寐以求！不错，多数情况下兹还仅仅是个梦想，如飞蛾扑火，但追求的努力却从未有止息过。莎剧塑造了许多这样的人物：亨利五世、勃鲁图斯、哈姆莱特、普洛斯彼罗……

人是靠思想成为万物之灵的，人的行为也是靠思想决定与驱动的；拥有思想才有可能拥有一切。因此，禀赋思想智慧的政治家乃最好的统治者，这也就成为政治文化的核心理念之一。哲学家王也好，开明君主也罢，一方面执掌正义利剑，一方面能思善行，那么还要再指望什么呢？

《哈姆莱特》应该是阐释该观念和象征其形象的最佳典范。剧中哈姆莱特经常处在有意识的疯癫或半疯癫状态，但道白似乎一如既往地一泻千里，即使癫痴也自有其逻辑，仿佛神灵借着他的口说话，其实堪为典型的哲学家言。他的含讥带讽通常发人深省，承载价值判断。当宫殿通宵传出伴随宴舞的铜鼓喇叭之声，他指斥这恶俗使丹麦备遭非议，蒙"酒徒醉汉"之名，"少量的邪恶足以勾销全部高贵的品德，害得人声名狼藉"；故"以为把它破坏了倒比遵守它还体面些。"[2]23 就克劳狄斯成为国王前向他扮鬼脸者现竟不惜花重金求其一幅小照，他向老同学说："这里面有些不是常理可解的地方，要是哲学能够把它推究出来的话。"[2]48 他词锋犀利、语带双关的"疯话"令御前大臣尴尬，令险恶奸王肉跳！

① "哲学家王"理念似乎蹈入了人治论泥潭，不过事实上柏氏的确并不看好"法治"这一社会管理手段，所以将之放到次等好的位置。至于民主政治，则和苏格拉底一样更持反对态度。他认为国家非一般人可以治理，各阶层应该恪守本分，干好自己该做的事，例如军士卫国、农民种田等。

国王：吃饭去了！在什么地方？

哈姆莱特：不是在他吃饭的地方，是在人家吃他的地方；有一群精明的蛆虫正在他身上大吃特吃哩。蛆虫是全世界最大的饕餮家；我们喂肥了各种牲畜给自己受用，再喂肥了自己去给蛆虫受用。胖胖的国王跟瘦瘦的乞丐是一个桌子上两道不同的菜；不过是这么一回事。

国王：唉！唉！

哈姆莱特：一个人可以拿一条吃过一个国王的蛆虫去钓鱼，再吃那吃过那条蛆虫的鱼。

国王：你这句话是什么意思？

哈姆莱特：没有什么意思，我不过指点你一个国王可以在一个乞丐的脏腑里作一番巡礼。（第四幕第三场）[2]93

疯言还是哲语？读者至少知道，这不是凡夫俗子能够说出的话。

在一般的意义上，王子愤世嫉俗的话正是站到了脱离具体事物的哲学的高度，尽管根源于具体事物，难听却直戳本质。代表了其宇宙观的改变，虽然此改变可能是暂时的。在这种改变里，一切皆荒诞，包括他自己，也包括奥菲利娅，第三幕第一场那一番“进尼姑庵去吧”之论表明他已不相信世间还有真情在！当然王子纯良的天性和思想家的睿智也在不时地校正他。这又使之逐渐地陷入于宿命论泥潭：“我们的结果却早已有一种冥冥中的力量把它布置好了。”“一只雀子的死生，都是命运预先注定的。注定在今天，就不会是明天；不是明天，就是今天；逃过了今天，明天还是逃不了，随时准备着就是了。”[2]122-129 他无奈地叹息，或为哲学的叹息罢！然而，假若可能，也许哈姆莱特为之向往的，乃是哲学家的超脱与旁观态度，他对霍拉旭坦言：“你就是我灵魂里选中的一个人，因为你虽然经历一切的颠沛，却不曾受到一点伤害，命运的虐待和恩宠，你都是受之泰然；能够把感情和理智调整得那么适当，命运不能把他玩弄于指掌之间，那样的人是有福的。”[2]66 兹何尝不是莎士比亚的愿望！在悲剧英雄身上，寄托了关于人君的最高理想，一个未践职的开明君主与哲学家王形象。大幕落下时，接续大统的挪威王子福丁布拉斯宣布给其以崇高的军人的葬礼，“因为要是他能够践登王位，一定会成为一个贤明的君主的；……”[2]136

“质本洁来还洁去”，哈姆莱特以他悲壮的死讴赞了个性的尊严，赢得了对旧制度及黑暗势力道义上的胜利，从而鼓舞着后继者的斗志；他那崇高的品格、忧国忧民的使命感和热情激昂的思想力量，作为一种永恒的精神财富，也必将为爱好正义的人们所珍视。

参考文献

[1] 阿尼克斯特. 1980. 英国文学史纲[M]. 戴镏龄，等，译. 北京：人民文学出版社.

[2] 莎士比亚. 2001. 哈姆莱特[M]//莎士比亚全集（七）. 朱生豪，译. 西安：陕西师范大学出版社.

[3] 弗・史雷格尔. 1985. 论哈姆莱特[M]//莎士比亚评论汇编（上）. 杨周翰，编选. 北京：中国社会科学出版社.

[4] 柯勒律治. 1985. 关于哈姆莱特的演讲[M]//莎士比亚评论汇编（上）. 杨周翰，编选. 北京：中国社会科学出版社.

[5] 赫士列特. 1985. 莎士比亚戏剧人物论[M]//莎士比亚评论汇编（上）. 杨周翰，编选. 北京：中国社会科学出版社.
[6] 泰纳. 2008. 莎士比亚论[M]//读莎士比亚. 张可，元化，译. 上海：上海书店出版社.
[7] 屠格涅夫. 1985. 哈姆莱特与堂·吉诃德[M]//莎士比亚评论汇编（上）. 杨周翰，编选. 北京：中国社会科学出版社.
[8] 弗洛伊德. 1996. 释梦（第五章第四节）[M]. 孙名之，译. 北京：商务印书馆.
[9] 辜正坤. 2019. 莎士比亚作品研究须突破之五大障碍[M]//中国莎士比亚研究（第 1 辑）. 李伟民，主编. 成都：西南交通大学出版社.
[10] 李伟民. 2019. 中国莎士比亚研究（第 1 辑）[M]. 成都：西南交通大学出版社.
[11] 黑格尔. 1984. 美学（第一卷）[M]. 朱光潜，译. 北京：商务印书馆 1984.
[12] 雨果. 1959. 悲惨世界（第二部）[M]. 李丹，译. 北京：人民文学出版社.
[13] 柏拉图. 1997. 理想国[M]. 郭斌和，张竹明，译. 北京：商务印书馆.
[14] 罗素. 1988. 西方哲学史（上卷）[M]. 何兆武，李约瑟，译. 北京：商务印书馆.
[15] 黑格尔. 1983. 哲学史讲演录（第二卷）[M]. 贺麟，王太庆，译. 北京：商务印书馆.

作者简介：王化学，山东师范大学文学院教授，博士生导师；山东省政府文史研究馆馆员；山东省外国文学学会副会长、山东省比较文学学会副会长。主要从事欧洲文学史和造型艺术史研究。

莎士比亚的《哈姆莱特》：一个基督教的隐喻

李伟民

【摘　要】莎士比亚在《哈姆莱特》中有大量的基督教隐喻。由于隐喻的隐蔽性使人们在解读《哈姆莱特》时更多地注意到主要人物哈姆莱特的人文主义特征，而忽视了他所处的基督教背景，以及他根据基督教教义和《圣经》思想、行动的处事原则。因此在评论中有意无意之间拔高了哈姆莱特的形象。从基督教隐喻角度解读，能够使我们得出不同的结论。更清楚地认识到《哈姆莱特》是从基督教的母胎中孕育出来的一部伟大悲剧。

【关键词】隐喻；莎士比亚；基督教；《哈姆莱特》

Hamlet: Metaphor of Christianity

Li Weimin

【Abstract】Shakespeare uses a lot of metaphors of Christianity in *Hamlet*. Due to the invisibility of metaphor, people may, when analyzing the work, pay more attention to the humanitarian features of Hamlet, neglect his Christian background and his life principles based on Christian believes and the Bible. Critics may thus even place Hamlet in a higher position than he deserves. If we read Hamlet from the perspective of Christian metaphors, we can reach different conclusions. We realize that it is Christianity that gives birth to *Hamlet*, the great tragedy.

【Key Words】metaphor; Shakespeare; Christianity; *Hamlet*

引　言

隐喻不但可以作为一种语言现象，而且从修辞的角度来讲，也可以被称为是一种人类了解世界、认识世界的认知现象。[①]人生大舞台，舞台小世界。将表演与语言结合起来的戏剧也因此被誉为人类认识世界的一个窗口（小世界）。所以，我们也可以毫不夸张地说，莎士比亚戏剧语言中的隐喻与人类的思维方式和思维发展过程密切相关，它是莎士比亚将社会悲剧、

① 束定芳：《论隐喻的本质及语义特征》，《外国语》，1998 年，第 6 期。

人生哲理的领悟通过舞台用来说明、理解、抒发精神领域情感的一种认识活动，在人类其他的文化和艺术活动中，我们到处都能看到隐喻的存在，莎士比亚的经典名剧《哈姆莱特》岂能例外。亚里士多德指出，修辞是说话的艺术，词汇的用法，如“清晰”“热情”“合适”和“华贵”等可以增进修辞的效果，它不但能使日常用语显得风格清晰①，而且在舞台上更能够发挥出强烈的艺术感染力。这些时时迸发出思想火花的隐喻，不但激活了《哈姆莱特》，也更加符合舞台艺术特定的表演规律和艺术创作规律。

一、《哈姆莱特》与基督教的隐喻

莎士比亚作品不仅在语言和戏剧领域取得了巨大的成就，而且它本身就是一座庞大的隐喻宝库。在这座庞大的隐喻宝库中，又以《哈姆莱特》由于争论最多、分歧最大又堪称所有莎剧中隐喻的集大成者。由于隐喻本身具有的间接性特点，致使我们在对《哈姆莱特》的解读中存在着多种可能。哈姆莱特究竟是一个人文主义者？还是一个非人文主义者？《哈姆莱特》究竟是一出复仇悲剧？还是一部人文主义者毁灭的悲剧？这样的争论自《哈姆莱特》诞生以来就从来没有停止过。但是，如果我们将《哈姆莱特》视为一个隐喻系统，将其中或隐或显透露出来的基督教思想看作是莎士比亚有意无意设置的隐喻，看作是作为创作者莎士比亚无论如何也不能够摆脱的隐喻，那么，我们是否还会为上述问题而争论不休？笔者的回答是：争论尽管还是会有的，但如果从《哈姆莱特》中的基督教隐喻入手，对其进行解读，至少能使我们获得一种新的视角。美国艺术科学院院士海伦·加德纳将莎士比亚悲剧称为“基督教悲剧”，因为“莎士比亚戏剧的确以最为优美动人的形式表现了显然是基督教的观念……它的一些最有代表性的特点，都是与基督教的宗教感情和基督教的理解相联系的……”②尽管他没有具体论述《哈姆莱特》与基督教之间的关系，但是，如果我们联系莎士比亚所生活的基督教环境和他对基督教的熟稔以及这部悲剧中随处隐喻的基督教的教义，通过物质和精神的极端存在，显示出来的基督教精神和思想，我们就会明白《哈姆莱特》在表面现象掩盖下的复杂，和《哈姆莱特》与基督教精神家园之间那千丝万缕的天然联系。我们通过《哈姆莱特》情节的开展，往往能够感受到冥冥中有一个主宰，这个主宰不是别的什么，就是基督教思想和精神指导着人物的思想和行动，尤其是在悲剧发展的紧要关头，莎士比亚往往用基督教思想来解释人物的思想，设置作品的情节，指导人物的行动，揭示人物的心理，安排人物的对话，调遣戏剧的结构，让观众以战栗的心聆观喋血的悲壮、啼血的悲泣。作为隐喻的基督教在《哈姆莱特》中是如此重要，而这一点正是我们理解《哈姆莱特》的关键。据统计《哈姆莱特》中引用或提到《圣经》，有三十九处，其中二十八处出于哈姆莱特之口。莎士比亚最熟悉的可能是 Miles Coverdale 约在 1539 年出版的《圣经》英译本，称为 Great Bible，以及 1560 年出版的 Geneva Bible（詹姆士一世的钦定本要到 1611 年才出版）。③

① 束定芳：《论隐喻的本质及语义特征》，《外国语》，1998 年，第 6 期。
② 海伦·加德纳：《宗教与文学》，成都：四川人民出版社，1989 年，第 73-74 页。
③ 莎士比亚：《哈姆莱特》（裘克安注释），北京：商务印书馆，1984 年，第 13 页。

二、哈姆莱特的基督教式背景隐喻

作为一个生活在基督教文化背景中的戏剧家，莎士比亚在《哈姆莱特》中将基督教作为悲剧的文化背景是再自然不过的事情了，处于基督教文化背景的戏剧观众也要求创作者这样做，但是，这种基督教式的背景在很多时候又是以直接或间接的方式体现在作品中的。哲学的自由是相对于必然而言的，宗教的自由是相对于信仰而言的。对于熟知基督教的英国观众来说，不管这种隐喻是直接的还是间接的，无论是从接受的角度讲，还是从信仰和心理的角度讲，都会得到他们的认同。而对于东方观众或读者来说，在缺少基督教浸染的文化背景下，就很难理解其中的基督教隐喻，而把注意力放在哈姆莱特的人文主义方面，使我们的解读天然存在着某种缺失。德国哲学家尼采认为，人的认识在原则上可称为是隐喻性的。思维要首先把世界变成同“自己一样的东西”[①]才称得上是认识。哈姆莱特的这种隐喻性思维兼有直觉思维和形象思维特征。主人公哈姆莱特所处的基督教背景在隐喻中的文化背景对理解隐喻的意义上起着关键作用，同时也给我们理解其形象带来了不确定性和困难。《哈姆莱特》隐喻中的基督教信仰背景、生活习惯背景，反映了他和他的周围浓重的基督教文化心理和基督教价值取向的文化背景，这绝不是一句简单化的“人文主义者”的断语所能概括得了的。我们看到《哈姆莱特》一开始就描绘出基督教的氛围，如第一幕第一场：“圣洁而美好”[②]，“神的恩典，是基督教义中一个重要概念”[③]在《哈姆莱特》也起到了渲染环境的作用，而这种被渲染的环境不是别的什么环境，正是弥漫在全剧中的基督教环境；即使哈姆莱特说：“我们进宫去好不好？”[④]，其中的言语（哈姆莱特发誓时常常把“上帝”挂在嘴边）也显示了他对“基督教信仰”[⑤]的无意识。我们在剧情中随时随地看到，哈姆莱特“以色列的士师耶弗他啊”[⑥]这样大量的基督教口头禅，其言语多见于《圣经》[⑦]。在《哈姆莱特》中基督教信仰的“神”“上帝”的意象是重要的，因为任何价值的评判都只成其为苍白的结果，宗教的判断才堪担当喻世警世醒世的作用，通过“神”“上帝”的隐喻，既能使戏剧中的人物的思想和行动得到合理的解释，渲染环境，又能使观众（读者）感受到圣洁、美好信仰，甚至看到哈姆莱特行动的力量的源泉。

莎士比亚在《哈姆莱特》中大量的人物对话都隐喻了《圣经》中的人与事。首先是对“人”的隐喻。莎士比亚的隐喻尽管有时是自觉的，有时是不自觉的，但是，这样的隐喻在客观上使观众（读）者获得了对基督教的认同感。悲剧开始时，鬼魂说：“淡薄而健全的血液凝结起来；它一进入我的身体，我全身光滑的皮肤上便立刻发生无数疱疹。”[⑧]来源于乞丐拉撒路“浑身生疮”[⑨]。“疱疹”隐喻《圣经》中浑身的“疮”。在《圣经》中有两个拉撒路，第一个是浑身生疮的乞丐。他被人放在一个财主门口，靠财主饭桌上掉下来的零碎充饥，靠狗来舔他的

① 弗里德里希·尼采：《权力意志——重估一切价值的尝试》，张念东、凌素心译，北京：商务印书馆，1991 年，第 691 页。
② 莎士比亚：《哈姆莱特》（英汉对照读本），朱生豪译，北京：人民文学出版社，2002 年，第 15 页。
③ 莎士比亚：《哈姆莱特》（裘克安注释），北京：商务印书馆，1984 年，第 17 页。
④ 莎士比亚：《哈姆莱特》（英汉对照读本），朱生豪译，北京：人民文学出版社，2002 年，第 85 页。
⑤ 莎士比亚：《哈姆莱特》（裘克安注释），北京：商务印书馆，1984 年，第 97 页。
⑥ 莎士比亚：《哈姆莱特》（英汉对照读本），朱生豪译，北京：人民文学出版社，2002 年，第 93 页。
⑦ 莎士比亚：《哈姆莱特》（裘克安注释），北京：商务印书馆，1984 年，第 105 页。
⑧ 莎士比亚：《哈姆莱特》（英汉对照读本），朱生豪译，北京：人民文学出版社，2002 年，第 50 页。
⑨《圣经》（简化字与现代标点符号和合本），南京：中国基督教协会印发，1989 年，第 90 页。

疮减轻痛痒，拉撒路死后进天堂，财主死后在阴间受苦。第二个拉撒路死后是耶稣使他复活，从此信仰耶稣的人越来越多。[①]《圣经》中的两个拉撒路尽管形象相当猥琐，最后都得到了好的结果。由鬼魂说出这样的话隐喻了他在被他的兄弟杀死以后（升天），也必将进入天堂或者活在“民众”的心里。即使是在世俗性的对话中，莎士比亚仍然不自觉地通过隐喻把人物对话和基督教或《圣经》联系起来。如《哈姆莱特》第一幕第一场：“那是扰乱我们心灵之眼的一点微尘”[②]，就是来自《圣经》中“为什么只看见你弟兄眼中有一粒灰，却不想自己眼中有梁木呢？”[③]悲剧中的鬼魂是“人”的隐喻，而“人”的思想和行动也是通过隐喻表现出来的，“鬼魂”的话就成为隐喻的隐喻。历经炼狱，才能有对人生过人的宗教审视和超越的眼光，哈姆莱特的许多对话性言语隐喻了基督教的教义：如“没有受过临终涂膏礼以前”[④]，在《圣经》中“基督徒临终前由牧师给吃一小块面包，代表耶稣肉身，并作感恩祈祷的仪式”[⑤]。再如，哈姆莱特说：“嗳呦，朋友，还要客气得多哩！”[⑥]此处又出现用圣餐用的未发酵的圆面包片代表耶稣肉身[⑦]，对白中两次出现“基督肉身”的隐喻，对身处基督教氛围中的观众来说既便于和现实世界联系起来，也是一件再自然不过的事情了。

如果说，隐喻有时还不足以点明基督教的文化背景，那么，莎士比亚有时就会直接将基督教与非基督教进行对比了。哈姆莱特对戏班子的话隐喻了他意识深处基督教的正统意识，他说：“他们既不会说基督徒的语言，又不会学着基督徒、异教徒或者一般人的样子走路，瞧他们在台上大摇大摆，使劲叫喊的样子，我心里就想一定是什么造化的雇工把他们造了下来：造得这样拙劣，以至于全然失去了人类的面目。”[⑧]异教徒天生就比基督徒低了一等，因为他们是上帝短期雇工造出来的。按基督教的说法，人是上帝造的，但这些角色的形象如此恶劣，竟像是上帝的雇工所造，而非上帝亲自动手造的，只有基督教造的人才是完美的。[⑨]通过对比，异教徒和基督徒一出生就有了优劣、高低之分。在对基督教事件的隐喻中，莎士比亚将《哈姆莱特》中所发生的事件涂抹上了一层基督教色彩，强化了剧中的基督教氛围。罗森格兰兹说：“那么那班戏班子们恐怕要来自讨一场没趣了”[⑩]，“源自，耶稣复活节前的四旬节斋期，一切从简”[⑪]，强调的是在风俗习惯上世俗社会的人也要按照基督教的那一套来生活。又如，大臣波洛涅斯报告哈姆莱特那班戏子已到……而《圣经》中大能的勇士……耶弗他用其女献祭则印证了，哈姆莱特的话既是疯话，也是对奥菲利娅一片深情的隐秘曲折的表达，同时，还暗中表达了哈姆莱特对波洛涅斯的厌恶之情[⑫]，波洛涅斯的行动也影射了《圣经》中用女儿献祭。再如“墓地”中两个小丑的谈话。用圣经典故暗讽人物，使隐喻因此达到了一石二鸟的效果，通过隐喻使观众得到了文化、精神上的认同感，嘲讽了戏剧演出中低劣的表演技巧，

① 《圣经》（简化字与现代标点符号和合本），南京：中国基督教协会印发，1989年，第118页。
② 莎士比亚：《哈姆莱特》（英汉对照读本），朱生豪译，北京：人民文学出版社，2002年，第11页。
③ 莎士比亚：《哈姆莱特》（裘克安注释），北京：商务印书馆，1984年，第13页。
④ 莎士比亚：《哈姆莱特》（英汉对照读本），朱生豪译，北京：人民文学出版社，2002年，第53页。
⑤ 莎士比亚：《哈姆莱特》（裘克安注释），北京：商务印书馆，1984年，第59页。
⑥ 莎士比亚：《哈姆莱特》（英汉对照读本），朱生豪译，北京：人民文学出版社，2002年，第99页。
⑦ 莎士比亚：《哈姆莱特》（裘克安注释），北京：商务印书馆，1984年，第113页。
⑧ 莎士比亚：《哈姆莱特》（英汉对照读本），朱生豪译，北京：人民文学出版社，2002年，第119页。
⑨ 莎士比亚：《哈姆莱特》（裘克安注释），北京：商务印书馆，1984年，第137页。
⑩ 莎士比亚：《哈姆莱特》（英汉对照读本），朱生豪译，北京：人民文学出版社，2002年，第87页。
⑪ 莎士比亚：《哈姆莱特》（裘克安注释），北京：商务印书馆，1984年，第99页。
⑫ 李伟昉：《莎士比亚与圣经》，《洛阳师范学院学报》2002年，第4期。

又使深受基督教浸染的西方观众看到这里，或者读者读到这里，就会想起圣经中的有关故事，在莎士比亚制造的基督教隐喻中联想到世俗社会的舞台演出中一些令人感到滑稽的场面，从而发出会心的微笑。基督教式的背景隐喻拉近了观众与戏剧之间的距离，使观众产生了一种认同感、亲切感，也使哈姆莱特的复仇无论是从基督教层面，还是从世俗的层面都更容易得到当时社会的观众的理解，从而产生出更加震撼人心的戏剧性，达到撼人心魄的艺术效果，同时也使《哈姆莱特》披上了一层基督教背景的薄纱。基督教思想自始至终笼罩着全剧。该剧以鬼魂谈话开始，而鬼魂本身就是宗教的产物，他的言语也成为隐喻的隐喻。如果，我们在研究《哈姆莱特》时忽视了其中的基督教隐喻，一味强调哈姆莱特身上的所谓人文主义精神，误读也就在所难免了。

三、隐喻中自觉或不自觉透露出来的宗教思想

《哈姆莱特》中的隐喻不仅仅表现为是一种语言现象，更重要的是还是一种思维特点。由于其本身的隐喻性使话语具有一种“不同寻常的”风格。从这种不同寻常的风格中，我们往往能够发现作者在语篇中通过隐喻透露出来的自觉或不自觉隐藏在其中的真实意图。而《哈姆莱特》中的这种不同寻常的语言风格或人物之间的言语风格的基督教思想和精神的呈现，正是其产生不朽艺术魅力的原因之一。这是因为，隐喻能取得特殊的修辞效果。它与感情、动机、意志等心理活动相联系，是以语言形式出现的“人认识事物的结果”[①]，这种自觉或不自觉隐喻的基督教思想在《哈姆莱特》第三幕中表现得尤为明显，如《哈姆莱特》中的人物直呼“上帝”，向上帝起誓，既要求自己又要求别人按照《圣经》的要求去做。如哈姆莱特：“上帝的慈悲保佑你们”[②]，“上帝保佑你们”这些随时随地的插入语，意思是上帝保佑你们做到这点，暗示如果违誓，后果不堪设想。[③]波洛涅斯叫着：“嗳呦”[④]，“指上帝起誓”[⑤]，王后：“阿门”[⑥]，“基督教祈祷的结束语和应声语，意为，但愿如此，心同此愿，源自西伯来语。”[⑦]相当多的起誓词“上帝”在汉语翻译中并没有译为“上帝”，而是根据上下文译成了各种语气词。在《哈姆莱特》中随处可见基督教用语，如：“我可以把这种家伙抓起来抽一顿鞭子，因为他把妥玛刚特形容过分，希律王的凶暴也要对他甘拜下风。”[⑧]古犹太希律王，曾为了扼杀耶稣，“差人将伯力恒城里并四境所有的男孩……凡两岁以里的，都杀尽了。”[⑨]中世纪欧洲神秘剧里把他演做大喊大叫的暴君。Out-herods Herod：比希律王还希律，是莎士比亚创造的词语，意思是“比暴君还暴君”[⑩]，隐喻的修辞夸张，语流的停顿和迂回在不知不觉中强烈地刺激着观众已经绷紧的神经。又如，国王祈祷：“我的灵魂上负着一个元始以来最初的诅咒，杀

① 李秀丽：《隐喻研究的误区》，《四川外语学院学报》2002年，第1期。
② 莎士比亚：《哈姆莱特》（英汉对照读本），朱生豪译，北京：人民文学出版社，2002年，第59页。
③ 莎士比亚：《哈姆莱特》（裘克安注释），北京：商务印书馆，1984年，第65页。
④ 莎士比亚：《哈姆莱特》（英汉对照读本），朱生豪译，北京：人民文学出版社，2002年，第63页。
⑤ 莎士比亚：《哈姆莱特》（裘克安注释），北京：商务印书馆，1984年，第71页。
⑥ 莎士比亚：《哈姆莱特》（英汉对照读本），朱生豪译，北京：人民文学出版社，2002年，第71页。
⑦ 莎士比亚：《哈姆莱特》（裘克安注释），北京：商务印书馆，1984年，第81页。
⑧ 莎士比亚：《哈姆莱特》（英汉对照读本），朱生豪译，北京：人民文学出版社，2002年，第117页。
⑨《圣经》（简化字与现代标点符号和合本），南京：中国基督教协会印发，1989年，第2页。
⑩ 莎士比亚：《哈姆莱特》（裘克安注释），北京：商务印书馆，1984年，第135页。

害兄弟的暴行！我不能祈祷。"[①]来自地上第一个亚当的长子该隐杀死其弟亚伯，受上帝诅咒。[②]克劳狄斯"表面上道貌岸然，内心却充满淫欲，或则为了觊觎王位而不惜犯弑君之罪，然而，他们的内心总无法完全摆脱罪孽感与自我谴责……克劳狄斯遇到了一个无法解脱的困境：他既想求得宽恕，又不愿放弃自己用罪恶手段获得的一切：慈悲的使命……"[③]从这里我们可以看到人物内心的冲突。这是经验与超验的撕裂、情感与理智的碰撞、迷恋权势与渴望宽恕的忏悔、灵魂超度与万世不劫的两难抉择；这是善与恶的搏斗，天使与魔鬼的交战。[④]显然，《哈姆莱特》的隐喻是对基督教的一个自觉认同，即使是恶人也不应该例外，也要受到基督教的约束。国家即其生命的终极认同，王位即国家，是不容"外人"染指的。"上帝的物当归还给上帝"，即国家的归于国家，终极的归于终极。只有这样，无论是现实社会还是神学世界才是正常的。在《哈姆莱特》中语言不仅是现实世界的符号，而且也是悲剧内部人物之间的符号，甚至是哈姆莱特身上各种因素被隐喻的结果，被隐喻的是一种生命的语言和基督教精神的完美结合。语言本性的互喻性、隐喻性，使现实世界与人类内心，基督教与世俗社会，一面在自身内部运动，又互指互喻，既有各自的运行轨迹，又在一定时间、一定场合上有所重合。

二者的重合构成了哈姆莱特和其他人物语言的基督教隐喻。在第三幕第三场国王："祈祷的目的，不是一方面预防我们的堕落，一方面救拔我们于已堕落之后吗？"[⑤]在新王的愿望中，祈祷既有预防的作用，又有重新拯救的作用，祈祷的目的重在后者。祈祷是基督世界，拯救是现实中的自己。克劳狄斯也强调谋杀的"罪恶"，又可以使熟悉圣经的观众联想到，亚当夏娃的长子该隐和次子亚伯一并给上帝敬献供物……该隐心生嫉妒残杀害弟，莎士比亚借用了这个典故。但是，按照基督教的教义，对平民和国王的祈祷是有所区别的："不能祷告。按基督教义，人若犯罪而能真心悔改，祈祷忏悔，是可蒙神恩宠的，但国王不能真心忏悔，就不得救赎，必下地狱。"[⑥]此处隐喻了克劳狄斯可鄙的下场。莎士比亚考问人性，考问人性中隐藏的恶，在考问中从基督教教义出发隐喻了新王的虚假和归宿，而且由于这种"虚假"，不论对于哈姆莱特来说，还是对于看戏的观众来说，都是很难得到饶恕的。不但，克劳狄斯用基督教和《圣经》在寻求得到饶恕和解脱，而且，哈姆莱特也用基督教教义和《圣经》来衡量自己复仇的正义性、合法性、适时性，以便获得指导自己的复仇行为通行证。哈姆莱特行动的依据是，是否合乎基督教准则，合乎基督教准则就是他行动的根据，反之就不能行动，如哈姆莱特说："他用卑鄙的手段，在我父亲满心俗念，罪孽正重的时候乘其不备把他杀死；虽然谁也不知道在上帝面前，他的生前的善恶如何相抵"[⑦]"指基督教原罪论所说的一般人都有的罪过"[⑧]，如果行动符合基督教准则就是合理的，反之就是不合理的。莎士比亚隐喻了基督教的原罪论，"满心俗念"和人人都会有的"罪"与谋杀比起来，显然是有一个孰轻孰重的问题，因而，前者与后者相比就显得微不足道了。莎士比亚试图用基督教的道德观念来解释社会、道德危机。哈姆莱特"你当初就不应该相信我，因为美德不能熏陶我们罪恶的本性；我

① 莎士比亚：《哈姆莱特》（英汉对照读本），朱生豪译，北京：人民文学出版社，2002年，第143页。
② 莎士比亚：《哈姆莱特》（英汉对照读本），朱生豪译，北京：人民文学出版社，2002年，第165页。
③ 莎士比亚：《哈姆莱特》（英汉对照读本），朱生豪译，北京：人民文学出版社，2002年，第145页。
④ 汪义群：《莎士比亚的宗教观初探》，《外国文学评论》，1993年，第3期。
⑤ 莎士比亚：《哈姆莱特》（英汉对照读本），朱生豪译，北京：人民文学出版社，2002年，第145页。
⑥ 莎士比亚：《哈姆莱特》（裘克安注释），北京：商务印书馆，1984年，第165页。
⑦ 莎士比亚：《哈姆莱特》（英汉对照读本），朱生豪译，北京：人民文学出版社，2002年，第147页。
⑧ 莎士比亚：《哈姆莱特》（裘克安注释），北京：商务印书馆，1984年，第167页。

没有爱过你”[①]，“比喻来自对野苹果的嫁接，其结果不能完全免除原来的酸味。这话的基础是基督教的原罪论，认为上帝造的第一个人亚当已经犯罪，以后他的子嗣无不带有罪恶的本性，因此需要耶稣基督的拯救。”[②]哈姆莱特秉承了希伯来—— 基督教的“原罪”及“失乐园”的观念，“泥塑的生命”，“像我这样的叫花子”，“世界是牢狱、荒原”这样的原罪思想从根本上是与人文主义思想相悖的。

隐喻性语言正是人们在头脑中把不同的事物 或观念联系起来的结果与体现。从某种意义上说，《哈姆莱特》中的隐喻使观众进一步获得更深层次的基督教精神的洗礼。在《哈姆莱特》中基督教精神可以说是无处不在，虽然很多基督教隐喻在戏剧的发展过程中可能仅仅是一带而过，但是，这样的隐喻多了，就会在整体上强化观众（读者）的感觉。如“即使石块也会感动的”，化用了圣经中的“石头必要呼叫起来”[③]；哈姆莱特：“国王是一件东西”[④]，化用了圣经中“他的年日如同影儿快快过去”[⑤]，目的是为自己打气。奥菲利娅唱：“毡帽在头杖在手”[⑥]的歌，隐喻了“英国民间传说，耶稣到一面包师富家讨面包吃，其妻要给，而女儿表现吝啬，后女儿变为猫头鹰”[⑦]。隐喻体现了哈姆莱特和剧中人物独特的基督教式的体验、思维方式和语境，而且成为观众了解《哈姆莱特》的上下文之间衔接、话题内容、说话的方式、人物地位及相互之间的关系、彼此熟悉的程度的一把钥匙。《哈姆莱特》中既包括了基督教式的语言环境，又包括了基督教式的言语环境，前者决定、涵盖了后者，后者进一步强化、说明了前者，二者相辅相成，不能截然分开。《哈姆莱特》中的隐喻作为一种以言行事的方式，作为一种传达信息、表达情感的方式，增加了剧中人物的艺术感染力，表现为悲剧中的人物能够根据现实语境中的情景及时取喻，创造出合适的、具有形象性的强烈基督教色彩的隐喻。[⑧]

基督教隐喻增强了人物对白的形象性、幽默感，在语气上也增强了分量，如小丑说：“你的《圣经》是怎么念的？《圣经》上说亚当掘地；没有两手，能够掘地吗？”[⑨]直接来自对“纹章的隐喻，有人认为亚当的锨是最古的纹章。”例如哈姆莱特说：“必须让它像棕榈树一样发荣繁茂，因为和平女神必须永远戴着她的荣冠”，《圣经》人要兴旺如棕榈树。[⑩]我们通过隐喻对哈姆莱特的一系列言语理解过程中，观众或读者对其中的基督教语境非常熟悉，观（读）者可以根据对说话人身份及话题的了解，预测了哈姆莱特将要表达的大概意思，然后根据哈姆莱特的言语，对原来的期待进行修正并做出反应，造成比较强烈的戏剧效果，从而给观众和读者留下形象、幽默的深刻印象。莎士比亚根据观众或读者对语境的熟悉程度，使观众或读者对话语的隐喻进行解码，根据哈姆莱特等人一连串话语的字面意义判断隐喻话语的语境意义和说话者的真实意图。哈姆莱特的隐喻通过某一领域的经验过渡到认知另一领域的经验，再使观众和读者得以将二者联系起来，一旦形象化的联系建立起来了，作者的目的也就达到了。同时，隐喻的过程也反映了基督教思想对莎士比亚本人和《哈姆莱特》的影响。

---

① 莎士比亚：《哈姆莱特》（英汉对照读本），朱生豪译，北京：人民文学出版社，2002 年，第 111 页。
② 莎士比亚：《哈姆莱特》（裘克安注释），北京：商务印书馆，1984 年，第 129 页。
③ 莎士比亚：《哈姆莱特》（裘克安注释），北京：商务印书馆，1984 年，第 179 页。
④ 莎士比亚：《哈姆莱特》（英汉对照读本），朱生豪译，北京：人民文学出版社，2002 年，第 167 页。
⑤ 李伟昉：《莎士比亚与圣经》，《洛阳师范学院学报》2002 年，第 4 期。
⑥ 莎士比亚：《哈姆莱特》（英汉对照读本），朱生豪译，北京：人民文学出版社，2002 年，第 179 页。
⑦ 莎士比亚：《哈姆莱特》（裘克安注释），北京：商务印书馆，1984 年，第 209 页。
⑧ 王松亭：《试谈语境因素对隐喻的影响和制约作用》，《外语研究》，2000 年，第 4 期。
⑨ 莎士比亚：《哈姆莱特》（裘克安注释），北京：商务印书馆，1984 年，第 243 页。
⑩ 莎士比亚：《哈姆莱特》（裘克安注释），北京：商务印书馆，1984 年，第 167 页。

在《哈姆莱特》中，很多隐喻是隐藏在祝福和诅咒之中的。卡西勒尔认为语言的权力也就是隐喻的权力，其共同的根基就是“隐喻性思维”。[①]隐喻不但表达了人们对真、善、美最基本的看法，同时，隐喻也表达了对邪恶的诅咒，促使、引导人们对假、恶、丑的憎恨与谴责。由于不相关事物和事件的并置，增强了语言的表现力和言语的力量，既对我们的想象产生巨大的影响，又对我们的理解能力形成了挑战。这就是《哈姆莱特》中基督教隐喻经常化、熟知化、陌生化所带来的效果。《哈姆莱特》中的隐喻在很多时候体现在祝福和诅咒的对白中。例如，祈求上帝“叫这杯撤去”[②]一样，哈姆莱特也是不情愿去死的。如同耶稣一样，他也是个不情愿但却是个称职的替罪羊……哈姆莱特被“钉死于十字架”，但他的死使丹麦获得了净化和新生……哈姆莱特的“救赎与耶稣的救赎目的是一样的”。《哈姆莱特》中的鬼魂就将那个杀害国王、欺骗世人的克劳狄斯称作“毒蛇”。哈姆莱特不仅将克劳狄斯比做“毒蛇”，而且还骂哪个叛变了他，替克劳狄斯盯梢，时时跟踪他的朋友称为“两条邪恶的毒蛇”。这样的诅咒式的隐喻对熟悉基督教的西方观众来说已经拥有了足够的分量。

四、基督教思想是哈姆莱特一切行动的根据

隐喻与诗歌特别是《哈姆莱特》这样的诗剧有不可分割的联系。可以这样说诗剧中如果缺少了隐喻也就不成其为诗剧了。“隐喻再也不是一种任意和微不足道的现象……隐喻成了出现在整个诗歌中‘说’和‘诗意化’的工具，它不再是一种词汇现象，而是一种话语现象。”[③]隐喻的艺术创作功能主要是指诗剧创作和隐喻之间构成的外在或内在的密不可分的关系。隐喻是诗剧《哈姆莱特》的生命源泉，隐喻是诗剧中飞扬的性灵，隐喻是诗剧中隐藏的思想，隐喻又是诗剧中美的时隐时现的体现，隐喻形成的美是诗人的情感的文本。隐喻将思维、语言诗意化，隐喻又将语言诗歌化。

莎士比亚戏剧特别是大悲剧《哈姆莱特》中，那充满激情、悲壮、缠绵、悲悯、圣洁、理性的经典演绎正是通过大量的隐喻体现出超越时空的魅力和激情的。在《哈姆莱特》中，隐喻已经不再是黏着于语言之内，游离于思想之外的华丽装饰，而是潜藏于戏剧台词中思想、精神深度的具体体现。《哈姆莱特》中的隐喻体现了以基督教思想形成和指导的悲剧的思维方式和戏剧中人物行为、行动的方式。用一个表示某事物的词借喻他物，这个词便成了隐喻词，其应用范围包括以属喻种，以种喻属，以种喻种和彼此类推。[④]《哈姆莱特》中大量的隐喻正是悲剧中的代表性人物哈姆莱特以基督教中特有的方式来指导自己的一切行动，基督教思想和精神隐喻成为他的一切行动的根据，并且以他物特有的含义引起观众和读者对基督教思想的认同和回溯。如果离开了对《哈姆莱特》中基督教思想的深度把握，显然，我们就不能很好地理解这个旷世未有的大悲剧了。

哈姆莱特之所以延宕是出于他对宗教思想的考虑，在宗教观念的影响下，他迟迟不采取果断行动，最终导致了他的悲剧。其他人的行动也要遵循基督教原则，马勒西斯话中的“耶

① 王一川：《语言的乌托邦》，昆明：云南人民出版社，2000 年，第 80-89 页。
②《圣经》（简化字与现代标点符号和合本），南京：中国基督教协会印发，1989 年，第 2 页。
③ 亚里士多德：《诗学》，北京：商务印书馆，1987 年，第 149 页。
④ 束定芳：《隐喻学研究》，上海：上海外语教育出版社，2000 年，第 122 页。

稣圣诞”，更是霍拉旭在挑战鬼魂时引用的基督教习语：“凭上天的命义，我命令你说话。”基督教隐喻表明，莎士比亚始终不能也不能抛开宗教的意识与基督教精神去塑造哈姆莱特和其他人的形象。哈姆莱特在整个复仇过程中，凡是关键时刻，他无一例外地按照宗教意识和上帝的旨意行事。为此，《哈姆莱特》就成为全部莎剧中宗教色彩最浓的一部戏剧。如此一来，我们还能无限地强调哈姆莱特是人文主义者，具有所谓的先进的人文主义思想吗？

从哈姆莱特一系列隐喻式的言语中，我们得知他是非常熟知《圣经》并习惯于按其行事的。例如，霍拉旭劝他不要做他不愿意做的事，但他最终还是按照《圣经》上说的去做了，“我们不要害怕什么预兆；一只雀子的死生，都是命运预先注定的。注定在今天，就不会是明天；不是明天，就是今天；逃过了今天，明天还是逃不了，随时准备着就是了。一个人既然在离开世界的时候，只能一无所有，那么早早脱身而去，不是更好吗？”[①]《圣经》中，两个麻雀不是卖一分银子吗？[②]这段话主旨思想的隐喻，告诉世人“不要怕他们。因为掩盖的事，没有不露出来的；隐藏的事，没有不被人知道的”。哈姆莱特相信事情总有水落石出的那一天，他相信，上帝能够洞悉生命的卑微，人只要按照上帝的旨意去做，那就不会有错，你只管照意志主宰者的指引做就行了。哈姆莱特在此处的隐喻构成了语言的原始隐喻，经由“有意识的思维产生的隐喻”[③]，成为指导其行动的指南。在哈姆莱特和霍拉旭的对话语境中，他们两人的话语所表达的意义已经超越一般的词汇意义，在哈姆莱特的意识深处呈现的是基督教教义中这段话隐含的意义，即事件必有真相大白的时候，作为接受者霍拉旭不会错误理解其中的隐喻。他们之间的对话是一个封闭的语境。哈姆莱特的回答（解释）是不需要接受者霍拉旭在达到对语篇的某种理解之外还有什么“弦外之音”，或者说，哈姆莱特的言语之外的意思，霍拉旭是相当清楚的，只不过哈姆莱特此时此地不能或不愿说出来罢了。诗歌语言与神学语言或宗教语言被认为是密切相关的，原因是它们都注重诗性隐喻，“即诗性隐喻在神学语言或宗教语言中都成为一个特别明显的标志。这是因为诗学隐喻表达意义的变形，最接近最具代表性的宗教语言”[④]。在《哈姆莱特》中，这种诗学隐喻的变形，首先，是哈姆莱特急于证明自己的清白，命运的安排是任谁也逃脱不了的，其次，他相信真相会大白于天下，再次，哈姆莱特也不得不顾虑到隔墙有耳。

由于现实的波谲云诡，在生与死的问题上，哈姆莱特对生命尊严和纯洁的捍卫，从来都是按照基督教原则思考问题的，如哈姆莱特说：“但愿这一副—— 这一副臭皮囊/融化了，消散了，化解成一滴露水吧！/又但愿永恒的天意并没有定下了/严禁自杀的戒律。上帝呀，上帝！/在我看来，人世的一切多么地无聊，/多么地腐败乏味，一无是处啊！”[⑤]哈姆莱特的思想活动的轨迹仍然是以宗教教义为皈依的。其一，是哈姆莱特出于对基督教的信仰而不能自杀。因为基督教教义是反对自杀的，也就是“永生的真神曾制定了禁止自杀的律法”。人应有对神圣的认同，也要有对自己肉身神圣性的确认，肉身之在为神圣，既神圣得不容侵犯，又不容任何异己之物的沾染。其二，是他悲伤至极甚至自杀也出自宗教的原因。其三，母亲的婚姻是乱伦。这种宗教观点是以神圣的婚姻誓言为基础的。世界充满了魑魅魍魉、光怪陆离，人的

① 莎士比亚：《哈姆莱特》（英汉对照读本），朱生豪译，北京：人民文学出版社，2002 年，第 237 页。
②《圣经》（简化字与现代标点符号和合本），南京：中国基督教协会印发，1989 年，第 12 页。
③ 胡壮麟：《诗性隐喻》，《山东外语教学》，2003 年，第 1 期。
④ 胡壮麟：《诗性隐喻》，《山东外语教学》，2003 年，第 1 期。
⑤ 莎士比亚：《新莎士比亚全集》（第四卷），方平译，石家庄：河北教育出版社，2000 年，第 232-233 页。

肉身的本体价值不可刈除，神圣的情感寓于神圣的肉身。这种宗教观点始出于《圣经》，但却在哈姆莱特身上得到了确认。

我们从《哈姆莱特》最著名的那一段对话中，哈姆莱特用悲怆的心灵寻觅迷失的精神家园，他将思考问题的落脚点归结到宗教意识“生存还是毁灭，这是一个值得考虑的问题；默然忍受命运的暴虐的毒箭，或是挺身反抗人世的无涯的苦难，通过斗争把它们扫清，这两种行为，哪一种更高贵？”[①]“生存—— 毁灭”“默默忍受—— 挺身反抗”构成了两对矛盾，在这两对矛盾中隐喻了是遵循基督教原则，还是违反基督教原则？哈姆莱特暂时选择的是前者。这也是他一再延宕的原因。对于人而言，如何生、如何死蕴蓄着深刻的哲理，领悟这哲理并付诸实践，意味着基督教生命意识的觉醒。生存和忍受是符合基督教教义的，反之，毁灭和反抗则是基督教教义所不赞成、不允许的。《圣经》劝人要忍耐，规定这是“基督徒的生活原则”，圣经说：“在指望中要喜乐，在患难中要忍耐”[②]“不要以恶报恶”，“因为经上记着：‘主说，伸冤在我。我必报应。’所以，‘你的仇敌若饿了，就给他吃；若渴了，就给他喝，因为你这样行，就是把炭火堆在他的头上。’你不可为恶所胜，反要以善胜恶。”[③]耶稣说：“惟有忍耐到底的，必然得救。”[④]约书亚说：“忍耐终将结下喜乐之果。”哈姆莱特似乎对人生有了更多的参透和顿悟，在此时此地他决心按照基督教的原则去做，虽然也经过了一系列激烈的思想斗争，在他心里多次掂量“这样做”或“那样做”的结果，但最终仍然不能做到超越自己的基督教背景。哈姆雷特流露出潜伏已久的强烈的厌世心理波澜，当他知道了叔父邪恶凶残的阴谋之后，也发现了自己的邪恶。浓烈的幻灭感笼罩了他，言前尘往事，依绪万端，顾当年行乐之时，觉世事无常，抟沙转烛，黯然于好梦易醒，盛宴已散，这一切与哈姆雷特的强烈的厌世情绪，与基督教所宣扬的“令人厌倦的人类处境”遥相呼应。哈姆莱特徘徊于两种选择之间，很难一时拿定主意。后者不是不可以选择，但前提是，如果选择后者也必须符合基督教教义所定下的原则，而这种遵从是以隐喻的方式显示出来的，是哈姆莱特思想深处的无意识的湍流旋涡的自然表露。哈姆莱特在这里所指的不可知国其实就是隐喻地狱。按照基督教教义，人死后，他的灵魂不是去天堂享受永恒的欢乐，就是下地狱受无尽的煎熬。哈姆莱特害怕死后去地狱，所以，他在话中有话中隐喻“地狱”，而不是直截了当地说“地狱”。哈姆莱特考虑更多的是死后的事情，并为之做准备。这是基督教的基本教义—— 复活（Resurrection）正在作用和影响着哈姆莱特的思想和行为。

这部作品的主题思想是基督教有关道德观念的延续与发展。《圣经》的核心是以绝对的人伦道德为本的人生价值观来贬斥邪恶与暴虐、弘扬善良与仁爱。它主张历史发展从根本上说是以对自然的驾驭征服乃至改造作为其核心的。哈姆莱特将灵魂深层的冲动与形式幻化用最悲怆也是最极端的方式表达出来，在重大事情的抉择上，他总是遵循宗教思想来惩恶扬善。哈姆莱特杀死波洛涅斯，被自己解释为是上天的意思表达了天意不可违的宗教观念，而“罕秣莱德壮烈牺牲之前，为丹麦王朝执行了劝善惩恶（poetic justice），把罪大恶极的奸君、杀兄篡位奸嫂的凶手明正典刑”[⑤]，也是“不要怜悯行诡诈的恶人”[⑥]的具体行动。

① 莎士比亚：《哈姆莱特》（英汉对照读本），朱生豪译，北京：人民文学出版社，2002 年，第 109 页。
②《圣经》（简化字与现代标点符号和合本），南京：中国基督教协会印发，1989 年，第 179 页。
③《圣经》（简化字与现代标点符号和合本），南京：中国基督教协会印发，1989 年，第 180 页。
④《圣经》（简化字与现代标点符号和合本），南京：中国基督教协会印发，1989 年，第 57 页。
⑤ 莎士比亚：《罕秣莱德》，孙大雨译，上海：上海译文出版社，1991 年，第Ⅻ页。
⑥《圣经》（简化字与现代标点符号和合本），南京：中国基督教协会印发，1989 年，第 549 页。

五、基督教隐喻：艺术想象的形式

莎士比亚通过隐喻，把语言、诗真理和美融合为哈姆莱特特有的隐喻性语言。亚里士多德认为，隐喻是以此物命名彼物，它“可以使我们最好地获得某些新鲜的东西”。想象的最终实现依赖于采取语言形式，而艺术想象的过程，也就是隐喻的实现过程。韦勒克在《文学原理》中认为，诗歌中起组织作用的两个原则是格律和隐喻。隐喻是诗的根基。隐喻表现出一种诗的特性，不仅是语言的特性，也是戏剧本质特性的体现，是莎士比亚使《哈姆莱特》的符号宗教化的过程。“隐喻就包藏着诗、真理和美”。

在《哈姆莱特》第三幕第三场中，“吃饭去了”①有被上帝招去的意思②，“天使吩咐我说：‘你要写上，凡是被请赴羔羊之婚筵的有福了！’又对我说：‘这是神真实的话。’”③。戏剧中的人物在面对死亡这件事上，不自觉地都是按照基督教的精神和具体的基督教教义来思考问题的，显然，他们都信仰基督教，熟知基督教教规。随着表达思想趋于复杂，生活言语被隐喻为基督教语言，既丰富了台词的内涵，又丰富了言语的表现力，有比较强烈的修辞效果。奥菲利娅唱起有宗教内容的歌，想象“他离开人间了，他离开人间魂归天”④之后的情景，雷欧提斯与教士争辩是否应有些什么其他的基督教仪式为他们的妹妹下葬，牧师强调：“我们要亵渎教会的神圣葬礼了—— 如果为她唱起了安魂曲，像对于平安死去的灵魂那样，”莱阿提斯则说：“我妹妹将要升天去，做天使，却罚你在地狱里号叫。”⑤哈姆莱特想象“它本来就是泥土，我仍旧让它回到泥土里去”⑥，人“本是尘，仍要归于尘土”。“因为你是从土而出的。你本是尘土，仍要归于尘土。”⑦哈姆莱特等人在隐喻的过程中不止一次地求助于基督教有神论，为观众呈现出一副可怕的想象的地狱，对死人幽灵的疑问困扰着哈姆莱特等人，甚至这种疑问还给哈姆莱特的拖延提供了借口，因为他不肯杀正在祈祷的奸王，是当时他似乎正承受着天恩。尽管他因为明确拒绝既定秩序认同自身理想的行为被视为当下王朝的异端遭到暗算，追求精神独立与思想自由也举步维艰，但哈姆莱特仍然不愿在克劳迪斯祈祷时杀他，因为克劳狄斯正在洗涤他的灵魂，如果这时候结果了他的性命，那么天国的路就会他开放。自己在肩负理想与现实相抵牾的狂乱与绝望后，在现行体制外建立崭新价值坐标的打算也就失去了根本的意义。

在《哈姆莱特》中事物的存在是通过比较、比照以别一人物或事物的存在来显示自身的，如果不通过这种对比，其中的人和物很难充分、完美地说明自身，更难在舞台上产生出强烈的艺术感染力和震撼力。而这种对比就构成了人与人、人与物、物与物之间用以说明事物的语言与所指之间、文本与舞台的表演之间、文本与文本之外作家的所指、此物与彼物之间均构成了一种互喻关系—— 互相说明对方，任何事物都是用以表明别一事物的喻体，同时又是用别一事物表明自身的本体。每一事物都兼具本体与喻体的双重特性，“人”与“上帝”互喻、

① 莎士比亚：《哈姆莱特》（英汉对照读本），朱生豪译，北京：人民文学出版社，2002 年，第 169 页。
② 莎士比亚：《哈姆莱特》（裘克安注释），北京：商务印书馆，1984 年，第 195 页。
③《圣经》（简化字与现代标点符号和合本），南京：中国基督教协会印发，1989 年，第 289 页。
④ 莎士比亚：《新莎士比亚全集》（第四卷），方平译，石家庄：河北教育出版社，2000 年，第 362 页。
⑤ 莎士比亚：《新莎士比亚全集》（第四卷），方平译，石家庄：河北教育出版社，2000 年，第 399 页。
⑥ 莎士比亚：《哈姆莱特》（英汉对照读本），朱生豪译，北京：人民文学出版社，2002 年，第 165 页。
⑦《圣经》（简化字与现代标点符号和合本），南京：中国基督教协会印发，1989 年，第 4 页。

“人”与“人”互喻、“人”与“物”互喻、“物”与“物”互喻，从而达到“万物互喻”。《哈姆莱特》中的许多人物尤其是哈姆莱特始终是把基督教中的“上帝”挂在嘴上，似乎他所做的一切都要得到上帝的批准。隐喻就是借助具体的事物谈较为抽象的事物，即以具体事物比拟抽象事物，使抽象事物更易被人所理解。隐喻是一种心理映射，哈姆莱特的基督教式的心理映射，是莎士比亚将对比事物的认识映射到基督教上，形成了向基督教的目标域的某种跨越。同时，这种基督教式的隐喻的心理映射也必然牵涉到此事物与彼事物的外在表象联系，涉及基督教与世俗社会、人世与鬼域、复仇与妥协之间的内在特性的关联，牵涉到两者或多者兼而有之的关系。莎士比亚在《哈姆莱特》中借用主人公之口说出了“人类是一件多么了不起的杰作!”这里借用了《圣经·创世记》中上帝造人这一说法。由此，我们可以得出在整个语篇中，最大的隐喻就是基督教的隐喻，不管喻体如何变化，本体的指射都离不开“上帝”。所以，如果离开了对基督教隐喻的清醒认识，我们在把握哈姆莱特形象上必然就会产生种种偏差。这也是历来对哈姆莱特形象认识产生巨大分歧的原因之一。

在《哈姆莱特》大量出现“凭着圣徒的名义”[①]这样的词句，当哈姆莱特装疯卖傻、瞒骗御前大臣波洛涅斯的时候，引用了“耶弗他的女儿”这一典故，耶弗他是以色列的勇士，后来当了元帅出征亚扪人。出征前他向耶和华许愿:“你若将亚扪人交在我手中，我从亚扪人那里平平安安回来的时候，无论什么人，先从我家门出来迎接我，就必归你，我也必将他献上为燔祭。”这一典故在莎士比亚手里得到了巧妙的运用。波洛涅斯实际上也就像耶弗他一样献出了自己的女儿。同时，这一典故也“预示了奥菲利亚的命运”和耶弗他的女儿一样，最后走向死亡[②]，这些类似的隐喻很多。又如雷欧提斯:“不过如此；因为一个人成长的过程，不仅是肌肉和体格的增强，而且随着身体的发展，精神和心灵也同时扩大。”[③]“你们的身子就是圣灵的殿。”[④]作为虔诚的基督教徒的圣徒，哈姆莱特的发誓相当有分量。精神的守望具有原始、古老、自觉、坚毅的执着和美丽。《圣经》说:“圣徒就是在基督耶稣里有忠心的人。”《圣经》中保罗在给哥林多基督教徒的信中，也尊称该地区的基督教徒为圣徒。哈姆莱特的话语中透露出天命观，霍拉旭不想让哈姆莱特跟着鬼魂前去，哈姆莱特说:“嗨，怕什么呢?我把我作的生命看得不值一枚针，至于我的灵魂，那是跟它自己同样永生不灭的。”[⑤]不料真的一语成谶，他的灵魂终于飞升天庭，永生不灭了。《哈姆莱特》中为数众多的基督教隐喻说明，莎士比亚对《圣经》了如指掌，根据其剧本中具有大量《圣经》引证和语录来看，他似乎比他同时代的大多数剧作家对《圣经》都精通得多，但他驾轻就熟地运用圣经语言这一事实，既指向说话者，又指向受话人的关联性[⑥]，只能说明他有着超凡的文学敏感性与不等摆脱的基督教背景。

莎士比亚在《哈姆莱特》中往往主动使用隐喻，作为一个语言大师，他已经意识到本体与喻体两种事物之间的差别，并懂得利用这种差异取得意想不到的修辞和舞台效果，虽然语言中存在着现成的词语或表达法，但为了生动、形象地传达他的意思和戏剧中人物的感情，获得更好的交流和共鸣效果，他选择用另一种事物来隐喻基督教，或者用基督教教义精神直

---

① 莎士比亚:《新莎士比亚全集》(第四卷)，方平译，石家庄：河北教育出版社，2000年，第259页。
② 张竹筠:《西方文化衍生与转型语境下的哈姆莱特》,《学术交流》，2004年，第10期。
③ 莎士比亚：《哈姆莱特》（英汉对照读本），朱生豪译，北京：人民文学出版社，2002年，第33页。
④ 莎士比亚:《哈姆莱特》(裘克安注释)，北京：商务印书馆，1984年，第37页。
⑤ 莎士比亚:《新莎士比亚全集》(第四卷)，方平译，石家庄：河北教育出版社，2000年，第250页。
⑥ 赵蓉:《隐喻阐释的两种新视角及其比较》,《四川外语学院学报》，2002年，第3期。

接表达、抒发剧中人物的感情。哈姆莱特终于未能超越灵魂不灭的来世观念及对天堂、地狱的设想；“生存”或是对死后灵魂的关注的基督教隐喻的悲剧性结局，其来自宗教的震撼力就更加强烈。同时，哈姆莱特的复仇的延宕在一定程度上与基督教的博爱主义有关。受到基督教思想浸染的莎士比亚使哈姆莱特放慢了复仇的脚步，其来自基督教的合理性也更加令观众信服。隐喻如同划破语言夜空迎来的一抹晨曦，但“隐喻不仅仅是语言的装饰，它含有显著意义的认知表达”[①]，在莎士比亚的大悲剧《哈姆莱特》中尤其如此。哈姆莱特的博爱、平等意识与希伯来—— 基督教的平等观有联系。[②]哈姆莱特说：“让我们称兄弟吧”，强化了基督教的，在终极意义上人没有高低贵贱之分，所有人的归宿都是在泥土中化为腐朽。无论是肥胖的国王……还是骨瘦如柴的乞丐。[③]但是，这样的观念终究不是来自人文主义思想，而是源自基督教式的隐喻。

结　语

解读《哈姆莱特》的关键是要弄清其中的基督教隐喻，正是由于隐喻的隐蔽性使过去的研究忽视了其中的基督教隐喻。通过对莎士比亚在《哈姆莱特》中自觉或不自觉反映出来的基督教思想，通过对《哈姆莱特》中背景、人物思想、行动的基督教隐喻的研究，我们发现那种认为哈姆莱特是一个人文主义者的结论是过于简单了，过分强调了哈姆莱特本人的人文主义者的先进性[④]，忽视了莎士比亚本人和基督教思想难以分开的联系，同时也忽视了哈姆莱特这个人物身上的基督教特征。

基金项目：本文为国家社会科学基金后期资助暨优秀博士论文项目“莎士比亚在近现代中国的传播与流变研究”（21FWWB008）阶段性成果。

作者简介：李伟民，四川外国语大学研究生院教授，中国莎士比亚研究会副会长，主要从事莎士比亚研究。

① 胡壮麟：《认知隐喻学》，北京：北京大学出版社，2004年，第11页。
② 张奎武：《圣经典故在莎剧中的艺术效果》，《外国文学评论》，1994年，第1期。
③ 宗亦耘：《悲剧与基督教观念——对莎剧〈哈姆雷特〉的分析》，《外国文学研究》1998年，第1期。
④ 李伟民：《从人民性到人文主义再到对二者的否定》，《重庆大学学报》（社会科学版），2004年，第1期。

发起人与代理人、主体与客体：伊格尔顿对《哈姆雷特》的社会关系解读

张　薇

【摘　要】英国文化唯物主义者伊格尔顿独辟蹊径从社会关系的角度解读《哈姆雷特》，他认为该剧的中心主题是“代理关系”，这种代理关系反映了主体与客体的关系，社会是一张人们彼此利用的网，是主体客体不断变化的网。伊格尔顿揭示了这一本质，但没有指明出路。出路在于针对社会的不同情况，主体应该采取主动的措施，或配合，或改变，而不是被动地被客体化。

【关键词】伊格尔顿；《哈姆雷特》；发起人；代理人；主体；客体

Source and Agent, Subject and Object: Eagleton's Interpretation of *Hamlet* from the Perspective of Social Relations

Zhang Wei

【Abstract】Eagleton, a British cultural materialist, made a unique approach to interpret *Hamlet* from the perspective of social relations. He believed that “agency” was a central theme in *Hamlet*, which reflected the relationship between the subject and the object. Eagleton revealed this essence, but did not point the way out. The way out should be based on different social conditions, and the subject should take active measures, or cooperate, or change, rather than be passively objectified.

【Key Word】Eagleton; *Hamlet*; source; agent; subject; object

英国文化唯物主义者伊格尔顿对莎士比亚情有独钟，他在《莎士比亚与社会》《威廉·莎士比亚》中专门评论莎士比亚作品，终极目的是借莎翁作品中所呈现的人与人的社会关系来警示当今社会。他的著作“不是简单地关注我们的时代，而是描绘形成我们看待莎士比亚的思维体验，莎士比亚所面对的问题很大程度上也是我们关注的问题……我们对莎士比亚的判断由我们在社会中所有的观念所决定”①。

① Terence Eagleton, *Shakespeare and Society*, London: Chatto & Windus, 1967, p.9.

伊格尔顿在两部专著中论述了社会的方方面面，对《麦克白》的解读主要集中在名分与越界、能指与所指上；对《科里奥兰纳斯》的解读主要集中在贵族与平民、个人与社会的关系上；对《特洛伊勒斯与克瑞西达》的解读主要集中在个人身份问题上；对《奥赛罗》的解读主要集中在“无中生有”、过度解读“证据”上；对《威尼斯商人》的解读主要是“法律精神”，对《一报还一报》主要解读在法律与社会的关系中个人经历的意义，而对《哈姆雷特》的解读主要集中在发起者与代理人、主体与客体上。

一、发起人与代理人

与大部分莎评学者（如约翰逊、柯勒律治、史雷格尔、别林斯基、基托、布拉德雷、阿尼克斯特）对《哈姆雷特》的关注点不同，伊格尔顿并不关注哈姆雷特忧郁、延宕、是否是人文主义者等问题，他独辟蹊径，从社会关系的角度来探讨这个剧的社会意义。伊格尔顿认为：“代理（agency）关系是《哈姆雷特》的一个中心主题，……既利用他人，又被他人利用，因此他们有两种自我意识，既为发起者（或指派人，source），又为代理人（agent）。”伊格尔顿不像传统的批评家分析人物性格，而是从人的社会功用、社会角色的维度来分析，他用“发起人”与“代理人”两个术语来指称社会关系中的两类人，来概括《哈姆雷特》中的两种人，这是伊格尔顿的创造。那么他笔下的发起人与代理人的关系有哪些情形呢？第一种情形是代理人的忠诚。戏剧一开场马西勒斯和勃那多将自己变成一个尽职的代理人向哈姆莱特转告“幽灵事件”，霍拉旭也充当代理人，如实地向哈姆雷特报告这非同寻常的异象。而剧终霍拉旭一方面作为哈姆莱特的代理人完成他的愿望—— 讲述故事，另一方面他牢牢地保持着自己个体完整性和正直的品质。

第二种情形，代理人的奴才相反映了王室的势利小人。波洛涅斯是全剧中最典型的代理人，伊格尔顿说他简直是一个皮条客（pandar），他完全充当了新主子克劳狄斯的工具，他为克劳狄斯刺探哈姆雷特是真疯还是假疯，鞍前马后尽阿谀奉承之事。然而波洛涅斯也是指使者，他提醒奥菲莉娅不要接近哈姆雷特，“从现在起，我不许你跟哈姆雷特殿下谈一句话”[①]。但同时他又将她作为钓饵将哈姆雷特诱上钓钩；他还指使雷纳尔多去监察雷欧提斯。另外，考尼律斯和伏底曼德被克劳狄斯委派做挪威国的大使，传递两国元首之间的指令，他们是被委派人、代理人。罗森克兰兹、吉尔登斯吞和奥斯里克除了作为代理人之外毫无存在感，他们身份的定位完全取决于社会使用他们的方式，他们单方面接受并执行这一定位。这一点在罗森克兰茨和吉尔登斯吞二人身上异常明显，他们有意识地把自己可能拥有的个人完整性交给了克劳狄斯，并视其为一种自由。他们二人都是自愿被使唤、被控制，并积极主动地答应成为克劳狄斯的傀儡，以讨新主子的欢心。在剧中他们两次充当克劳狄斯的代理人，第一次是试探哈姆雷特真疯还是假疯，第二次是押送哈姆雷特去英国欲除之。奥斯里克也是一个代理人、唯命是从的人，即人们想让他变成什么样的人，他就成为什么样的人。他转达国王的指令，通知哈姆雷特比剑，哈姆雷特完全了解此人的一贯的奴才品性，故意要弄他：

① 莎士比亚：《莎士比亚全集·增订本》（5），朱生豪译，南京：译林出版社，2011 年，第 295 页。

奥斯里克：谢谢殿下，天气真热。

哈姆莱特：不，相信我，天冷得很，在刮北风哩。

奥斯里克：真的有点儿冷，殿下。

哈姆莱特：可是对于像我这样的体质，我觉得这一种天气却是闷热的厉害。[①]（第五幕第二场）

奥斯里克完全失去人的主体性，他不敢得罪主子，以致认热为冷、认鹿为马，成了代理人。在“比剑”一场戏中，雷欧提斯是克劳狄斯的代理人，克劳狄斯要借他的手除掉哈姆雷特。

第三种情形是代理的传递性。在剧中有一系列连续的代理，这种代理有传递性，像击鼓传花，克劳狄斯—波洛涅斯—奥菲莉娅—哈姆雷特，中间的两位都是代理人，探寻的终点是哈姆雷特的疯狂问题。为了说明代理的传递性，伊格尔顿引用了第五幕第二场克劳狄斯的一段话来类比。

……把杯子给我；鼓声一起，喇叭就接着吹响，通知外面的炮手，让炮声震彻天地，报告这一个消息，“现在国王为哈姆雷特祝饮了！”[②]（第五幕第二场）

鼓声—喇叭—炮手—炮声—消息—祝饮，要完成“祝饮”这个仪式必须要一系列连续的动作，中间的都是代理行为。同样哈姆雷特从海上逃脱回来的信首先经水手，水手给克劳迪奥，克劳迪奥交给使者，使者给了国王克劳狄斯。中间也经历了几个环节，水手、克劳迪奥、使者都是代理，是哈姆雷特的代理。这种代理的传递性在任何时代、任何社会都是普遍存在的。

在整部剧中主要的动作发起人是鬼魂和克劳狄斯，他们是一正一反、一善一恶的形象。鬼魂发出复仇的指令，哈姆雷特也就成了鬼魂的代理人，哈姆雷特艰难地完成这一使命，最后与克劳狄斯同归于尽。克劳狄斯常常“借刀杀人”，利用他人来达到自己阴险的目的；伊格尔顿指出：“社会被呈现为一个由起因、代理人和结果组成的接连不断的网络，它是一个人们相互利用的网络。”[③]在这一过程中代理人消解了自己的身份而去完成别人指派的任务。

剧中有些是自觉自愿做代理人的，如波洛涅斯、罗森格兰兹和吉尔登斯吞，但也有被迫成为代理人的，如奥菲莉娅，奥菲利娅被克劳狄斯和她的父亲当作棋子，来试探哈姆雷特，但当她面对哈姆莱特时，真实的她忘记了自己代理人的角色从而变回了自己。

伊格尔顿发现：与发起和代理相联系的是剧中还有“看”—“代理”—“被看”的关系。克劳狄斯怀疑哈姆雷特的疯狂，派奥菲莉娅去试探哈姆雷特，他和波洛涅斯躲在旁边偷窥，这里“看者”是克劳狄斯和波洛涅斯，“被看者”是哈姆雷特，奥菲莉娅既是“代理”又是“被看者”。在“戏中戏”一场，哈姆雷特要验证克劳狄斯是杀父凶手，他安排霍拉旭在一旁观察克劳狄斯的反应，这里“看者”是哈姆雷特，代理是霍拉旭，“被看者”是克劳狄斯。“戏中戏”与“装疯”一场的主动和被动的情势正好颠倒了。在“寝宫”一场中，波洛涅斯躲在帷幕后面偷听偷看，进一步验证哈姆雷特的疯狂，波洛涅斯是“看者”，哈姆雷特是“被看者”，

① 莎士比亚：《莎士比亚全集·增订本》（5），朱生豪译，南京：译林出版社，2011年，第391页。

② 莎士比亚：《莎士比亚全集·增订本》（5），朱生豪译，南京：译林出版社，2011年，第397页。

③ Terence Eagleton, *Shakespeare and Society*, London: Chatto & Windus, 1967, p.40.

王后既是“代理”，又是“被看者”。笔者认为伊格尔顿所指的“代理关系”包含命令与服从、指派与被指派、主动与被动的关系，代理人往往是中介或工具，是接受者、被动者。在《哈姆雷特》中，这种“代理关系”存在于善恶两方，从哈姆雷特这一方说，他们代表的是正义、智慧、谋略，而就克劳狄斯一方来说，他们代表的是邪恶、奸诈、歹毒，“代理关系”被善恶双方都利用了。这部作品告诉我们“代理关系”普遍存在于人的社会，无处不在，只是我们很多人并没有意识到。伊格尔顿揭示了人的社会关系中的一种形态，笔者认为他的着眼点和出发点应该是马克思主义对人的论述，马克思在《关于费尔巴哈的提纲》提出过著名的论断：“人的本质不是单个人所固有的抽象物，在其现实性上，它是一切社会关系的总和。”[①]伊格尔顿对《哈姆雷特》的分析生动地演绎了马克思的这一论断。

二、主体与客体

发起人与代理人的关系本质上是主体与客体的关系，发起人是主体，代理人是客体。伊格尔顿进一步探讨主体与客体的关系。

首先看幽灵与听者。伊格尔顿强调“言说（speak）”这个词在主客体中的作用。幽灵对马西勒斯和勃那多沉默不语，最开始幽灵也是一个沉默的、拒绝询问的客体。“因为它只是作为一个客体被呈现给他们，但它对哈姆雷特说话，从而揭示自己是一个有意志的主体，也使哈姆雷特成为客体，幽灵要求他听，然后让他担负责任，使他成为代理人。”[②]幽灵分别以两种不同的存在状态出现：白天它被关在炼狱里，晚上它四处游荡。在它被迫遣返炼狱之前，它必须迅速向哈姆雷特表明自己的身份；因此，当它面对马西勒斯、勃那多和霍拉旭时，它就陷入了用言语表明自己和迫使它保持沉默的压力这二者的张力之间。从本质上讲，这种张力是我们在其他人物身上看到过的，在作为主体和客体的自我之间，在自由的自我表达和自我隐藏之间。作为主体的幽灵在黑夜是浪游的有罪的灵魂，在这种情况下，它是可以说话而且为人所知的；白天被囚禁在炼狱里的它则是沉默的。幽灵是主体，听者是客体。

为了论证主体、客体的关系，伊格尔顿引入了感觉器官，“眼睛”“声音”和“耳朵”。“‘眼睛’或‘声音’和‘耳朵’在整个戏剧中被用作符号，用来区别自我作为主体和自我作为客体的符号。人们用自己的眼睛所看到的才是最真实的个人（感受）：看（‘眼睛’）或说（‘声音’）就是作为主体。”[③]“耳朵”作为被动的接受者，是客体。马西勒斯和勃那多因为亲眼所见幽灵，相信幽灵的存在。他们向霍拉旭的耳朵讲述见鬼魂一事，霍拉旭开始不信，当他亲眼见到幽灵后，他说：“当着上帝起誓，倘不是我自己的眼睛向我证明，我再也不会相信这样的怪事。”[④]（第一幕第一场）

霍拉旭先作为客体，后来作为主体，因为他又转告了哈姆雷特，哈姆雷特起初也将信将疑，但当他目睹鬼魂，并亲耳听到鬼魂的讲述后，他也信了，从客体变成了主体，他向鬼魂允诺复仇，并担当“重整乾坤”的重任。

---

① 中共中央马克思恩格斯列宁斯大林著作编译局编译：《马克思恩格斯选集》第一卷，人民出版社 2012 年，第 135 页。
② Terence Eagleton, *Shakespeare and Society*, London: Chatto & Windus, 1967, p.44.
③ Terence Eagleton, *Shakespeare and Society*, London: Chatto & Windus, 1967, p.44.
④ 莎士比亚：《莎士比亚全集·增订本》（5），朱生豪译，南京：译林出版社，2011 年，第 281 页。

其次，剧中也有拒绝成为客体的例子，比如第二幕第二场，波洛涅斯要试探哈姆雷特是否疯狂，但哈姆雷特看穿了他的意图，故意不按照波洛涅斯的套路去回答。

波洛涅斯：啊，恕我冒昧。您好，哈姆雷特殿下？
哈姆雷特：呃，上帝怜悯世人！
波洛涅斯：您认识我吗？殿下？
哈姆雷特：认识认识，你是一个卖鱼的贩子。
波洛涅斯：我不是，殿下。
哈姆雷特：那么，我但愿你是一个鱼贩子一样的老实人。
波洛涅斯：老实，殿下？
哈姆雷特：嗯，先生，在这世界上，一万个人中间只不过有一个老实人。
波洛涅斯：这句话说得很对，殿下。
哈姆雷特：要是太阳在一头大可亲吻的死狗尸体上孵育蛆虫—— 你有一个女儿吗？
波洛涅斯：我有，殿下。
哈姆雷特：不要让她在太阳光底下行走。怀孕是一种幸福，可是你的女儿要是怀了孕，那可糟了。朋友，留心啊。①（第二幕第二场）

哈姆雷特故意曲解问题，并回答得含混不清，他不仅令波洛涅斯更加迷惑，而且还利用波洛涅斯，让他误以为自己的疯狂完全是由于失恋，从而把这一信息传给克劳狄斯，以便迷惑克劳狄斯，用疯狂来自我保护。在这场“反试探”的戏中，哈姆雷特表现出智慧和高超的伪装能力，他变客体为主体，嘲弄帮凶。

第三，除了人与人之间有主体和客体，自我也有主体和客体。伊格尔顿认为：“作为主体的自我（self as subject）和作为客体的自我（self as object）之间的张力（tension）是内在的，这种内在张力存在于这样的两极之间：即一个人如何看待自己，以及别人如何看待他或他如何被人利用。”②奥菲莉娅就时刻生活在这种张力之中，她一方面将自己视为波洛涅斯的乖女儿，服从他的意愿，另一方面在她对哈姆雷特的爱中维护真实的自我（authentic self），她就夹在这两种不相容的力量之中，两种力量拉扯着她，主客体无法分身。她无法承受父亲暴毙所带来的沉痛打击，而父亲的暴毙恰恰是哈姆雷特所造成的，他们两个都是她深爱的人，最后她丧失理性，走向死亡。

在第三幕第四场中，哈姆雷特与母亲的对峙强烈地揭示了自我作为主体和自我作为客体的冲突。刚开始，他们两个人都是充满强烈的自我肯定和自信的主体。他们在开场快速、有力的交锋证实了这一点：

王后：哈姆莱特，你已经大大得罪了你的父亲啦。
哈姆莱特：母亲，您已经大大得罪了我的父亲啦。
王后：来，来，不要用这种胡说八道的话回答我。

① 莎士比亚：《莎士比亚全集·增订本》（5），朱生豪译，南京：译林出版社，2011 年，第 313 页。
② Terence Eagleton, *Shakespeare and Society*, London: Chatto & Windus, 1967, p.43.

哈姆莱特：去，去，不要用这种胡说八道的话问我。[1]（第三幕第四场）

这段对话你来我往，针锋相对。哈姆雷特要擦亮母亲的眼睛，让她认识到事情的真相，为此，他对比了母亲的两任丈夫，他觉得母亲真是有眼无珠而选择克劳狄斯，即使是没有主体性的人，自我选择也不会如此之盲目。葛特露德终于恍然大悟："我看见我灵魂里那些洗拭不去的黑色的污点。"[2]（第三幕第四场）哈姆莱特的话像一把匕首刺进她的耳朵，迫使她把自己的罪过客体化，用主观来审视它。然而当幽灵出现，情况就截然不同了，幽灵同时客体化了哈姆莱特和葛特露德两个人，它注意到了葛特露德的惊讶并指责哈姆莱特的延宕；它将哈姆莱特作为自己的代理人去宽慰葛特露德。因此，哈姆莱特又回到葛特露德身边去安抚她；这时他发现母亲很关心他，因为她将哈姆雷特客体化为一个疯子。双方都认为是对方看错了：葛特露德认为哈姆莱特幻视，哈姆莱特却不明白为什么自己的母亲看不到父王的亡魂。这两个自我的主体再次发生冲突，他们都各自主张自己的观点而反对彼此。最后，哈姆莱特重获控制权：葛特露德听从了他的建议保守秘密，他给她提供一些道德上的建议（不要上叔父的床钻入乱伦的衾被），他把母亲视为主客体的统一体，他既请求她的原谅，也规劝她；这样，他既使自己成为她原谅的客体，也使她成为他说教的客体：与此同时，他想和她建立一种良好的真诚的母子关系。从中我们看到主客体是可以互为转换的。在"调包计"里哈姆雷特想操控那些试图控制他的人：

我倒要瞧瞧他们的能耐。开炮的要是给炮轰了，也是一件好玩的事；他们会埋地雷，我要比他们埋得更深，把他们轰到月亮里去。（第三幕第四场）

哈姆雷特成功地实施了"调包计"，这是剧中他最值得夸耀的战绩，本可以从被动转为主动，九死一生回来，可以趁克劳狄斯没有防备之心而除之，但是哈姆雷特再一次葬送了主动权，居然先让人送信告知克劳狄斯自己活着回来了，让克劳狄斯有时间去准备新的阴谋，这一行为实在莫名其妙！本来哈姆雷特完全可以成为发起人、主体，像阿姆莱特那样，可是他又一次放弃了大好机会（前一次是克劳狄斯忏悔，哈姆雷特未下手），使自己处于被动状态，变成任人算计的客体。他非但不能改变社会，连自己的性命也保不住，这是双重悲剧——社会悲剧、个人悲剧。也就是说，这个故事完全可以写成社会正剧、个人正剧！而这个剧的性质和趋向取决于哈姆雷特把自己放置在一个什么样的社会角色。

笔者赞同伊格尔顿在《威廉·莎士比亚》一书中对哈姆雷特忧郁和延宕的原因的结论，"事实上，他花了几乎全剧拒绝用克劳狄斯的命来偿还他父亲的命"[3]。他听了鬼魂的指令后苦恼地说："唉，倒霉的我，却要负起重整乾坤的责任。"（第一幕第五场）这反映他是不得不接受这一任务和使命，他的主体并不想这么做，也并不想成为客体，但复仇和重整乾坤的重任责无旁贷地落到他的肩上，他在主体的意愿和被客体化之间左右摇摆，于是延宕就发生了。

既然从剧情看哈姆雷特大部分时间处于代理人、被动和客体的情境，那么怎么改变为发起人、主动和主体的情境呢？我们不妨从《哈姆雷特》的题材来源去看，原来的历史故事是

① 莎士比亚：《莎士比亚全集·增订本》（5），朱生豪译，南京：译林出版社，2011年，第350页。
② 莎士比亚：《莎士比亚全集·增订本》（5），朱生豪译，南京：译林出版社，2011年，第352页。
③ Terry Eagleton, *William Shakespeare*. Oxford: Basil Blackwell, 1986, p.73.

怎么处理主客体的关系的。《哈姆雷特》取材于萨克索的《丹麦史》，阿姆莱特为保护自己，装疯，伺机报仇……阿姆莱特改国书，要求英王处死两个使臣，并将公主嫁给他。不久，阿姆莱特脱身回国，在为他举行的丧宴上，他趁众人酩酊大醉、卧地不醒之际，用一条大毯盖住他们，并把毯子钉死在地下，放火把芬根等统统烧死，然后宣布自己为王。[①]哈佛大学的斯蒂芬·格林布拉特说："(原故事中)阿姆莱特不需要鬼魂来告知他，也不会有对叔叔是否有罪的怀疑，因为(芬根)杀兄是公开的、众所周知的。"[②]因此原历史中没有鬼魂，自然也没有"戏中戏"。这样我们就看到与莎士比亚《哈姆雷特》完全不一样的情况。阿姆莱特始终是主体，他不存在被鬼魂指派而成为客体的现象，他的复仇完全是自觉的、主动的、心甘情愿的、出于道德伦理的孝顺父亲，他很好地保护自己，最后伺机复仇，他聪慧、果敢、雷厉风行，并尽量使自己处于主动的情势而非被动的情势。尽管奸王和帮凶所组成的社会势力很强大，但最终阿姆莱特报了仇，当上了王。整个历史故事呈现的是正剧，而不是悲剧。我们可以这样说，阿姆莱特正直的自我与黑暗的社会发生激烈的冲突，阿姆莱特并没有把自己边缘化，也没有逃避复仇的重任，他一直忠实于自己，拉着主体的缰绳，驾驭着横冲直撞的烈马。当他从英国回来，神不知鬼不觉，潜伏于宴会角落，最后把凶手和爪牙一并歼灭。他掌握了自己的命运，更重要的是他改变了社会，使黑暗的社会重新回归正义、有序。个人与社会虽然有冲突，但最终可以是良好的结局。而现在的剧情都是莎士比亚的主观意愿而为之，不是哈姆雷特延宕，而是莎士比亚要他延宕！他把本来主客体最终统一的关系改写成主客体的悲剧。或者说，主客体最好的出路是主体掌握主动权，像《丹麦史》中所描写的，但他放弃《丹麦史》里好的主客体出路，而选择这样一种让人纠结、迷惑、悲摧的情状。

伊格尔顿在书中要探讨个人如何在社会中保持主体性的问题，他认为个人与社会有三种关系：一是在社会边缘活动重新建构一个真实的自己；二是在社会中活动，按照公众对自己的定位，出卖自己；三是冒着被毁灭的危险继续做原本真实的自己。"在《哈姆雷特》中，这三种情况都尝试过，但它们都不够。"[③]我们发现，伊格尔顿实际上认为真实的自我无论在社会内还是在社会的边缘都很难实现，将自己置于完全客体的位置，那就是出卖自己的主体性，而做真实的自己，就险象环生，意味着自己将面临哈姆雷特式的追问：生存还是毁灭的问题。在《哈姆雷特》中存在着两种人，一种是认清在社会中所处的位置，自觉扮演其社会角色的人，另一种是生活于社会对立面，拒绝被客体化的人。前者，如朝臣；后者，如哈姆雷特，"哈姆雷特绝不是一个人的悲剧，在他身上，由于他的王子身份，个人与社会的关系比普通人来得更紧密，个人与社会的矛盾体现得最典型、最充分。"[④]

英国思想家、哲学家霍布斯区分了作为感觉者的主体以及作用于主体产生感觉的感觉对象。法国思想家笛卡儿明确把主体自我意识同客观现实世界相对立，并把它作为分析认识特别是论证可靠知识的出发点。与他们的认识有联系，但又不同，伊格尔顿在这篇论述中，把主体与客体用于人与人的关系之中，从掌控与被掌控、主动者与代理人的角度去理解。当某人要传达别人的话语，受人指示时，他就成为客体；当他指示别人时，他就成为主体。每一个人都处在这种主客体的关系中，有时同时扮演两种角色。

---

① 参见张泗洋、徐斌、张晓阳：《莎士比亚引论》(上册)，北京：中国戏剧出版社，1989年，第354-355页。

② Greenblatt, Walter Cohen, Jean E. Howard, Katharine Eisaman Maus, *The Norton Shakespeare,* New York & London: W·W·Norton & Company. 2008. pp.1685-1686.

③ Terence Eagleton, *Shakespeare and Society*, London: Chatto & Windus, 1967, p.52.

④ 张薇：《当代英美的马克思主义莎士比亚评论》，北京：中国社会科学出版社，2018年，第78页。

伊格尔顿通过“发起人”（指派人）和“代理人”这两个意象，通过主体和客体的二元对立和转化的精当分析，得出人无法脱离社会单独存在、社会是一张相互利用、相互牵制、互为主客的关系网的结论。

不过，伊格尔顿在详细地分析《哈姆雷特》中主体和客体的困境之后，并没有指出理想的主体和客体的关系的出路，即便他探讨忠实于自己的自我和虚伪的社会之间的冲突，也并没有明确地指明出路，他的探索只停留在揭示主客体的复杂的、动态的状况，分清楚谁是发起人、谁是代理人，而且他更多地侧重探讨“自我”如何对待社会，并没有侧重于探讨社会应该怎样满足人这一主体的需求，因此论述有单向度的嫌疑。同时，社会也不是一个虚空的抽象物，它是由无数的“自我”“个人”所构成的，因此社会这一客体是由无数各具特色、各有思想的主体构成。

那么理想的主体与客体的关系到底应该怎样？这个问题既容易回答又很难回答。容易的回答是：社会这一客体应该是个完美的、健康的、正义的、能够满足任何一个个人主体的愿望的社会，而个人主体能自觉地、主动地、以真善美的姿态成为社会的一分子，构建美好的社会。但人性是复杂的，对权力、金钱、性的欲望是无止境的，这些欲望滋生出许多邪恶、黑暗的东西，这样，就把那个答案化成了乌托邦式的幻想。不切实际的回答，等于没有回答。

探讨完作品和伊格尔顿的评论，笔者得出这样的结论：当社会比较和谐、有序的时候，作为主体应该配合和维护这种和谐，这样社会也能更好地惠利于个人；当社会一片混乱、邪恶当道时，作为主体应该采取智慧、果断的方式去“重整乾坤”，这或许就是我们从伊格尔顿的社会关系解读中所得到的启示。

参考文献

[1] GREENBLATT W C, HOWARD J E, MAUS K E. 2008. The Norton Shakespeare[M]. New York & London: W. W. Norton & Company.

[2] EAGLETON T. 1967. Shakespeare and Society[M]. London: Chatto & Windus.

[3] EAGLETON T. 1986. William Shakespeare[M]. Oxford: Basil Blackwell.

[4] 中共中央马克思恩格斯列宁斯大林著作编译局. 2012.《马克思恩格斯选集》第一卷[M]. 北京：人民出版社.

[5] 莎士比亚. 2011. 莎士比亚全集·增订本（5）[M]. 朱生豪，译. 南京：译林出版社.

[6] 张泗洋，徐斌，张晓阳. 1989. 莎士比亚引论（上册）[M]. 北京：中国戏剧出版社.

作者简介：张薇，上海大学文学院副教授，博士，哥伦比亚大学访问学者。研究英美文学，主攻莎士比亚研究。近期著作有《当代英美的马克思主义莎士比亚评论》。

《驯悍记》中的性别表演与身份焦虑

陈　静　　杨林贵

【摘　要】莎士比亚的《驯悍记》重点描写了一段两性婚姻的缔结，探讨了早期现代英国社会变革时期，通过性别身份的表演性，折射出这种表演性带来的主体身份焦虑问题。本文将文本置于历史语境之下，审视剧中个体如何抗拒或迎合社会规约，即悍妇如何演绎“悍”，投机者如何投机，展示对社会规约下自我的认知，在不断调整自我行动中重复排演实践，以求定位自我。正是这种身份表演塑造过程中的不确定性催生或加剧了人物的身份焦虑，而这一焦虑虽在悍妇与投机者的联姻中呈现出了解决的态势，对比消失的“局外人”斯赖，一段婚姻带来的圆满结局引发的更是对身份焦虑是否只是一时解决的思考。

【关键词】《驯悍记》；性别表演；身份焦虑；社会流动

Gender Performance and Anxiety in *The Taming of the Shrew*

Chen Jing　　Yang Lingui

【Abstract】*The Taming of the Shrew*,in the depiction of an unexpectedly settled marriage, explores the performativity of patriarchal anxieties of identity in early modern England through performative actions by different gender roles who employ various self-identification tactics. Situating the play in its historical context, this article examines how Katharina has breached social expectations imposed on women and how Petruchio has carried the responsibility of conserving patrilineal inheritance. Under those performative actions, what motivates major characters to conduct perfor mative disguise or exaggerated performance through repetition exactly lies in the hidden anxieties over identity. Although anxieties are temporarily circumvented in marriage, they are not resolved, as seen in the play's framing of the shrew taming within an Induction that ends with Sly's unsettled status. In a comparative view, thus, the performative features of gender identities and anxieties are antithetically reinforced.

【Key Words】*The Taming of the Shrew*; performativity of gender; anxiety over identity; social mobility

引　言

在以“唯一符合作者创作意图”的权威版本为旨归的传统批评中，莎士比亚的早期戏剧《驯悍记》一向被认为是一部不成熟的喜剧，甚至是一部老式闹剧①，而激进的女性主义者更是对本剧的带有女性歧视的剧情和对白耿耿于怀②。前者从内容与形式的和谐统一的对位解读中未能看到主题的严肃性，而后者由于对性别意识的过度敏感和偏激理解，忽略了本剧的元戏剧特性。本剧在伊丽莎白时代的英国舞台取得成功固然离不开流行戏剧元素的巧妙利用，但在笑闹背后隐藏的丰富思想内涵远远超出闹剧的形式范畴。然而，这种内涵却极容易被表面化解读，甚至被误读，得出莎士比亚为女性歧视张目的结论。实际上，《驯悍记》的结构设计以剧中剧形式③不断提醒观众剧中夸张的驯悍内容的表演性，即以戏剧化的形式和真假身份的转换手法演绎“此象非真”的哲理内涵：话语及其描述的包括性别角色在内的社会身份表象本身就是一个不断构建的过程。这也是戏剧文本为观众和读者设置的一个谜题。莎剧演绎的这个谜题直到20世纪后期才在后现代哲学中得以揭示，也说明了莎剧创作及其思想的超前性。正如当代女性主义理论家巴特勒（Judith Butler）所论，性别身份具有构建性，是通过角色表演来实现的，而这种表演性需要在一个重复性的过程中去理解，也就是说性别即是“表演”，是一连串的身体行为对社会规范的重复排演实践的结果，性别成形与区分性的管控性实践构建了什么是身份，建构了主体性④。从这种意义上看，莎士比亚戏剧早在400多年前就具象地预示了后现代哲学家关于女性身份的结论。

本文探讨莎剧《驯悍记》如何以戏剧的形式演绎了社会身份的表演性。这部剧的元戏剧特征与其社会身份表演性的主题相互交织，构成了这部剧的喜剧意趣和美学成就。表演性的主题镶嵌于戏剧结构之中，通过表演的主题勾连了戏本内外的意识形态场域，揭示了男女主人公，甚至“局外人”斯赖，都有的身份焦虑。戏剧人物以不同形式表现出的焦虑，体现在个体为了在社会中生存，大多做出迎合社会主流意识形态的期待的表演，而剧中男女主人公反其道而行，逆向表演造成的笑料和冲突，在表演中归顺主流意识形态。因此，本文将首先探讨人物主体如何受自我认知的影响，在迎合或抗拒身份角色的社会期待中，或展露自我真实性格，或一时以面具示人，在不断调整自我行动中重复排演实践，以求定位自我。然而，性别身份塑造表演过程中的不确定性催生或者加剧了人物的身份焦虑，在这些焦虑的推动之下，剧中的男男女女都产生了精彩的交锋，最终通过主要人物悍妇与投机者的联姻呈现出了一时的解决。

---

① 例如，新批评的强有力捍卫者海尔曼（Robert B. Heilman）反对根据现代现实主义戏剧传统对《驯悍记》的美学价值进行否定，力图为本剧辩护，将其认定为闹剧，认为是莎士比亚这部剧的成就就是将“一个老套的流行闹剧情境打造成了一部他自己的结构合理、情节紧凑、颇为复杂的闹剧”（158）。见海尔曼论文 “The Taming Untamed, or, The Return of the Shrew”, *Modern Language Quarterly* 27 (1966): 147-61.

② 例如麦克拉斯基（Kathleen McLuskie）专注于对剧中男权意识形态的解构，见 “Feminist Deconstruction: The Example of Shakespeare's *Taming of the Shrew*”, *Red Letters* 12 (1982): 33-40.

③ 本剧的驯悍内容是以戏中戏形式呈现的，虽然戏中戏在本剧的不同版本中的分量有所不同，但结构上都是让一个假贵族斯赖看一出驯服悍妇的闹剧。1623年出版的对开本的 *The Taming of the Shrew*“引子”中的斯赖后来神秘消失，让观众分不清哪个是正戏哪个是副戏，而早期版本（*TheTaming* of *A Shrew*，1594年印刷出版，1596年和1609年重印）中斯赖这个“戏外”人物的内外穿插，让我们对于本剧的结构以及与表演相关的手法和主题能够有进一步的认识。

④ “... performativity cannot be understood outside of a process of iterability, a regularized and constrained repetition of norms. And this repetition is not performed by a subject; this repetition is what enables a subject and constitutes a temporal condition for the subject...”，原文引自 Judith P. Butler. *Bodies that Matter: On the Discursive Limits of "Sex"*, New York: Routledge, 1993, 95.

一、早期现代悍妇的离经叛道式角色表演

莎翁所处的社会人文主义思想盛行，宗教改革家们也提倡女性与男性相当的自由。[①]但在社会主导意识形态中，传统女性顺从的观念仍旧存在。清教在宣扬婚姻的同时，也热衷于提倡妻子完全自愿的顺从。[②]这些强调在布道书、婚姻手册和行为手册中都可以略窥一二，如《关于婚姻的劝诫》这一结婚仪式上的布道文，威廉·惠特利的《已婚者指南》以及威廉·古执的《论家庭义务》等。[③]因此，凯瑟丽娜未被驯服之前有多讨人嫌可想而知。

但是关于她为什么会成为闻名的悍妇似乎没有得到太多关注。随着新兴资本主义工业的兴起，以家庭为单位的生产经济逐渐衰落[④]，女性因此更加被表现为一种被欣赏与渴望的对象[⑤]。而在《驯悍记》中，这种视觉美的代表显然是令路森修一见钟情的比恩卡。而对比之下逊色的凯瑟丽娜又因外貌无法吸引到适龄英俊，那么在她父亲眼里，她就是一件由于交换价值较低而不好在婚恋市场上流通的货物[⑥]。根据 16 世纪中期的保护女继承人法令，女儿是父亲和家庭的巨大财产的一部分[⑦]，而一个嫁不出去的女儿就成了吃白饭的存在[⑧]。更何况巴普提斯塔请了教师来家中培训两女，而像比恩卡这种又会音律，又能够学习希腊文、拉丁文的待遇在伊丽莎白时代的上流阶级都不是常见的[⑨]。因此在耗费金钱心血之后，凯瑟丽娜还是迎合不了社会对于女性贞静温婉的期待，也难怪她父亲的心会一偏再偏，难怪在二幕一场的父女争执中，她会指责到父亲偏爱她小女儿。因此，剧幕拉开，凯瑟丽娜这样一位和父亲叫嚣，对着外男撒泼的形象跃然纸上。她像是意识到自己不管是作为一个女儿，还是作为一位女性，都只能算差强人意的存在，从而筑起了悍妇的心理防线，像是发泄愤懑，又像是在掩饰着什么。

除了违抗偏心的父亲，面对眼里只有妹妹的帕度亚未婚男士，她言辞激烈地反驳他们对她的不齿，借以表达自己对他们看不上她的不屑，她甚至粗暴地砸破霍坦西奥的头，像是知道只要自己言行激烈，就可能打破刻板印象的桎梏。而她作为一个已经出格的悍妇，需要压制的仅仅只有这么几句接踵而来的男性嘲讽吗？在一幕一场中，葛莱米奥在回答巴普提斯塔的求婚凯特的言论时说道，有一句“还不如送她上囚车（cart）”[⑩]的台词涉及了 16、17 世纪英国城镇的生活。当时一种名为“浸水刑凳”（cucking stool）的惩罚方式已被用来惩罚违反群体等级秩序的女性。那些被评判为在乡间邻里作威作福的悍妇，会被绑上一辆外形似椅子、有轮子的“囚车”（cart），接受当街游行的惩罚。而等到惩处地点之后，整个装置又会被沉进

---

① Dusinberre, Juliet. *Shakespeare and the Nature of Women*. New York: Palgrave Macmillan, 1996, 41.
② Dusinberre, Juliet. Shakespeare and the Nature of Women. New York: Palgrave Macmillan, 1996, 82-85.
③ 杨洋：操控与协商——《女人的奖赏》和《驯悍记》中的婚姻关系，四川戏剧，2016，第 6 页。
④ Korda, Natasha. “Household Kates: Domesticating Commodities in *The Taming of the Shrew*”, *Shakespeare Quarterly*, 47. 2(1996): 110-111.
⑤ Newman, Karen. “Renaissance Family Politics”, in *Essaying Shakespeare*, Minneapolis: University of Minnesota Press, 2009, 30.
⑥ Dusinberre, Juliet. Shakespeare and the Nature of Women. New York: Palgrave Macmillan, 1996, 109-120.
⑦ Ross, Charles. “Shakespeare's *Taming of the Shrew* and England's Heiress Protection Statute”, *Foreign Literature Studies*, 34. 2, (2012): 8-17.
⑧ McDonald, Russ. “Men and Women: Gender, Family, Society” in *The Bedford Companion to Shakespeare* 2nd ed. MacMillan, 2001. 263.
⑨ Hutcheon, Elizabeth. “From Shrew to Subject: Petruchio's Humanist Education of Katherine in *The Taming of the Shrew*”, *Comparative Drama* 45. 4 (2011): 315-337.
⑩ 莎士比亚：《莎士比亚喜剧集 I》，朱生豪译，哈尔滨：北方文艺出版社，2019 年，第 80 页。本文所有关于《驯悍记》的文本出于此书。以下引用自本书的注释以“《驯悍记》，第×页”形式标注。

水中，上下没过那些女性的头顶三四次，直看着她们像鸭子一般挣扎，达到羞辱与训诫的目的[①]。因此，葛鲁米奥在面对凯瑟丽娜目中无物的脾性时，不似其父，骂几句就作罢，他的提议更像是要直面挑战并付诸行动，以此捍卫整个社会中的男性权威与尊严。也只有还未体验到这种惩罚严厉性的悍妇才会试图公然挑衅父权制社会中男性统治力的不容抗拒性与女性顺从的义务性。

与此同时，在四幕一场中，彼特鲁乔也说道，“我就这样克制（curb）她的狂暴倔强的脾气”[②]，此处可以联想到一种更为严酷的惩治措施则是“悍妇的口套”（scold's bridle），指的是是一种类似马笼头的器具，悍妇的头将被锁在一个金属笼头里，舌头被一块金属块压着，她们除了会反胃干呕，再无法随意言语[③]。莎翁创作此剧时，见证了父权制的核心家庭的家庭模式，这一模式在 1580 年到 1640 年达到鼎盛时期。在王国式的家庭里，婚姻的统治权就像国家的统治权，男性无论是以父亲或丈夫的身份，对他的孩子抑或妻子得到了极大强化，使他作为家庭君主的角色合法化[④]，女性的位置可想而知。因此巴普提斯塔看似纵容凯瑟丽娜挑战核心家庭中的男性权威，但彼特鲁乔的宣言是对家庭两性关系中丈夫对妻子绝对权威的直接捍卫。所以，凯瑟丽娜在家对婚恋市场上炙手可热的妹妹随意打骂，愤恨自己的商人父亲对妹妹宠爱有加，无法体验到现代社会普遍的家庭关怀。对外强势地站在社会常规的对立面，用带刺的话语叫嚣着不稀罕男性的求爱。她以一种极端的方式宣泄反抗着生存环境中收到的负面反馈，她在社会的目光里、男性的审判里越发格格不入，不知她在这样一个过程中内心究竟是否有过一丝担忧与害怕。

二、男权焦虑下投机围猎的技巧磨炼

如果探讨凯瑟丽娜的视野只能囿于个人的家庭归宿，那么男主人公彼特鲁乔就将话题范围拓宽到了个人的社会归宿。莎士比亚生活的英格兰正处于封建社会崩溃和新兴资产阶级出现的时期。这时，人们的等级、地位等身份特征不再由法律界定，称号、财富等都是可变的因素。[⑤]这也是为什么莎剧中 fashion（塑造）以及 nature（天性）两个词是经常被提及的词，体现了定规动摇之后个人对于身份不确定性的焦虑。[⑥]斯通（Laurence Stone）指出这种社会剧变深刻体现在社会流动中。社会流动包括水平迁移与垂直流动，前者更多是从地理位置层面出发，后者更看重社会等级与财富累积的隐含意义，而其中向上的社会流动所蕴藏的奖励对于一些名利追寻者来说更是有着无法拒绝的吸引力。因此，当大量土地得以私有制后，绅士阶层开始兴起，其社会地位也得到了缓慢但稳步的提高，证实了财富的累积可以实现地位的提高。[⑦]关于绅士这一词背后代表着的社会发展与观念包容，拉尔夫（Berry Ralph）也指出，它是现代早期英格兰阶层分层的重要术语，涉及其他阶层中

① Fletcher, Anthony. “The Taming of the Scold: the Enforcement of Patriarchal Authority in Early Modern England”, in *Order and Disorder in Early Modern England*. New York: Cambridge University Press, 1985, 116-136.

②《驯悍记》，第 127 页。

③ Boose, Lynda E. “Scolding Brides and Bridling Scolds: Taming the Woman's Unruly Member”, *Shakespeare Quarterly* 42. 2(1991): 199.

④ Stone, Lawrence. *The Family, Sex and Marriage in England 1500-1800*, New York: Harper & Row, 1977, 41.

⑤ Wrightson, Keith. *English Society, 1580-1680*. e-book, Taylor & Francis e-Library, 2005, 7.

⑥ 杨林贵，周亚，曹丽娟：驯与训——《驯悍记》中近代早期妇女之身份构成，人文杂志，2015(2)：第 73-78 页。

⑦ Stone, Lawrence. “Social Mobility in England, 1500-1700”, *Past & Present*1 (1966): 29-31.

所没有的关于自我的定义的张力。[1]那么对于一个有着良好声名的青年男性彼特鲁乔来说，如何能够实现财富的快速累积，实现自我社会地位的不断进阶，从而将自己塑造成一个合格的文艺复兴时期的绅士的呢？

婚姻在这一过程中就扮演了重要角色，被作为一种常见的手段来为男性自我博彩。在《第十二夜》中，托比在规劝安德鲁爵士继续他那追求富有的侄女时说到，"她不要什么公爵不公爵……老兄，还有希望呢"[2]，甚至连管家马伏里奥都能做这种黄粱美梦。在《温莎的风流娘们》中，福斯塔夫被频频戏弄也是因为他不甘放弃两位夫人的"全部富源"[3]。其中的范顿之向安妮求婚，一开始也是被她父亲的收入所吸引，财富作为挤入这一新兴阶层的门槛，其重要性不言而喻。据记录，从 15 世纪以来，大概只有 18%的绅士阶层得以成功维持家族威望[4]，其中，正因为社会不断流动带来人人皆可通过财富实现自我地位上升的可能性，身份的彰显开始不仅限于财富的累积，更多的财富被用于炫耀自我的珠宝首饰等等的花销[5]。在一幕二场中，彼特鲁乔说道，"家父安东尼奥已经不幸去世，所以我才到这异乡客地，想要物色一位妻房，成家立业"[6]。他作为长子，必须瞄准时代的机遇，利用婚姻这一有效方式巩固世代相传的父系资产[7]。而在早期现代英国，由于经济这一主要因素，中下层阶级的男女拥有一桩满意的婚姻远不如拥有大量财富资源的上层阶级来得容易[8]。因此，彼特鲁乔在听闻一有钱人家的妙龄女子正待嫁后，才会马不停蹄前往拜访，实现自己出门闯荡的目的。

但是当周围人再三强调那未来妻子是一位难以驾驭的女子，不要见钱眼开时，他是否担忧过婚后的社会目光？为何彼特鲁乔显得与其他追求贤妻的绅士们格格不入？他无须担忧，他在清醒地下一场回报率极高的赌注。他终究作为一名外乡人，谈了一桩外人眼里好不到哪里去的姻缘，那么就算有了财富的累积，他该如何快速融入、获得当地上层阶级的认可成了问题。摩尔人奥赛罗通过通婚与叙述话语这两条途径，快速地融入当地文化和主流社会，建构起属于自己的文化身份[9]。只不过与摩尔人遭受种族偏见导致其婚姻悲剧走向不同的是，帕度亚对出格的悍妇有多厌恶不再赘述。悍妇那喋喋不休的舌头所意味的不仅仅是话语自由权的争取，更是对话语本身象征着的父权社会秩序的干扰[10]，这样的话语反抗显然与男权社会赋予女性的"贞洁、幽静、顺从"的箴言不符[11]。而在当时的村落社群文化中有一种"道德体系"的存在，即邻里之间除了互帮互助，更承担着任何僭越行为规范的责任[12]，那么明显悍妇这一

① Brockman, S. L. "Tranio Transformed: Social Anxieties and Social Metamorphosis in *The Taming of the Shrew*", *Journal of Early Modern Studies* 4 (2015): 217.

② 莎士比亚：《莎士比亚喜剧集III》，朱生豪译，哈尔滨：北方文艺出版社，2019 年，第 107 页。

③ 莎士比亚：《莎士比亚喜剧集II》，朱生豪译，哈尔滨：北方文艺出版社，2019 年，第 276 页。

④ French, Henry. "'Gentlemen': Remaking the English Ruling Class", in Wrightson, K. (Ed.), *A History of England, 1500-1750*. Cambridge: Cambridge University Press, 2017, 273.

⑤ French, Henry. "'Gentlemen': Remaking the English Ruling Class", in Wrightson, K. (Ed.), A History of England, 1500-1750. Cambridge: Cambridge University Press, 2017, 274.

⑥《驯悍记》，第 87 页。

⑦ Sokol, B. J. , and Mary Sokol. *Shakespeare, Law, and Marriage*. Cambridge: Cambridge University Press, 2003, 30.

⑧ McDonald, Russ. "Men and Women: Gender, Family, Society", in *The Bedford Companion to Shakespeare* 2nd ed. MacMillan, 2001, 264-265.

⑨ 张德明：《奥瑟罗》：一个西方"他者"的建构，浙江大学学报（人文社会科学版），2003，33(1)：第 8 页。

⑩ Korda, Natasha. "Household Kates: Domesticating Commodities in The Taming of the Shrew", Shakespeare Quarterly, 47. 2 (1996): 115.

⑪ Malcolmson, Cristina, and M. Suzuki. *Debating Gender in Early Modern England, 1500-1700*. New York: Palgrave Macmillan, 2002, 141.

⑫ Stone, Lawrence. The Family, Sex and Marriage in England 1500-1800, New York: Harper & Row, 1977, 145.

破坏性的因素对于整个社会的安定来说是一个巨大的隐患。倘若彼特鲁乔成功将她收服，使得非法僭越男性主导的女性舌头重新被压制，不仅使得两性关系中女性话语重新被男性管控，驯服的意义更将体现在彼特鲁乔作为男性，其自身的话语权威借助悍妇这一女性主体在父权制社会中也能得到快速的确认与巩固。

因此，教育悍妇的责任虽是从父亲辗转到丈夫身上，但通过这段婚姻，悍妇这一不和谐因素引起的社会焦虑仍有希望处于掌控之中，无论是两性中的男性权威还是群体中的男性主体模式都将得以巩固，也难怪葛莱米奥夸赞猎手彼特鲁乔有个好胃口。那么这样一对在伊丽莎白时代的社会规约的视角下，急需男性权威改造的女性个体与急需女性个体确立男性主体的男性个体如此看来正好凑成一对“佳偶”。

三、身份焦虑的避风港：早期现代婚姻机制的佳偶良缘

因此，正如前文所探讨的，凯瑟丽娜作为规则破坏者又是否如表面显示的一般诞妄不经，漠视桎梏她的女性社会身份与即将面临的何种严苛的生存环境？从二幕一场她逼问比恩卡，“向你求婚的男人中间，你最爱哪一个”[①]，可以看出她内心其实艳羡妹妹的异性缘，她并非一个排斥婚姻与家庭的异类。她时不时释放出对比恩卡的敌意证明了她其实也认同自己作为长姐，倘若真被自己那受欢迎的妹妹抢先嫁了人，她的长女地位与颜面荡然无存[②]。三幕二场中，她由于新夫久未到场，哭诉道，“谁也不丢脸，就是我一个人丢脸”，“人家现在将要指点着苦命的凯瑟丽娜”[③]，可以看出，她也并非不惧怕外界的刻薄指点，担忧另类的自己被口诛笔伐。相反，正如帕度亚的青年才俊，如她的父亲一般，她内心对于婚姻能够带来的声名财富甚至是十分认同的。从 1363 年的《饮食和服装法令》开始，在其后的 200 年间，陆续有 7 部关于着装规范的法令颁布[④]，而这些抑奢法的共同点包含了女性的着装由她丈夫的地位而定。所以她才会在新夫姗姗来迟，又要带她匆匆离席之时，隐晦地控诉他是故意装出一副破破烂烂的样子，表明她内心无法接受彼特鲁乔那在婚礼上的那一身不太合“身份”的邋遢打扮；表明她再怎么荒唐，也渴望一段受认可的体面婚姻。那么，她此前种种我行我素的行为就并非她真实性格的彻底流露，更像是她在自身无法迎合周围环境的许可后，自我角色认知发生偏离时的强化，借以得到她作为女儿、作为女性未能享受过的替代性关注。在她的系列行动中，矛盾如蛛丝马迹般流露而出。这表明已有的“悍妇”身份已无法完全支撑个体角色认知，无法指导自我行动形成自我认同，那么她就必将产生个人身份危机，她对于无法拥有明确个人身份的焦虑暴露无遗。

而她的身份焦虑正好被冒险投机的彼特鲁乔误打误撞洞悉了一般，继而他采取了一系列的与文艺复兴时期的驯马术相连的驯服措施[⑤]。他不像《驯悍记》的民间故事来源，如《一张

---

①《驯悍记》，第 95 页。

② Spicksley, Judith. “A Dynamic Model of Social Relations: Celibacy, Credit and the Identity of the ‘Spinster’ in Seventeenth-century England”, in French H. & Barry J. (Eds), *Identity and Agency in England, 1500–1800*. New York: Palgrave Macmillan, 2004, 116.

③《驯悍记》，第 112-113 页。

④ Hunt, Alan. *Governance of the Consuming Passions: A History of Sumptuary Law*. New York: St. Martin's Press, 1996.

⑤ Joan Hartwig. “Horses and Women in *The Taming of the Shrew*”, *Huntington Library Quarterly* 45. 4(1982): 285-294.

羊皮裹悍妇》[①]里描写的一般，直接对悍妻进行毒打，而是在潜移默化中，将其物化为马。他先是在婚礼上大闹一场，牵了头一幕二场中葛鲁米奥口中的破落老马（old trot），上头的“马鞯”“用小钉嵌着她名字的两个字母”[②]，让人不得不将悍妇凯瑟丽娜联想成一头没什么价值的病马，却等着被彼特鲁乔这个好手发现价值，只有靠他她才能在市场上重新流通。其后，作为主人兼饲养员，他有权不让凯瑟丽娜吃一顿饱饭，睡一个好觉，更何况是打着关心的名义，从而在生理上先将她驯服。因此彼特鲁乔虽然不似老式驯悍故事中的男性形象，这段外来投机者收服悍妇所呈现的互惠共利[③]其实也展现了彼特鲁乔的残忍之处[④]，这在他的言语间也不自觉被流露。四幕一场，彼特鲁乔说道，“我已经……把她驾驭(reign)起来”，此处“reign”如（统治）谐音“rein”（缰绳）[⑤]，两者形成了一个双关语，流露出他在制服凯瑟丽娜这头不尽人意的悍马之时，对于男性统治力的绝对自信，对于巩固男性权威的成竹在胸，这也正是他为何敢于迎娶一位悍妇的原因。他不仅要在社会流动年代完美承担家族遗产承继人的责任，更以这一段两性关系为载体，通过“消灭”悍妇，得到群体的认同，他追名逐利的离乡之行才算是完全打消身份焦虑，迎合了社会规约，构建了自我身份。他夸张的驯悍表演也因此显得合情合理，符合了当时的宗教、伦理文本中所宣扬的两性婚姻中“男性需要巧妙地驾驭自己那逾矩的妻子从而强势保护自己手中的权力”的要求[⑥]。至此，生理上的驯服手段使悍妇无心无力再用诉诸犀利的言辞打造自我。彼特鲁乔继而在心理上通过指日为月、老头变少女等刺激，潜移默化她的发言权已被剥夺的事实，不断强化悍妇对于反抗就意味着更为强势的残忍压制的认识，在思想上重塑悍妇的角色认知。而他的残忍也正是因为他追求消除悍妇这一特殊女性主体的价值意义，从而确认个人身份，在夸张的驯悍表演中不断呈现了对父权制社会秩序的维护与巩固。

因此，凯瑟丽娜自知悍妇无法迎合文艺复兴时期理想的贞洁、沉默、顺从的女性行为。[⑦]她凭着僭越男性权威话语铸就的面具示人，企图掩盖无法定位自我社会角色带来的身份焦虑。恰逢彼特鲁乔自知身处男权社会，必须迎合社会期待规范的两性关系中的男性话语的造就，并借以巩固群体中的男性权威，在主动行动中压制“悍妇”这一社会干扰因素。至此，悍妇的贞洁有了送出的对象，她无法再用暴躁的言语武装自我，无须再向外界传达出关于她探求个人身份无果的焦虑。而彼特鲁乔也凭借着对男性身份的渴求，不仅实现了名利的投机，也扳正了凯瑟丽娜对于女性本位的偏离，为社会群体的稳定性做出了贡献。但是，关于个人身份危机导致的焦虑是否真的伴随着夫唱妇随的圆满结局的到来而终止？在这样一个完美结局中隐匿的其他参与表演的男男女女的身份焦虑是否也得到了化解？如果没有，那么在戏份最多的男女主角的衬托之下，这种焦虑又以何种方式被增强？剧本中个人身份的追求与社会群体的稳定之间的动态平衡下充满张力的潜在行动都值得进一步评议。

① Jan Harold Brunvand. “The Folktale Origin of *The Taming of the Shrew*”, *Shakespeare Quarterly* 17. 4(1966): 345-359.
②《驯悍记》，第 114 页。
③ Ramsey-Kurz, Helga. Rising above the Bait: Kate's transformation from bear to falcon. English Studies 88. 3 (2007): 262-281.
④ Mathie, Elizabeth. “Critiquing Mastery and Maintaining Hierarchy in The Taming of the Shrew”, *SEL: Studies in English Literature 1500-1900*, 60. 2 (2020): 268.
⑤ Boose, Lynda E. “Scolding Brides and Bridling Scolds: Taming the Woman's Unruly Member”, *Shakespeare Quarterly*, 42. 2(1991): 199.
⑥ Lloyd Davis. *Sexuality and Gender in the English Renaissance: An Annotated Edition of Contemporary Documents*. New York: Routledge, 1998, 198.
⑦ Newman, Karen. “Portia's Ring”, in *Essaying Shakespeare*, Minneapolis: University of Minnesota Press, 2009, 71.

四、身份焦虑的破框：戏外人斯赖的戏中情

在《驯悍记》的引子中，补锅匠斯赖一睁眼就成了高贵的主人。虽一开始斯赖大叫着人家把他当作疯子，可是当贵族安排小童温顺地站在他的面前扮演他的妻子，他转头就安心地当起了他的贵族老爷，真情实感地演起了戏。因此，在这个引子里，斯赖的身份流动的方式看似与彼特鲁乔经历的别无二致，都是一朝发了大财，实现了自我社会地位的上升，紧接着又借“温顺”的老婆，打消了内心的忧虑，更加巩固确认了自己的主体身份。而莎翁对于斯赖的戏份的处理只有引子这个开端，在斯赖同意看彼特鲁乔如何驯服凯瑟丽娜这部戏中戏后，圆满的结局中斯赖的结局反倒没了踪影，让人不禁浮想联翩。那么不知自己早已成为戏中人的斯赖的春秋大梦又能做到几时？

斯赖的结局在首次出版于1594年的四开本中的 *The Taming of a Shrew* 可得以一窥。关于 *A Shrew* 与 *The Shrew* 之间的关系众说纷纭，George I. Duthie①与 Raymond A. Houk②都认为两者都是基于时间更早、但已无从考证的驯悍题材的戏剧改编而来。而在 *A Shrew* 的戏中戏里，斯赖在三幕四场，四幕一场、二场中不时有出场戏份，比起莎剧中设置的单一引子，前者更像是在时刻提醒观众带着到底是谁在演戏这一疑问，对剧中发生的情节保持警觉。而在收场白中，斯赖的结局更是一目了然，穿回旧衣服睡在路边的他才感慨原是自己做了场美梦。老板娘也提醒他道：“你还是赶紧回家吧，小心你老婆又骂你一顿。”而斯赖的回答也耐人寻味，“我已经知道怎么驯服悍妻了……我这就回去给她点颜色瞧瞧”③。戏剧到此，以斯赖在梦醒时分既没有飞黄腾达，又有悍妻在家画上句号。那么从“戏外人”斯赖的遭遇联系到戏中情，是否圆满结局仅限于戏中戏，其性别表演下身份焦虑解决的定论是否有待商榷？

答案是肯定的。斯赖的存在似乎完全被男女主人公代表的大结局所掩盖。但等观众从戏中反应过来时，就会发问，斯赖消失的悬念与既定的结局有何关系。思索之中，各方蛛丝马迹都只会更显耐人寻味。首先，悍妇是否已驯服。剧中大幅描写悍妇的行为表演背后隐藏的个人身份焦虑，以及她所引起群体中男性主体为代表的权威的担忧等，虽最终以其被更为强势的男性表演所驯服而结束，但到尾声，比恩卡、寡妇、斯赖的“悍妻”又开始浮出水面，一时得到维护的男性权威同时面临着更大的隐患。其次，剧中彼特鲁乔确实在利益的驱使下冒险使美梦成真，那么通过这种手段得来的声名地位又能维护多久？整个帕度亚，难道就没有再像为了追求比恩卡，甘愿易装，折辱自降身份的霍坦西奥了吗？没有年纪一把仍想娶个美娇妻的葛莱米奥了吗？就连临时扮演斯赖老婆的小童，都能完美演出高贵的妇女的言行谈吐。更别提完美胜任主人的举止规范，帮助他抱得美人归，最终却落得啥也没有的下场，只能空口抱怨主人几句，向彼特鲁乔表达艳羡之情的特拉尼奥。因此，只要有时机，帕度亚流动出多个彼特鲁乔没有可能吗？一对情侣的安定无法定论整个社会能够就此和谐安定，反倒在大篇幅描写身份焦虑通过悍妇的消灭，名利得以双收而一时解决的对比之下显示出讽刺性。在看似稳定和谐的集体之下，生活在其中的每个人都有参与表演的能力与行动的倾向，使得

---

① Duthie, George I. “The Taming of a Shrew and the Taming of the Shrew”, *The Review of English Studies*, XIX. 76(1943): 337-356.

② Raymond A. Houk. “The Evolution of the Taming of the Shrew”, *PMLA*, 57. 4(1942): 1009-1038.

③ 自译，原英文台词参考 http: //elizabethandrama. org/wp-content/uploads/2020/01/Taming-of-a-Shrew-Script. pdf

这一外部环境无法给予个人身份以确切保证，这种藏匿于圆满结局下的不确定性才是引起身份焦虑的最大因素。

结　语

就这样，在喜剧的气氛中，斯赖、彼特鲁乔们的身份焦虑带有反讽意味地得到了一时的解决。然而，本剧的聚焦人物凯瑟丽娜焦虑的解决似乎呈现出另外一种格局。她在两姐妹的既定外貌与品行的对比中黯然失色，在无人问津中矫心饰貌，表演成了疾言怒色的悍妇形象，最终成了父亲的负担，成了男权社会的威胁因素。但在文艺复兴时期悍妇是与世俗相悖的存在。在男权社会的审判之下，在森严残酷的惩戒面前，凯瑟丽娜的内心并非不恐惧，一个在拒绝迎合社会期待中，对于个人身份产生焦虑、剑走偏锋的女性主体形象跃然纸上。而投机者彼特鲁乔适时出现了，虽然交易对象是个悍妇，但他对巴普提斯塔给出的嫁妆筹码甚为满意。他也并不担忧未来妻子会怎样不合社会规约，反而迫不及待想成婚，因为他必须消灭悍妇才能维护男性群体的尊严，也只有消灭悍妇这一附加荣誉才能帮助外乡人的他更快迎合社会期待的同时确认主体身份。因此在夸张的驯悍表演中，渴望迎合性别身份期待的男性焦虑与无法迎合女性身份的悍妇焦虑相辅相成，在行动中解决焦虑，实现了自身性别身份的认同。

同样，这种焦虑的解决只能是一时的，观众、读者更需要发现的是隐匿在这种喜闻乐见的喜剧结局之下的疑团。引子中与彼特鲁乔经历相似的斯赖何去何从？虽说凯瑟丽娜终成贤妻，但结尾的寡妇、比恩卡、凶悍的老板娘及斯赖的悍妻，这些人的结局又如何？虽然彼特鲁乔美梦终成，但乔装打扮的霍坦西奥、路森修，完美胜任主人言行规范的小童、特拉尼奥等同样具有表演能力的青年们呢？他们同样有着在产生他们的权力结构中占据一席之地的期待①。在性别表演的基础上，传递的是更深层次的社会表演。社会变革时期个人身份焦虑的暂时解决使得社会安定更具讽刺性。群体中每一个具有表演的能力与目的的个体都能行动起来，通过完成社会规约，以期实现主体的确认，而这恰恰是个人身份焦虑无法缓解的根源。没有时代浪潮不能抛弃的人，而时代有的是一批又一批赶潮人。

作者简介：陈静，东华大学外语学院，主要从事英语语言文学研究。

杨林贵，东华大学外语学院教授，中国外国文学学会莎士比亚研究会副会长，主要从事莎士比亚研究。

① Amy L. Smith. "Performing Marriage with a Difference: Wooing, Wedding, and Bedding in *The Taming of the Shrew*", *Comparative Drama*, 36. 3-4(2002): 290.

第三编

莎士比亚与西方文学

达菲诗歌中的莎士比亚印记

周　洁

【摘　要】英国前桂冠诗人卡罗尔·安·达菲擅长通过诗歌创作致敬经典，其十四行诗及自由体抒情诗中均有莎士比亚印记。她的十四行诗以莎士比亚体十四行诗为主。她早期最受读者欢迎的《祷告》只是形式上与莎士比亚十四行诗贴近，诗歌《安妮·海瑟薇》、十四行诗组诗《狂喜》则在形式、主题及变体的创新上都能看到莎士比亚十四行诗的影响。她以莎士比亚为题创作的十四行诗及在新冠肺炎疫情书写中对莎士比亚创作的暗指则表达了她对莎士比亚的赞美和羡慕。达菲诗歌中的莎士比亚印记表明莎士比亚的诗歌影响深远。

【关键词】莎士比亚十四行诗；卡罗尔·安·达菲；影响

Shakespearean Imprints in Duffy's Poetry

Zhou Jie

【Abstract】With talent of writing in traditional poetic forms to pay tribute to the classics, former Poet Laureate Carol Ann Duffy inherits influence from William Shakespeare in both her sonnets and free verse. Most of her sonnets are written in Shakespearean sonnet form. Her early success in sonnet, “Prayer”, is close to Shakespearean sonnet in form. “Anne Hathaway” and the sonnet series in *Rapture* are Shakespearean not only in form, but also in theme and in her innovation in “quatorzains”. Her poem entitled “Shakespeare” and the allusion to Shakespeare's writing in her poem written during the Covid-19 shows her praise of, and respect for, Shakespeare. Shakespearean imprints in Duffy's poetry show the influence of Shakespeare throughout history.

【Key Words】Shakespearean sonnet; Carol Ann Duffy; influence

卡罗尔·安·达菲（Carol Ann Duffy，1955—）是2009—2019年英国桂冠诗人，也是英国历史上第一位女性桂冠诗人，其诗歌创作中时常出现莎士比亚的影子。她创作了很多莎士比亚体十四行诗，主题涉及爱情或宗教信仰，如早期的《祷告》[①]和《世界之妻》[②]中基于莎

① Duffy, Carol Ann. *Mean Time*. London: Anvil, 1993: 52.
② Duffy, Carol Ann. *The World's Wife*. London: Picador, 1999.

士比亚婚姻生活创作的抒情十四行戏仿诗作。而诗集《狂喜》[1]，不仅在形式和内容上与莎士比亚十四行诗产生互文，还有一些莎士比亚十四行诗变体。她后期以莎士比亚为题创作十四行诗向莎士比亚表示赞美，并在新冠肺炎疫情期间的诗歌暗指莎士比亚的创作，表达对莎士比亚创作才能的羡慕。

一、早期十四行诗创作中的莎士比亚十四行诗印记

达菲早期创作的十四行诗数量较少：《站立的裸女》[2]和《出卖曼哈顿》[3]里分别收录了她基于但丁首创的交叉连韵十四行诗体（Terza Rima sonnet）和基于彼特拉克十四行诗体创作的诗歌；她在早期诗集里，还创作了几首不规则的莎士比亚十四行诗，如《出卖曼哈顿》里的《远隔千里》（“Miles Away”，Duffy，1987：57）；而《祷告》则是一首较规则的莎士比亚十四行诗。《祷告》是 2003 年英国最受喜爱的诗歌之一[4]，在形式和内容上都能看到莎士比亚的印记。

莎士比亚体十四行诗由 3 个四行体和 1 个对句组成，押韵格式为 ABAB CDCD EFEF GG。内容上，前 12 行用来陈述事物，最后用一个对句作为结语点题。《祈祷》在结构和押韵格式上也是莎士比亚体十四行诗，但格律虽基本都是每行十个音节，除了第 11 行，其他各行都不是莎士比亚十四行诗五步抑扬格。

Prayer

- \ - \ - \ - \ - \ -
Some days, although we cannot pray, a prayer
\ - -\ \ - \- - \
utters itself. So, a woman will lift
- \ - - \ - - \ - \
her head from the sieve of her hands and stare
- - \ - \ -- \ - \ - \
at the minims sung by a tree, a sudden gift.

- \ - \ - - \ - - \
Some nights, although we are faithless, the truth
\ - - \ - \ -\ - \
enters our hearts, that small familiar pain;
- - \ - \ - \ \ - - \
then a man will stand stock-still, hearing his youth

① Duffy, Carol Ann. *Rapture*. London: Picador, 2005.
② Duffy, Carol Ann. *Standing Female Nude*. London: Anvil, 1985.
③ Duffy, Carol Ann. *Selling Manhattan*. London: Anvil, 1987.
④ Dowson, Jane. *Carol Ann Duffy: The Poet for Our Time,* London: Palgrave Macmillan, 2016: 9.

- - \ - \ - \ - - - \
in the distant Latin chanting of a train.

\ - - \ - \ -\- \
Pray for us now. Grade 1 piano scales
-\ - \ - \ - - -\
console the lodger looking out across
- \ - \ - \ - \ - \
a Midlands town. Then dusk, and someone calls
- \ \ - \ - \ - \
a child's name as though they named their loss.

\ - \ - \- - \- \
Darkness outside. Inside, the radio's prayer -
\ - \ - \ - \ - -
Rockall. Malin. Dogger. Finisterre.

不齐整的格律似乎没有莎士比亚体十四行诗的五步抑扬格流畅，但是，第 2 行、第 6 行、第 9 行，第 13 行和第 14 行都出现的扬抑格，使得该诗较为“通俗”[①]，更适合表达人们的在日常生活中，人们感到绝望而空虚，因为“不能祈祷”，也更容易表现出某种神秘的感觉。而莎士比亚体的押韵格式则使该诗读来像教堂里人们做祈祷。

诗人一开始就指出，在“某些白天”，即使人们“不能祈祷”，祈祷也会自行发生：于是女人从筛子样捧着脸的手里抬起头看着外面，有棵树发出微小的像歌一样的声音，这一刻便像一份“礼物”，振奋她的精神，自然世界使她恢复了一种平静的心态。此处对女人的头的描写让人联想到达菲的诗歌《小小的女性的头骨》（“Small Female Skull”）第一行“我把我小小的女性的头骨放在手中”（I balance my small female skull in my hands）和第二节重复描述的“头在手里”（with my head in my hands），于是便与哈姆雷特联系起来[②]。

第二节中，诗人继续描述另一种祈祷。在“某些夜晚”，即使人们“没有信仰”，真理仍然进入人们的心间，来缓解压力和痛苦。这是一种启示：一个人经历的痛苦是“熟悉的”，而“熟悉”便是一种安慰。然后，静静站着的男人听到火车慢慢驶向远方的歌声，想起年轻时的拉丁语，回到快乐的时光。这一刻强调了记忆和经验的重要性，告诉人们，可以通过日常生活中的声音联想到自己的青春时光，与周围的世界建立联系。该节中的拉丁语是可以与基督教联系起来的。

第三节直接呼唤世人为自己祈祷，说钢琴曲可以安慰看着英格兰中部小镇的房客。至此可以发现，从第一小节的树像唱歌的声音，到第二小节把火车的声音描写为“歌声”（chanting），

① 聂珍钊：《英语诗歌形式导论》，北京：中国社会科学出版社，2007 年版，第 123 页。

② 详见 Horner, Avril. “Small Female Skull”: patriarchy and philosophy in the poetry of Carol Ann Duffy, Angelic Michelis & Antony Rowland. (eds.). *The Poetry of Carol Ann Duffy: Choosing Tough Words*. Manchester: Manchester University Press, 2003: 99-120.

再到第三小节的钢琴曲，都让人联想到莎士比亚戏剧《驯悍记》中“音乐被授以神职”“振奋人的思想”[①]的描写，从而增加了音乐在日常生活的神秘性。

第三节里提到的“黄昏，有人叫/孩子的名字仿佛叫出了他们的失落”（as though they named their loss），由于使用了“named”的过去时形式，表明是一种回忆，又让人联想到莎士比亚戏剧《皆大欢喜》中的“赞美失去的东西使回忆变得珍贵”[②]，自然使人得到安慰。

而诗人在第二节提到的“真理”和在最后的对句中提到的“黑暗”让人联想到《麦克白》里的“黑暗的工具告诉我们真理”[③]。在达菲的诗里，黑暗的工具就是无线电广播，关于航运的预告也能给人带来一种平静，成为一种祈祷。

总之，达菲的诗歌《祈祷》在诗体结构、押韵格式、每行音节和音步数上可以算作莎士比亚体十四行诗，而女性的头、反复出现的音乐声、失落、黑暗和真理等都有莎士比亚的印记。

二、基于莎翁婚姻生活诗性思考的戏仿十四行诗

莎士比亚是戏仿能手，他的很多作品是对其他经典作品的戏仿。其戏仿基于诗性的思考而成：“他的《泰特斯·安特洛尼克斯》是对马洛的《马耳他的犹太人》的戏仿”；“《理查三世》在更大的程度上是对马洛的‘不知不觉的回忆’”。[④]

1999年达菲出版了她最成功的戏剧独白诗集《世界之妻》，诗集按照时间顺序编排，反映了诗人个人的内心变化。从诗集的标题看来，似乎是奥维德的《古代名媛》的戏仿，不过诗集的叙述人不仅仅是古代名媛，还有当代著名的女性，而且是世界名人之妻或女性朋友、亲人；她们写的不是给自己的情人或爱人的书信，而是她们如何看待这些名人、她们自己及经历的改变。诗集中的戏剧独白诗，是达菲戏仿经典文学作品，进行女性主义重读和改写的文本，被看作是“翻新和进一步强化女性主义思想的新尝试”[⑤]。联系莎士比亚的戏仿，达菲《世界之妻》的戏仿应该是她在女性主义思想意识下对经典作品的诗性思考，或者也可以说，是在一定程度上对经典作品的“不知不觉的回忆”。按照瑞奇从女性作家角度所提出的“改写是对经典的‘修正’（revision），是以新的视角走进古老的文本”，达菲“以一种全新的眼光走近历史和经典”[⑥]，“让原有的沉默和边缘者发声”[⑦]，成功地挑战了男性霸权并超越了其藩篱，走进了属于“她者”的被解放的创作空间。

引人注意的是，《世界之妻》里巧妙地收录了四首十四行诗，《安妮·海瑟薇》（“Anne Hathaway”，Duffy，1999：30）、《魔鬼之妻》中的第三部分《圣经》（“Bible”，Duffy，1999：44）、《弗洛伊德夫人》（“Frau Freud”，Duffy，1999：55）和最后一首《得墨忒耳》（“Demeter”，Duffy，1999：76）。

---

① “Preposterous ass, that never read so far to know the cause why music was ordain'd! Was it not to refresh the mind of man, after his studies or his usual pain?”详见 *The Taming of the Shrew,* act 3, sc.1, l.9-12. Lucentio to Hortensio, 1593.

② “Praising what is lost makes the remembrance dear”，详见 *All's Well that Ends Well* (1603-4) act 5, sc. 3, l. 19.

③ “The instruments of darkness tell us truths.”详见 *Macbeth*(1606) act 1, sc. 3, l. 123.

④ “诗性的思考被诗与诗之间的影响融入具体语境，即使是在才能最高的诗人莎士比亚那里也是如此”。详见[美]哈罗德·布鲁姆：《读诗的艺术》，南京：南京大学出版社2010年版，第9页。

⑤ 张剑：《改写历史和神话——评当代英国诗人卡罗尔·安·达菲的〈世界之妻〉》，《外国文学》2015年第3期。

⑥ 陈宏薇：《西方文论关键词：改写理论》，《外国文学》2016年第5期，第62页。

⑦ 陈宏薇：《西方文论关键词：改写理论》，《外国文学》2016年第5期，第65页。

《安妮·海瑟薇》以莎士比亚的妻子安妮·海瑟薇的口气，讲述她与莎士比亚的爱情记忆，是诗人从当代女性的视角对莎士比亚夫妻生活的诗性思考。

Anne Hathaway

"Item I gyve unto my wife my second best bed..."
(from Shakespeare's will)

The bed we loved in was a spinning world
of forests, castles, torchlight, cliff-tops, seas
where he would dive for pearls. My lover's words
were shooting stars which fell to earth as kisses
on these lips; my body now a softer rhyme
to his, now echo, assonance; his touch
a verb dancing in the centre of a noun.
Some nights I dreamed he'd written me, the bed
a page beneath his writer's hands. Romance
and drama played by touch, by scent, by taste.
In the other bed, the best, our guests dozed on,
dribbling their prose. My living laughing love —
I hold him in the casket of my widow's head
as he held me upon that next best bed.

在《安妮·海瑟薇》的标题下，达菲引用了莎士比亚的遗言“我给我妻子之物：我次好的床……”对于莎士比亚夫妻关系的考证，有人认为，由于“父亲生意上的失败”，莎士比亚“不得不辍学帮助父亲务农。他在 1582 年同安妮”结婚，“在 1585 年左右离开家乡到了伦敦”[①]。达成共识的是：安妮·海瑟薇（1556—1623）比莎士比亚大八九岁，两人是奉子成婚。安妮·海瑟薇“身体强壮，甚至颇有几分招人眼目的男子气度的女子”，“有足够本领让她那年轻的丈夫多年之中无所适从，醋意屡生；后来又时而令他发疯，时而让他生趣，并最终让他生厌。如果这是事实就是的生动描绘，威廉逃往伦敦就无须多作解释了”[②]。陈黎在为该诗汉译本所做的导读中提到“夫妻长年分离，有人认为他们感情不睦，有人甚至认为安妮曾红杏出墙，因此莎士比亚在遗嘱黎未留给她什么遗产，只留给她一张‘次好的床’，当作是对妻子的惩罚或侮辱”[③]。作为现代人的达菲，对与丈夫长期分离的安妮给予理解和同情，她还让安妮在正文中把她与丈夫的床描述成“是他潜寻珍珠的”的天地。表明安妮对这张床乃至他们的爱情的珍视。她对于他们最好的床做出了这样的解释：“我们的客人在另一张床，最好的床上打盹，/流着散文体的口水。”也就是说，即使他们最好的床上让客人用，客人的存在也只能像是散文，只有他们夫妻二人在次好的床上才能做出诗。陈黎认为，达菲以此诗为安妮正名，让当事人

① 聂珍钊、杜娟、唐红梅、朱卫红：《英国文学的伦理学批评》，武汉：华中师范大学出版社 2007 年版，第 96 页。
② 苏福忠：《瞄准莎士比亚》，北京：人民大学出版社 2017 年版，第 336-337 页。
③ 陈黎、张龄芬：《野兽派太太》，北京：外语教学与研究出版社 2017 年版，第 24 页。

“述说她与莎士比亚的亲密关系”，并将“次好的床”解释为“一种爱的表白，因为那张床象征了两人昔日爱的印记”[①]。

该诗充分运用隐喻。诗歌开始于“床”作为“爱情”的隐喻，之后出现了一系列相关隐喻：用“旋纺的天地”喻指夫妻之间的激情时刻；用“珍珠”喻指他们爱情的珍贵；用“流星雨”喻指他们爱情的壮丽；用“较柔的韵”喻指她的阴柔和他的阳刚；用“回声”和“和鸣谐韵”喻指他们的和谐；“名词”和“动词”则把他们之间的爱情比作了一首诗—— 他与她像“名词”与“动词”一样彼此不可分离，共同在爱情的诗歌中舞蹈；用“夜”和“梦”喻指他们的分离和思念；由于他“写我”，“床”又成了“稿纸”，他写成的都是“传奇”和“戏剧”—— 不是世人所看或听的，而是只有他们两人才能触、嗅、闻到的“传奇”和“戏剧”；而他们的客人在他们最好的床上打盹时只能流出“散文体的口水”；最后，他被纳入她“寡妇的头棺”喻指他“生动欢笑的爱”永远活在她的心头，就像他给她的拥抱一样永远温暖。达菲让安妮把莎士比亚的话语描述成“坠落大地的流星雨，化为吻”，把她自己的身体描述成“柔软的韵，/时而是回声，与其和鸣谐韵”；仿佛她也是诗人，与莎士比亚一样，可以灵活运用语言，把他的触摸描述成为“动词，在一个名词中央舞蹈。”她通过“梦”来表达思念。隐喻的运用一方面说明达菲在试图让莎士比亚的妻子在言说时表现出与莎士比亚相媲美的语言运用能力，一方面也说明莎士比亚对当代诗人的影响。

从该诗的形式上看，戏仿莎翁婚姻生活的《安妮·海瑟薇》也有与莎士比亚体十四行诗类似的地方：前四行基本算是五音步，而且形成了 ABAB 的尾韵，最后也以押韵的对句结尾，赋予该诗以十四行诗的特色，为安妮表达对莎士比亚的感情提供了便利条件。

三、诗集《狂喜》唤起的《莎士比亚十四行诗集》记忆

达菲 2005 年出版的《狂喜》由 52 首爱情十四行诗组成，按照时间顺序讲述了一段爱情故事，出版商评价此书为感人的个人情感历程的印证。人们称该书为“一张真爱的地图”（a map of real love），它将直率与精细结合，是一首由痛苦写成的歌。达菲一度拒绝对其中表达的各种矛盾—— 醉心、渴望、激情、许诺、怨恨、分离和痛苦做出解释，但在一次采访[②]中说她生活中有三件重要的事情：一是女儿的出生；二是喜欢她的诗歌的母亲因癌症病逝；三是恋爱—— 她爱得心醉神迷，全身心投入，找到爱情又痛苦地失去。达菲没有透露她的恋爱对象是谁，也不想讲述这段爱情故事，而是希望读者集中于她的诗歌，而不要过多地关注她个人。有人认为，这部诗集是达菲写给女作家杰基·凯（Jackie Kay）的[③]。

这部基于个人感情经历（包括同性爱）写成的诗集唤起了读者对《莎士比亚十四行诗集》的记忆。《莎士比亚十四行诗集》最早于 1609 年编辑而成的诗集共有 154 首十四行诗，每首诗都有相对的独立性，合在一起又构成整体，“重复着相同的主题—— 总是离不开时间、友谊

---

① 陈黎、张龄芬：《野兽派太太》，北京：外语教学与研究出版社 2017 年版，第 88 页。

② 为了了解该诗集的创作背景，Jeanette Winterson 对达菲进行了采访，详见 http://www.jeanettewinterson.com/journalism/can-you-move-diagonally-jeanette-winterson-interviews-poet-laureate-carol-ann-duffy/（2019 年 10 月 16 日读取）。

③ Catherine Lanone: “Baring Skills, Not Souls: Carol Ann Duffy's Intertextual Games” at: https://journals.openedition.org/erea/94（2019 年 10 月 16 日读取）. 杰基·凯（Jackie Kay）是非裔苏格兰诗人兼小说家。

或爱情、艺术（诗）”①，表达真、善、美。一般认为，其中前 126 首写给诗人的一位少年朋友，诗人竭力称颂他的美；后 28 首写给一位性情放荡、不忠于爱情的女郎，体现了人文主义的爱情观。总之，诗集真实地记录着莎士比亚的情感生活和隐秘的内心世界。因此，可以说，达菲的诗集《狂喜》由于集中以爱情为主题、基于个人感情经历而作、采用莎士比亚体十四行形式而在某种程度上与《莎士比亚十四行诗集》类似。诗集中的十四行诗变体，包括一些十二行、十五行、十六行、十八行的诗歌和一些有七节组成的诗歌，应该也是步莎士比亚“准十四行诗”（quatorzain）②的后尘而且有所发挥。现以诗歌《狂喜》和《爱情诗》为例，探讨其中的莎士比亚影响。

与《祈祷》一样，诗歌《狂喜》的押韵格式和每行的音节数都符合莎士比亚十四行诗的标准，只是在开始的一些诗行中没有使用完全的抑扬格。

\ - - \ - \ - \ - \
Thought of by you all day, I think of you
- \ \ - - \ - -- \
The birds sing in the shelter of a tree.
- \ - \ - \ -\ - \
Above the prayer of rain, unacred blue,
- \ -- \ \ - \ - -
not paradise, goes nowhere endlessly.
\ - - \ - - - \ - \
How does it happen that our lives can drift
\ - - \ - \ - \ - \
Far from our selves, while we stay trapped in time,
\ - - \ - \ \ - - \
Queuing for death? It seems nothing will shift
- \ - - - \ \ -- \
the pattern of our days, alter the rhyme
- \ - \ -\ - - - \
we make with loss to assonance with bliss.
- \ - \ - \ - \ -\
Then love comes, like a sudden flight of birds
- \ - \ - \- \ - \
From earth to heaven after rain. Your kiss,
- \ - \ - \ - \ - \
recalled, unstrings, like pearls, this chain of words.

① 莎士比亚：《莎士比亚十四行诗 》（英汉对照），屠岸译，北京：外语教学与研究出版社 2012 年版，第 9 页。

② 罗益民（2016）将“quatorzain”称为“准十四行诗”（34），指出托马斯·沃森创作的十八行诗（34；41）、斯宾塞使用的“十二行体”（39）和十五行的“无韵诗”（39）、莎士比亚十四行诗中十五行的第 99 首和十二行的第 126 首及其由四音步抑扬格构成的第 145 首（62）都是“准十四行诗”。

- \   - \   - \   - \   - \

Huge skies connect us, joining here to there. 13

- \   - \   - - -   \ -   \

Desire and passion on the thinking air. 14

(Duffy, 2005: 16)

在形式上不同于莎士比亚十四行诗传统的是，虽然该诗从押韵格式上每四行成一个单位，但是只有第一个四行是完整的断句，除第 1 行外，第 2~4 行描述了一个鸟儿歌唱却不是天堂的自然景象；第 5~7 行是一个问句，提问了一个人生的哲学问题："为什么生命总会游离/我们自己，我们又被时间困扰/束手待毙？"第 7 行后半部分直到第 9 行结束，是个否定句，断言"无事似可代替/我们的生活方式，即使和谐中充满/失落，也不能被幸福的半和谐代替。"第 10~13 行与第 2~4 行形成对照，表现了爱情的力量："此时爱情来临，像鸟儿突然飞起/雨后，从地面到天际。你的亲吻/回味中，散落出，珍珠般，这串文字。"最后两行又回到了莎士比亚十四行诗的习惯，既押韵，也与第 1 行呼应，表达主题："苍穹连接我们，连接这里与那里。/欲望和激情弥漫在思念的空气里。"

《爱情诗》是一首写爱情诗的自由体诗。达菲用英国文学史上不同年代的爱情诗歌中的著名诗句创作了一部文学"拼贴画"，以表达爱情的普遍性。标题用定冠词"the"表示该诗包含了所有的爱情诗的内容，可以代表所有爱情诗。

该诗由三个十二行的诗节组成，诗行长短不一。诗人使用了大量的破折号，将引用的诗句与自己的诗句区分开来，形成一种微妙的、不规则的韵律，与情感的不规则性一致。每节都以"直到……"（Till...）开头，形成一个完整的句子。整首诗中，著名经典爱情诗中的只言片语嵌入不和谐、破裂的现代诗节。而最初的一处引用就是莎士比亚的"我情人的眼睛"（my mistress' eyes）：

Till love exhausts itself, longs
for the sleep of words —
my mistress' eyes —
to lie on a white sheet, at rest
in the language —
let me count the ways —
or shrink to a phrase like an epitaph —
come live
with me —
or fall from its own high cloud as syllables
in a pool of verse —
one hour with thee.

诗人开始就表达了一种让"词语休眠"（让这首诗成为爱情诗的终结者）的渴望：读过莎士比亚十四行诗第 130 首的读者，看到"我的情妇的眼睛"自然会联想到"一点也不像太阳"，而达菲在下一行写到“躺在白纸/床单上”，由于第二行和第五行分别是“for the sleep of words”和“in the language”，可以断定诗人在第四行是想表达“躺在白纸上”。随后，诗人引用巴雷特·布朗宁的“让我来细数一番”（let me count the ways），让读者联想到“我多么爱你”（How much I love you），而诗人却在下一行写到“或缩减成一个墓志铭的短句”。接下来引用了马洛的“与我同住”（come live with me），然后又说“或如一池韵文里的音节，从它/自己的云端坠落——”，并引用司各特的“与你共享一个时辰”（an hour with thee）。

在第二节，诗人先后引用了怀亚特的“你觉得怎么样”（how like you this）、西德尼的“问你的心，然后再写”（dear heart/how like you this）和坎皮恩的“她的脸上有一座花园”（there is a garden in her face）。在第三节，又引用了多恩的“我的新大陆”（my new-found land）、圣经《雅歌》里的“看哪，你多美”（Behold，thou art fair）和雪莱的“飞蛾对星星的渴求”（the desire of the moth for the star）。全篇由各时期的爱情诗句拼合而成，成为一个著名爱情诗句的合集，体现出英国文学中爱情诗传统对达菲的影响。在这些引用中，诗人以莎士比亚十四行诗开始，可见莎士比亚十四行诗在她心目中的位置。

总之，达菲的诗集《狂喜》中充满了“发生于读者／观众记忆层面上的叠刻性互文现象”[①]，能唤起读者对莎士比亚十四行诗及其他经典作品的记忆，使读者“在心理上获得一种重复记忆时的快乐和愉悦”[②]。

四、对莎士比亚的赞美与疫情书写能力的羡慕

2014 年收录在《仪式光芒》（*Ritual Lighting*）里的《莎士比亚》也是一首十四行诗，达菲在诗中对莎士比亚极尽赞美。而在 2020 年新冠肺炎疫情期间，达菲又在《花园》一诗中表达了对莎士比亚当年在瘟疫期间完成戏剧及诗歌作品的羡慕。

Shakespeare

Small Latin and less Greek, all English yours,
dear lad, local, word-blessed, language loved best;
the living human music on our tongues,
young, old, who we were or will be, history's shadow,
Love's will, our heart's iambic beat, brother
through time; full-rhyme to us.
Two rivers quote your name;
your journey from the vanished forest's edge
to endless fame — a thousand written souls,
Pilgrims, redeemed in poetry — ends here, begins again.
And so, you knew this well, you do not die —

① 陈宏薇：《西方文论关键词：改写理论》，《外国文学》2016 年第 5 期，第 66 页。
② 陈宏薇：《西方文论关键词：改写理论》，《外国文学》2016 年第 5 期，第 65 页。

courtier, countryman, noter of flowers and bees,
War's laureate, magician, Janus-faced —
But make a great Cathedral, genius, of this place.

该诗既表明莎士比亚在达菲心目中的位置，也说明莎士比亚对达菲的深刻影响。达菲认为莎士比亚是语言大师，说“小拉丁文和更小的希腊语，所有英语都是你的，”（第 1 行）又亲切地称他为“亲爱的小伙子，当地人，被字祝福的，最被语言爱的”（第 2 行）和“兄弟”（第 5 行），因为他创造了“我们舌头上活生生的人类音乐，”无论年轻与年老，无论过去与将来，他都在“历史的影子”中，把“爱的意愿，我们心里的抑扬格节拍/通过时间；全韵给我们”。达菲用“两条河流引用你的名字”（第 7 行）来表现莎士比亚的世界闻名，用“旅程”来描述莎翁的生命，把他的出生地比作“消失的森林的边缘”（第 8 行），以突出他成为“无尽的盛名”（第 9 行），因为他在作品中创作了数以千计个有灵魂的人物，像“朝圣者”（第 10 行）一样在他的诗歌里被完成，又被赋予新的生命。因此，达菲认为莎士比亚“不会死”，因为他是“受宠遇者，同胞，鲜花和蜜蜂的记录人/战争诗人，魔术师，两面神”（第 12~13 行）。这里的“两面神”（Janus）又被译作“雅努斯”，是罗马人的门神，也是罗马人的保护神。据说，他有前后两个面孔或四方四个面孔，象征开始。作为起源神，他执掌着开始和入门，也执掌着出口和结束，同时他又被称为“门户总管”，象征着世界上矛盾的万事万物，所以，他的肖像被画成两张脸，有“双头雅努斯”或“两面神”的说法。可见，在达菲心目中，莎士比亚是文学艺术之源头，其作品内容丰富，包罗万象，可以穷尽一切。为此，达菲在诗的最后说，莎士比亚用自己的天才把这个地方变得神圣，变成了“伟大的大教堂”（第 14 行）。

2020 年新冠肺炎疫情期间，4 月 23 日是莎士比亚诞辰，达菲创作了诗歌《之后发现的碎片》（Fragments found after），为疫情期间剧院无法开门以及自己无法写出佳作而表示伤感。诗歌在莎士比亚时代的瘟疫与当下的新冠肺炎疫情之间切换。诗人以“感恩花园”开始，但是随即提及“黑死病”，无疑暗指莎士比亚在黑死病期间的戏剧及诗歌创作[①]。第一行后的短横线之后，第二行便回到了现实：“早晨，我走进绿色的、有呼吸的空间/避难-”，第三行最后的短横线之后，“努力成为花园的一部分”表达了诗人对于莎翁艺术创作能力的敬佩和自己在花园里创作出精彩作品的愿望。

五、结　语

回顾达菲的诗歌创作，从达菲十四行诗的 3 个四行体和 1 个对句、押韵格式和不完全的五步抑扬格，到基于诗性思考对文学经典的戏仿；从各种隐喻，到爱情诗集中的互文，都能看出“对经典的一种接受和回归”[②]。这些莎士比亚印记表明，达菲诗歌中有一个“说不尽的

① 李伟民在《瘟神难掩戏剧烟火 文艺筑赋人世悲喜——莎士比亚戏剧的瘟疫书写》（《中国莎士比亚研究》2020 年第 1 期，第 28-42 页）中指出，“在《哈姆雷特》《李尔王》《奥赛罗》《罗密欧与朱丽叶》《亨利四世》《第十二夜》《特洛伊罗斯与克瑞西达》《裘里斯·恺撒》《约翰王》《无事生非》《终成眷属》《辛白林》《理查二世》《亨利六世》《亨利八世》《安东尼与克莉奥佩特拉》《克里奥兰纳斯》，以及《十四行诗集》中都涉及了“瘟疫话语”的叙事，莎剧中的“瘟疫意象”往往成为莎氏对人与人性的瘟疫隐喻。

② 陈宏薇：《西方文论关键词：改写理论》，《外国文学》2016 年第 5 期，第 64 页。

莎士比亚”[①]。由此可见，莎士比亚的诗歌对当代英国诗歌的深刻影响。

基金项目： 国家社会科学基金项目“达菲诗歌文体研究”（项目编号：17BWW060）阶段性成果。

作者简介： 周洁，山东财经大学公共外语教学部教授，外国语学院硕士生导师，中国文体学研究会常务理事，山东省外国文学学会常务理事，主要从事英国诗歌研究。

① 李伟昉：《说不尽的莎士比亚》，北京：中国社会科学出版社 2004 年版。

面具帷幕遮掩着多少热情而丰富的戏文①

——布鲁姆"影响的焦虑"视角下《沃尔特·惠特曼的美国》中莎士比亚戏剧对惠特曼的影响

鲁跃峰

【摘　要】使用布鲁姆"影响的焦虑"诗歌理论、社会文化研究、历史学、叙事学、比较文学等方法，本文梳理了大卫·S. 雷诺兹的《沃尔特·惠特曼的美国：文化传记一种》中有关莎士比亚对惠特曼影响的有关论述，并还原了美国 19 世纪上半叶莎剧演出现场，以莎剧中诸多角色、场景、演员为背景，以当时的演出风格象征的文化艺术方面的流行时尚为研究对象和纽约阿斯特广场暴乱为突破口，分析莎士比亚戏剧对惠特曼的深刻影响。

【关键词】布鲁姆；影响的焦虑；大卫·雷诺兹；《沃尔特·惠特曼的美国》；莎士比亚；戏剧表演；惠特曼；《草叶集》

The Passionate Teeming Plays This Curtain Hid

Lu Yuefeng

【Abstract】Using Bloom's Poetry Theory of The Anxiety of Influence, social and cultural research, history, narratology, comparative literature and other methods, this paper combs the relevant discussions on Shakespeare's influence on Whitman in *Walt Whitman's America:A Cultural Biography* by David S. Reynolds (US), and restores the performance scenes of Shakespeare's performances in the first half of the 19th century. Taking many characters, scenes and actors in Shakespeare's plays as the background, as well as the fashion of popular culture and art symbolized by the performance style at that time as the research object, and taking the riot in Astor Square in New York as the breakthrough, this paper analyzes in detail the real influence of Shakespeare on Whitman, and puts forward in-depth opinions on the deeper influence of Shakespeare on Whitman. It is instructive for us to understand Shakespeare and Whitman better.

【Key Words】Bloom; The Anxiety of Influence; David S. Reynolds; *Walt Whitman's America: A Cultural Biography*; Shakespeare; theatrical performances; Whitman; *Leaves of Grass*

---

① Whitman, Walt. *Leaves of Grass, Comprehensive Reader's Edition*. Harold Blodgett and Sculley Bradley. Ed. New York, 1965.（惠特曼，《草叶集综合版》，第 381-382 页。）

引 言

莎士比亚对惠特曼的影响一直是一个既引人注目又让人望而生畏的问题，你无法逃避，但又不敢轻易涉足。众所周知，王佐良先生一直都认为英语诗歌史上有过三次高潮，这早已得到学界的公认：莎士比亚是英语诗歌史上第一次高潮的杰出代表。华兹华斯、柯勒律治、拜伦、雪莱、济慈这批浪漫主义诗人是英语诗歌史上第二次高潮，而惠特曼及其众多的追随者是英语诗歌历史上的第三次高潮。而引领着这第三次高潮的惠特曼不可能没有受到前边第一次高潮中的杰出代表莎士比亚的影响。而布鲁姆这样一位文学艺术评论界的巨擘则提出著名的“影响诗歌理论”，后辈诗人面对受前驱、前辈诗人及其成就影响的现实，陷入一种“影响的焦虑”，从而以自己的创造性“误读”前人，开辟新的诗歌空间，以达成自我肯定并跻身强者行列。这个问题如此重大，以至于像布鲁姆这样的大师竟然连续写了《影响的焦虑》《影响的剖析》这两本书来论证这个问题，可见其有多么重要、多么艰难以及多么有意思，而且布鲁姆除了在前者数次提到惠特曼以外，还自称他的《影响的剖析》一书中，自始至终，都专注于这两位高大的文学前辈（莎士比亚和惠特曼）。这就更不能不让我们慎重，因为，对于莎士比亚和惠特曼这样两位文学巨人来说，仅仅是莎士比亚对整个世界的影响力到底有多大，还有，惠特曼受到的所有的影响到底有多少，这两者本身各自就是一个无比艰巨的任务，可能耗去一个顶尖学者的一生的心血，根本无法在此篇小小的论文里完成。而他们之间特定的影响与接受又没有那么简单，既有表面的、可以看到的影响，又有隐藏很深的、表面上看不到，但又非常根本的影响；而这种影响之间的梳理比上一个更为严峻、更为难以处理。但这又不能成为轻率处理他们之间关系的理由，我们还是要先搞清楚莎士比亚的影响的哪一部分与惠特曼接受的影响中的哪一部分有直接的缘分，然后再逐步梳理这两部分的直接关系、间接关系、表面原因和深层的原因。或者说，我们目前只能从我们力所能及的、目前能够占有的那部分材料所涉及的领域来展开论述、进行此种处理，才能有所收获。为了起到应有的作用，为了解决本文所关心的问题，我们在讨论之前，必须耐下心来先来做一番细细的前期调查工作，厘清其各种概念、定义、分类与功用及其互动变化关系，还原当时具体情形，了解其种种动机及其手段，达成共识，然后方可进行问题的讨论。这个极为复杂的问题使我们可以更清楚地意识到这两位巨人的魅力，从中汲取他们二位的营养。

虽然这个问题是如此艰巨，但也不是不能探讨，更何况大卫·S. 雷诺兹的著作《沃尔特·惠特曼的美国》[①]一书中有相当多的篇幅直接间接地描述了这种影响，书中牵涉的方面比较多，资料也比较权威。虽然雷诺兹也会有一些失误和不足，但是这本书也确实有很多真知灼见，在一定层次上，大致可以指出莎士比亚对惠特曼的影响。至于其失误、遗忘与不足等，如果笔者发现，或是笔者的观点与其不同，将会在行文里随时指出。

1 莎士比亚的影响和惠特曼受到的影响最基本评估

1.1 莎士比亚的影响

莎士比亚的影响从戏剧和文学延伸到现代电影、西方哲学和英语本身。威廉·莎士比亚

① Reynolds, David S. *Walt Whitman's America: A Cultural Biography*. New York: Vintage Books, 1995.

被广泛认为是英语史上最伟大的作家，也是世界上最杰出的剧作家。他通过在人物塑造、情节、语言和体裁等方面的创新，扩大了人们对未来的期望，从而改变了欧洲戏剧。多年来，莎士比亚的作品也影响了许多著名的小说家和诗人，包括赫尔曼·梅尔维尔、查尔斯·狄更斯和玛雅·安杰洛，甚至在今天也继续影响着新作家。莎士比亚是英语世界历史上被引用最多的作家，仅次于圣经中的各种作家；他的许多语录和新词已成为英语和其他语言的日常用法。根据《吉尼斯世界纪录大全》，莎士比亚仍然是世界上最畅销的剧作家，据信，在他去世近400年的时间里，他的戏剧和诗歌的销量超过了40亿册。他也是历史上第三位翻译最多的作家。

1.2 惠特曼受到的影响

按照山姆·沃利（Sam Worley）[①]的说法，惠特曼受到的影响范围之大势无与伦比的。为什么？惠特曼追求表达存在的整体，包含诗意的整个人类经验的过去和现在，他提出的目标是：写一个新的圣经，涵盖人类的起源和命运，将表达字面上和隐喻的生活的目的和意义，并在这个过程中提供一个统一的愿景。所以惠特曼会从许多地方获得灵感，但对他最深刻的影响是那些恰恰提供了这种全面愿景的事物，其中主要有宗教：自然神论，贵格会，伊曼纽尔·史威登堡的神学，还有美国非常流行的各种神秘实践，如灵魂说唱、催眠术等。哲学：黑格尔，艾默生。历史进程中的整体的政治、经济、军事、科技、新闻、文学、文化艺术、风俗、等时代的整体状况，还有各类具体的艺术风格流派的影响：戏剧、演说、诗歌、小说、报纸、歌剧、流行音乐、摄影、绘画、印刷、新闻、戏剧流行音乐歌剧等。

2 莎士比亚对惠特曼影响程度的基本评估

在影响研究中，研究者们最容易失误的地方是，任意夸大这种影响的程度，将本来无关的东西牵强附会、强拉在一起、拔高其意义；另外一种倾向是只看到表面影响没有看到深层影响，特别是那些看似无关紧要的东西中的最关键的东西往往被忽略。这也是我们特别需要注意的。

莎士比亚对惠特曼影响程度的基本评估如下：第一，个别领域有相当影响，但不是至关重要。这是一个不证自明的真理，如果莎士比亚对惠特曼的影响是至关重要的话，那么他只能成为莎士比亚的模仿者和学徒，而不会有本文最前边所引用的王佐良先生和布鲁姆把他们放到同样重要地位的那种评价。第二，从艺术技术层面上来说，从所列范围覆盖部分可以清楚地看出莎士比亚的戏剧、诗歌对惠特曼有特殊的影响。第三，从民族层面上说莎士比亚在剧中所表现出来的追求自由、反抗专制暴政的灵魂对处于独立战争、南北战争期间的惠特曼有着特定的影响。第四，莎士比亚不知是有幸、还是不幸，没有读过惠特曼的东西，所以莎士比亚对他会做出什么评价不得而知；但是从表面看，惠特曼虽然很欣赏莎士比亚的才华，但对其描写内容不满，甚至是极为不满。

我们已经谈到过莎士比亚了。在我看来，他似乎是星际的天才，而且是一流的，并且完全适合于封建主义。他的贡献，尤其对于激情文学的贡献，是巨大无比的，对于人类来说永

① Sam Worley, “Influences on Whitman, Principal” (Criticism) - The Walt Whitman Archive.

远弥足珍贵—— 而且他的名字会在美国一直受到崇敬。但他身上有很多与民主相抵牾的东西。莎士比亚不仅与封建主义相一致，而且我还要说，莎士比亚就是封建主义在文学中不折不扣的化身。①

但是，在笔者看来，这只是表面现象，这之下隐藏的真实原因反而倒过来证明了莎士比亚对惠特曼的影响很大。因为，这一点上，如果按照布鲁姆"影响诗歌理论"进行考察的话，这一评价可以视为后辈诗人惠特曼受到前驱、前辈诗人莎士比亚及其成就影响，陷入了一种"影响的焦虑"，从而以自己的创造性"误读"前人，开辟了新的诗歌空间，以达成自我肯定，并跻身强者行列一种必然的做法。按照这个影响的焦虑理论来说，惠特曼对莎士比亚的这种欲擒故纵的批判，反而说明了他受莎士比亚影响深厚，这表面的批判只不过是一种可以达到他自己那种目的的手段。用布鲁姆的术语来说，就是以那种防御机制逃离前人的影响，不做他的学徒，而是要与他们平起平坐。

3　19 世纪莎士比亚戏剧演出对惠特曼的启示

成就了惠特曼《草叶集》的平等主义和民粹主义的参与精神；以戏剧为代表的不同的文化风格之间存在着流畅的互动，打破了社会各阶层之间界线。惠特曼说过，年轻的自己"每一个毛孔都在吸收戏剧"，喜欢观看戏剧"一切：高雅的，低级的，普通的"，和林肯一样，惠特曼对莎士比亚同样喜爱。林肯非常熟悉莎士比亚，能一连背诵好好多段不出错误。惠特曼常去的剧院是纽约波威里剧院，在那里他领略了当时戏剧表演所代表的流行的艺术风尚，这种风尚后来在几个不同的层面影响到了他的《草叶集》创作。

1832 到 1836 年，惠特曼常去观看戏剧。那时他还是个生活在布鲁克林和曼哈顿之间的一名少年；另外，还有 1842 年到 1849 年，那个时期，他在纽约，成了一名记者和作家。小的时候得自己买票，只坐在廉价的第三层楼里，也就是顶层楼座里，与粗鲁无礼的人们，或妓女们坐在一起。第二个时期，19 世纪 40 年代做记者的时候，日子好过多了，有了记者的身份，可以坐在剧院一楼的剧场正厅座位上，是剧场里最好的座位。雷诺兹在自己的《沃尔特·惠特曼的美国》一书中详细描写了波威里剧院的演出实况。对我们理解惠特曼所受到的莎士比亚戏剧的影响有相当的帮助：

那时候，那些剧院都很简陋，环境很糟，入口处黑得很，观众坐在一排排粗糙的木凳上。演出时，男人都没有脱帽的习惯（"自己之歌"中的"我"就像他们一样，在室内和外面都戴着帽子）。观众吃着食物。坐在上层的穷人观众时不时地把骨头和残渣剩饭扔到下层的观众区域。演出时，观众和表演者之间的互动是一个惯例。早期剧院虽然也尽力考虑到区分开不同阶层的观众，富人和受人尊敬的人被安排在第二层的包厢里，再上面的人地位和身份就差了一些，而下面的人群则鱼龙混杂，什么人都有，但实际上，一旦演出开始，大家变得都一模一样，一起激动起来，根本分不清这是礼貌还是热情。这些观众里面有些人，比如说，那些

① Whitman, Walt, *Complete Poetry and Collected Prose* . New York: Library of America, 1982. p.1058.

鲍厄里男孩儿们、那些粗人们，与其说是去看戏，不如说是去找开心。他们看到高兴处就拼命地叫好，不开心时就会拼命地喝倒彩，表达他们的赞扬和不满，真的是跟着感觉走。这种喧闹往往会让大家听不见台词。观众中有些人很过分，一旦不满，就会往台上扔东西。大家对此习以为常，谁都不会在意：这是观众的参与习惯。[①]

当时观众和表演者之间亲密关系、演员与观众亲密互动是当时戏剧界的风气，也是当时美国的文化艺术潮流中的倾向。最有趣的是，表演十分自由轻松，多数演出是按照剧本，但不少时候还会出现观众和演员对话，而演员也以插科打诨的方式来对答几句，但很快就回到戏中原题上来了。这是典型的参与式风格，演员和观众的互动往往会充满了人称代词：用“你们”“你们的”或“我”“我们”自由沟通。著名演员朱尼厄斯·布鲁图斯·布斯[②]可以随时随地与观众互动，比现在这种拉开距离的表演要强大得多，场面也自然得多，观众的投入参与都是很自然的事情，所以观众已经变成了戏剧的重要元素，观众可以随时与演员互动，叫好，起哄，不满意时甚至会往台上扔西红柿。演员站在这样一个舞台上，与庞大的观众群相比，处于非常弱势的地位，所以，他们最大的任务是取悦观众，而不是优雅地演出。因为当时竞争非常激烈。演员必须很卖力，观众才能满意。现场冲击力极强。但是演员们都会很累，演出会比较粗糙，但是一定是张力十足，否则就会卖不出票，就会失败、关门。惠特曼非常喜欢布鲁图斯，那是他最喜欢的演员，惠特曼经常表达他对这位演员的感激之情，认为他的表演揭示了艺术家与民主国家人民之间关系：当这种关系非常个人化和亲密时，大家会为这种关系鼓掌；当这种关系变得冷酷或疏远时，大家会予以谴责。

当时的演员生活和演出是紧密结合在一起的，布斯在台上的疯狂有时让他自己都分不清什么是现实什么是戏剧。他做出了许多令人啼笑皆非的事情。当时的报纸往往会报道：那个疯狂的悲剧演员又来了。布斯于 1796 年出生于英国，在 20 岁之前，他就已经可以和埃德蒙·基恩在莎士比亚戏剧演出中一较高下了。布斯赢得了美国最重要演员的声誉—— 同时也是一个有着疯狂癖好的酒鬼。全国各地的剧院经理都知道在演出前把他锁起来，这样他就不会跑到当地的酒馆去了。有一次，他喝醉了去表演，观众发出嘘声，他从舞台上摔了下来。还有一次，在一艘开往查尔斯顿的船上，他到了一个演员朋友自杀的地方，他告诉大家，他要去给他的朋友送个口信儿，然后就跳入水中，大家不得不把他救上来。对惠特曼来说，布斯富有灵感的天才，对传统的藐视，等于是建立了一种新的风格，打破了所有规则和传统，超越了普通层面的生活。布斯给惠特曼的另一个巨大启示是他的激情。惠特曼认为没有人能比布斯更能强烈激发他的整个情感。

20 世纪初表演流派大致有两种：一种是所谓的茶壶派，以彬彬有礼的演员为代表，优雅而精致。演员努力表现的是微妙的情感而不是戏剧性，通常一只手放在臀部，另一只手来回做着手势，就像个茶壶一样。另外一种流派采用了一种狂暴的风格。演员们不得不与那些喧闹的流行文化中的其他娱乐形式的演员相竞争。所以，莎士比亚的戏剧当时根本不是高高在上的经典，而是经常与吟游歌手、闹剧、歌曲等一起同台演出。在这种情况下，布斯拒绝了

---

① 特劳贝尔，《沃尔特·惠特曼在卡姆登》，第一卷，第 455 页。

② 朱尼乌斯·布鲁特斯·布斯（Junius Brutus Booth，1796—1852）是当时美国最著名的悲剧演员，本质上是一个感性而非理性的演员，最能表现野心、嫉妒、仇恨、恐惧和复仇的激情。他出演得最好的角色都是恶棍和半恶棍，如理查德三世、伊阿古、夏洛克等。他的儿子约翰·威尔克斯·布斯也是一位著名的演员，也是刺杀林肯的那位刺客。

古板的茶壶派表演风格，用自己那本能的热情去赢得观众的热情。纽约波威里剧院，演员朱尼乌斯·布鲁特斯·布斯，开始了《理查三世》表演。站在舞台中央，这位身材瘦削的演员，古代的服饰，低着头踱步沉思，观众在痛苦的期待中等待着。然后他抬起头，用自己蓝色的眼睛扫视着礼堂，表情凶狠，他以低沉而坚定的声音，开始了自己的表达，音量逐步加强，观众被激活，直到结束，观众们激动无比，自始至终情绪都随着他的情绪而改变。表演是如此的成功，以至于在打斗的场景中，其他演员都害怕他还真的会杀掉自己。

这就是惠特曼在波威里剧院看到的主演理查三世时的布斯。惠特曼从未忘记那一夜的表演。到了极端的时候布斯会完全投入到自己所扮演的角色之中去，这实际上是 20 世纪斯坦尼斯拉夫斯基的演员修养理念的提前体现。他对这个角色很投入，投入得很彻底，彻底地打破了生活和艺术之间的界限。他入戏很深，大家都很害怕他很可能会像奥赛罗一样，想用枕头闷死扮演苔丝狄蒙娜的女演员，大家不得不把他拉开，怕他真的会一不留神闷死那位女演员。

在 19 世纪 20—30 年代，纽约各个剧院的表演风格，表演方式，现场互动气氛，各阶级观众混杂在一起那种现实情况在某种意义上代表了美国流行文化中自由奔放、常常有些喧闹的风尚，是真正的民主式风气所导致，戏剧与社会阶层之间的关系表明了平等主义和民粹主义占上风的时代特征，给了惠特曼那种参与精神，这种内战前就渗透到美国人的生活中的参与精神成就了惠特曼，他的《草叶集》是这种参与精神繁荣时期的顶峰。以戏剧为代表的不同的文化风格之间存在着流畅的互动，打破了社会各阶层之间界线。它真实地反映了一种前大众传媒文化，在这种文化中，美国人经常自娱自乐，互相娱乐。惠特曼会在公共汽车上吟诵莎士比亚，在海边朗诵荷马和奥西恩[①]，在街上哼唱咏叹调，这些都是当时日常生活中的典型表演。他对诗歌的定义是诗歌必须有激情的互动性的参与。“读者也总是要扮演他们自己的角色。”[②]

4 福特剧院[③]演员刺杀林肯暴乱：演员、高贵目的、真实激情

艺术家如果不能把生活和艺术分开，在今天可能会被人当成是一种很可笑的怪癖为大众所鄙视。但是正是由于这种发生在莎士比亚戏剧表演中演员身上的艺术与生命合而为一的风尚，极为巧合地导致了亚伯拉罕·林肯被刺身亡的悲剧，而又幸运地孕育了惠特曼的《草叶集》中反专制反暴君平等自由民主思想。朱尼乌斯·布鲁特斯·布斯的儿子约翰·威尔克斯·布斯[④]继承了父亲的狂野表演风格。约翰·威尔克斯·布斯，和大多数南方人一样，认为林肯是一个暴君，正在毁灭美国的前途。他的性格之所以与众不同在于他也是一位极为优秀的莎剧演员，在这一点上与他的父亲相同，他入戏也很深。在福特剧院的总统包厢，他用手枪刺杀了林肯，然后从包厢里跳到舞台上逃走，逃走之前都没忘了喊一句他自己演出时常说的台词：“Sic semper tyrannis!”（Thus always to tyrants！这就是暴君的下场！）然后才迅速地跑向外面

① 传说中的爱尔兰诗人。

② 惠特曼，《散文集，一八九二》，第二卷，第 725 页。

③ 福特剧院（Ford's Theater）在美国华盛顿。1865 年 4 月 14 日林肯（Abraham Lincoln）在此遇刺身亡。从那时到如今，该剧院为了怀念林肯，完全维持 19 世纪 60 年代的旧观。

④约翰·威尔克斯·布斯（John Wilkes Booth，1838—1865）是美国戏剧演员，他于 1865 年 4 月 14 日刺杀了林肯。他同情南部邦联，对南北战争的结局甚为不满。在逃脱的过程中被国旗绊倒，跳到舞台上时，大叫：“这就是暴君的下场。”当时全场皆惊。1865 年 4 月 26 日，凶手约翰·威尔克斯·布斯在逃亡途中被警察击毙。

等着的那一匹马，爬上马背逃跑了。这件事情本身在好几个层次上完全是戏剧性的。可惜雷诺兹并没有进一步展开。在笔者看来，首先，他把自己当成了剧中主人公之一，就是暗杀暴君恺撒的布鲁图斯，这个角色他演过很多次。其次，刺杀高贵的林肯总统这种卑鄙行为背后的目的却是杀死暴君这种高贵的念头。最后刺杀这种行为是极为愚蠢的，但是激情是极为真实的。

在林肯遇刺这件悲惨的事件中，其中生活和艺术的交集没能逃过惠特曼敏感的眼睛。他没有办法不把这悲惨事件视为一出激情冲动的悲剧。他总是把这个事件看作是一出感情强烈、充满悲剧性的戏剧。在早期版本中的《草叶集》的情感高峰似乎有着他最崇拜的演员朱尼厄斯·布鲁图斯·布斯风格的影子。惠特曼就像塑造他的那位大演员一样，将激情的表达推向了一个新的高度。

雷诺兹认为，从某种意义上说，惠特曼本人在日常生活和诗歌创作中都是一位演员。这一点对于普通人来说，也许只是一种怪癖特性，但是对于惠特曼这样一个奇特的民族诗人来说，这一点却是一个难得的契机，成功地解决了他诗歌中的大问题，让《草叶集》特点突出、浑然天成、转换自如并包容一切。所以惠特曼才会不仅在大街上和海边慷慨激昂地朗诵戏剧段落，而且为其精妙的诠释感到自豪。东河渡轮的船长托马斯·A.基尔回忆说，惠特曼会用莎士比亚式的独白来取悦同船的乘客，有时他会中途停下来，说“不对！不对！不对！坏演员才是这样的。”[①]然后又重新开始。“在我看来，”基尔说，“说到阅读那些激动人心的诗歌和莎士比亚精彩段落，很少有人能超越他。”他特别喜欢《理查三世》《李尔王》《科里奥兰纳斯》中的那些暴风骤雨般的场景。他会在纽约公共马车上滔滔不绝地朗诵莎士比亚的段落，这反映出他与美国生活中那些充满激情的动荡事件息息相关。他的一个朋友威廉·罗斯科·塞耶称他为：“一个真正深深入戏的装腔作势的人物，一个习惯于扮演某个角色的人，久而久之，他就不再意识到自己是在扮演这个角色了。”

雷诺兹认为这种角色扮演意识可以说明《草叶集》中的“我”的身份这个令人困惑的问题。因为以前有些人认为这是自传体的，认为他的诗歌是其个人焦虑和欲望的忏悔或升华。还有另一些人则认为那纯属虚构。雷诺兹认为，从演员这一点出发，可以从诗人惠特曼和真实的人的惠特曼之间的许多不同之处看出。“真正的”惠特曼，因为参与了种种文化潮流，在很大程度上实际上是一个演员，还有，他的诗歌是他最宏大的舞台，是他最有创意的表演的中心，所以雷诺兹认为用这种方法我们就可以在某种程度上解决这种困惑。

还有 1835 年以后，在同一出戏中扮演多个不同角色的快速转换角色特技开始风靡一时，查塔姆广场的富兰克林剧院尤为如此。这种随意的特性挑战了性别界限。惠特曼诗歌中那些形象多变、雌雄同体的人物在当时并不罕见。在一个角色扮演可以灵活多变的时代，惠特曼证明了自己也拥有和其他人一样的灵活多变能力，随时准备将自己融入多种身份，而不必考虑性别。这确实是莎士比亚戏剧对惠特曼实实在在的影响。可惜的是雷诺兹只从戏剧扮演这个角度提出来惠特曼受到了演出的影响，但实际上，戏剧对于惠特曼来说有更深的影响。

如果我们从叙事学角度出发，如果我们从叙事者内在身份性格成熟发展的角度看去处理这个问题，可能会更适合《草叶集》中那个诗意的“我”的真实情况。当年，人们的身份比较单一、莎士比亚的叙述者隐藏在背后，然而随着时代的发展、大气候的改变、自我意识的

① 乔尔·迈尔森编，《惠特曼和他的时代：基于朋友和同事的回忆、回忆录，和采访的惠特曼传记年表》（底特律，1991），第 33 页。

增强、民主社会里法律所允许的多重自我身份需要在不同的领域里满足不同的要求这样一个现实，使得这个自我，逐步露出水面，并在法律允许范围内，在不同的情景中，展现出自己的不同身份，变为那个明显的诗意人格的我。这就不仅仅是技巧的借鉴而是内核的合理发展了。不过这还是在技巧层面，再从诗人本身所承担的神圣的角色这一更高的层面上说，莎士比亚的那个我已经初具神性，可以在诗歌中征服死亡，让朋友不朽，而惠特曼则将自己作为一个基督一样的人物，不仅要解放自己的朋友，而且要为所有人指出他们的发展的可能性，解放所有的人，神性的内涵也在这个诗意的“我”中得到了充分发展。

虽然当时那种充满真实激情的表演风格起源于国外，但它却具有一种独特的美国特色，在某些方面促成了惠特曼的民族主义。“英国”风格通常有些温顺和势利，“美国”风格则富于热情和民主。后来“英国”风格和“美国”风格之间起了一场冲突，这场让人激动的文化战争的主角是英国演员威廉·查尔斯·麦克雷迪和美国演员埃德温·福里斯特。冲突高潮是著名的阿斯特广场骚乱[①]，在这场骚乱中，不同的表演风格和对国家的忠诚发生了碰撞而导致了冲突。迈克尔·道布森在2007年8月2日《伦敦书评》上面，对这场骚乱的详细分析，此处恕不赘述[②]。

这次骚乱涉及阶级和文化冲突，涉及民族自豪感民族自尊心，这也与惠特曼的《草叶集》在主题上有重合之处。在阿斯特广场骚乱之前，反英情绪时常在剧院爆发。当阿斯特广场歌剧院于1847年11月开业时，它很快成为上流社会炫耀他们优雅的服装和白羊羔皮手套的地方，充满了上流社会势利的气息，污名远传。1849年5月，英国贵族反美演员麦克雷迪宣称他会在那里出演《麦克白》，而美国本土演员福雷斯特也宣布将在民粹主义的百老汇剧院扮演同样的角色，在这样的时刻发生这样的巧合难怪会出麻烦。阿斯特广场的骚乱是一个分水岭，美国文化中爆炸性的元素与克制的、保守的元素发生了冲突；英、美两国的新旧制度发生了冲突。这里边暗含着一个极为深刻的悖论：反对英国的美国的广袤大地需要英国的伟大的莎士比亚，英国的莎士比亚戏剧需要当年逃避英国莎士比亚戏剧的那些美国人的后代的狂放不羁的舞台。

结　语

惠特曼对戏剧的热爱是疯狂的，但也是短暂的。因为，1840年以后，戏剧已经开始变质，不再是全国各阶层共同分享艺术的放松的时刻，而是开始堕落。廉价节目和低俗节目开始流行。可以理解的是，1849年阿斯特广场骚乱之后，惠特曼对戏剧的兴趣急剧衰退。然而，莎士比亚戏剧还是在不同层面上给了惠特曼以不同的影响。这是谁也无法否认的。

作者简介：鲁跃峰，河南师范大学外国语学院讲师，中国外国文学学会莎士比亚研究分会“2019莎士比亚教学与演出国际研讨会”《莎士比亚之夜》总导演，主要从事赛珍珠、惠特曼、莎士比亚、英汉戏剧欣赏表演创作翻译导演研究。

---

① 阿斯特广场歌剧院骚乱：当时两位著名的莎士比亚演员威廉·查尔斯·麦克雷迪（William Charles Macready, 1793—1873）和埃德温·福雷斯特（Edwin Forrest, 1806—1802）之间的小争执演变为1849年5月10日的那场暴力血腥的阿斯特广场公众骚乱，美国历史上最致命的一次，致25人死亡，100人左右受伤。

② 迈克尔·道布森（Michael Dobson），《伦敦书评》，2007年8月2日（London Review of Books, August 2nd 2007）。

第四编 续史贯珍

莎士比亚与弥尔敦

George Eloit（著）　任于锡（译）

诗的大路，经过了弥氏诗歌的中心又经过了莎氏的作品而前进；这莎氏并非十九世纪与我们同时存在的莎氏，而是被认为天赋以高超于弥氏诗歌生命的。这种平凡的信仰，或者就是现在在我们与我们所需要新诗的趋势间的一种界限。在诗歌中对于不自觉和自由份子的十九世纪热，现在已经变成一种弱症，可是反把莎氏培养肥了。我们真是不幸的很，关于诗人个人创作的态度，他给我们极少的说明，而弥氏却给我们极多。为此莎氏的沉默和弥氏的饶舌，很可认为是外来的情形，因为都是字面的学识太多，以致太直解了。关于他们个人创作上一种卓越的蒙昧，我们可以从莎氏读进去而从弥氏读出来。在这一方面，他二人被比的好像太高了，也太勉强了，很易使人不相信；尤其是常识告诉我们说一位诗人无论说什么或是不说什么论到他的作品必需永远认为其中有很多的意义。事实是这样假设我把莎氏与弥氏的名句并列在一起，那么很明显的是都有这同样自知与不自知的性质。当我们整个去比较一个伟大的莎剧和《失乐园》的时候，我想，并非结果不同。设若我们从莎氏浪漫主义的崇拜里把他举出来，放在世界名诗的光明中解释一下，可以臆断的说莎氏正式的自知他写《麦克倍司》时候所作的事情，就如同弥氏正式的不知他写《失乐园》时候所作的事情一样。

这种背驰的关于弥氏的臆断，因为他与莎氏间有假对比的缘故，自然造成《失乐园》整个形式是机械的模仿的一种见解。这篇诗一半认为是逊于荷马的叙事诗，一半是认为逊于但丁的宗教幻象。实在，它是来源于这两种形式；但天然的它又是一个新的独立的形式。是弥氏对他所作事情重要的蒙昧所创造出来的。弥氏在他曾谈到的所谓“英雄诗”中并未有这种新形式适当的记载。他也从未给一个适当的名字。代替这种名字，我们可以叫它作象征的叙事诗。问题是弥氏想试验着无论他知道与否去找一种诗的新形式，从其中能够造出一个叙事诗纲要的精解来用于极端的象征观念的主张。他愿意写一首“意义丰富”的诗，意义极丰富，“就没听说过”的，但他并不愿写首不周密的讽刺诗，直接像他的老师施本修一样。他对思想的检束，他年年想得到诗歌紧密而合理的形式的努力，有了增厚他作风里象征程度的效果。他的诗，全体与细分，是极暗示读者之能事的，这反而是他专注意到形式而未同时注意到暗示方面的缘故。在另一方面，他并非最先构成诗歌，然后像他说的再不自然的把作风加在我们常认为他那种字义过敏的语气上。无论在思想或作风上都是一种先觉的了解，这是要证实在形成他象征叙事诗观念的唯一动作里他正发展着他向真实方法去的作风。他培养“自由发生”正确“和谐诗歌”的思想和意象，也培养正确紧张的和感情的诗词。一个预思的伟作潜伏在他的“未预思的诗歌”下面。他构成他的诗，构成他的精神，是在他向着那“思赐”的诗神的时候，他说：

她夜间未得恳请来访至，
并且口授给我不留意的或者容易
感悟我未预想到的诗。

比英国别的诗人更显著的一点是他经过沉思走进自然里去。现在很多的作家都是经过一种沉思境地的苦搜枯肠而堕入自然。这当然是一条旧路。但现在它成为被公认为极广大极独断追求一种改新想象的方法。事实是经过十九世纪文学流下来的自然思想的混杂思潮，现在分解成一种油雾遮暗了自然思想的高处。弥氏，所以，是一位在现代富于诗思真正革新的人们所应研究的学者以上的英国诗人。他是这种革新的一个伟大的提议者，设若莎氏有几分用尽了诗思，那么弥氏就把它革新了。他完成了顶好的诗歌盲目的努力到现代的事务上。用自由而广涵传说的态度，他创造诗歌的一个新形式。并且当某部分诗人已经置妥了十八世纪新古典派因习主义基线的时候，他却开了自由诗思一时最高最有力的根源，那是无甚价值的，因为因习的自由吓示为现代诗壤最坚牢的结果。

但莎氏最高的自然思想也有和弥氏同样的性质且是同方得到的。我们应当避免些这二位诗人中间荒诞无稽的对冲。规检的莎氏在一方面被上世纪的诗人和批评家崇拜着，使他惊讶的是设若他不能再在舞台上出现。爱默生的朋友，西浪逊阿尔克特，在莎氏作品里发现了一种超宗教的幻想。沙尔司莱姆是很能合乎中庸之道当他宣布说“基督的忽然再现使我们跪倒——莎氏，使我们起立”。他不记载接待弥氏拜访适合现代的态度，——而抵进或者跑进“过度的狂想”中去。设若莎氏走进这屋来，无疑的我们都要起立；但这种致敬莎氏他自己倒反觉着很不适了。他的精神也不喜欢加莱尔的要求说弥氏的想象同他个人比较（而含意是，同加莱尔的）是十分机械的，因为莎氏精神中惊人的糅性，是十九世纪试验再生不出来的，而集中在批评纯洁的思想上。莎氏，不像他很多的崇拜者们一样，他有个人目的范围异常明白的认识，并且他是第一位从弥氏认识出他个人不能达到的一种诗力（包括诗的自由思想）一致的极度。

然而，经过剧场图书馆学校和书院的作用，在我们与弥氏中间发生了莎氏非常骄矜的一个形象。萧翁和其余偶像毁灭者要刺穿那形象的尝试是预言的。但这些说“箭”都没有用。他们仅会刺到这巨像的身旁。在《它下部叆叇的边上》：

因为最崇高的山，
并不对星去冠戴它的尊严，
它那牢固的足迹放在海里，
把众天之天造成它的住址，
仅留下它下部叆叇的边际，
给人类去作践踏的寻觅。

对他个人这种壮严的形象莎氏的肺能像公鸡一般的叫颤。阿诺特的商籁体（十四行），是在上世纪中叶产生的，表示出对莎氏崇拜的高潮。但是在诗人的批评中以后，英国文学的大学教授们都出来了，“他们牢固的足迹，放在海里”。他们结合的努力有地方能够捉住非批评家仰慕的一船重货。虽然“在人类事务中是有潮的”。船必需到海里去，而这“最崇高的山”

必需向着地平退去。当我们的诗歌从它现在的浅峡里释放出来的时候，它前程一个重要的形势全恃乎在实景里看莎氏作品最普遍的努力。

但是，因为我们过度的个人主义，使普通的想象仍然被莎氏个体人物似真的束缚着，并且被他作风的幻变流动着，在这种作风里人物是活动的，喘气的，而有他们的存在。例如：我们可以拥护“奥赛洛悲剧”，因为它好像是把它的纯直给了我们。但是我们仍然很坦白的被它主要人物奇异的“心理学”（因为这是我们现在常叫的名词）所迷惑住了。在这整个作品中我们真并不发生多少兴趣。我们可以觉到在它的语气中有某种急进的不一致—— 这是因为在此时各方面有一种积极抵抗的意义，他在此正努力着，但并未十分成功，限制他幻思的范围成为一种心灵上的污光。我们还可以进一步觉到在动作的极心有一种巨烈的非实性，戏剧抵抗自由的可信处。我不是说情形一定如此。问题是这种困影，虽然他们关于整个作品，而实在就是莎氏诗人的价值所在，大概能够觉到而未必向难普遍兴趣的前部。因为我们的兴趣还未很决断的从奇异的意象和人物的创造者莎氏发生出来而到了整个诗的作家莎氏。对他这种观察的一个适合的基础是被十八世纪批评主义立下的，但是不久浪漫的洪流又把它拂过了。在这洪流的水痕里，一种过度的怀疑主义发生到相当程度，莎氏“大流的冲力”，现在仍然迷住了很多人，可是已经被少数人讽讯的发问了。这种想象的真正流露将至若何限度，而这种完全修辞的能力又将有何结果，这重要问题已经从最近拿莎氏当作一个普遍的伊利沙白时代写剧家的研究里得到了相当的显著。但这种研究，结果因为抗议他诗意的缘故，而研究发掘他，使所有的舞台把戏，所有的浅薄动机，都变成最后的儿戏，把它们散布在我们面前的棹上，并且把他的修辞形成了假的浮雕。设若我们愿意见见真正莎氏以前著作的习惯，我们就被请来看它们在面前的集会。在这次集会里，阿诺特的莎氏——

别人等候我们的问题。你却在自由
我们发问又发问，你只微笑而默幽……

是被拒入内的。我们现在明了的是真莎氏在等候我们的问题，并且他是一个太着实际的人而永远是高尚地在“默幽寂静着”。十八世纪初叶梦幻的莎氏，只致意于汉默雷脱，否司托夫，麦克白斯夫人，道倍雷，与其他幻变的呼唤，是很可靠的一种浪漫派的幻想。但是我们不能就满意来把那个魔鬼代替上一个在电线上活跃戏剧家的骨骼。我们完全应当被逐着走向伟大的诗人那里去，他是在这两个凡俗的人物以后：我的意思是莎氏在他每个佳剧里努力着去“形成”一种坚固的诗意—— 一种“非冷淡的理智所能了解”的观念，但是由理智而形成的。他可以很盲目的得到他的中心思想，而多少破碎的，用许多修辞和时间的导演把它构造出来。但它的存在成为剧中诗的价值的主要来源。它是唯一能供给他想象之流的泉水，而这水流是既非幻惑的又非寻常的。并且他的思想就像他的作品一样前进深入而澄清了里尔和麦克倍斯。

至于，这两个剧形成思想的结果已经比较的微小了。这种有力的形成观念是厌恶近代幻想的主要趋势。里尔被称为“伟大的童话”；麦克倍斯为“伟大的准乐剧”。这是对它们的现代看法一个最好的撮要。很多爱读莎氏的人心里接受了而他们口里可还是拒绝着。他们不感觉这两个剧像完全的诗一样，整个的影射出它们的前辈《汉默雷脱》和《奥赛洛》来；而他们感觉出一种个人主义控诉决然的哀微。但后两个悲剧是莎氏对前两个最深彻的批评。它们把他的辩证输送在《汉默雷脱》和《奥赛洛》的心理学覆育着“灰白愁思形成的病态”悲情里；并且设若这剧主要，设若他要成功一个悲剧而使其整个的结果伟大的时候，这种像伊亚勾和汉默雷脱精细而狡狯的主角—— 这种“青年的才智”—— 是应当被废弃的。

《里尔》悲剧，人物简单而情感紧张，是莎氏离开《奥赛洛》闷室的束缚而写的。它是逃到较大的真实里去的。哈兹里特曾觉到了，他说在《里尔》这篇剧里莎氏是很美的被捉在他个人想象的网里了。更确切的一点是，莎氏在此处跑出了曾经缠绕他直到现在的那个网：他努力地默思而使他个人自由，并且能很自由地追随着他想象的高流。他确曾被很多的灵巧“围绕住”了，而现在呢，在他能够作出“他脑筋中的序言”以前，它们已经开始编成剧了。在《汉默雷脱》和《奥赛洛》中，他并未深切地注意到整个的故事。所以在哪些剧里滑稽博笑的美术特性表现出来了，而特别是在主要题旨破碎或暧昧的几段里。当然在《里尔》和《麦克倍斯》里有很多失错的地方，但是作者的心并未注意到；他的较高的想象压住了它们，预先占据了全题。

莎氏重要悲剧《麦克倍斯》的题旨实在同《失乐园》的题旨一样：是权力欲望与和平力量之争。这种题意自然表现在莎氏的早年作品里，我们可以说现在是继续表现着的。但是他把它几乎很凶的推到前景上而用他一种空前绝后集中的力量把他自己放在里面，好像它是完全了—— 好像他忽然觉到这个题意，只有它，才能要表现，而且是超过他灵魂所能达到的思想以外的标准。我们应当同样的去想象，创造他象征的想象，而影响到他身上去。换言之，我们必须同样重要的去接近《麦克倍斯》的情形如同我们需要接近他伟大的继续者弥氏的魔王一样。我们需要拿全诗概念的眼光去看他。

以梗概简明去论《麦克倍斯》悲剧无疑是十分古典的；但是它的象征特质是中古的。而《汉默雷脱》是中古的故事浸入了现代独人剧中的。这种剧是暗示的，也是夺魂的；但以全体论，不管现代训诂上一切同情的作品，它是很明显的并未成功。莎氏他自己，不像他的崇拜者们，并不对它十分热诚。他拥护他的结构的中古观念：

我已经这样听说了，并且有一部分信仰；
但是，瞧，清晨披上赤褐色的外大氅
蹒跚在东方高速山岭的露滴上。

他仍然是狂喜在大自然鲜明的光里，在他那时候晨曦曾经照耀在中古的事物上；他的心很高兴地去排列人类动机纷扰的全幕，而于引渡的栈道无关。在《麦克倍斯》趋向于想象的中古方式以前刚引的和雷瘦的言语是莎氏普通态度一个够好的表征。然而在《麦克倍斯》里，他用一种使他可以在一五九〇年笑的辩证把他个人投入这种方式里，当时他就开始作成了《汉默雷脱》。

《麦克倍斯》如同《失乐园》一样都有那种文艺复兴时期最高的满足他旅行到最后绝顶的梦想。所以就成了《麦克倍斯》无比的带象征特质的作风。作者梦想的极度使他的诗堆满了象征的印象。这些印象，同现代个人主义深切地合作，把它在舞台上歌剧的风味借给了这个戏剧。麦克倍斯夫妇的言语并非“舌讷”的讲出来；他们凄惨精神的性格是被两个著名俳优的艺术家详论而扮演过的，他们取了角色而引得观众的注意。我们都爱集中这种“英雄”与“女侠”的病态心理；并且因为这种特点它自己就不是诗里惊人的作风上一个充足的根源，这种心理必需在我们诚实的时候，完全或十分打击我们有点像假的战争一样，“表示出满是呐喊”，而并不太多，表示出我们回忆的时候，单个的人类“在舞台上傲然阔步的消磨他的时光”，而又马上转下去，或者，转进“在一切东西里运动”的一种力里去。

事实是我们拿《伊亚勾》和《汉默雷脱》的态度去看《麦克倍斯》。应当看这篇剧诗《麦克倍斯》像看剧诗《汉默雷脱》的谈话一样，而注意它思想和作风整个的方式。《汉默雷脱》是戏剧心理的作品。《麦克倍斯》是戏剧象征的。麦克倍斯一方面他个人就是一个象征的人物，—— 不仅在程度方面—— 那是与汉默雷脱没什么关系的。假设《汉默雷脱》遗去汉默雷脱而不成剧的话，那就等于麦克倍斯没有戏剧全体的动作而不成角色一样。我们应当把它拉回来记住。经过他的言语而表现惊人的印象，应当认为，不但是他自己脑筋复杂主要的诗歌所能完成的中古与古典派混杂的壮严。它指明了现代诗的大路。它的意义是想象的两种不同方式的一个真正接合：极大的严密性与象征的激烈性。这位诗人的想象转动在一个十分精密的轨道里，像一颗行星围绕了它的太阳一样。

他觉到，在他故事动作的每一点里，他中心思想的推动—— 设若我们以带有柏拉图意义的“思想”这名词去解释，立刻指明它是属于整个心灵，想象和智识的东西。这种思想，就是在诗人好像远离它的时候，也在每个插话里放进它的光明。这种插话可以完全在它自己的轴上分解；诗人可以耑致意于精细的个别的我们所谓现代的考究—— 例如在刚要杀党堪以前麦克倍斯和他的短刀一幕里；或是在刚要杀无辜的夏娃以前魔王和他的毒蛇一幕里！但每段插话里珍贵的力量是来自支配他时的那个“思想”，使诗人努力得到向心的推力。它是这样地被在他面前特别的人类环境占据了，所以他不能屈下于唯一的象征主义，他也就是这样地预先被一个伟大的人类思想占据了，所以他不能屈下于他的幻想。它经过幻想而流露出真正“世界上没有的”光明。

诗并不是纯粹有诗意的，当她很知道有像十九世纪初叶那种神秘的光辉的时候；或者，当，按结果同现在一样，她知道追随下意识的光明的时候。上文讲的那两个伟大诗意插话的象征性质是，至其极的，超意识。麦克倍斯的短刀是一把“心理的刀”，而魔王的蛇也是一条心理的蛇，这是诗人不能自觉地注意到一个比较完全的解释。人心是独自在傀儡以上出现的，人心是在它最可怕的进退两难里。这是“心在继续狂喜里的痛苦”，在人类最大的欲望与不承认和平的力量之间的一种痛苦，而和平的力量单独地能克服这种欲望使它适合于人类的快乐——这种力量是“宇宙间人类在忿怒之下找到唯一的和平”，像弥氏这样的说法，比他知道的还多哩。

麦克倍斯，自然，很显明的是“忿怒的人类”。我所谓和平的力量在他的故事中是没有范围的。魔王的力量掌握了一切而使空气黑暗。在弥氏的伊甸乐园里，恶魔沿着地皮“像一片低下蔓延的黑雾”跑进来了；在《麦克倍斯》里，从开端它就翱翔“于浓雾与污秽的空气中”。最显明的理由是莎氏写了个浪漫派的剧，而浪漫的和戏剧的魔鬼人生对他与他的观众有一种自然的诱惑：它成了舞台上的好材料。但这不算这首诗的特别伟大处：因为辩证声调的严酷，想象逻辑的是可怕，使他发展而表示出邪欲的力量。在这个题目上莎氏在他能写《麦克倍斯》以前作了很多的苦思。寻常的莎氏与诗人的莎氏最近很怪的彼此分离了。传奇家把他当做想象的怪物；最近考古家表彰他是位实行者。近代审美家，最注重这种区分，当他浸入艺术家的梦的时候高兴把他想象成完全脱离公民天性的个人。但最显明是事实是莎氏的天性一致集中在他少有的判断力上。一方面他把这判断力运用到经济的事业上，另一方面用在他想象的事业上；虽然，他被环境促进以后感到在他作品里常把他的判断力放在一边而在他的事业里却永没有过（有事实的记载证明）。可是当他组成《麦克倍斯》的时候他并未把它放在一边。他最后奋然决绝地把他的判断力带到那错误欲念的题目上去。

事实对平常读者与观众的心就够明显的了。但还有人反对，他们，受了现代艺术家定理的影响，认为莎氏在此处的态度仅是一个戏剧的虚构；还有，另走极端的人看出他由麦克倍斯的口里喊出他个人对人类的失望："人生不过是个走路的影子"，等等。这一段，关于这个剧的全部动作，不仅表示出他对麦克倍斯的判断，并且表示出普通人类天性不能统治欲念的结果，所以若以为在这首诗里莎氏的态度正是在他悲剧时期的早年作品里所表现罪恶深思的结果是不正确的。我敢说在那些作品里流露着连续不断的谈话是作者离开附近的故事用一种刺激的活泼把个人所有肉体上承受的痛苦和罪恶都说出来了。但是那些连续不断的谈话在《麦克倍斯》里并没有接续下去；那种话是落伍的了。莎氏在此处超出了他自己的感觉。他的思想凌驾于对恶魔灵性一个明显现象所生的"千万自然惊惧"之上。他拿它当做难以束缚的欲望，征集想象而破坏了人类快乐和平。以前他自己这种作恶的天性里他就没有这样被恶魔的力量很快地预先占据过。所以他失去了辛辣的滋味，那是以前他认为加给别人一种"鄙陋，忍耐，应受蹴踢"的痛苦。莎氏以沉静的态度去观察麦克倍斯加给无辜人的罪恶。他被每个人类天性悲惨的堕落所占据着。他很超然的看出意志错误的人在他内心仅有一种恶浊情感的观念。所以这剧中可怕的讽刺集中在这样一个事实里：麦克倍斯把一个纯粹外部情感方面的解释当做辩证；还是莎氏自己，在动作全体里，用在人性内部的："我们仍在此处有判断力"。

自然在莎士比亚悲剧里已经找到判断人类动作的"精神规律"或是"道德通行的法度"或这种同类名词意义的人是合理的。反对这种主张的批评家也应当反对莎氏用他的悲剧引诱我们去沉思人类情海里唯一的意义。在无边无际的海里，没有真雷。而常常在莎氏悲剧英雄里却有很多剧场上的暴风雨，"惊雷似的呼喊""狂怒的呻吟"和"溺风眼泪"。但是由他可以听到心的深处，它是人类感情撞到岸边的奔腾澎湃巨浪之声。这个岸也已经为莎氏在十六世纪中被道德思想的大复兴早就造坚固了。有时候，无疑的，他带着一种公民的满意态度站在那岸上，点缀着灵巧的诗感，这种诗感在现在很能使公民高兴，并且很能激动萧伯纳和反公民的全族。但我们应当注意在莎氏作品里出平民的绮丽的地方就是它的浪漫情热主义的全部。因为他站在岸上这样安舒，他能够很容易被海里风浪的纯洁壮观引起愉快的情绪来。这种现象在现在我们客厅里的原始人（和原始女人）中再现了。然而他们咬那只喂他们食物的手：他们蔑视那种供给他们和纵情他们文学幻想中病态情热主义在安全地带的平民道德。毕竟，莎氏的态度走向传统习俗的简单标准是属于一种伟大□品的简单标准。他把这些标准放进他的想象中，并且拿它们去修养而在它们以上。设若他是很幼稚很习俗地去写：

虽然公平是你的辩护，请想想这个吧
在公正的程序中，我们没人
可以看见拯救。
……

他仍然是在向着他最伟大的悲剧极端辩证的途上走去。这个悲剧和他的动机有同样的思想在纯美的形式里：

我们可以跃过将来的生活。但在这些情形当中
我们仍然在此处有判断力。
……

他走向“精神的规律”最好的态度好像是一种淡泊克情的信仰，剥夺了淡泊的傲慢性而接近了极端的基督教，但是并未很为基督教的和平意义所照明。这种东西并不在他的天性里，也并不在他戏剧作品的特性里，去捉住了最高人类和平的概念，而是“在忿怒之下为人类找出的和平”。但是在《麦克倍斯》悲剧里他不能够想到目睹人类情感中的大怒不发，同时，沉入唯一和平力量的境界内。他对这故事的概念要求的是这种力量应当有战栗的闭幕。还要有战栗的蒙蔽。那才是这剧的特别伟大处。它氛围中未曾有的紧张并非完全来自极端邪恶的认识。而是来自极端和平的认识。天永远是在“经过夜的黑幕窥着喊呼，抑制，抑制”。最初，麦克倍斯对于和平的人生有一种很强的认识。他并不像莎氏所臆想的那个天生异常简单，凡俗，而有气质的人物。这种观念把这个戏剧剪成了碎片，而在平常的读者并不注意他全部结果的旨趣。除非我们承认著者把他的“自由意志”集中在麦克倍斯的思想上，这个很单纯的并不是系统化。麦克倍斯被认为一个十分平常的人，他，用他意志可怕的动作，使他个人不平常。我们看出他努力使他的想象力去服务他的大欲望。并且远离开了他那和平的事实。那么，当这种欲望实行的时候，和外界没有真正威逼他成功的东西之时，我们听到他说：

顶好同亡人在一起
我们可以把他们（亡人）
送到和平去以便得到我们的和平
殊胜于心受着痛苦而卧
在不安的狂喜中。

在弥尔敦的作品里魔鬼有同样的失望，造成适方象征叙事诗的作风，展露在无限的景色里：

我所逃的路是地狱；但我自身就是地狱；
并且，在最低的深处，一层更低的
威吓着阔开着要吞食我的深处，
我遭受着这个地狱好像一个天堂。

在这两方面的结果是相同的：“唯有在破坏里我才找到我惨酷思想的安慰”是魔王说的。在两方面发言者都是变成一个最可怕的讽刺标准，因为在人类天性中永远是：要完成我们快乐中的继续努力——或是我们的生活力，设若我们愿意暂时这样叫的话——必须与我们的和平冲突，而引导到混沌的途上去；并且以后，我们思想的努力真的生存在混沌中，思想自然的移动宛如我们天生的元素，而不是在众心之心里最可恨可怕的那个东西。当莎氏写《麦克倍斯》的时候，他已经完全觉到那种讽刺。那是一个用戏剧形式表现出来最好的题旨，并且它在《麦克倍斯》里比在《失乐园》里更使我们情绪有坚信力。另一方面，讽刺所根据的和平题旨是“非戏剧的”，而且需要《失乐园》的形式。《麦克倍斯》的戏剧象征是走向《失乐

园》的叙事象征一条路上去的。我们说莎氏天才的主要趋势，必须从他写《理查第三》（一篇在读《麦克倍斯》以前的预备作品）那几年开始，我们知道，就是向着我们在《麦克倍斯》里找出来的那时的艺术走去，而这种趋势又是整个文艺复兴精神发展的一部分向着我们在《失乐园》里找出来的那种诗的艺术走去。

这种发展已经被现代诗浸没在艺术里，在另一方面，被“历史力量”的影响重压在诗史上的嗜好所蒙蔽。那么，这种公认为清教徒的“历史力量”已经表现出绝对与艺术和诗相抗衡。阿诺特很推崇这个见解，以诗与文化的概念置于道德行为的概念之上，并且用后者与清教徒的鄙陋和悭吝去联合。矫正这种均衡，他主张“行为是人生的四分之三”，并且在他晚年，觉到颓靡自然主义的散布，他主张“背抗道德概念的诗是违叛人生的诗”。但是不幸这位大批评家他自己太受自然主义的影响。他类别人性，像博物学分类家一样。他隔着善恶，并且赞美它！他使它好像成为：不是一个有生气而永久存在的物质，而是一个必需而不甚有趣的性质，—— 人生树的“四分之三”淡然地支持作诗的纤枝嫩叶之坚木。那么，我们 可以这样说，德行（以这个字的含义讲）是仅占全树大小的四分之一或百分之一。它是有生命的一种白木质汁。叶子不能用它去分配。当芽般的小作家把它用在木质的公民里的时候，他们不过为一个有热病的生命，不久便变跛了。这就是为什么二十世纪初叶很盛行的诗歌运动现在成了红叶——

它是同类中最后的一个
在能舞多久就舞多久地舞着哩。

它不仅是“背抗道德概念的诗……远叛人生”。它是隔离诗歌唯一生命的诗。这种辩证，或是与此相接近的理论，曾支配了我们从阿诺特以来两位伟大批评思想家，伊尔文巴比与保罗爱穆尔。虽然人们曾感透了人类想象的真理比他更深些，但并不像他那样想象的阔大。他们搜查和图绘那块他已经证明过和割过边界的中地：就是道德的智慧和想象合一的深处。现代诗思在我们能有无论哪种伟诗的再生以前必须经过这块地方。这个事实每年愈来愈明显了。但是诗唯一概念不幸继续的反抗宗教和道德的思想。特别是美国，这种清教徒主义盲目的反动坚持地存在下去。

清教徒运动（与稗史所云）在英国文艺复兴时代使诗歌从她的疾进奔驰上坠下马来。她在莎士比亚的时候挥舞着，并且被英国清教徒主义捉住的那个阿克狄若望不幸被烧，假若没烧完，还在它狰狞的火里。但是稗史缺乏那种那所要求的似是而非的事实。若望颠覆在火里太突然了。并且火本身就是不可信的敌对。较真实一点的神话是这样，诗的火，采用清教徒主义的力量，不可思议地降在“历史的势力”上。这个火来在英国天然的祭坛上，燃尽了石头和牺牲品，甚而和那些伊里加的门徒在一起保险敌抗世间所有的火海。在英国文艺复兴时代诗的精神—— 就是自从伟大希腊时期以来它最有力的一个现象—— 包括人生之全力，培养它们而以它们来发育自己。这些力量是如此复杂广布以致诗的艺术在散漫里有失踪之险。同时它唯一的阔大性能使它内部发展一个坚强的批评力。诗变成它自己散漫的批评，而努力集中着。换言之，在十七世纪韵文中表现严格的集中力，必须首先注意到，不是“宗教和道德要素”的结果，而是一种自然的发展，在诗力的高峰—— 因为是特殊的高峰—— 诗不能在它自己相当的国土（范围）内完成。

因此有了从《汉默雷脱》的特殊散漫到《麦克倍斯》的特殊集中的莎氏转变。在规则的时候，几乎，诗人用道德改善人生的方法来调和他的浪漫故事；因而在他的戏剧里他整个的伦理主张都是动摇不定的。换言之，《汉默雷脱》有英格罗撒克逊民族中流行的浪漫态度和清教徒感情的十字记号一类的东西。在《汉默雷脱》的表面上，莎氏举起了一面反照当代“年龄与体形”的镜子。在《麦克倍斯》里他集中努力去通透当时的思想和辩证的深处：是“我们在此仍有判断”的辩证；是在与人类和平战争里讽刺人类欲望的思想。这种人生观，是从象征文艺复兴的全部经验里生出来的可以正式称为清教徒（而不是“清教徒的”）。在《麦克倍斯》里我们看出诗的火焰降落到清教徒在极度专心时建造的思想上而采取为已有。这种进行上的继续和完成就是弥尔敦《失乐园》的步骤。莎氏从《汉默雷脱》到《麦克倍斯》的转变是到了普通运动的顶端，在英国诗里（可以说）从一五八〇年和一六六〇年前进，它把象征的叙事诗从施本修仙女王无先例的散漫里带到《失乐园》苛刻的集中里去。

施本修的伟诗耑论伊利沙白时“完全绅士”的思想，参透在莎氏经营的前半期作品里，而在《汉默雷脱》里完成这种思想。《汉默雷脱》的人格可以认为是一个亚沙王所代表的多方面人格形式的试验发生在人类和诗的或然范围内，但是，若在施本修手中，这种试验就在一种多倍象征主义惊人的阵势里失踪了。文艺复兴的诗普通是代表在一般人天性以外和以上的欲望里透露着一个人的全部天性。施本修，实在是，开始经过插话和角色的阔大全景去解释人性中所有的显著性质，而很宽舒的集中在亚沙王理想的人物里。他愿用“能力是多么无限”来表示出“人是块什么东西”，同样的欲望在莎氏的作品里活动着，当他写《汉默雷脱》的时候；并且引起一个同仙女王一样主要的进行来。他写过一套散漫的对话和独语集中在汉默雷脱人物上，而以伟大的嗜好，代表在另外一个人格以后的一种性质。这套话，因为它在莎氏的想象里奔驰着，真正无穷尽呵。在戏剧里我们觉到他可以很容易的插上几段外加的句子（三幕一景百二十九行）。因为事实，此剧已经被特殊的减成适合台上两点钟以内的限制了。而哥德关于麦扣收的注解最好是用于汉默雷脱：莎氏被迫着把他杀了（是用一个不适当歌舞剧的方法），不然他也要把剧来弄坏了。

汉默雷脱王，是亚沙王的承继者，受益于剧形所要求的压缩性。但是在戏剧的《汉默雷脱》里，如同在象征的亚沙尔里，人类代表的想象被繁多复杂软化了。很明显的是莎氏他个人的意见：他次大的作品，《奥赛洛》的形式表示出《汉默雷脱》推论方法的一个忽然激变。以《汉默雷脱》的全部特性和方法论是莎氏作家在他前半事业里多方面发展的灿烂终曲。同时他很可以回顾一下认为它是一件有点古怪“费力的巧事”。自然汉默雷脱个性神秘的复杂又是莎氏的副产物。他对于现代个人主义者已经努力摘出的神秘思想是显然并不经心的。当他写剧的时候，他自己的希望是在乎所谓人这块东西的“无限能力”：是这个而不是常来往于幕间汉默雷脱的特征。事实是在这篇诗里把人类属性惊人的阵容集合起来，但不在《汉默雷脱》人物里表现集中，或很疏的找出焦点来。光线的放射超过了他而永不能相遇。它们向着人格伟大而多荫的周围放射出去；而莎氏用一种挫折的显意在戏剧的全部里追求着。

从这种热烈的实验里他去明了去追求是无用的，或是至少诗的康庄大道，而特别是悲剧的诗，趋向于中心去而不趋向于人性的周围—— 不向人的“无限能力”去而向穿过他身体中心的那重要部分去；因此他的最伟大处和最鄙陋处都在不可分的表现出来：“知道是很像一尊神—— 但是……这仅是遗骸的一种精华”，自然这种内在的部分，也是轮廓上的考查，在《汉默雷脱》悲剧里传递出来：在接近这剧的大段以后的地方。我们看见了人性的遗骸，它不是被“情梦”激动着“兽性的埋没”；而是一个“纯粹合理”的题旨，按此已超出其上，和着淡泊的兴奋态度从诗歌里流到《汉默雷脱》的尾声去，“余皆默然”了。但是这种人类本性的重要二面（二重人格），设若可以这样叫法，是在《汉默雷脱》的背景里保存着的。它在下边两个悲剧里表现出来。在《麦克倍斯》里它握住戏台前面的中心。在《失乐园》里它表现着成为宇宙的中心—— 宇宙的是因为当它已经发展了一世纪而在它全力的高潮里被幻变的思想充分寻找着的时候，它出现了。

总而言之，《失乐园》不是一个在诗意的情感方面对清教徒的征服，而是一个文艺复兴的实行。它的缺点是，像弥尔敦他自己说的一样（卷四的序）：表现着他对他的伟大题目给了不适当的意见。但是在他辩证题目的本身，他故事的全部思想，是十分诗意的一方面，他同样是合理的。它仅是一个愈变愈显著的题目最终的集中，如文艺复兴的诗，在它适当地代表人类的努力里，从四周走到人性的中心去。少年的弥尔敦看出了人类感情与和平的冲突是很显明地在他老师施本修的作品里表现着。但是设若莎氏，像他走向《麦克倍斯》一样地注意到《汉默雷脱》特殊散漫的时候，弥尔敦也像他年幼时为创作“英雄诗”题的缘故去寻找材料和待时成功的时候，一定可以觉到在仙女王里有像混沌一样的东西。无疑的经过思考以后他会拒绝亚沙王的故事当作他自己的诗。事实是他必需用可怕的困难经过文艺复兴带有诗意的混沌而找到他自己的出路——

被天上的诗神教着冒险去走下
这个黑暗的斜坡，并且再走上来，
经过些苦难和罕遇的颠踱。

这些“天上的诗神”用生命中期困苦的方法去教他。此时他从诗歌里转了方向，是件被浪漫派的□□者悲伤的事，而他却有带诗意的幸运。他自己一生必需敌抗人类国家宗教政治各方面的混沌；他内在的每一个形成能力都必须努力地去练习；尤其是在他能用尽辩证去创造他伟大的诗以前。他必须有伟大宗教和道德的能力去形成个人人格的经验，并且他必须拿诗意的美丽去形容它们。在他诗幻的中心有这种事实，对他，诗歌和道德是既不混杂而又不分离。自从他这时候以后，爱迭生派的作家会试验着“使道德时髦化”，而惠特曼派的作家则用续文的方法努力使它不时髦。但是弥尔敦的目的—— 至少在我们现在还是这样很叹美那个深奥而不知的地方—— 永不是道德家的或非道德家的教训。他的目的是用象征叙事诗的形式表现人格内部形成的神秘性。当他说无论何人若愿写首真实的诗“应当他自己就是一首真诗”的时候，他是用很谦逊而非人称的说法。但是事实是他所蓄志想作的新诗必需他应当创造他个人的生活比无论哪个诗人所作的都要努力些。文艺复兴的重要题目是他从杂乱里抽出来的，是这样，在它要在诗歌里得到一个著名的形式以前，它必须在他自己生活里很显著的挣扎到底。它要求的是他应当满饱其眼福，而后再把它遮蔽起来。他必须“感觉”出那个“极重要像灯的光明”是在文艺复兴诗歌阔杂光辉的中心里—— 是一个人类伟大和平超越的伟大感情的神秘。莎氏在这个闪光内所见到现而隐的东西是经过《失乐园》大幕里全部光和暗的更替而确实感觉到的：人类如何就是“尘土的精华”（卷七第五二五行）—— 而且当他的明了都属于和平的时候“在明了中如何像一位神”。

弥尔敦的诗途真是“困难而罕遇”。它可以认为从古代以来在欧洲诗话里最严格的旁语。

他的诗必须从一个想象的混沌里形成出来：

一个普遍的凶猛呐喊
是震耳的声音和言语完全混沌杂着。

荷马听到的诗音是细微，清晰，而简单的。但是荷马的世界，有时候弥尔敦用一种约束的渴慕回顾着，现在可是永不见了。“古代的整齐”已经在一方面被北欧的原始能力攻破了（可以这样说），而在另一方面被东方广大精神上的渴慕破裂了。在文艺复兴里欧洲人格是一个重要成熟的混沌。但丁在静止神秘的远景视线里把它完全看出来了。莎氏，活动其中，在经验里拿它当作一个多形的剧影。弥尔敦，“站在大地上，并非站在两极上失神”，最初爱古代调和道德简单化；但是在他的人格里也有但丁内心的思想和莎士比亚写剧的能力一类的东西。所以，他初步的幻想就是人类感情最美的形成，像希腊人在它简单的普遍性里，在所有消灭的纷扰和曲解的雾后，看见的时候一样。但是他更去寻找它最内的方式；并且他看出来这不像静止的东西，而像一篇不断的戏剧。

他的题目确是从内心继续创造出来的人类个性；换言之，是人类极重要极快乐的创造，破坏，再造的神秘。他附属于人类社会中，使人类变成单个人出现。他把希腊时候欧洲文化中长成极大的社会复杂现象用最简单而最简约的几句话表示出来。他给我们一种弥尔敦内部生活的简单现象，代替了荷马外界的简单生活，在一个象征的故事里表现出来。在荷马的作品里，上界和下界的神都参加人类的社会行动。在弥尔敦的作品里，他们参加在他人格无穷的形成里。在荷马，社会生活是神圣的重要和有趣味；但神是“降下来相遇的”。在弥尔敦，社会生活是比较小点，但神却成功很多主要的神事。弥尔敦的诗不比荷马的诗少有那些难免的病。这是自然的结果，不仅是从英国文艺复兴，而是从欧洲诗歌的全生命到现在的成绩。

——1930 年 10 月 20 日，译自《伊丽阿脱现代诗的循环》

原载《励学》1933 年第一卷第一期

谈莎士比亚悲剧《马克白》

毕基初[①]

悲剧《马克白》是生命里的火灾，在它强烈的燃烧下，毁灭了一个高贵纯洁的灵魂。而且由于它的借镜，使你颤栗，使你反省，使你审判了你自己内心的犯罪。然而什么是造成这火灾的因素，是谁放了第一把火？不是社会的制度，不是时代的背景，不是因果律，不是哲学体系推理出的必然的逻辑，更不是客观的物质对生命的投影，而是一个蕴藏在生命内抽象模糊偶发的印象，由于第三个女巫的一句话所启发出来的。

祝福，马克白，你将要是国王。

这印象是内心的自发的如电光一闪的一个动机，也可以说是模糊，不完全，不自觉，然而却是形而上的。我们也常有类同的感觉，当我们在受着别人的压迫侮辱与损害的时候或是欣羡于别人的荣誉与尊贵的时候。可是这种动机如爆散的火星消灭于理智的约束与传统的道德观念中，我们接受过祖先的信条，告诉我们勿苟予，勿苟取。

对于马克白则不然，那动机似一粒种子，落在他如河流三角洲地带肥沃的强烈想象力的领域上，更加上适宜的气候与湿度，我想那该是环绕于他周遭的氛围与时机—— 他的凯旋，邓肯的懦弱—— 还有按时的灌溉与耕刈，无疑的那是马克白夫人的煽惑，于是这粒种子开出了罪恶之花，表现了阴谋，表现了暗杀，表现了罪恶。它是一块化石，显示出整个人性的丑恶。观众在博物院里可见到我们人类骨骼的标本，在舞台上莎士比亚却解剖了人类的灵魂。是的，我们要特别注重马克白夫人的煽惑，假设班柯有马克白夫人那样一位妻子，那么，这悲剧的主角该由班柯扮演，而绝不是马克白。同一的怂恿，同一的动机，因为女巫也预言过班柯要为一个帝王世系的始祖，可是班柯只有一个模糊的不完全的不自觉的行而上的动机；但，在马克白的胸里却孕育了一个罪恶的化身，接受着马克白夫人含有毒素的由胆变成的乳汁的哺乳，慢慢成长起来，成为强有力的主宰，支配了整个悲剧，执行了暗杀的残酷事业。

罪恶，你就是我的善良了。

孕育于马克白胸里罪恶的化身，不仅是弑杀国王邓肯的凶手，暗害同僚班柯的凶手，蔑视真理的凶手，背弃正义的凶手，更是勒毙马克白的凶手，它第一个伤害的不是别人而是马

① 毕基初（1919—1976），山东威海人，毕业于北京辅仁大学西语系，20 世纪 30 年代末期开始发表文学作品，40 年代是毕基初文学创作活动的兴盛期，这期间他发表了大量的小说、诗歌、散文和文艺评论，他的文学创作曾受到当时华北文坛的关注。

克白自己。在动物的生殖里，我知道蝎子是裂开它自己的背生产第二代，以它的死为种族的延续，马克白也是这样做了他孕育的罪恶的化身的第一个牺牲。然而那是怎样不情愿的牺牲。最伟大的战争场面不是在丹新南堡垒外马克白与全付披挂的马克德夫的最后的战斗，而是在马克白的心里他与一个膨胀的罪恶的动机的角力。像是受了传染病的病人，病菌刚侵袭了他清白的灵魂，他就发出了悔恨的太息。

星群，隐匿了你们的火焰
别让光亮看见我黑而深的欲念

就在马克白拔出了匕首要暗杀邓肯的时候，他内心的冲突达到白热的顶点，终于高贵的勇敢的誓忠的将军马克白是死了，死于一个占据着他灵魂的新生的野心的卑鄙的觊觎着王位的背信者的手里。邓肯是死在可见的匕首下，马克白却更早的死在心灵幻象的产物不可见的匕首下。

我去，干了吧，钟声招唤我呢。

钟声，马克白夫人敲出的暗杀的信号，我们如果似马克白所说的那样把它当做了邓肯的丧钟，倒不如说是马克白自己的丧钟。它为马克白敲开了地狱的门，它宣布了勇敢而人性的将军的死亡。此后的马克白是一个与魔鬼签订了契约的罪犯，他用邓肯的血签名于出卖灵魂的合同上，他用他自己灵魂的死亡，荣誉的丧失，把良心当做了冻疮（暴风雨里那个坏蛋安图尼欧的话）买来了一个溅满血的暴君的王位。在封神榜里那个蛊惑暴君的妃子，我们都叫她做妲已，实在妲已是冤枉的，因为就在妲已入宫的前夕，她的灵魂让一个九尾狐狸吃掉，那九尾狐狸借着她的尸还了魂。是的，马克白也是如此，在马克白夫人召唤的钟声里，真正的马克白为他自己内心所孕育的妖怪吞食了。是否马克白完全让罪恶支配，像黑暗的夜覆盖着他的生命，不，却又有一点星光，那就是被杀死的善良留下了血淋淋的尸痕，当他说“所有的伟大海神的海洋能从我手上洗净这些血吗？”你以为那是邓肯的血，不，邓肯的血是可见的，也就是可以洗净的，像马克白夫人所说的只要一点水就可以把他们洗刷干净，那是马克白自己的血，一个高贵善良万人喝彩的将军做了魔鬼的献祭的血，那血是不可见的，也就是不能洗净的了。

第二幕第三景的开场（也可以说是第二景的结尾）门外的敲门声，按着情节的逻辑，那该是麦克德夫与兰诺克斯；依着象征的暗示，可以解释做正义，真理，光明，我们可以随便说它是个人的良心、传统的道德，或是宗教的启示，我却要说那是马克白的鬼谴责着活的马克白，那是被杀死的善良的马克白在敲着地狱的门，不信，你听守门人的独语：

这里的确有敲门的，倘若一个人是地狱之门的守门者，他老得要转动这把钥匙。

也许这一景的安排是为了调剂观众紧张的情绪，投合流行的趣味。甚至于柯勒瑞治（Coleridge）怀疑守门人的独语不是莎士比亚的写作而是出于别人的手笔；可是站在我们的观点上，抛弃了考据学修辞学的引证，只从这个剧的本身上着眼，它不是插曲，也不是无关紧要的噱头，而是全剧的关键（Keystone）。我们可以给这景加上个小标题："马克白的灵魂敲着地狱的门"。犹如歌德的《浮士德》里那博识的学者与梅菲斯特签订出卖灵魂的契约那场面。

马克白这样的杀死了自己。

然而，马克白的鬼却曾再度出现了一次。那是在筵席上班柯的鬼出现的时候。你以为那是班柯的鬼？不，那是死去的马克白的鬼，马克白的良心，变做了班柯的形状来谴责他。——这是马克白心的穹窿上最后的一颗星，从此后他完全遮盖在罩棺材的黑布里，他是那占据着他的心的凶手的奴隶，他的善良的灵魂永远幽禁在地狱里。

卑鄙的凶手登上了王位，也占据了一个清白的灵魂，把它染上夜的黑。直到马克德夫砍下了他的头，他始终被魔鬼控制着。

我们恨马克白吗？我们憎恶马克白吗？倘若我们有了这种情绪，马克白不能成为一个悲剧的主角，那是违反了亚利斯多德的悲剧的规则。事实上却正相反，马克白的手指敲在我们同情（Sympathy）的键子上。我们为他叹息，为他难过。为什么我们会为一个杀人的凶手难过叹息，那是因为马克白蒙了不白之冤，他被人性里的奸细所出卖。正如我们应当可怜妲己，而恨那借尸还魂的狐狸。那潜伏于马克白品性的病菌，很自然地已蟠据了我们的灵魂。很可能的，你或是我在莎士比亚的透视镜里观察马克白时，已经为一个小的欲望（却更黑）占据住，我们没有马克白的才力，不敢向王冠宝座有所企图，可是我们也有我们小的领土，小的尊严与荣誉，你听，魔鬼在我们胸里磨刀的声音，我们的灵魂也即将遭遇到支解的不幸了。

别怜惜这肉体的生命，因为马克白说过：

如其在这意外的事前一个钟头死去，
我便是幸福一生。

那意外事不是邓肯的死，不是阴谋的展开，而是杀了他自己，杀死了优越崇高的灵魂。

原载《文艺世纪》1944 年第 1 卷第 2 期

论莎士比亚的《马克柏司》

斯米吞（著）　东方蓝（译）

《马克柏司》是莎士比亚的三个伟大的悲剧中的一个；那其余的两个是《奥忒罗》和《利尔王》。那三个剧本表现着我们的世界所已经看到过的最洪大的天才的创造力，被看做能及得上他们的仅有的作品是希腊得伊士奇的《伯罗米修士的命运》和德意志的歌德的《浮士德》。

古怪之至，在近十八世纪末（一七七九年）一个为弥得尔敦所作的叫做巫女的戏剧的原稿本被佐治·斯提汾斯先生，莎士比亚学的学者，在托马斯·披尔逊先生的收藏中发现着。使他惊异的，他注意到在巫女中所表现的巫术的场面同在《马克柏司》中的巫术的场面是一式一样的。从巫女的一个致辞的辞句可看到它是远在一六〇三年以前写就的，斯提汾斯推知《马克柏司》直到一六〇六年才写，所以莎士比亚是一定抄袭了弥得尔敦的。可是任何人只要对于莎士比亚学的解释学稍有一些经验的一看就一定会知道是弥得尔敦剽窃莎士比亚，并不是莎士比亚剽窃弥得尔敦。在巫女中的笔触的怯弱。不稳定的描写，以及尤其语句的松弛，一切都表征它是剽窃来了的材料。内在的证据全然胜于那柔弱地断为真实的证据，那剑桥的编辑者们，随在斯提汾斯和李斐德以后；所以举出了的。要说《巫女》的巫女是先于《马克柏司》的三巫女会等于说水能升得比它自己的水平线更高。

作为一个剧本的《马克柏司》已引起欧罗巴所有的国家的伟大的心的赞美。比如，那博学的德意志批评家 A. W. 希勒格，说到它：

谁能赞美尽这个崇高的作品？从伊士奇的《狂暴》以来，所已编写过的什么都没有这样宏大而且可惊的。巫女实在并不是神圣的复仇之神，而且也并没有这样做的意向；她们是地狱的不高贵而且庸俗的工具，莎士比亚意欲表示善与恶的冲突在这个世界上那只有在天意的许可之下才能产生，那使各个的凡人所有的咒诅变成一种对别人的祝福。

哥尔利治说：

《马克柏司》从头到底都同《汉姆列德》对照着：尤其在开头的形式上。在后者，从那最单纯的对话的形式在逐渐上升到有一种奋激的智能的语句，然而那种智能依旧存留在热情的位置上；在前者，那诉求是同时使想象与情绪连在一起的。因此那行动从头到底是莎士比亚所有的戏剧中的最迅速的。在整个的剧本中双关语和字眼的戏弄是完全戒绝了的，喜剧的成分也全然绝迹，甚至讥讽与哲学的沉思也没有，《马克柏司》是整个地，纯粹地悲剧的。

克累息也说：

至于思想的丰富，《马克柏司》还列在《汉姆列德》之下；它欠缺着在《朱理亚·恺撒》中所有的广博的，自在的，历史的完美。在完满，结构的深沉，或者人物的充分表演上，它不能同《奥忒罗》比。可是，我们以为，在和谐的单纯的力量上，在它的动作的从高的顺流上，在它的计划的透彻上，在它的语句的神经质的权力与胆大的观察上，以及在奢侈的方能与诗意的色泽上，它超越着莎士比亚或者任何别的诗人所尝创造过的一切。

斯托泼福耳德·勃鲁克博士加着说：

马肯的试询马克达夫的忠诚以显示他自己是一个好色的，贪吝的，无德性的王子，而且问这样的一个人适不适宜于统治，还有那关于那国王的罪恶的一节，都是同这样地不必要的，而且又是拖延的。……那戏剧的这些部分都提示着莎士比亚所原来写的《马克柏司》还要长，然后把使它拖长的一切都割去，于是把余下的紧凑起来而成为这个剧本，如我们现在所有着它的。所以，《马克柏司》现在是莎士比亚的戏剧中的最短的。而迅速，每一个人都说，现在是它的主要的特性。

莎士比亚于《马克柏司》仿效着伊士奇和马逻，尤其在他集中他所有的悲剧的力量在只描写两个主要的剧中人物，而让别的人稍胜于仅有外形，这一点上。马克柏司和他的妻子是两个必得相并地被分析的人物。他们是像同一个钱的正面和反面。这两个人在他们的一生的大部分中被所有的人尊崇着而且敬仰着：他是皇室的大首领与屏藩，她是，自从当坎的王后的死亡以来，全国的首要的夫人。骤然，由于巫女的指示，他把一切都抛弃—— 财富，幸福，荣誉，心的平安—— 为要得到一个王位，那从他一坐上去的时候就开始倾向着它的毁灭。马克柏司夫人是一块比她的丈夫更坚强的质料。她应该是那男子，他是那女子。马克柏司是太想象的，他对于做一个残酷的，深谋远虑的犯罪人秉有着一种太强烈的幻想，以致他不会像一个东方的暴君似的从他所有的谋杀了兄弟的血液中平静而硬心地封上他的王位。马克柏司能计划，可是他不能向结果闭着他的眼睛。他看到他的过去的罪孽使它们自己幻化成那些他所尝杀死了的人的血污的鬼形。在谋杀当坎的以前，他看见一把匕首在它前面的空中，而在一切都做好了以后；他想象着声音在叫喊着，"不要再睡眠，马克柏司要谋杀睡眠"，而且他不能走回去看看他的犯罪的场面—— 他的神经坚强的妻子不得不代他去这样做。他的想象重新创造着那可畏的过去，而为他建立的地狱已开始。在别方面，他的妻子，在这个决断的时期内，从不显示一条筋肉的战栗。她以一个基督徒的殉道者的紧张的坚忍经历着这一切暴厉的行为与经验，决定着不让有稍微的畏缩的现象显示。她甚至在他的悔悟的苦楚与精神的恐怖中，在变成一个怯者的时候，用她的剩余的决意来支持她的丈夫，她还激励他显示一种更好的，一种更胆大的面容去正视着那已经可疑的人。然而那第一个沮丧下来的是她。为什么这样？为了这个缘故，马克柏司已变得同恐怖熟习着，而他的望进那不可见的境界的精神的视觉由此失去着它的锐敏性。她在别方面，从没有同那恐怖的和血的景象变得熟习；她一向就比她的丈夫受着更甚的痛苦，可是，患着一种女子的崇高的自己牺牲的精神，她也不用言语也不用行为来显示她的苦楚，而且甚至强迫他自己做使她的非常艺术而审美的天性感受到不可言说的痛苦的事情，即，带着匕首回到那死室中去，而面对着那谋杀的当坎的刀痕深深的，遍体染血的尸首。所以在马克柏司的精神恢复它的常态的时候，在他以一种不屈不挠的决意与坚毅面对着那反对他的集团，而一切来自无恨的深渊的鬼和精灵都被他的坚决的实际的需要赶出他的心的时候，那在马克柏司夫人的心中的可畏的内省的性能，它的反应比那袭击着她的丈夫的他的罪孽的化形要可怖到十倍的，在腐蚀着她的感觉的灵魂的装出来的坚忍，直到她的理性由于极度的恐怖在它的高位上蹒跚着。随带着他的全副武装在他的背上勇敢地战斗到最后的马克柏司的死可说是登天堂，而马克柏司夫人在那无名的恐怖的火焰中死去可说是入地狱。这两个伟大的人物的死在全世界的文学中达到了悲剧的恐怖的最高的地位。马克柏司承受着他的苦楚，他的身体满充着精力，他的生机也是最饱满的，而他的妻子也坚如岩石地站在他的后面，以支持起他的在消失下去的坚毅：马克柏司夫人，在别的方面，历受她的苦楚，由于使他坚强起来的辛劳，在灵魂和身体两方面都一样地枯竭了。她当是更坚强的，可是在她的纷扰的日子来到的时候，在那犯罪的灵魂的不可想象的恐怖临到她的身上来的时候，她不再贮有那用来加强她的感觉的坚忍的力量了，而地狱的忏悔的火焰也把她的理性烧走了。

卜拉德赉教授说：

这两个角色，马克柏司和马克柏司夫人，是被一种而且同一种野心的热情激动着；而且到一个相当的限度他们是一样的。每一个人的性情都是高慢的，骄傲的，而且指挥的。他们都是生就来管理，即使不是统治。他们对于低下于他们的人是专断的或者轻蔑的。他们并不是光的孩子，像布鲁特斯和汉姆列德一样；他们是世界的孩子。我们观察到他们对于国家没有爱，对于他们的家庭以外的任何人的福利也没有兴趣。他们的习惯的思念与目的是，而且，我们想象，早已是，只有地位与权力。而且虽然在他们二人都有一些，而且在一个有得更多，高超，尊敬，良心，与人性，他们并不意识地生存在这些事物的光亮中或者讲到它们，并不是他们是利己主义者，像易阿哥一样：或者，要是他们是的话，他们的是一种利双人主义。他们并不有分开的野心。他们相互地支持而且相爱。他们分开着受痛苦。而且要是在时间过去的时候，他们势所有些分开的话，他们并不是庸俗的灵魂，不会在他们经验他们的野心的无结果的时候疏远，而且互相责备。他们到终了都依旧是悲剧的，甚至宏大的。

嘿兹力特说：

马克柏司似乎为他的命运的暴厉所驱使，正如一条船在一个狂潮前漂流一样；他像一个喝醉酒的人似的摇来摇去；他在他自己的目的的重压和别人的暗示下蹒跚着；他随遇地处着他的穷境；从那由于三巫女同他的交通所给与他的迷信的恐惧与喘息的悬虑，被一种勇敢的忍耐赶受着，以证实她们的预示，而且用虔诚而血污的手撕开那把未来的不确定遮掩着的幕。他对于同命运与良心的挣扎并不是匹敌的。……他的能力生长自在他的心里的忧虑与骚扰。他的盲目地向他的野心与复仇的目的物冲前去，或者他的从它们的退后来，都同等地泄露着他的感情的被蹂躏的情景。他的性格的这一部分由于同马克柏司夫人的性格的接触是可赞美地设置着的，她的意志的执拗的强有力和她的男性的坚决，使她有一种优越以支持她的丈夫的踌躇的德性。她立刻攫住着那可使他们完成他们所急盼的伟大事件的机会，而且被不从她的目的物退缩，直到一切都做好为止。她的决断的分量几乎可抵消她的犯罪的分量。她是一个我们所憎恨的伟大的坏女人，可是我们恐惧她更胜于我们憎恨她。她并不像里干和衰涅立尔似地激起我们的憎嫌与厌恶。她所以做恶事以便达到一个伟大的目的。

龙斯柏立教授在《作为一个戏剧的艺术家的莎士比亚》中（第四至五页）说：

马克柏司夫人的天性，比他的要更绞裂得多，虽然在起初是更决断的，终于在悔恨的白天和无眠的晚上充分报与破坏法律的责罚。在马克柏司逐渐变成一个那在伦理的斟酌上会毁灭他的感染性的更坚强的男子的时候，在她一方面这种的感染性增大着以完成她所已在急速地进行着的行为，而且在其中她已采取了决定的部分。那女子不能全然使她自己失去女子的本性，而终于屈服于一个她所不适于担受的久延而且沉重的负担之下。

乌利际也说：

那真正的犯人，他，如他的行动所显示的，并没有意志，却只为他自己的兴趣，在他的实在的天性上是孤独的。因此马克柏司和他的妻子单独在一边，而他的国度的反对他的贵族们，整个的国家和人民，都聚拢来站在又一边；简之，以及一切的人种。因此，那行动的道德一部分依附在这个在那从上帝犯了罪的人与他的所有的人们之间的不可除去的而且逐渐地加深着疏远上，还有一部分附在，由于一种本质的必然性，马克柏司的犯罪的在接连不断地扩展而且成长着的加速的恐惧上，直到它达到它的不可避免的报应与死亡的目的为止。

关于别的人物，他们同两个马克柏司的可怖的活动比起来只是影子而已。当坎每一时都是一个国王—— 高贵，尊严，而且堂堂不凡，在感情上是这样，在行为上也是这样，谋杀这样的一个国君所以是有“繁重的可恶”的。虽然在历史上的当坎，像在历史上的邦廓一样，是一个作恶而且残暴的人，莎士比亚已偏向地把当坎和邦廓描写成具备着各种善良的性质的人物。当坎在治理的智慧与政治的先见上都照耀着卓越的光亮？邦廓既是一个勇敢的战士，又是一个忠心的朋友。虽然他的心关于当坎的谋杀决不确信于马克柏司的无辜，邦廓在治理国家的事件上是准备着给与他所有的忠诚的支持与扶助。然而马克柏司不能忘记虽然他自己，依照着那三巫女的预示，要做国王，邦廓的后裔此后要执掌王位，有那样的事意思就是马克柏司的家属或者会被消灭或者被革除权力。要得到确切的保证，他计划着杀戮邦廓和夫利恩斯，他的“谋杀者”，在前一事件是成功的，可是在后一事件是失败了，这样就使得他的一切努力的无效。

马克达夫也是一个忠诚的，心迹高贵的人，对于做各式各样的错误的事情都永远露着不悦的表示的。他所以准备着冒险，不但牺牲生命本身，去坐上苏格兰的王位做一个会值得受人的尊敬的国王。在谨慎地试着马肯的心以后，甚至像后者试着他的心，马克达夫像用一只铁钩似的使他自己黏附着他。关于他乌利际写道：

马克达夫的妻子和孩子们为了他们的天然的保护者的自私自利遭受着痛苦，他忘却了他的一个丈夫和一个父亲的责任，已离弃了他们以获得他自己的个人的安全。因此他受到失去他所有的小孩们的处罚，而那落在他的妻子身上的命运辛酸得并不是全然不当的，她用它来为他的离弃她攻击她的丈夫。

马肯是这样的一种统治者的典型，就是他并不赋有治理的大天才，却秉有一种甚至更有价值的才能，即，一个被伦理的纯洁，忠诚与真理所渗透着的灵魂。把这些好像当做一件袍子穿着，他为他的继承的位子向前又向上地斗争着，那位子那篡夺者已从他劫夺去，而他为它们争并不因为他有为统治的缘故统治的野心，却因为那位子是上帝赋予他的，而且他是要为它负责任的。关于马肯，乌利际说：

善良需要着时间与忍耐；德性的行为为它的完成要求着许多预虑，成熟的准备，与平静的心的泰然，仿佛为要对于这个重要的真实引起注意似的，莎士比亚有意使马肯的逡巡而多思的迟疑正对照着马克柏司的暴烈而躁急的敏捷。……他已把这两种有历史性的行动的形式美丽地描写着。在一方面是那种一决定就做的火速的行为，而且像一个敌对的侵略凭蹂躏与惊慌达到它的目的：在又一方面，是一种它来预筹与估计一切可能发生的事件的迟疑。

讲到在那戏剧中的鬼的出现，那在《汉姆列德》中既然已被接受下来，在《马克柏司》中也不能被反对。那出现，正如它同马克柏司有关系的，只有他看得见，因为那所需要产生的反应就是要用来造就他的影响。关于这一点，H. T. 洛兹捺尔说："邦邵的鬼的出现是直接出于马克柏司的心的状态；所以那鬼只有他看得见。"……

原载《文学研究》1940 年第 1 卷第 4 期

中国学生对于研究西洋文学应有的认识*

余楠秋

今日之中国学生，无论是在大学或在中学，对于世界的文艺似乎甚是注意。在一个时期当中，有一班人几乎像发狂似的来读文学的作品；他们也不管文字之优劣，作品之有无价值，只要书店里有一本新书，就争先恐后地去买来看。这个时期，在无论何国何地，当新思想输入之时，总是必有的现象；中国恰当文字革命，新奇学说盛行的时候，这种情形，自然也不能免。但是到了近来，一般读者因看的书多，辨判力亦渐加强，不像从前黑白不辨；对于选择书籍，批评文稿，均是有理智的而不是盲从的，有思想的而不是乱说的。这诚是中国文艺界的一大进步。不过在各学校里，仍是有许多学生对于研究世界文学，不知目的之所在。当先生们的，不在事先为他们详细说明；当学生的，如是只知一味乱读，标准毫无。每逢谈论起来，信口开河，称赞几声莎士比亚，又批评几句拜龙 Byron，对于西洋文学的皮毛，恍惚略略晓得一点，而于西洋文学的背景及意义，实则尚未窥堂奥。这种情形，对于研究西洋文学者，诚是一大危机。兹篇所谈，即系讨论中国学生对于研究西洋文学应有的认识，其目的在希望研究西洋文学有兴趣的人，能拿定宗旨，看清目标，庶几时间不至白费，所得的结果，比较上或者有点价值。

普通讲来，文学之能引人兴趣者，有五种来源。第一，文学给吾人以过去的思想；前人的生活以及他们对于生命作何感想，我们都可于他们所做的文章中得来。大概文学上的作品，能够留传下来的，必定是当时的结晶品，可以代表那个时代的思想；一代有一代的思想，一代有一代的生活，因其各异，所以研究文学者，越觉得有味。第二，吾人生来就欢喜听故事，看小说，不拘年龄的大小，男女的性别，这种习惯，无论何人都有的。大文豪史悌文生 Stevenson 说："吾人爱读小说，就如爱食肉一般。"由是可以想见这种爱听爱看的习惯，原来是吾人生来就有的天性。而况且小说故事，很可以长进知识，增助情感，为益至大。第三，研究文学，能使吾人知道前此影响世界促进文化之幻想及思潮，因是而唤起吾人之想象能力。吾人以前的历史，至伟且大；今日之光荣，纯靠过去的成绩为基础。但是过去的成绩，是前人用他们的理想造成的。吾人欲知道他们的伟大的思想，唯一的方法，是研究文学。因为前人给我们以伟大的思想，于是吾人运用心灵，使自己的脑海中，增加想象的能力；结果或能造就更伟大的思想，更永久的精神。第四，文学最易引起吾人的审美观念。爱美之心，人人有之；但是没有什么东西可以引起吾人的美感，则吾人的爱美性，不足以发扬光大，真情露骨地表现出来。在世界能有永久性的东西，惟有文学足以激起人家的美感，唤醒吾人的情绪。一篇有意义的文章，几句好吟玩的诗词，反复朗诵，其味无穷；生活之有兴趣，男女之有情感，世界之有生命，胥赖乎此。第五，对于文学有兴趣的人们，借此可以发展其天才，更能增加其愉快。有些人生性对于文学相近；如有机会使他们能充分地发展这个生性，他们必感受无穷的快乐，或因是而能造就更伟大的文学家。密尔登 Milton 并非生来就是一个诗人，迭更司 Dickens 也不是出世就是一个小说家；然而他们都能成为世界上的大文豪者，无他，不外乎最初对于文学上发生特殊的兴趣，然后渐渐尽量发展他们的天才。

根据以上五种来源，吾人对于文学之研求，自然会感受兴趣。但是现代的中国学生，既然对于文学上感受兴趣，则对于西洋文学一方面的研求，自不可不有一定的方针，看清他们的宗旨。能有一定的方针，能知他们的宗旨，然后才能得到相当的益处与较好的结果，此所以我特地提出“中国学生对于研究西洋文学应有的认识”的问题来讨论一讨论。我认为我们研究西洋文学，必须（一）具有时代的眼光，（二）了解东西思想，（三）明晓作品的背景，（四）懂得文字的运用，（五）尊重人生的观念。能够先有这几种认识，则我们所看的，方不至于白费时间，枉用脑力。今特将这五项应有的认识，更为详细解释以便大家讨论。

一、须具有时代的眼光

文学的作品，无论何时，必定是表示一个时代的思想。当我们研究一篇作品时，我们须先认清它的时代性，看它是否能够代表那个时代的精神？它的力量，是否能够影响到后代？古典派的文豪，自有他们研究的特点；浪漫派的作品，另有他们放肆的理由。各有各的精神，各有各的优点。到了现在，有些人还是跟着他们的思想做去。我们试把现代的文学与他们的作品拿来比较一比较，看现在的趋向如何？看人类的思想进步如何？民族主义的文学，是否得到相当的地位？民权主义的精神，是否表现得恰当？民生主义的实行，是否表演得真切？凡此种种，均足以试验研究西洋文学者，有无时代的眼光。

二、须了解东西的思想

研究西洋文学者，应知东西的思想，有迥然不同之处。有时东方人认以为是者，据西方的观念，则以为完全错误；而是有时西方人认为不错者，照东方的观察，则似应根本推翻。例如对于女子的觉念：在中国往者普通人的心理，一个女人应当时常守在家里，克尽妇职，才不愧于贤妻良母；进一步说，所谓“三从四德”必须件件做到，方能称为理想中的妇人。然而在西方人的眼光里，却是大谬不然。所谓理想中的妇人，她应当绝对自由，时常出现于交际场中，多交朋友，不分男女，使人家崇拜她，称她做“安琪儿”。社会上的事业应当参加，个人的浪漫行为，毋需拘束。照这种的样子，东方人简直会说她是发狂。这个就表现东西两方面极端矛盾的地方。如果研究西洋文学者，不懂得他们的哲学，在情势上，自然不会同他们表同情，自然不能见到他们描写情绪的用意。所以读西洋文学者，必须要另换一副眼光，来考察他们的心理，寻求作品的妙处，然后才能够得到相当的结果。

三、须明晓作品的背景

文学家所出的作品。一篇有一篇的用意，一篇有一篇的背景；无论其改良社会，增进道德，宣传主义，总是有一定的目的。研究西洋文学者，应当先把这一点看清，同时并应将作者的生平事实，详细查明，然后才能够见得到在当时文坛上的地位，以及他的文章在文学上的价值。否则随便乱读，只等于看字认字而已！又何配谈起“研究”两字？譬如迭更司所著的《贼史》*Oliver Twist*，我们要是不晓得他做这本小说的用意，是在描写当日英国社会的腐败情形，以冀促起政府的改良，则我们读了这本书，可算毫无意义，绝不会觉得迭更司思想的伟大，这篇作品的真正价值。所以我们每读一篇作品，必须要明晓它的背景，才能得到实益。

四、须需懂得文字的运用

第四，研究西洋文学者，应知道文字的运用。所谓文字的运用者，在每篇文章的里面，每章，每段，每句，各有其衔接之处，而个人的想象力，尤不可不注意及之。一句有一句的道理，一字有一字的需要，并不是随便乱凑，写到多长，便称它为一篇文章。有时引用成语，有时增加词藻，读者尤须细心揣想，务必得到作者的原意。譬如中国人常用的“白云苍狗”“闭月羞花”“沉鱼落雁”等等辞句，要是读者不懂得它们的意义，自然地不会觉得有何妙处。像这样的用法，在西洋文学中，引用之处亦甚多；所以读者应当加倍留心，揣摩到他们文字的巧妙，则自能渐渐心领神会矣。

五、须尊重人生的观念

研究西洋文学者，最要紧的是能尊重人生的观念。生命是多么的美丽！人生是怎样的可爱！试问吾人生活在世上，究竟所为何事？这一点秘诀，惟有文人能够在他们的作品里面，详细地讨论研究，把它发扬光大起来，能使读者豁然贯通，了解人生的真谛，不至中道迷途，混沌一世。有时诗人骚客，借文字的运用，把他们的情绪一一写出来，至无聊赖时，或且高歌朗诵以发泄他们满胸的悲愤；这个正是以见文章之妙用。而文字虽经过几千年的历史，仍能有永久价值者，亦原是故。所以我们读西洋文学者，须要看他们对于人生的观念，是否代表他们的民族性？他们的地位何在？他们的价值何存？必如是方能得到文学的真味，方能懂得西方的伟大思想。

以上所述中国学生对于研究西洋文学应有的五种认识，不过仅就其大者要者而言；若是细细地把它分析起来，当就不止这几种。但是我以为如果读西洋文学的中国学生，只要能够把这五种认识放在他们的心里，我敢相信他们纵不能到如何的伟大思想，然而也不至于白费时间。拿定宗旨，看清目标，这是我一点很诚恳的希望。

原载《暨大文学院集刊》1931 年第 1 期

*注：余楠秋（1897—1968），名箕传，字楠秋，湖南长沙人。1914 年，赴美国留学，先后入菲力普大学和伊里诺大学，获伊里诺大学文学学士学位。1921 年回国。历任江苏省省立商科大学英语部部长，省立东南大学商科教授等职。1923 年，任私立上海复旦大学文学院院长，兼西洋文学系主任，并兼任私立中国公学英文教授，国立暨南大学讲师。余楠秋 1921 年 9 月由中国公学新聘为商科教授，且对于中国公学的校务非常积极，在开学典礼上被指定为代表发言。（见《中国公学开学记》，《民国日报》1921 年 9 月 14 日，第 11 版）。1931 年 11 月 29 日，上海各大学教授成立抗日救国会，余楠秋等人被选为理事，沈钧儒等人被选为候补理事。1934 年 4 月 1 日出版的《清华校友通讯》在介绍即将毕业的校友时，刊出余楠秋等人的照片。余楠秋在《我的读书经验》（载《读书月刊》）一文中谈到："我 12 岁去北京清华学校……我认为读书必须要感觉到读书的乐趣，一个人如果是觉得读书是一桩很苦的事情，他根本就不应该读书。"余楠秋著有《中日美间之国际关系》《演说学 ABC》《演说学概论》《中国学生对于研究西洋文学应有的认识》，合著《读书经验谈》等，译著则有《暴风雨》《近代欧洲史》《英国史》《欧洲近代现代史》《史学概论》《法国革命伟人传》《德意志意大利统一小史》等。余楠秋虽然曾任复旦大学西洋文学系主任等职，但一生译著主要集中于史学领域，余楠秋与王淑瑛译《暴风雨》可谓在史学译著之外不多的文学译本。余楠秋与王淑瑛以五言诗体译《暴风雨》是莎剧翻译史上的一次大胆的尝试。余楠秋与王淑瑛以五言诗体译《暴风雨》的出版本身就彰显出，中国人以更加民族化的文体、语言形式参与到莎氏经典化过程中的主动作为。余译《暴风雨》出版已经几十余年，但是坊间对余楠秋与王淑瑛以五言诗体译《暴风雨》的研究并不多见。仅有李伟民发表了《〈暴风雨〉五言诗体中译——民国时期莎剧经典化的尝试》，《外国文学研究》2020 年第 3 期。为了纪念这位中国莎学研究先贤，为中国莎学研究提供坚实的史料基础，经多方发掘，寻觅到余楠秋先生的《中国学生对于研究西洋文学应有的认识》，同时涉及对莎氏的认知。他在该文中强调，如果仅知西洋文学的皮毛，而于背景及意义不深入了解，实则尚未窥堂奥。要了解西洋文学须有时代眼光；须了解东西方思想；须明晓作品的背景；须懂得文字的运用；须尊重人生的观念。浙江越秀外国语学院我的学生助理王茜婵、朱思伊、张昌德承担了文字录入工作，现出版以飨读者。（李伟民）

第五编

翻译研究

林译《吟边燕语》的副文本研究

朱安博　张凯月

【摘　要】副文本是翻译研究中不可分割的一部分，它可以帮助读者获取原作的写作背景和历史背景，揭示文本不能体现的内容，为翻译研究提供新的角度。《吟边燕语》作为早期莎剧进入中国最重要的译著之一，对莎士比亚在中国的传播与接受具有重要意义。本文拟借杰拉德·热奈特提出的副文本理论，通过对林译《吟边燕语》副文本的分析解读林纾的翻译思想和翻译动机。
【关键词】副文本；林纾；《吟边燕语》；翻译研究

A Study on the Subtext of *Yinbian Yanyu* Translated by Lin Shu

Zhu Anbo　Zhang Kaiyue

【Abstract】Subtext is an integral part of translation study, as it can help readers understand the writing background and historical background of the original work, reveal the content that the text can't reflect, and provide a new perspective for translation study. As one of the most important translations of Shakespeare's early plays in China, *Yinbian Yanyu* is of great significance to the dissemination and acceptance of Shakespeare in China. This paper intends to interpret Lin Shu's translation thought and motivation through the analysis of Lin's translation of the subtext of *Yinbian Yanyu*, based on the subtext theory proposed by Gérard Genette.
【Key Words】subtext; Lin Shu; *Yinbian Yanyu*; translation study

莎剧进入中国对莎士比亚在中国的接受具有重要意义，自《澥外奇谭》第一次对莎剧进行翻译开始，已经有林纾、萧乾等多个《莎士比亚戏剧故事集》的中译本出现。作为首个全译本，林译《吟边燕语》向中国学者传播了西方文学和西方文化，深化了中国人对于西方文学的认识，也让读者体会到了莎士比亚的魅力。副文本为译者提供了现身的平台，揭示了译者的翻译动机等内容，对于推进译本的研究和传播具有重要价值。本文拟分析该副文本对于译本在中国之译介和传播的重要作用。

1 翻译研究中的副文本视角

“副文本”的概念最早由法国文艺理论家热拉尔·热奈特（Gerard Genette）在 20 世纪 70 年代首次提出，1982 年他进一步明确了副文本的内涵，1987 年，他出版了《门槛》(*Seuils*)，形成了较为成熟的副文本理论，1997 年，《副文本：阐释的门槛》(*Paratext: Thresholds of Interpretation*) 出版，副文本理论也逐渐引起了学界的关注，该理论也逐渐应用于翻译研究之中。2018 年，凯瑟琳·巴彻勒（Kathryn Batchelor）出版了《翻译与副文本》(*Translation and paratexts*)，该著作系统介绍了副文本理论，为翻译研究提供了重要的基础。巴彻勒提出，副文本指的是诸如标题、小标题、笔名、序言、题词、题名、前言、尾声、后记等围绕或组织文本的因素。按照不同的分类方式，副文本可以分为以下几种类型。根据副文本相对文本的位置来分，可分为“内副文本”或“边缘副文本”(peritext) 和“外副文本”或“后副文本”(epitext)。

热奈特指出，“一个没有副文本的文本，有时就像一头没有赶象人的大象，无法拥有所有的力量；一个没有文本的副文本，则是没有大象的赶象人，不过只是一场愚蠢的炫耀(parade inepte)。”①副文本有助于帮助读者了解原作的写作背景和历史背景，深入理解作品以及作者的写作意图，准确把握文化和历史的深刻影响，是连接作者、译者、读者三位一体的桥梁，因此研究副文本有助于更好地阅读和了解作品内涵。

2 《吟边燕语》的内副文本分析

2.1 标题的重构

林纾（1852—1924）与魏易合著的《吟边燕语》(译自《莎士比亚戏剧故事集》) 自 1904 年以来，已经出版多次，深得读者喜爱。②在《吟边燕语》之前该著作也曾被译为《莎氏乐府本事》，该书为英汉对照版本，附有许多英文注释，对于英语初学者来说是一本难得的读物。后由商务印书馆出版的著作名为《吟边燕语》。也曾有学者认为“英国诗人吟边燕语”才应是全名，但是李伟民先生曾指出“英国诗人吟边燕语”的题目不准确，原译本封面及扉页上都没有“英国诗人”四字，《吟边燕语》才应该是规范的名字。③

林纾没有将作品直译为“莎士比亚戏剧故事集”，而是通过对翻译风格的转变，为其赋予了具有中国特色的标题《吟边燕语》。标题“吟边燕语”拟出自宋末诗人黄庚的一首诗，名为《吟边》(如下)。通过对标题的重构，使其更贴近汉语的表达方式，让译入语读者更易接受。

---

① Gérard Genette, *Paratexts: Thresholds of Interpretation*, Trans. Jane E. Lewin. New York: Cambridge University Press, 1997. p410.

② 刘炳善，《兰姆在中国有了自己的知音》，《读书》，1989 年第 4 期，第 146 页。

③ 李伟民，《中国英语教育史上的重要读物：莎士比亚戏剧简易读本》，《语言教育》，2013 年第 3 期，第 74—75 页。

吟　边

宋・黄庚

落尽荼蘼燕未归，

小园寂寂掩柴扉。

吟边正苦无诗料，

风递杨花扑客衣。[①]

2.2　出版说明

在出版说明中，首先介绍了林纾的基本情况，指出“林纾是我国以古文翻译外国小说的第一个人，译作有一百八十四种之多”[②]，可见林纾在我国翻译史上的地位。但是林纾本人对外语知之甚少，甚至可以说对外语毫无兴趣，但是在朋友的帮助下，他翻译的西方文学作品曾“一时纸贵洛阳”[③]。我国著名翻译家郑振铎也曾提到，“在中国恐怕译了四十余种的世界名著的人，除了林先生外，到现在还不曾有过一个人。”[④]由于林纾没有直接读英文原著，而是通过他人先翻译成简单的汉语然后自己进行文字的润色，所以其译著大多采用归化的翻译策略。林纾本人虽然不懂英文，但是对西方文学和文化背景了解透彻，加之对文言工笔的擅长，其著作也是十分受读者喜爱，“不胫走万本”[⑤]。林纾“善于领会原著的风格，译笔传神而流畅”[⑥]，在翻译史上的地位可见一斑，虽然其译文多为文言文，但由于其译文通俗易懂，因此现当代时期仍有不少读者喜欢阅读其译著。由于新文化运动的冲击，林译本在 1923 年之后便没有再版。而伴随“西学东渐”，近代西方学术思想向中国传播，林译小说于 1981 年重印再版。[⑦]

林纾首次将外国文学名著大量译入中国，“在我国旧民主主义革命阶段起过相当大的影响”[⑧]。深受儒家思想懂得熏陶，林译《巴黎茶花女遗事》将法国爱情故事进行了中国化再创作，小说中爱情描写与爱国主义交织在一起，具有强烈的反封建意义。通过对美国小说《黑奴吁天录》（*Uncle Tom's Cabin*）中黑奴悲惨遭遇的描写，展示出其爱国动机，希望通过文字来警醒众人奋起反抗并引起了当时社会的强烈反响。

在翻译技巧上，虽为文言，也有值得令人研究和借鉴的地方。因此即使不少作品已有现代汉语译本，而林译仍具有独立存在的价值。以《吟边燕语》为例，曾有许多译者都对 *Tales From Shakespeare* 进行重译，但是林译本一直经久不衰，在翻译史上具有重要的地位。翻译作品风格因人而异，可见林译本无论是在翻译风格还是在翻译技巧方面都有其独特性。

出版说明是译本副文本中极其重要的一部分，包含作者情况介绍、翻译背景介绍等内容。这些副文本内容不仅交代了作者身份和基本情况，也能够起到帮助读者了解创作背景的作用。历史背景的介绍也能够将读者代入当时的历史时期，以便更好地理解翻译作品。

---

① 黄庚，《吟边》，http://www.samoya.net/shi_detail/473643.html.

② 兰姆，《吟边燕语・出版说明》，林纾、魏易译，北京：商务印书馆，1981 年，第 1 页。

③ 兰姆，《吟边燕语・出版说明》，林纾、魏易译，北京：商务印书馆，1981 年，第 1 页。

④ 奚永吉，《莎士比亚翻译比较美学》，上海：上海外语教育出版社，2007 年，第 566 页。

⑤ 兰姆，《吟边燕语・出版说明》，林纾、魏易译，北京：商务印书馆，1981 年，第 1 页。

⑥ 兰姆，《吟边燕语・出版说明》，林纾、魏易译，北京：商务印书馆，1981 年，第 1 页。

⑦ 赵稀方，《翻译与新时期话语实践》，北京：中国社会科学出版社，2003 年，第 19 页。

⑧ 兰姆，《吟边燕语・出版说明》，林纾、魏易译，北京：商务印书馆，1981 年，第 1 页。

2.3 从序言分析林纾的翻译观

序言是译作副文本研究中不可缺少的一部分，其作用主要是向读者介绍原作及译作的创作背景和时代意义，是沟通原作与译作之间的桥梁。热奈特指出，序言的主要功能是“确保文本得到正确的解读”①。彭林祥和金宏宇在其文章中也曾提到：“序跋是参与正文本意义生成和确立过程中的最重要的副文本。它为读者进入正文本营造了阅读空间和审美氛围。”②序言是译者向读者传达思想的重要途径之一，促进了译作的传播和译本的正确解读。

2.3.1 译者翻译动机

《吟边燕语》序言部分是林纾自序，首先介绍了作者的翻译动机。“欧人之倾我国也，必曰识见局，思想旧，泥古骇今，好言神怪；因之日旧沦弱，渐即颓运；而吾国少年强济之士，遂一力求新，丑诋其故老，放弃其前载，惟新之从。”③从林纾笔下可以得知，在当时的社会人们开始学习西方文化，导致对本国文化持有全盘否定的态度，认为应全面学习西方的文化。“英文家之哈葛得，诗家之莎士比，非文明大国英特之士耶？顾吾尝译哈氏之书矣，禁蛇役鬼，累累而见。”④因此林纾想通过翻译作品来寻找中西文化文学作品之间的共同之处，英国著名作家诗人莎士比亚笔下的作品也有神怪的描写，“莎氏之诗……立义遣词，往往托象于神怪。”⑤林纾认为：“盖政教两事，与文章无属。政教既美，宜泽以文章。文章徒美，无益于政教。”⑥可以看出，林纾认为一味追求西方文学的学习对政教没有益处，西方国家“惟政教是务”⑦，文学是在政教繁荣的基础上发展起来的。以此来展示出自己对于学习西方文化的态度，认为人们应在学习本国文化的基础上了解西方文化，取其精华去其糟粕。翻译是一种文化的传递现象，通过序言中翻译动机的描写，林纾赋予了莎士比亚故事集新的意义，使其不只是作为故事集呈现给中国读者，而是一部具有历史意义的西方翻译作品。在林纾笔下莎士比亚被塑造成为一个好言神怪的英国伟大诗人，在一定程度上促进了作品的接受。

2.3.2 译者对于原作者评价

林纾对哈葛得和莎士比亚都给予很高的评价，曾多次将两位文学家的作品译入中国，《迦茵小传》《吟边燕语》等作品都对社会产生了重要的影响。序言中林纾将莎士比亚与“中国最伟大的诗人”杜甫相比较，将莎士比亚诠释为英国最伟大的诗人，使其作品更加具有代表性和说服力。

2.3.3 小说体重构

“诗家之莎士比”“莎氏之诗”⑧，在林纾的译序中可以看出，他并不是误将莎剧理解成小

---

① Gérard Genette, *Paratexts: Thresholds of Interpretation*, Trans. Jane E. Lewin. New York: Cambridge University Press, 1997. p197.

② 彭林祥、金宏宇，《作为副文本的新文学序跋》，《江汉论坛》，2009 年第 10 期，第 81 页。

③ 兰姆，《吟边燕语·序言》，林纾、魏易译，北京：商务印书馆，1981 年，第 1 页。

④ 兰姆，《吟边燕语·序言》，林纾、魏易译，北京：商务印书馆，1981 年，第 1 页。

⑤ 兰姆，《吟边燕语·序言》，林纾、魏易译，北京：商务印书馆，1981 年，第 1 页。

⑥ 兰姆，《吟边燕语·序言》，林纾、魏易译，北京：商务印书馆，1981 年，第 1 页。

⑦ 兰姆，《吟边燕语·序言》，林纾、魏易译，北京：商务印书馆，1981 年，第 1 页。

⑧ 兰姆，《吟边燕语·序言》，林纾、魏易译，北京：商务印书馆，1981 年，第 1 页。

说体。林纾清楚地知道莎剧是诗体，但是其翻译目的并不是想简单地翻译其内容，而是想通过小说这种在当时社会受欢迎的语体来表达自己的思想，为了让读者更能接受莎剧，林纾便采用了小说体的形式进行了改写。通过林纾小说体的“再创造”，译本更容易被当时的社会所接受，将莎剧重构为鬼神小说，加深了中国人对于莎剧以及西方文学的认识，在一定程度上促进了莎士比亚在中国的传播与接受。

2.3.4 合作翻译

“挚友仁和魏君春叔，年少英博，淹通西文。长沙张尚书既领译事于京师，余与魏君适厕译席，魏君口述，余则叙致为文章。计二年以来，予二人所分译者，得三四种，《拿破仑本纪》为最巨本，秋初可以毕业矣。”[①]

林纾对英文并不通晓，其多部译作都是通过与别人合作完成的。因此读者也不难理解林纾使用归化方式进行翻译的原因。通过魏易的口述，林纾进行了如此翻译，添加了自己对于原文的理解，通过其翻译将原著进行了重构，文本风格也发生了改变。在自序中林纾提到了魏易，两人曾合作翻译多本著作，除了《吟边燕语》以外，自序中还提到了《拿破仑本纪》。除魏易之外，林纾曾与陈家麟、王庆通、曾宗巩、毛文钟等多人合译并出版过多部著作。其中，曾与魏易合译过学术著作《民种学》、长篇小说《迦茵小传》《黑奴吁天录》等多部作品。林纾的作品对社会、政治、教育等多方面都有所影响。他不断翻译西方小说，其小说也促进了国家和社会的觉醒。[②]其著名译作《黑奴吁天录》(原名《汤姆叔叔的小屋》)在社会上引起强烈影响。林纾在其序跋中批判了美国的暴行，对唤醒民众起了积极的效果，让人们认识到国力的衰弱，激励中国人民开启救国的道路。林纾和魏易两人的译著多是带有爱国主义、救亡图存的呼吁以及对当时社会的批判。[③]在《吟边燕语》序言中，林纾提到：“盖政教两事，与文章无属。政教既美，宜泽以文章。文章徒美，无益于政教。”[④]以此呼吁中国人开启强国的道路，而不是仅仅提倡学习西方政教文化，认为这并不会促进中国走上富强的道路。副文本是呈现译者翻译思想最重要的方式。林纾在序言中提供了与翻译重构的相关信息，促进了读者了解作者的翻译背景和理念。

从以上分析得知，序言部分虽然简短，却涵盖了作者的翻译动机和翻译目的、对原作者及原作的评价等多方面的内容。译者自序作为译作副文本的一部分，为译者现身提供了平台。《吟边燕语》的译序体现了译者的翻译思想和翻译观，也反映了译本在目的语历史和文化环境中的生产和接受机制，因此对于译序对于译著内容也有一定的影响。林纾的著名译著的副文本也是后人研究林纾翻译思想的重要史料。通过研究副文本，可以让译者充分现形[⑤]，揭示文本本身所不能体现出来的东西。

---

① 兰姆，《吟边燕语·序言》，林纾、魏易译，北京：商务印书馆，1981年，第2页。
② 薛卓，《林纾前期译书思想管窥——读“林译小说”序跋札记》，《福建师大学报（哲学社会科版）》，1980年第1期，第71页。
③ 薛卓，《林纾前期译书思想管窥——读“林译小说”序跋札记》，《福建师大学报（哲学社会科版）》，1980年第1期，第70页。
④ 兰姆，《吟边燕语·序言》，林纾、魏易译，北京：商务印书馆，1981年，第1页。
⑤ 肖丽，《副文本之于翻译研究的意义》，《上海翻译》，2011年第4期，第18—19页。

2.4 小标题命名

林纾在其“林译小说”的副文本中都对其译著的原作品进行了文本框架的重构，通过对著作标题、小标题、译序等部分的重构彻底转变了原作品的风格。①在林译《吟边燕语》中，作者不仅将原著的著作名《莎士比亚戏剧故事集》改写为富有中国诗意的名字“吟边燕语”，而且对于小标题，林纾也进行了重命名，将小标题都简化成为两字的传奇式题目，例如将《哈姆雷特》译为《鬼诏》，将《罗密欧与朱丽叶》译为《铸情》，文中也增添了许多对鬼神的描写。小标题的命名突出了故事的主题，同时契合了其对莎剧鬼神的描写，风格与《聊斋》的命名相似。（见表 1）

表 1　译本与原著题目对比

《吟边燕语》标题	*Tales From Shakespeare*
肉券	*The Merchant of Venice*
驯悍	*The Taming* of *The Shrew*
孪误	*The Comedy of Errors*
铸情	*Romeo and Juliet*
仇金	*Timon of Athens*
神合	*Pericles，Prince of Tyre*
蛊征	*Macbeth*
医谐	*All's Well That Ends Well*
狱配	*Measure for Measure*
鬼诏	*Hamlet, Prince of Denmark*
环证	*Cymbeline*
女变	*King Lear*
林集	*As You Like It*
礼哄	*Much Ado About Nothing*
仙狯	*A Midsummer Night's Dream*
珠还	*The Winter's Tale*
黑瞀	*Othello*
婚诡	*Twelfth Night or What You Will*
情惑	*The Two Gentlemen of Verona*
飓引	*The Tempest*

① 柯彦玢，《“外史氏”：文本框架的重塑之道——评林译〈贼史〉》，《外国文学》，2015 年第 4 期，第 34 页。

在《吟边燕语》的序言中可以看到，林纾在翻译的过程中夸大了文中对于鬼神的描写，因此对标题的表达也类似于中国《聊斋》的标题，对标题的重译也可以看出作者的翻译风格。兰姆姐弟在改编故事集时并没有改变其标题，但是林纾对标题也做了特殊处理，根据其译文给每个故事都重拟了标题，使标题呈现出鬼神的风格的同时又能起到吸引国内读者的作用。从读者接受的角度来看，林纾改译的题目更符合中国人的接受心理，符合社会的需求。因此文明戏时期对《吟边燕语》故事的剧本改译也有部分剧名沿用了林纾的标题。①兰姆姐弟沿用了莎士比亚的标题，其中有几个剧名是直接以人名来命名的，例如 *Hamlet*，*Macbeth*，*King Lear*，*Othello* 等，但是林纾都改译成了故事型标题，从而让读者更加关注故事情节的发展。②汪笑侬对于林译本喜爱有加，更是以书中传奇式的标题为题目为该书创作了二十首诗。③但是朱东润曾对林译本两字的标题翻译提出批评，认为两次表达不符合中文表达习惯，并提议在每个标题后都加一个“记”字，三字的标题更符合中国古代戏剧的命名方式。④

3 《吟边燕语》读者评价

热奈特认为，外副文本不限于正文本的形式，因此比内副文本更能起到推广和传播正文本的作用。⑤译作的读者评价作为作品外副文本的一部分，对译作的传播和接受具有重要意义。林译本在莎剧译入史上具有开拓性意义，也有不少学者是通过林译本了解莎士比亚的。众多翻译家和读者对林纾的译本从不同角度给予了客观的评价。著名文学家、学者郭沫若曾给予林纾很高的评价：

“Lamb 的 *Tales from Shakespeare*，林琴南译为《英国诗人吟边燕语》，也使我感受着无上的兴趣。它无形之间给了我很大的影响。后来我虽然也读过 *Tempest*，*Hamlet*，*Romeo and Juliet* 等莎氏的原作，但总觉得没有小时候所读的那种童话式的译本来得更亲切了。”⑥

郭沫若是中国新诗的奠基人之一，中国历史剧的开创者之一，在文学史上具有崇高地位。在郭沫若的文字中我们看到他对林译本的评价之高，他认为林译本比莎剧原作研究更有价值，强调了林译本对于莎剧传播的启蒙作用。林纾与郭沫若同为翻译家，两人虽在翻译策略上不同，但是都强调对主观感情的投入。郭沫若对于林译本的肯定推动了林译本在学界的传播。

相比之下，朱东润给予其译本客观性评价。朱东润指出，林译本《莎剧故事集》文字“倩丽有余而雄直之气不足，好尚奇谲俶诡之事。”特别是在翻译 *Hamlet* 和 *King Lear* 的时候。在他看来，林纾并没有传达莎士比亚的悲剧精神，而是增加了很多鬼神的描写。此外，他还对林译本的标题进行了批判性的分析，认为林纾虽然将标题进行了归化翻译，但两字的标题不

① 安凌，《文明戏时期莎士比亚戏剧的改译及演出》，《外语与外语教学》，2012 年第 3 期，第 78 页。
② 曹新宇、顾兼美，《论清末民初时期莎士比亚戏剧译介与文明戏演出之互动关系》，《戏剧艺术》，2016 年第 2 期，第 41 页。
③ 汪笑侬，《题英国诗人吟边燕语二十首》，《晚清文学丛钞：小说戏曲研究卷》，阿英编，1960 年，第 588-590 页。
④ 李伟昉，《朱东润〈莎氏乐府谈〉价值论》，《外国文学研究》，2019 年第 41 卷第 2 期，第 158 页。
⑤ 张逸琛，《〈红楼梦〉法语全译本的外副文本》，《曹雪芹研究》，2020 年第 4 期，第 145 页。
⑥ 郭沫若，《少年时代》，北京：人民文学出版社，1979 年，第 114 页。

能体现中国的特色，因此提出三字标题的建议。朱东润在《莎氏乐府谈》中对林译本进行了较为客观的分析，对莎剧传播与接受的研究具有重要借鉴意义。①

除了以上对于林译本的直接评价之外，汪笑侬也曾以林纾拟的 20 个标题为题为此处创作了 20 首诗。②由以上作品评价中可以看出多数学者都给予了林译本高度的认可和评价。综上所述，读者评价作为译作外副文本的一部分，对于译本的传播接受与学术研究具有借鉴意义。

4 结 语

《吟边燕语》是莎剧进入中国最重要的译本之一，得到了众多学者的肯定。林纾作为中国著名的作家、翻译家，虽不通晓英语却在翻译界小有成就。其译本文笔优雅，特色鲜明，因此其副文本也具有研究价值。热奈特说有些文本可以被认为是原著的副文本，因为这些译本总是以某种方式评论原著。这样的译本通常都是经过作者修订或核查过的，或者干脆是作者自己译的。因为译者代替了作者修改文本，做了大量的评论。《吟边燕语》的标题、小标题、译序在某种程度上来说正是对原著的评论，有些内容不是原著固有的，而是译者加入或改写的。这种评论既是对原著的评论，也是对当时中国社会的评论。从以上对林译《吟边燕语》副文本的分析，我们可以清楚地看到副文本对于连接作者、译者和读者的桥梁作用，有助于我们更好地理解林纾的翻译风格，全面客观地揭示林译本的价值。

作者简介：朱安博，华北电力大学外国语学院教授，主要从事莎剧汉译研究。
张凯月，华北电力大学外国语学院研究生，主要从事翻译学研究。

① 李伟昉，《朱东润〈莎氏乐府谈〉价值论》，《外国文学研究》，2019 年第 41 卷第 2 期，第 158 页。
② 汪笑侬，《题英国诗人吟边燕语二十首》，《晚清文学丛钞：小说戏曲研究卷》，阿英编，1960 年，第 588-590 页。

莎剧百年译介之路探微

—— 以译者为中心

李　靖

【摘　要】莎士比亚研究被称为世界文化学术的奥林匹克。自 1921 年《少年中国》刊发田汉翻译的莎剧《哈孟雷特》起，莎士比亚戏剧在中国走过整整百年译介之路。针对学界对莎士比亚在中国的传播阶段看法各异，文章采用历时描写法，以译者为中心，补遗一些被学界忽视的译介成果，将莎剧在中国的传播划分为述介、译介与新生三个阶段，其中译介阶段又可分为三个时期，并总结特点。

【关键词】莎士比亚；戏剧；译者；百年

Translation and Review of Shakespeare's Plays over the Past Century: Translator as the Center

Li Jing

【Abstract】Shakespeare study is called “the Olympics of world art and culture”. Since Tian Han's translation of Shakespeare's Hamlet was published in Young China (1921), Shakespeare's plays have gone through a hundred years of translation and introduction in China. Scholars have different views on the stages of Shakespeare's spread in China. This paper divides the spread of Shakespeare's plays in China into three stages: introduction, translation and rebirth, among which the translation stage can be divided into three periods. Taking the translator as the center, this paper adopts the diachronic description method and supplements some translation achievements neglected by the academic circle, then focusing on the translation and rebirth of Shakespeare's plays in the past hundred years and summarizing their characteristics.

【Key Words】Shakespeare; drama; translator; century

1　引　言

马克思称誉莎士比亚是最伟大的戏剧天才。马克思、恩格斯在给斐迪南·拉萨尔的信中更是先后五次提到莎士比亚，要求拉萨尔的剧本“要更加莎士比亚化”（马清福 1979：147），使得“莎士比亚化”成为马克思文艺思想的标识性概念。由此可见，莎士比亚及其作品在革命导师心中的地位。自 1921 年《少年中国》刊发田汉的莎剧[①]译作《哈孟雷特》起，莎剧在中国走过整整百年译介之路。

最早整理莎士比亚戏剧在中国的传播情况是 1954 年——《戏剧报》资料室在《戏剧报》发表《莎士比亚戏剧在中国》。1964 年，莎士比亚 400 周年诞辰时，《世界文学》刊发戈宝权文章《莎士比亚的作品在中国（翻译文学史话）》。1994 年，东北师范大学出版社出版孟宪强专著《中国莎学简史》。学者对莎士比亚作品的考察、研究不断深入，针对个别译者或译作的全面研究也有不少，但从历时角度系统考察莎剧译介的研究仍不充分。笔者以为，站在新时代的历史发展阶段，回顾莎剧在中国的传播历程，以历时研究为经，以译者中心为纬，考察莎剧百年译介之路，并借此讨论我国译者对莎剧翻译的贡献，是有必要和价值的。

2　莎剧在中国的百年译介之路

世界上第一部莎士比亚剧作集[②]问世已近 400 年，莎士比亚来到中国的时间并不久远，莎士比亚作品被翻译成中文的时间更不过 100 年。

不同学者对莎士比亚在中国的传播阶段看法各异。孟宪强（1994：2-50）认为可分为：发轫期（1856—1920）、探索期（1921—1936）、苦斗期（1936—1948）、繁荣期（1949—1965）、崛起期（1978—1988）等阶段；国外学者濑户宏（濑户宏著，陈凌虹译，2017：2-3）则从中国接受莎士比亚的角度划分为清末到五四新文化运动前后、五四新文化运动到 20 世纪 80 年代及 1990 年林兆华导演《哈姆莱特》至今三个阶段。二位的观点都有可资借鉴之处，但笔者认为划分莎士比亚及其作品在中国的传播阶段，应当考虑具有重要影响力的译者和译作的出现时间，及其所处社会背景与文化思潮两大方面因素。

笔者管见，宜以中国共产党早期组织成立及真理标准大讨论时期作为时间节点划分为述介（1840—1920）、译介（1921—1977）与新生（1978—2021）三个阶段。本文在简要回顾、补遗述介基础上，重点阐释译介与新生两个阶段，即译介以来的百年。

2.1　述介（1840—1920）：最初阶段

笔者之所以将中国共产党早期组织成立作为划分节点之一，是因为 1919 年爆发的五四运动进一步促进新文化运动的发展，中国自此走上新民主主义革命的道路；1920 年中国共产党早期组织应运而生，马克思主义的传播成为新思想潮流，真正意义上的莎剧译介就发端于这一思潮背景之下。而在此之前，莎士比亚及其作品在中国文人、学者乃至百姓的学术、文化及社会讨论中，大多是以是以人物记述、日记纪事、梗概故事等形式出现，对此戈宝权与孟宪强都做过细致梳理。既如此，故笔者认为此为第一阶段——述介。

戈宝权（1964）和孟宪强（1994）认为，莎士比亚的名字最早是由传教士介绍进入中国。

① 莎士比亚作为世界大文豪，享誉古今，学界常用莎翁、莎氏及莎剧等简称，本文按此行文。
② 即 1623 年第一对开本《莎士比亚戏剧集》，被认为是最接近莎士比亚戏剧舞台的版本。

李长林、杜平（1997：146）考证后“发现在中国最早提到莎士比亚的是林则徐”[①]。不过，现有的文献表明“莎士比亚”这个译名最早出现在梁启超（1902：83）著的《饮冰室诗话》中：“希腊诗人荷马，古代第一文豪也……近代诗家，如莎士比亚、弥尔敦、田尼逊等，其诗亦动数万言，伟哉!”这个译名沿用至今。

孟宪强(1994:8)指出“中国对莎士比亚生平和戏剧作品进行较为详尽的介绍出现在1916年孙毓修的《欧美小说丛谈》(商务印书馆出版）中”。李伟民（2013：88）则认为“王国维的《莎士比传》堪称中国最早出版的莎士比亚传记”。笔者发现，1913年，孙毓修(1913：47)就在《小说月报（上海1910)》第4卷第7期刊文《欧美小说丛谈续编：英国戏曲之发源》，其中写到：“……至15世纪而极盛。莎士比 Shakespeare 之戏曲，实道源于此。”1916年，商务印书馆出版的《欧美小说丛谈》实际上是汇集之前诸多丛谈而成。此外，1918年，《南京高等师范学校校友会杂志》第1卷第1期刊有汤志谦的文言译作《莎士比亚之历史》，该文译自豪斯所著的 *A Brief English Literature*，主要述介莎翁生平、创作四期及作品类型等。

另一方面，李伟昉（2016：31）认为“林纾翻译的《吟边燕语》是中国以完整的戏剧形式并用白话文翻译莎士比亚作品前最重要的莎士比亚戏剧故事翻译，对推动莎士比亚在中国的传播产生了极为深远的影响”。不过，林纾一生笃工古文，不通英文，《吟边燕语》实际由他与魏易合译而成。陈历明（2016：87）则认为1903年出版的《海外奇谭》[②]比林译本还早，是最早的莎剧汉译本。而这两个译本共同之处在于都是文言译本，且都译自兰姆的 *The Tales from Shakespeare*（《莎士比亚故事集》，旧通称《莎氏乐府本事》)。

另有一位被学界忽视的译者——甘作霖。继林纾与魏易之后，他于1916年至1917年间独自用文言翻译兰姆本中部分故事：《威内萨之商人》《麦克伯》与《丹麦太子哈姆来德》，陆续在《英文杂志》发表。

2.2　译介（1921—1976)：最难阶段

清朝后期先后推行洋务运动、维新运动及清末新政，但都是为维护封礼旧制而生。直到五四运动的爆发，直到中国共产党早期党组织的出现，新文化运动才真正、全面地到来——以李大钊为首的中国共产党早期组织领导反对旧道德，提倡新道德；反对文言，提倡白话；反对旧文学，倡导新文学。笔者认为莎剧在中国的译介就孕育与发端于这一思潮与时代背景。

笔者通过“超星发现”[③]高级检索方式，设定检索项为“全部字段”，输入“莎士比亚”；检索年份：1921—2021；语种：中文及外文；文献类型：图书、期刊、报纸、学位论文及会议论文。检索得到41751项结果，其中图书5473项、期刊30638项、报纸3756项、学位论文1683项、会议论文201项。选择可视化查看，可见：总体而言，各类学术发展百年趋势基本一致。1930年代前期产出微量；1930年代中期至1960年代中期各产出相对均衡；1970年代末期后，各类学术发展重获新生，图书出版、学位论文和报纸文章量逐步攀升，期刊载量

---

① 林则徐在广东主持禁烟时，辑译的《四洲志》中有“沙士比阿”一词。邹振环（2020：82）认为“《四洲志》当时有无单行本刊行，至今仍是一个谜。”，但据考约出现在1840年前后。

② 戈宝权（1964）认为是《澥外奇谭》。就笔者所知，古文“谭”同“谈”，“渤海”古称“渤澥”。

③ “超星发现”是一个拥有近10亿海量元数据，涵盖清末至今的在线资源检索库。虽未必全面采集全部数据，但笔者多方查找，鲜见类似资源。本文相关检索最后访问时间均为2021年8月31日。

增势尤其明显。(详见图 1)

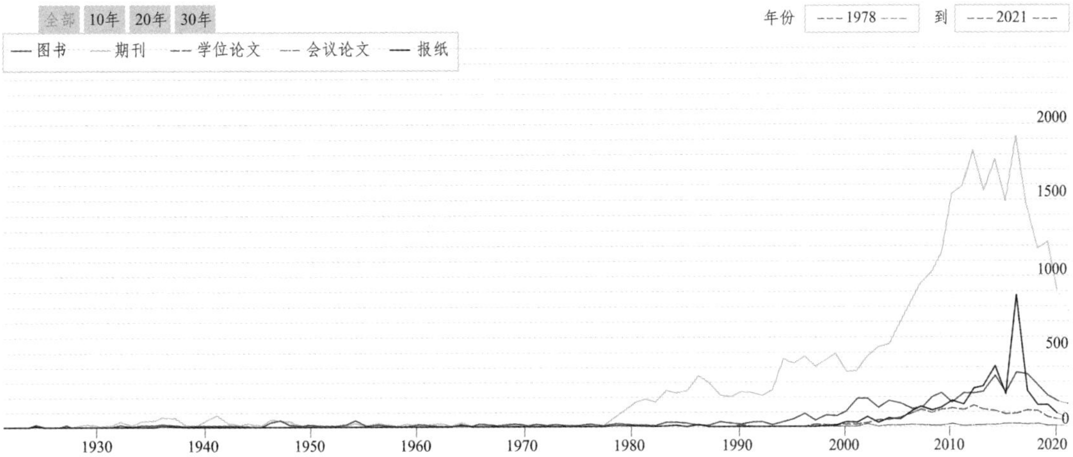

图 1　莎士比亚各类型学术发展图(1921—2021)

(注:趋势图从最早有数据的年份开始显示。)

基于此,并根据莎剧作品翻译、译述与评介的发展情况,笔者将 1921 年以来的 100 年以 1978 年出现的真理标准大讨论为节点一分为二,即译介与新生两个阶段,译介阶段大致又可分为发端共鸣、译介高产及曲折前行三个时期。

2.2.1　发端共鸣的十五年(1921—1935)

1921 年,田汉在《少年中国》第 2 卷 12 期上发表用现代白话文翻译的《哈孟雷特》(第一幕第一至三场),可以说这是莎剧翻译真正意义上的发端。经过整理,1922 年 11 月,中华书局出版《莎翁杰作集 第一种 哈孟雷特》单行本。译本开体例之先河,是首部莎士比亚剧作集问世近 300 年后,我国首部以剧本形式用散文体完成的莎剧白话文全译本。笔者认为,这是田汉对中国戏剧翻译的最大贡献,中国莎学者由此开启莎剧的翻译、评论与演出之路——田汉堪为中国莎剧翻译的先驱。

田汉在《译序》(1922:1)中对莎剧有简单述评,认为“莎翁的作者生涯略可分为四期:(一)习作期,(二)喜剧期,(三)悲剧期,(四)老成期……读 *Hamlet* 的独白,to be or not to be,that is a question。不啻读屈子离骚”。田汉作为莎剧首位译者,应该也是首位明确指出这一经典独白文学价值的中国译者。此外,1924 年,中华书局再次出版田汉译著——《罗密欧与朱丽叶》,笔者没有发现比该译本更早的完整译本,且田汉的译名沿用至今。

值得指出的是,之前学界(戈宝权,1964:140;孟宪强,1994:13;王林,2003:134)一致认为,田汉仅翻译过以上两部莎剧。但笔者研究发现,1923 年,《革新评论》第 2 卷第 3 期还刊载过田汉译作《莎翁杰作集 第三种 恺撒》第一幕,译文文末还提示“未完”。该刊第 2 卷第 4 至 6 期,笔者多方查找无果,但第 7 期上再刊田汉文章《曹锟篡国与艺术家的态度》。当时常见译者以连刊形式发表长篇译文,笔者推测,很可能第 4 至 6 期刊有田汉续译的《恺撒》译稿,这当然需进一步考证。

1929 年,田汉还在自己主编的《南国月刊》上发表长篇译文《莎士比亚剧演出之变迁》,

系日本人 Nakamura 原著，该译文后与另两篇文章一并收入田汉译著《欧洲三个时代的戏剧》。田汉的莎剧译作问世后，逐渐引发文人、学者对莎剧的热情关注、讨论与共鸣。

1922 年 7 月中旬，余上沅曾用“上沅”之名，在《晨报副刊》上连刊译文《〈汉姆列〉少了汉姆列》，将 *Hamlet* 译为“汉姆列”；10 月中下旬，又逐日连续发文《过去二十二戏剧名家及其代表杰作》，其中 10 月 18 日第八篇为《莎士比亚与〈汉姆列〉》，认为“无论如何，莎士比亚，总是戏剧史上数一数二的人物，我们绝不能不重视他”（1922：2）。后来还在《新月》上刊文《翻译莎士比亚》，提及日本坪内雄臧历时 43 年，终于在 1928 年完成莎士比亚全集的翻译，认为“创作和翻译两种艺术相距虽不可以道理计，而完美与完美是相近的”，而当前“新文字新技术的应用，不但未到纯熟，并且还时常感觉不够，工具不练到精纯充足的地步，再好的思想，再好的意境，也是不能圆满的表现”（余上沅，1930：11）。

1925 年，《现代评论》刊发田汉《论翻译答江绍原先生》一文，该文提到“试译者”的初衷，并表达了田汉对批判译本的文论持欢迎的“就正”态度。可惜，笔者遍寻而不得江绍原所作的原文文献。此外，1926 年，焦尹孚在《洪水》连刊《评田汉君的莎译——〈罗密欧与朱丽叶〉》。

1928 年，《新月》发表梁实秋译文《莎士比亚时代之英国与伦敦》，记述莎士比亚身处的时代背景、社会环境及其戏剧之路。1932 年，梁实秋还在《图书评论》刊文《莎翁名著哈姆雷特的两种译本》，这时他已开始着手翻译莎剧。该文将邵挺文言译本《天仇记》（邵译本）与田汉译本《哈孟雷特》（田译本）对比，采用译名“哈姆雷特”，可见作者对剧名译名不同于田、邵二位的态度，并认为田译本较佳：“田译本和邵译本可不能同年而语了……我觉得此书有广为介绍的必要。”同时按甲、乙、丙、丁之顺序列举尚需斟酌的十处译文，并认为田译本没有交代翻译所依据的版本，故在文末提出观点：“所以翻译莎士比亚的作品，应先研究莎士比亚的文字。”（梁实秋，1932：61-64）

陈铨在《清华学报》刊发长文《十九世纪德国文学批评家对于哈孟雷特的解释》，该文沿用田汉译名“哈孟雷特”，剖析德国文艺批评家、剧作集雷兴（今译莱辛）、歌德等对哈孟雷特的解释所带来的价值，认为“在欧洲文学里边最有趣味的人莫过于莎士比亚的哈孟雷特，最复杂的人莫过于哈孟雷特，而同时最难解释的也莫过于哈孟雷特”（陈铨，1934：913）。

这一时期，有关莎氏作品的评论与研究也在不断走向深入。《译文》杂志多次刊发苏联莎士比亚学者和戏剧家的论文的译作，比如魏猛克翻译的狄纳莫夫的讲稿《学习莎士比亚》（1935）等。这些文章基于马列主义分析莎士比亚及其作品，指出莎士比亚是伟大的人道主义者，其作品乃现实主义的光辉榜样，对于当时文艺工作者起到巨大的作用。

田汉莎剧译本的问世，引发的关注、讨论乃至争论，某种意义上是一种共鸣与共情。可以说，莎剧读者、译者以及学者合力掀起了新文化运动里莎剧翻译、介评的第一波浪潮。总的来说，这一时期莎剧译介可以概括为三个特点：以田汉为代表，正式开启莎剧翻译之路；莎剧译者、译著及著作数量上升；莎评文章出现马列主义与中国立场的视角与观点。

2.2.2 译介高产的三十年（1936—1966）

发端共鸣的十五年，虽有莎剧译著陆续面世，但不少是复译。译界各自为政，对莎剧缺乏有计划和系统的翻译。或许是受日本莎剧全集翻译出版的影响，或是民族危难，爱国气节使然，1930 年代起，在中国翻译莎剧全集的共识逐渐形成。朱生豪、梁实秋与曹未风是这一代译者中最具代表性的拓荒者，几年之后，中国迎来翻译莎剧作品的高潮。

朱生豪翻译莎剧之初受到前辈同事詹文浒的鼓励。他从 1935 年开始翻译莎剧，1936 年完成首部译作《暴风雨》。其时国难当头，战乱纷飞，而他流离失所，疾病缠身。在 1944 年 4 月，编完《莎士比亚戏剧全集》1~3 集后病情不断恶化，12 月便含怨离世，英年 32 岁。朱生豪以常人不可想象的坚毅，以只争朝夕的果敢，以妙笔生花的文字，共译出 31 个剧本，仅剩 6 个历史剧未竟。1947 年，世界书局分上、中、下三卷本出版《莎士比亚戏剧全集》，除 4 部历史剧之外，共收录 27 部译作。1954 年，作家出版社出版《莎士比亚全集》31 种，共计 180 万字。1964 年，人民文学出版社组织杨周翰、方重等教授，先后译出朱生豪未译完的 6 个历史剧，以及莎士比亚的全部诗歌。但随之而来的“四清”运动与“文化大革命”中断了《莎士比亚全集》的出版。即便如此，堪为译界楷模的朱生豪已然成为中国翻译史上永远的丰碑。

1930 年，梁实秋为顾仲彝翻译的《威尼斯商人》校阅，开始接触莎剧翻译。在胡适的推动下，1931 年起开始着手翻译莎剧，由此走上翻译莎翁作品的漫漫长路。梁实秋最早译成《暴风雨》等七部，1936 年 5 月至 11 月之间陆续由商务印书馆出版。1967 年，全部译出的 37 部莎剧在台湾地区出版，梁实秋成为中国首位以一己之力译完莎士比亚全集的翻译家。历时三十多年，从讲授莎剧，到发表莎评，再到翻译莎剧，梁实秋堪为中国研究莎士比亚的研究权威，翻译莎剧的领军人物。

李伟民（2015：100-101）认为 “曹未风是中国第一个计划翻译出版莎士比亚戏剧全集的翻译家”，“自 1931 年起翻译莎士比亚剧本与十四行诗，计划全部译出莎士比亚戏剧”。1935 年到 1944 年，他先后译出《该撒大将》等 11 部，除《该撒大将》由商务印书馆出版外，其余各部由贵阳文通书局以“莎士比亚全集”总名出版。1946 年，新译的《安东尼与枯娄葩》连同之前译本，由文化合作股份有限公司冠以“曹译莎士比亚全集”之名出版。1959 年，在《外语教学与翻译》期刊上连载《翻译莎士比亚札记》，讲述其近 30 年翻译莎剧的困境与心得，对人物性格的把握等。不幸的是，1963 年因病故去。1950 年代至 1980 年代初，新文艺出版社、上海文艺出版社及上海译文出版社连续再版发行其译作，可见影响甚广。

孙大雨是一位对莎剧翻译具有独特贡献的译者，他一生译有《黎琊王》等八部莎剧。早在 1931 年，他就在《诗刊》上发表《译 *King Lear*》《罕姆莱德》（第 3 幕第 4 景）两部节译诗体译作。孙大雨（1931：32）在译文后的“跋”说道：“我的方法不是直译，也不像意译，可以说是‘气译’—— 原作的气质要是中国文字里能相当地保持，我总是尽我的心力为它保持……，我以为用诗行翻译诗行是可以允许的。”他运用自创的“音组”的办法来翻译原文里的“素体韵文”（又称素诗体，Blank Verse），颇费苦心，独具贡献。1944 年，还在《中山文化季刊》上发表长文《莎翁悲剧“黎琊王”底最初版本写作年代于故事来源》，考证详尽。1948 年 11 月，《黎琊王》译注版（上、下二册）终于由商务印书馆出版。1957 年后，孙大雨遭遇长期不公，其莎剧译著终于在 1990 年代由上海译文出版社出版，并将《罕秣莱德》《黎琊王》《奥赛罗》《麦克白斯》收入《莎士比亚四大悲剧》出版。孙大雨的一生，虽历经坎坷，但钟于莎剧与诗歌，自创理论，对莎剧译介极为用功，足见其造诣精深。

同时代的莎剧译者还有曹禺、卞之琳。1944 年，文化生活社出版曹禺译作《柔蜜欧与幽丽叶》。这也是一个诗体译本，是为演出而译，故在台词中加入了“舞台指示”。译文一出，李辰冬即在《文化先锋》上发表书评文章《柔蜜欧与幽丽叶》，陈列三点理由赞誉曹禺先生的译文为最佳版本。1947 年，署名陈瘦竹的文章《〈柔蜜欧与幽丽叶〉研究》刊发在《文潮月刊》，该文逐幕、逐景甚至逐段地剖析了剧目跌宕起伏、变幻莫测背后的深刻原因。1949 年，上海文化生活出版社再次出版曹译本。此后，1954 年，1960 年，作家出版社与人民文学出版社也分别再次出版。方平也称赞曹译本“这一优美的诗体译本，向读者展现的艺术境界是一般散文体难以达到的”（甘险峰，2010：52）。卞之琳 1954 年才开始研究与翻译莎剧，晚于其他同时代的译者。1956 年初，《文学研究集刊》第二册刊载卞之琳长文《莎士比亚的悲剧〈哈姆雷特〉》；8 月，作家出版社出版其译著《哈姆雷特》，这也是一个诗体译本，堪称莎剧中译的经典。1964 年，《文学评论》第 4 期刊载卞之琳长文《莎士比亚戏剧创作的发展》，论及莎士比亚的人道主义及“未定型的资产阶级倾向”的阶级属性。接着，张永忠在《文学评论》第 5 期刊发表评论文章《对于〈莎士比亚戏剧创作的发展〉一文的意见》，认为卞文“未能紧紧扣住它的阶级内容”“没有把个人主义的实质揭示出来”（张永忠，1965：77-78）。

方平与吴兴华，是读着第一代、第二代莎剧译者的作品成长的新生代杰出译者。早在 1948 年，方平就选译过莎士比亚的诗歌《维纳丝与阿童妮》（*Venus and Adonis*），发表在《诗创造》上；1952 年，全部译出后，由上海文艺联合出版社出版。1953 年，方平译注的《捕风捉影》由平明出版社出版，该译本还分别于 1957、1961 年由新文艺出版社、上海文艺出版社出版。1955 年，平明出版社出版方平译著《亨利第五》，该部译著还于 1958 年由人民文学出版社出版。1961 年，上海文艺出版社出版方平译著《威尼斯商人》。1957 年，人民文学出版社出版吴兴华译著《亨利四世》。1956 年，《北京大学学报（人文科学版）》刊发吴兴华长文《莎士比亚的亨利四世》，文章从故事描写的历史事件切入，分析莎士比亚的创作方法。1963 年，吴兴华在《文学评论》再刊长文《〈威尼斯商人〉—— 冲突和解决》。吴兴华文章犹如抽丝剥茧，层层深入，读之畅快人心。

这一时期，除了上述杰出代表，还有不少为莎剧译介做出贡献的译者，如 1937 年，方重翻译西林考特所作文章《莎士比亚与民族理想》连续刊载在《奔涛》。1959 年，人民文学出版社出版方重译著《理查三世》。此外，周庄萍、孙伟佛、蒋镇、邱存真、张常之等先后翻译过不同莎剧，详见《戏剧报》资料室及戈宝权整理成果，不再赘述。

总的来说，这一时期莎剧译介呈现三个特点：译著和译者明显增多，犹如雨后春笋，成果丰硕；从翻译单行本到翻译全集的开拓；由散文译本到诗体译本的探索。

2.2.3 曲折前行的十年（1967—1977）

1966 年，十年“文化大革命”开始。2004 年，孟宪强补正之前观点，称这一时期为中国莎学史上的“延续期”。笔者认为这段时期的莎剧译介既有大陆地区的曲折，也有港台地区的精进，是曲折前行的十年。

笔者通过“超星发现”用同样方法检索 1967—1977 范围值，仅得结果 47 项，其中报纸 1 项，期刊 9 项，图书 37 项。图书中除 2 项外，其他均是莎剧或诗歌译著。47 项检索结果，笔者剔除 1 项英文、1 项日文、1 篇报纸文章外，其余 44 项文献资料出版机构或作者地域的分布情况是：香港 1 项，大陆 10 项，台湾 33 项。10 项大陆文献中有 6 项发表或出版于 1977 年，即在粉碎“四人帮”后。管中窥豹，可见一斑，“文化大革命”十年期间大陆莎剧的翻译、介评与传播几近停滞。好在港台地区的莎剧译介活动不断发展。例如，1969 年，台湾地区由世界书局出版了由朱生豪的译本及虞尔昌的补译汇集而成的《莎士比亚全集》；1970 年代，梁实秋诸多莎剧译本分别由爱眉文艺出版社、远东图书公司出版；1976 年，周兆祥在香港大学完成学位论文《汉译哈姆雷特研究》并出版。

囿于平台数据限制，上述数据并不能全面反映这一时期港台地区莎剧译介、研究的全貌，加之个人学识和精力有限，没能在更大范围检索整理，但是有关大陆地区数据相对具有可信度。

2.3 新生（1978—2021）：最快阶段

邓小平（1994：144）认为："关于真理标准问题的争论，的确是个思想路线问题，是个政治问题，是个关系到党和国家前途和命运的问题。"笔者将真理标准大讨论时期作为划分时间节点，正是因为通过这场大讨论，莎剧翻译、研究及演出等传播活动才得以蓬勃发展。

如前所述，自 1978 年起，各类学术发展重新迎来春天。2016 年，在莎士比亚逝世 400 年时各类学术发展达到高峰。笔者再次通过"超星发现"用同样方法检索 1978—2021 范围值，得到 40493 项结果，可见，这一阶段的各类成果可谓车载斗量，汗牛充栋，限于篇幅，笔者简要介绍主要译作和学者成果，辅以图表方式，以便读者管窥全貌。（详见图 2、图 3）

图 2、3 可见，这一时期各类型文献总量占百年（1921—2021）各类型文献总量 41753 项近 97%，可见发展之迅猛。40493 项中，期刊项数量占比最高，近四分之三，显示出莎剧研究走向深入和广泛。以莎翁 400 周年诞辰的 2016 年为例，全年图书类文献数量（357 项）接近于 1978 年之前图书类文献数量之和（384 项）；而期刊类文献数量（1936 项）则比 1978 年之前期刊类文献数量之和（863 项）还多 1073 项。

译作方面，逐渐涌现出分门别类、系统编辑的莎剧全集，而不再以零散、个别的单行本为常见。这一时期，多种莎剧全集先后出版。1978 年，人民文学出版社出版的以朱生豪译本为主体（经吴兴华等校订），由吴兴华、方平、章益、杨周翰等补译的 11 卷本《莎士比亚全集》终于面世，这既是中国大陆出版的第一部莎剧全集，也是第一部外国作家作品全集。朱生豪矢志不移的心愿终得实现，时至今日，朱生豪仍是当今中国最有影响力的莎剧翻译家。

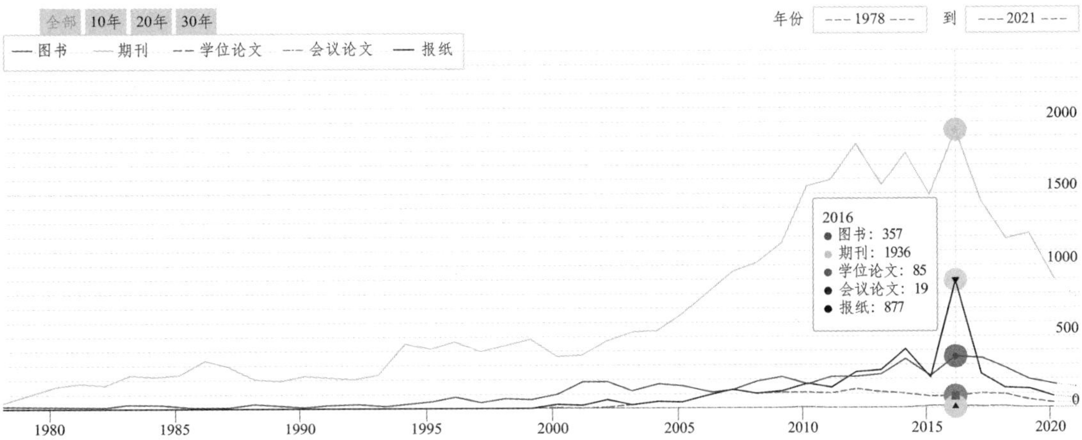

图 2　莎士比亚各类型学术发展图（1978—2021）

（注：趋势图从最早有数据的年份开始显示。）

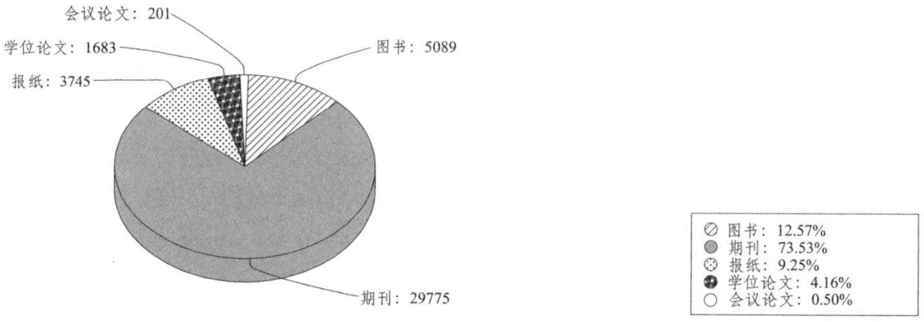

图 3　莎士比亚各类型学术成果数量占比图（1978—2021）

1995 年，中国广播电视出版社出版梁实秋译的《莎士比亚全集》。2002 年，中国广播电视出版社联合远东图书公司再次出版梁实秋译的 40 册中英对照版《莎士比亚全集》。

1998 年，译林出版社出版以朱生豪翻译（裘克安、何其莘、沈林、辜正坤等校订）为主体，由索天章、孙法理、刘炳善、辜正坤补译的 8 卷本《莎士比亚全集》，全集包括了莎士比亚的全部三十九出戏剧、两部长诗、一部十四行诗集，及一些杂诗和片段。此前，未有如此完整中文全集译本。2016 年，译林出版社基于该全集版，还出版过限量 2000 套的《莎士比亚全集》典藏版，全集共 12 卷，按喜剧、悲剧、历史剧、传奇剧和诗歌分类。

2000 年，方平主编和主译的诗体译本《新莎士比亚全集》（12 卷）由河南教育出版社出版；2014 年，上海译文出版社再版。该全集还由猫头鹰出版社在台湾地区出版。1993 年 6 月起，由方平主译，屠岸、汪义群、辜正坤等合译，《新莎士比亚全集》历时 4 年余，即告完成。新全集不仅是译著，还有编著的性质，每部剧之首都冠有一篇“前言”，剧末附上一篇“考证”，既有学术评介价值，又兼有资料编著的特质。1999 年，方平在《〈新莎士比亚全集〉译后记》一文中回顾在已有散文体莎士比亚全集的情况下，为何还要“呼唤新的全集诞生”的初心。新全集竭力实现莎剧精神风貌（形式）与艺术风格（内容）的有机统一，是莎剧翻译史上又一个里程碑。

2016 年，外语教学与研究出版社出版辜正坤主译，许渊冲、罗选民、傅浩、曹明伦、刁克利及彭镜禧等合译的《莎士比亚全集·英汉双语本》（39 册）。该全集整体上采取“以诗体译诗体，以散体译散体”的翻译基调。同年，浙江工商大学出版社出版我国第一部四卷本《莎士比亚全集》，四卷分别为喜剧、历史剧、悲剧、传奇剧和诗歌。该全集集朱生豪译出的 31 种戏剧及陈才宇补译的 8 种戏剧、154 首十四行诗、两首长诗和若干短诗而成。应该说，2016 年出版的全集是为纪念莎翁逝世 400 周年而生。

值得一提的是，2014 年，台北商务印书馆出版傅光明新译的中英对照本《罗密欧与朱丽叶》——傅光明计划以一己之力，用十年时间完成新译《莎士比亚全集》的宏大工程由此开始。至今，天津人民出版社已出版《哈姆雷特》等十八部，已接近完成一半。傅光明新译《莎士比亚全集》每部作品都有一篇长篇导读，并且添加大量注释，有助于读者理解作品的隐含意义和时代背景，相信众人都对傅氏译竣莎剧全集满怀希望，并期待见证。

这一阶段，期刊文献与学位论文数量均有显著增加。概括而言，可分为两类，一类是与莎翁、莎剧文本相关的成果，比如莎翁的身世、作品的历史背景、版本校勘、文本注疏、演出史、批评史等，另一类是针对莎剧译者、译本的成果，比如翻译思想、文化取向，译作的语言风格及译本对比等。1980 年代到 1990 年代，王佐良、李赋宁、孙家琇、孟宪强等都是莎学研究杰出代表。笔者通过“中国知网”以“莎士比亚”为主题词检索 1978 年以来文献成果，从期刊发文数量和被引频次来看，李伟昉、李伟民、胡开宝、陈国华、蓝仁哲、罗益民、曹明伦、曹树钧、杨林贵等学者的莎学、莎剧研究成果具有代表性。学位论文则以龚芬、庄新红、张威及辛雅敏等为代表。因这一阶段以来的研究文献方便查阅，均不再赘述。

总之，这一时期的莎剧译介研究重获新生，突飞猛进，研究边界不断拓宽，研究视野愈显开阔，成果也日益丰硕。

3 余 论

自田汉的莎剧译本《哈孟雷特》问世至今，完整意义上的中国莎剧翻译走过百年历程。回顾莎剧在中国的传播所经历的述介、译介与新生三个阶段，不同阶段特点各异：述介，为最初阶段，发展缓慢；译介，是最难阶段，译评丰硕；新生，乃最快阶段，百花齐放。

放眼百年的莎学译介、研究成果，可以说浩如烟海，更勿提横向共时的比较研究了—— 这也是本文不足之处，比如对同时期港台地区的莎剧研究叙述显然不够，澳门地区是何情况，更无从谈起。此外，笔者实属刚刚迈入莎学这一宏大学术殿堂，学力颇有不逮之感，故文中观点难免有谬误之处——谨此求教于同仁、方家斧正——当然文责自负了。

参考文献

[1] 《戏剧报》资料室. 1954. 莎士比亚的戏剧在中国[J]. 戏剧报（4）：40-42.

[2] 卞之琳. 1964. 莎士比亚戏剧创作的发展[J]. 文学评论（4）：52-79.

[3] 陈历明. 2016. 莎剧最早的汉译本：《海外奇谭》[J]. 外国语（1）：87-95.

[4] 陈铨. 1934. 十九世纪德国文学批评家对于哈孟雷特的解释[J]. 清华学报（4）：913-939.

[5] 邓小平. 1994. 邓小平文选（第 2 卷）[M]. 北京：人民出版社.

[6] 甘险峰. 2010. “我与莎士比亚 60 年”—— 方平论莎士比亚翻译史[J]. 文学界（专辑版）（9）：52-53.

[7] 戈宝权. 1964. 莎士比亚的作品在中国（翻译文学史话）[J]. 世界文学（5）：136-143.

[8] 濑户宏. 2017. 莎士比亚在中国：中国人的莎士比亚接受史[M]. 陈凌虹，译. 广州：广东人民出版社.

[9] 李长林，杜平. 1997. 中国对莎士比亚的了解与研究—— 《中国莎学简史》补遗[J]. 中国比较文学（4）：146-152.

[10] 李伟昉. 2016. 论林纾对莎士比亚的接受及其文化意义[J]. 文学评论（1）：31-35.

[11] 李伟民. 2013. 文以纪传，曲以吊古—— 王国维的《莎士比传》[J]. 外语研究（6）：88-92.

[12] 李伟民. 2015. 被湮没的莎士比亚戏剧译者与研究者—— 曹未风的译莎与论莎[J]. 外国语（5）：100-109。

[13] 梁启超. 1902. 饮冰室诗话[J]. 新民丛报（9）：83-92.
[14] 梁实秋. 1932. 莎翁名著哈姆雷特的两种译本[J]. 图书评论（2）：61-64.
[15] 马清福. 1979. 关于“莎士比亚化”[J]. 戏剧创作（5）147-148.
[16] 孟宪强. 1994. 中国莎学简史[M]. 长春：东北师范大学出版社.
[17] 孟宪强. 2004. 中国莎学史上的“延续期”——《中国莎学简史》自补遗之二[J]. 四川外国语学院学报（3）：34-41.
[18] 莎士比亚. 1922. 莎翁杰作集 第一种 哈孟雷特[M]. 田汉，译. 上海：中华书局.
[19] 莎士比亚. 1923. 恺撒—— 莎翁杰作集第三种（未完）[J]. 田汉，译. 革新评论（3）：7-24.
[20] 孙大雨. 1931. 跋[J]. 诗刊（3）：23.
[21] 孙大雨. 1954. 莎士比亚悲剧《黎琊王》和它对于我们的意义[J]. 文艺报（10）：17-20.
[22] 孙毓修. 1913. 欧美小说丛谈续编：英国戏曲之发源[J]. 小说月报（上海 1910）（7）：47-51.
[23] 豪斯. 1918. 莎士比亚之历史[J]. 汤志谦，译. 南京高等师范学校校友会杂志（1）：4-9.
[24] 田汉. 1925. 论翻译答江绍原先生[J]. 现代评论（30）：17-19.
[25] 王林. 2003. 论田汉早期的外国文学接受与译介[J]. 中国比较文学（2）：126-137.
[26] 余上沅. 1922-07-20. 《汉姆列》少了汉姆列[N]. 晨报副刊（1-2）.
[27] 余上沅. 1922-10-18. 过去二十二戏剧名家及其代表杰作（八）莎士比亚与《汉姆列》[N]. 晨报副刊（1-2）.
[28] 余上沅. 1930. 翻译莎士比亚[J]. 新月（5-6）.
[29] 张永忠. 1965. 对于《莎士比亚戏剧创作的发展》一文的意见[J]. 文学评论（5）：76-78.
[30] 邹振环. 2020. 舆地智环：近代中国最早编译的百科全书《四洲志》[J]. 中国出版史研究（1）：78-104.

基金项目：本文受湖南省教育厅科研项目（项目编号：17C1310）和长沙师范学院教研项目（项目批准号：PX-16201002）资助。

作者简介：李靖，长沙师范学院外国语学院讲师，中山大学博士研究生。主要研究方向：戏剧翻译，商务法律翻译。

《仲夏夜之梦》的儿童剧源语改编

刘昌茂　徐圣琳　吕　晟

【摘　要】国内外莎士比亚剧作的改编已趋于成熟，但绝大部分的观演群体都以成年人为主。本文借鉴国内外儿童剧改编的经验，对莎翁的经典喜剧《仲夏夜之梦》进行儿童化源语改编。从剧情筛选、角色删减和台词创新三方面，采取针对不同需求分别对待的方式，本着姚斯“期待视野”的创作原则，尽可能在保持原著中的美学价值、哲理性等精髓的同时，对情节和台词做了“去成人化”处理，让复杂台词简单化，使改编的剧作从观演双方都满足国内受众群体的需求，为儿童群体提供了表演与欣赏莎剧的机会。

【关键词】莎士比亚；儿童剧改编；《仲夏夜之梦》

Adapting *A Midsummer Night's Dream* for Children in English

Liu Changmao　Xu Shenglin　Lyu Sheng

【Abstract】Although adaptations of Shakespeare have developed prosperously and been mature at home and abroad, the majority of the audiences and performers are mostly adults, and there are few researches on adapting Shakespeare into children's drama domestically. Enlightened by the experience of adapting children's plays at home and abroad, this paper focuses on the measures of adapting *A Midsummer Night's Dream* in English for children, in which plots' selection, characters' simplification and lines' innovation are included. Meanwhile, based on Jauss' “horizon of expectations”, this paper manages to childrenize the plots and lines, saving the essence of aesthetic value and philosophy from the original version, on the purpose of satisfying the audiences and performers' needs and providing the children in our country with more opportunities of performing and appreciating Shakespeare's plays.

【Key Words】Shakespeare; adaptation of children's drama; *A Midsummer Night's Dream*

在中国，莎翁的作品不仅是被搬上舞台最频繁的外国戏剧，改编自莎剧的相关影视作品和戏曲在国内也屡见不鲜，但其受众群体仍然以成年人为主，以英语作为台词语言，对莎剧进行儿童化源语改编的研究却是寥寥无几。在儿童化莎士比亚的道路上，兰姆姐弟于

1807 年出版了《莎士比亚故事集》(*Tales from Shakespeare*)，作者在努力保持对改编版本忠实性的同时，将莎士比亚的戏剧语言改编成通俗易懂的叙事性散文，不仅删去了原著中可能对儿童产生不良影响的不雅语言和禁忌文字，还消除了妨碍儿童和青少年读者顺利阅读的语言障碍。除此之外，国内外的专家也通过绘本的方式将莎剧儿童化编写后出版，以达到向儿童群体传播莎翁经典作品的目的，如法国儿童作家卡罗琳·吉约(Caroline Guillot)的《写给孩子的莎士比亚》和罗益民的《给孩子讲莎士比亚》。两位作者都只保留了主要的故事线和重要角色，大大简化了台词，最终使故事更加轻松简洁。但遗憾的是，以剧本为体裁对莎剧进行语内改编的研究却从未有人涉足。确实，既要忠实于原著，平衡创新与传统的“度”，又要进行儿童化改编，是一项非常艰难的任务。本文将结合国内外儿童剧改编经验，论述如何力求在不改变原著主旨的前提下，通过筛选情节、调整角色、简化台词等手段对原著进行儿童化改编，并结合排演与最终舞台呈现的结果检验改编版《仲夏夜之梦》的适用性与实用性。

1 情节的筛选

作为世界文坛的瑰宝，莎士比亚戏剧拥有极高的文学价值。我国著名莎学专家李伟民教授曾这样评价莎剧：“在重读经典的呼唤声中，莎士比亚毫无疑问是应该重读的经典之一。”“它的经典地位显示出一种长期的稳定性，不仅在世界范围的文学经典文本研究中独占鳌头，而且在舞台上常演不衰。”(2008：36-37)然而，并不是所有的剧本都适合儿童剧改编。在选择剧本时，莎翁的喜剧因为其轻松诙谐又不失深刻性的特点，成为改编者们的第一选择。在莎翁众多优秀的喜剧作品中，笔者选择了具有魔法元素的《仲夏夜之梦》(以下简称《仲夏》)。《仲夏》讲述了古代雅典四个年轻人为了追求真爱，在机缘巧合下先后来到雅典郊外的树林，在误入精灵的领地后，因“爱懒花汁”魔力的作用，发生了一系列令人啼笑皆非，但最终有情人终成眷属的故事。美国著名心理学家布鲁诺·贝特尔海姆在其著作《永恒的魅力：童话世界与童心世界》中提出：“没有经历一个相信魔力的阶段，儿童长大后难以经受成年生活的疑难和困苦。童话故事是向儿童提供魔力幻想的最好资源。”[①]正因如此，贯穿着魔法和精灵元素的故事情节才能够完美契合孩子们热爱思考，天真烂漫的性格，并满足他们对一切日常生活中难以接触到的事物天马行空般的想象。

亚里士多德把戏剧的主要元素分为：情节、性格、言语、思想、戏景、唱段。“在这六大要素中，最重要的是情节。情节就是叙事作品中的故事。它与生活中原生态故事的不同在于，它是由作者根据生活素材加工创造，并已获得了自身的因果关系和审美特性。”(亚里士多德，1996：64)改编者在选择原剧本中的情节时需要格外谨慎。

《仲夏》是一部开放式结构戏剧，故事线多条且相互交织。然而，并不是每一个情节都值得保留。汪流在谈改编的时候提出“浓缩”的理念，针对“那些篇幅长、内容丰富、头绪繁杂的原作，改编者又不想从中节选一段，而要全部搬上银幕”，提出“需要对原作做浓缩工作。此种方式抓住与主题有关的人物事件，以主人公思想情绪的脉络为贯穿线，对原作删繁就简，

① 转引自舒伟、丁素萍：《20 世纪美国精神分析学对童话文学的新阐释》，《外国文学研究》2001 年第 1 期。

去枝砍蔓，以适应电影结构单纯、集中、简捷、明了等特点”（汪流，1995：21-23）。其电影改编理论亦适合用于舞台剧的改编。

1.1 优选精彩冲突

笔者对原著情节做以下调整：没有冲突便没有戏剧，一个带有精彩冲突的故事才能成功吸引观众的注意，满足目的观众的“期待视野”①：文学艺术作品的接受过程在作家进行构思创作时便已开始，无论是创作者还是改编者，都需要预先考虑自己的作品能否对目标观众或读者产生吸引力并引起他们的兴趣。与成年人不同，相比安静平和的故事线，孩子们更喜欢夸张的肢体动作和热闹的舞台气氛。如果一部儿童剧中的冲突不够精彩，或是情节拖沓、冲突间隔太长，都有可能随时失去观众，难以成为一部合格的儿童剧。

原著分三条故事线展开。第一条主线，父亲 Egeus 带着女儿 Hermia 前来请雅典公爵 Theseus 主持公道，希望公爵说服女儿嫁给青年 Demetrius；而 Hermia 爱恋的是 Lysander，迫于雅典法律的严苛，两人决定私奔。Helena（Hermia 的好友），为了创造更多和心上人 Demetrius 见面的机会，最终还是将这个秘密告诉了 Demetrius，就这样，为了追寻自己心里坚守的真爱，四人都在晚上来到了郊外一片神秘的树林。第二条主线，为了保证能在公爵婚礼上顺利演出，由不同职业的工匠们组成的戏班成员来到郊外安静的树林排练，织工 Bottom 不幸被调皮的小精灵误施魔法，长出驴头。第三条主线，树林中的仙王仙后因为争夺同一个仙童而闹得不可开交，仙王命令小精灵 Puck 使用具有魔法的爱懒花捉弄仙后，让她疯狂爱上睡醒后第一眼看到的生物。最后，三条线中的人物同时在夜晚出现在树林里，大家因小精灵误施魔法而演出了一场场闹剧：在爱懒花汁的作用下，Lysander 和 Demetrius 同时爱上了睡醒后第一眼看到的 Helena，完全将 Hermia 抛之脑后，而仙后也爱上了被施了魔法长出驴头的 Bottom，于是他们同时对心爱之人展开了强势的追求，发生了一系列令人啼笑皆非的故事。考虑到三条故事线过于复杂，容易在舞台呈现时导致换场困难等技术问题，笔者总结了原著中的冲突点，删除了对于总体情节发展没有推动意义的戏份（如第一幕中雅典公爵宫殿中的戏），最后保留了三个：Hermia 与父亲的冲突、仙王 Oberon 与仙后 Titania 之间的冲突以及在小精灵 Puck 误施“爱懒花”魔法后两对恋人：Lysander 和 Hermia、Demetrius 和 Helena 间的冲突。冲突之间按先后顺序叙述，存在着因果关系，环环相扣，在保持主要剧情不变的同时使整体剧情紧凑有看点。

1.2 “吸睛”的开场

“戏剧式改编理论”②要求改编文本必须要有一个戏剧性的基调，遵循三段式戏剧结构的规律，有交代、危机和高潮。一部优秀的戏剧往往伴随着足够吸睛的开场，满足观众的期待视野。我国著名儿童文学作家陈伯吹认为“一个有成就的作家，愿意和儿童站在一起，善于

① 由德国文艺理论家姚斯（Hans Robert Jauss）提出。

② 戏剧式改编理论由梅里爱和格里菲斯初创，是基于戏剧及戏剧与电影的关系的认知所形成的一套理论，它是按照冲突律为情节和结构基础，并依此建构起善恶分明的阵营及代表人物、冲突的中心事件、起承转合的情节线索、有头有尾的完整故事等如此一套改编程序的理论。

从儿童的角度出发，以儿童的耳朵去听，以儿童的眼睛去看，特别以儿童的心灵去体会，就必然会写出儿童能看得懂、喜欢看的作品来。”（陈伯吹，1956）对于成年观众来说，一个富有意境的开场镜头或是一句富有生活哲理的台词就能暂时留住观众继续等待剧情的推进和价值输出，然而，儿童观演群体所处的年龄阶段对于观看和演出戏剧的心理诉求不同，他们渴望看到更具有喜剧性的开场，也更愿意参与其中的表演，无论是亲自演出还是看到剧中主人公们有惊无险的冒险、神秘的魔法元素以及在魔法作用下演员们的滑稽表现，都能使他们的娱乐和游戏心理得到满足。（在下文将提到的角色调整部分，笔者保留精灵的角色也正是出于孩子们生性喜欢魔法的考虑。）

原著中的第一幕发生在雅典公爵的宫殿之上，从雅典公爵向未婚妻宣布婚期开场，到 Egeus 说服女儿嫁给 Demetrius 未果结束。但这样的开场呈现，调度会比较呆板，婚期与爱情的主题和冲突并不能成功吸引儿童观众的注意。为了创造一个满足儿童观众期待视野的开场，笔者调整了剧情的顺序，将工人们在树林里排练的戏份设置为开场第一幕。这样做的原因首先在于由工人们组成的戏班人数较多，当演员们在舞台上表演时能够增加舞台热闹的氛围；其次，这出戏因为有丑角的戏份，表演更夸张，更加吸引眼球：痴迷表演的织布工 Bottom 为了争取到每一个自己心仪的角色，在导演面前一次次夸张滑稽地模仿各种不同的角色；最后，为了增添剧本情节的趣味性，烘托闹剧气氛，利用“魔法”“冒险”和“追逐”的元素满足孩子们的游戏心理，笔者特增加了一个情节—— 调皮精灵 Puck 变身老虎整蛊戏班，让舞台氛围瞬间活跃起来：正在排练的工人们拿到的剧本当中有老虎的角色，调皮的精灵 Puck 也变成老虎混入其中，让其他工人们误认为他也是演员之一，在大伙围观着足以以假乱真的虎皮戏服赞叹不已的时候，真正扮演老虎的工人 Sandy 进场了，Sandy 担心自己的戏被别人抢走，争着上前与老虎理论，途中才发现老虎是真的，工人们顿时被吓得四处逃窜，等众人离开后调皮的精灵 Puck 才显露真实的身份。该处工人们四处逃窜的剧情刚好能够接上故事高潮部分—— Bottom 与队员走失后误入精灵们居住领地的情节。

1.3 合适的戏份

当主要情节、冲突与开场确定后，需要根据观众的年龄和心理发展阶段筛选合适的戏份。儿童观演群体正处于世界观和价值观逐渐形成的关键阶段，改编者需要在不改变原著精神的前提下“去成人化”，删改少儿不宜的情节，选择更利于舞台呈现的戏份。《仲夏》作为浪漫爱情喜剧，很难避免谈及主人公之间的爱情关系。对此，笔者将整出戏的关注点转移到了“爱懒花”的魔力上，而主角之间的“爱恨情仇”则被弱化。经过这一处理，原文中关于仙后因魔法爱上驴头 Bottom 的戏份被极大地简化。

原剧本花了共两页半的篇幅描写仙后睡醒后看到 Bottom 的场景，在魔法的作用下，仙后疯狂地爱上 Bottom，用世界上最美的语言去形容对方，并让贴身伺候自己的小精灵们把好吃好喝的东西拿来招待 Bottom：

Titania：What angel wakes me from my flow'ry bed?
什么天使使我从百花的卧榻上醒来呢？

Bottom：[Sings]

The finch, the sparrow, and the lark, 鹌鸽，麻雀，百灵鸟，
The plain-song cuckoo grey, 还有杜鹃爱骂人
Whose note full many a man doth mark, 大家听了心头恼，
And dares not answer nay- 可是谁也不回声。……

Titania：I pray thee, gentle mortal, sing again.
温柔的凡人，请你唱下去吧！……

Titania：Thou art as wise as thou art beautiful.
你真是又聪明又美丽。……

Titania：Out of this wood do not desire to go...
请不要跑出这座林子！……
That thou shalt like an airy spirit go.（Shakespeare, 2003：91-93）
使你身轻得像精灵一样。

改编版台词中省去了仙后和 Bottom 之间大部分的对白，用六句简单的对白将这出戏呈现出来：

Bottom：Hee-haw, hee-haw, hee-haw... 嗯昂~嗯昂~嗯昂~

Titania：How dare! Too much noise! Who is... 胆子也太大了！吵死了！谁在……

Bottom：Hee-haw, hee-haw, hee-haw... 嗯昂~嗯昂~嗯昂~

Titania：It's you! 是你！
（Bottom denies with his waving hands 波顿极力摇手否认）

Titania：It's you! Honey! Your voice is so sweet~
是你！亲爱的！你的声音也太优美了~

Bottom：Hee-haw... 嗯昂~

Titania：Come on! Let's have a dance! 来吧！一起跳支舞！[①]

显然，相比原著中的情节，改编版的情节更利于小演员们表演，仙后的扮演者通过邀请 Bottom 跳舞来体现自己“坠入爱河”，这一改编不仅成功避免了谈及“两性关系”，还将复杂的场面化为舞蹈，在背景音乐的烘托下，巧妙通过声画结合提升了整部剧的看点。

在原著中，仙王在发现错施魔法之后要求精灵 Puck 分别引开两位男青年。然而，这出戏的台词过多，情景转换也较复杂，不利于观众理解剧情。笔者直接将消除魔法的戏份浓缩成以下三句台词：

Oberon：Puck，what have you done! 帕克，你都干了些什么！

---

① 改编版《仲夏夜之梦》第二幕，第三场。

Puck：I'm sorry... 抱歉……

Oberon：We must break the magic. Spell~ 我们必须解除掉魔法！[①]

2 角色的调整

亚里士多德将戏剧六要素之“性格”排在第二位，可见其重要性仅次于情节。排在其后的言语、思想、戏景和唱段也都为塑造人物性格服务。人物性格是角色塑造的核心。《仲夏》原著中共有21个角色，从各种平民工人到雅典公爵，从女儿到父亲，再从凡间年轻男女到精灵世界的仙王仙后和各类精灵。对于大多数成年人而言，莎翁的作品无论是阅读还是观演都存在着相当的难度，不是所有的角色都能被大多数观众记住，更不用提儿童观演群体。针对改编过程中遇到的角色调整问题，笔者借鉴了夏衍在改编长篇小说问题上提出的三点建议：“一、抓主线，舍其余。二、分段写。三、以个别人物为中心来写。”（夏衍，1979：266-267）最后，对改编后的剧中角色做如下调整。

2.1 保留必要角色

从故事的主线出发，保留四位主人公从雅典城到雅典城外树林中的精彩戏份，删去对故事发展和舞台呈现效果没有贡献的角色，如雅典公爵与其未婚妻、精灵世界中的其他精灵的角色等。最终，除了由六个不同职业的工人，木匠 Quince，工匠 Snug，织布工 Bottom，风箱修理匠 Flute，补锅匠 Snout 和裁缝 Starveling 组成的戏班成员与两位精灵群演外，改编版一共保留了八个角色：父亲 Egeus，女儿 Hermia 及其恋人 Lysander，Demetrius 和他的追求者 Helena，仙王 Oberon，仙后 Titania，和精灵 Puck。他们是整个故事线的承载者。

2.2 替换角色名

改编者在改编之初需要考虑到受众的“期待视野”，根据受众个体条件，如受教育程度、生活经历、艺术欣赏水平等来采取不同的改编手段。改编时“除了要处理文化融合、文化差异等问题外，还要在对原著的忠实与创造之间，在观众的期待视野和自身的美学表达之间，找到最佳的平衡。”（周仲谋，2015：71）《仲夏》原剧中的角色名都具有浓厚的古希腊特色，虽然具有异域风情，但一些名字的发音却十分拗口，不利于演员记忆，也不方便观众对应角色。Jacqueline M. Pacyk 在其荣誉论文中阐述道：“为了减轻孩子们的语言负担，可将更常见、易发音的名字替换掉剧中主角们拗口的雅典式名字；由于戏班角色名发音难度相对较低，最终得以保留。”（Jacqueline，2009）但在笔者看来，主角的名字并不适合更改，有必要保留他们名字中的“雅典腔”，增加异国情调，反之，戏班角色名比较接地气，则可以更改成中国观众熟悉的名字，以便发音和记忆。如 Flute、Snout、Snug、Starveling 被分别改为中国儿童熟知的名字 Frank、Smith 、Sandy 和 Steven。但由于 Quince 和 Bottom 发音没有难度且戏份较

---

① 改编版《仲夏夜之梦》第二幕，第三场。

重，他们的名字保持不变。这也是笔者在处理方式上与 Jacqueline 的不同之处。对于精灵的名字，如 Oberon、Titania 和 Puck 等，笔者和 Jacqueline 所持态度相同，“为了突出剧中精灵的特殊身份，与‘凡人’区别开来，他们的名字应该保留”[①]（Jacqueline，2009）。

3 台词的“儿童化”

戏剧是语言的艺术。台词是搭建起剧本的基石，“是按照戏剧的内在特性构思的，台词本身就是戏剧内在特性的体现。它决定着演出的形态与风格，本质上，它已经就是戏剧。”（1987：179）莎翁的戏剧作品自问世以来就因其呼之欲出的描写、富含“深度”的哲理性台词以及对“文字游戏”的巧用而闻名，无形中给改编者造成了巨大的压力。在对莎剧台词进行“儿童化”改编的过程中，改编者首先得明确儿童语言的特征，才能使得儿童剧文本中的语言紧密贴合儿童的现实生活和思维特征，做到去“成人化”。在句式上，儿童剧本台词要“文句浅显为贵，以单纯句为最合宜。”（陈学佳，1934：170）这一点与剧本台词的双重性，即可读性与可表演性不谋而合，在修改台词时应尽量避免长句和发音困难的单词。在风格上，“不仅是平顺无疵的白话，还得是泼刺的，美丽的，dynamic 而且明快。”（茅盾，1990：402）由此可见，改编版儿童剧的台词必须简洁自然、轻松明快而又不失美感。具体步骤如下。

3.1 化冗长为简短

关于台词的删减处理，夏衍先生认为“可以删去舞台上为了交代时间和人物关系的某些不必要的对话，并要将话剧中的整场戏切碎”（夏衍，1980：111）。但如果一味地将这些“不必要”的对话删去，会使剧情发展欠缺必要的信息，让观者莫名其妙。因此，笔者将演员烦琐的台词改写为短小精悍的旁白，使小演员们记忆台词的压力得以减轻，同时也清楚地给观众交代了前因后果。被删除了的原著开场讲述了公爵宣布婚期、父亲想要包办女儿的婚姻……这段戏是整场戏的“前因”。原著中对于该场戏的叙述就花了六页的篇幅，如果将此段戏删掉，虽然整场戏的戏剧节奏能够被推进不少，但观众却无法得知为何 Hermia 会因为婚姻问题和父亲争论，为何男女主角要选择私奔，最后观众也将因为缺乏对故事背景的了解，难以跟上情节发展的节奏，甚至选择“弃剧”，影响观感体验。在改编版本中，故事背景直接通过几句简单的旁白引出：

Narrator：Long long ago, there was a sharp law in Athens: any girl who refused to marry according to her father's wishes would be put to death. Hermia and Lysander loved each other, but Hermia's father wished her to marry another man, Demetrius.[②]

---

① *A Midsummer Night's Dream: As Told in Rhyme for Children Just around the Age of Nine.* 存档于美国印第安纳州鲍尔州立大学（Ball State University）。

② 改编版《仲夏夜之梦》第二场。

旁白：很久很久以前，在雅典有这样一条残酷的法律：任何在婚姻问题上不听从父亲意愿的女子都将处于死刑。赫米亚和拉山德深爱着彼此，但是赫米亚的父亲却希望她嫁给另一个男子—— 狄米特律斯。

除了将不同角色的台词浓缩成旁白之外，同一个角色的部分台词也因过长而被精简成旁白。如：仙王 Oberon 向精灵 Puck 讲述“爱懒花”的故事并安排 Puck 前去寻找此花，以达到捉弄仙后的目的。该戏份中仙王的台词加起来就有两页的篇幅，一共不下 200 词：

Oberon：That very time I saw（but thou couldst not）
就在那个时候，你看不见，但我能看见
Flying between the cold moon and the earth
Cupid all armed
持着弓箭的丘比特在冷月和地球之间飞翔
…
And ere I take this charm from off her sight
（As I can take it with another herb）
我可以用另一种草解去这种魔力，
I'll make her render up her page to me.（Shakespeare，2003：76）
但第一我先要叫她把那个孩子让给我。

为了尽可能增加改编版的表演性，减轻演员背诵台词的压力，仙王的台词被划分为两部分，一部分用旁白叙述，一部分则作为演员的台词，最后演员只需要记忆 29 个单词即可：

Narrator：One night，Oberon saw Cupid flying in the sky...The purple flower is magical，if its juice is put on someone's sleeping eyes，they will fall in love with the first creature they see when they wake up.

旁白：一个夜里，奥布朗看见爱神丘比特从夜空中飞过……这朵紫色的花十分神奇，把它的花汁滴在任何一个睡梦中的人的眼皮上，他们将会爱上睁开眼睛后看到的第一个生物。

Oberon：I will use the juice on Titania,
我要把这个花汁用在提泰妮亚身上，
then when she wakes,
等她醒来后，
she will fall in love with something silly,
她将会爱上任何一样第一眼看到的东西，
like a bear, a lion, a wolf, or a sheep! ①

① 改编版《仲夏夜之梦》第一幕，第三场。

可能是一只熊、一头狮子、一匹狼又或者是一只绵羊！

3.2 同义词替换

在改编台词的过程中，改编者为了在简化台词时尽可能减少其中寓意的流失，可以采取“语内翻译”[①]（或同义替换）的方式，以儿童演员和观众更能接受的“语言符号”去解释原著当中的台词，这不仅便于演员和观众加深对故事的了解，而且给表演者们提供了一个适合练习口语表达的情景。

例如，在原著中，Lysander 的台词“A good persuasion；therefore，hear me.”（你说得很对。听我说吧。）被改写为“I have an idea.”（我有一个主意。）；“I have a widow aunt，a dowager of great revenue.”（我有一个寡居的伯母，很有钱。）被改写为“I have a rich widow aunt.”（我有一个有钱的寡居的伯母。）；倒装句“From Athens is her house remote seven leagues.”（她的家距离雅典有七里格远。）被改写为“Her house is about twenty miles away from Athens.”[②]（她的家离雅典有二十里路。）。虽然七里格和七公里所表示的长度不同，但后者更能被儿童群体接受，使用公里不仅能让我国观众理解，也能增加孩子们的实用词汇。

3.3 保留“智”与“美”

“好的改编应该能够形神兼备地再现原著的精髓。”（巴赞，1987：99）要想在改编本当中再现莎剧原著中的精髓，改编者必须保证在改编过程中原剧台词所传递的思想哲理不被折损。莎翁笔下的台词经历了时间和空间的洗礼，在四百多年间不断被世界各地的人们传颂，可以窥见其深刻的哲理性。如果全剧的台词都用现代英语来表达，难免会少了些许韵味；但若长篇的古英语台词保持不变，也难以被观演群体理解和消化，更别提吸收其中的养分。考虑到这点，《仲夏》原著中一些传颂度较高的哲理性名句被保留在改编剧本当中，如“The course of true love never did run smooth.”（Shakespeare，2003：60）—— 真爱之路从无坦途。此外，为了丰富改编版台词的深意，笔者也将一些出自其他剧本中的经典台词纳入改编版的《仲夏》当中，如《罗密欧与朱丽叶》中经典楼台会。《罗密欧与朱丽叶》片段被用作工人们在树林里排练的剧本，希望借此机会能够让演员们在排演《仲夏》的同时也能够表演这出传唱度较高的经典片段，同时也给观众以新奇的体验，让那些了解《罗密欧与朱丽叶》的观众在沉浸观看《仲夏》的过程中因为意料之外、不期而遇的惊喜而会心一笑：

Juliet：O Romeo, Romeo, wherefore art thou Romeo?
罗密欧啊，罗密欧！为什么你偏偏是罗密欧呢？
Deny thy father and refuse thy name, ...

---

① 由雅各布森（Jakobson）提出，指的是在同一种语言之内以属于同一语言的某种语言符号去“翻译”（解释）另一种语言符号。语内翻译也同样作用于语内台词改编，两者同样是在同种语言之内进行语言符号转换。

② 此段引用自莎翁原著的台词均出自 Shakespeare, *A Midsummer Night's Dream*. Cambridge: Cambridge University Press. 2003：61，其余出自笔者改编版《仲夏夜之梦》第二场。

否认你的父亲，抛弃你的姓名吧

Romeo：Shall I hear more, or shall I speak at this?

我是继续听下去呢，还是现在就对她说话？

Juliet：What's Montague?

姓不姓蒙太古又有什么关系呢？

It is nor hand, nor foot, nor arm, nor face,

它又不是手，又不是脚，又不是手臂，又不是脸，

nor any other part belonging to a man.（Shakespeare，2004：71）

又不是身体上任何其他的部分。

《哈姆雷特》的经典独白 “To be，or not to be，that is the question.”（Shakespeare，2003：127）—— 生存，还是毁灭，这是个问题。这句话也在改编版的第二场中被改写为 Helena 的台词：“To tell，or not to tell，that is the question.”—— 告诉她（指赫米亚），还是不告诉她，这是个问题。在 Helena 得知 Hermia 与 Lysander 要私奔之后，她开始徘徊于是否告诉 Demetrius，因为她既渴望再一次见到 Demetrius，又担心自己的行为会伤害 Hermia，在做与不做之间，她陷入了沉思。此画面正与 Hamlet 在思考为父报仇时陷入的纠结情绪相对应。第二场中 Egeus 的台词 “What's done is done”（Shakespeare，2013：93）也是出自《麦克白》中麦克白夫人的台词。Egeus 以父亲的身份和雅典的婚姻法威胁女儿 Hermia 嫁给自己心仪的男青年，尽管追求自由恋爱的 Hermia 不愿自己的幸福沦为冰冷法律桎梏下的牺牲品，努力说服父亲，但却被告知木已成舟，接受事实，若一意孤行，只有牺牲性命，别无他法。在这样的情境之下，Egeus 说出了这句经典名言—— “What's done is done！”木已成舟，不可挽回！

这些经典的语句让孩子们“在接受过程中通过美的享受，获得经验、知识以及新的价值观”[①]（瑙曼，1976：87），在改变他们的知觉、情感、意识以及思维方式的同时，帮助他们对事物获得新的、更加正确的认识。例如，“The course of true love never did run smooth” 告诉观众要想获得真爱或是成功都将接受挫折的洗礼，让人们更加珍惜当下来之不易的一切，带着积极乐观的心态眺望未来，相信风雨过后会有彩虹。而“What's Montague? It is nor hand，nor foot，nor arm，nor face，nor any other part belonging to a man.”则引发观众更深的思考：名字不过是一个代号，真正代表一个人身份的到底是什么？是虚化的名利还是一颗热忱的心与一路走来的人生阅历？“To tell，or not to tell，that is the question.”和“what's done is done”则启发人们培养“三思而后行”的行为习惯和心思细腻的性格，以及对于已成定局之事坦然处之的态度与对所犯之错的总结以及对人生经验的积累。

4 结 语

莎士比亚创作的剧本“主要是用于舞台表演呈现的，并不是用于发表的精雕细琢的文学

① 瑙曼等学者合著论文集，《社会—— 文学—— 阅读》。

作品”（Bate，2008：5）。剧本不同于其他文学体裁，没有最后的舞台呈现，其中的特点与价值将无从实现。为了检验改编版《仲夏夜之梦》是否适合儿童表演与观看，并进一步探索其中的教育意义，笔者在厦门市青少年宫的“儿童英语戏剧表演”课程中进行了近三个月的课堂教学，并组织学员参与排演和舞台呈现。学员们对故事情节表现出浓厚的兴趣。令笔者惊讶的是，班上 80%的学员能够在表演训练的过程中根据当下语境自如地使用剧本当中的经典台词，真正做到了从根本上理解台词寓意，学以致用。在最后的汇报演出上，小演员们也不负众望，成功将儿童莎剧《仲夏夜之梦》搬上了舞台。

从改编和组织排演剧本的过程来看，莎剧儿童化改编十分具有挑战。改编者需要在保证剧本台词精简的同时努力诠释原著中的主旨，在遣词造句上调整英语台词的难度，照顾到儿童观演群体的语言接受能力；在情节设置与台词调整时将目的观众的期待视野考虑进来。对此，改编者可采取“筛选情节”“调整角色”和“简化台词”等手段使改编过程中原著主题思想与精彩内容的流失降到最低，确保改编版剧本的适用性和实用性。这样的儿童化改编方式不仅能够消除莎剧中令儿童群体感到生涩难懂进而望而却步的台词障碍，将莎剧以一种喜闻乐见、娱乐性十足的方式献给孩子们，使其拥有更多表演和欣赏莎剧的机会，在提升语言熟练度和表现力之余让孩子们接受人文主义的熏陶和人生哲理的启发，同时，还能为国内儿童剧改编选材提供更多思想源泉，为国内相关改编研究提供参考。

参考文献

[1] BATE J. 2008. The Genius of Shakespeare[M]. New York: Picador.

[2] JACQUELINE M. 2009. A Midsummer Night's Dream: as told in rhyme for children just around the age of nine[D]. Muncie: Ball State University.

[3] JAKOBSON R. 1971. On linguistic aspects of translation [A]. In Jakobson, R. (ed). Selected Writings. 2. Word and Language [C]. The Hague: Mouton.

[4] SHAKESPEARE W. 2003. A Midsummer Night's Dream[M]. Cambridge: Cambridge University Press.

[5] SHAKESPEARE W. 2003. Hamlet[M]. Washington: Folger Shakespeare Library.

[6] SHAKESPEARE W. 2013. Macbeth[M]. Washington: Folger Shakespeare Library.

[7] SHAKESPEARE W. 2004. Romeo and Juliet[M]. Washington: Folger Shakespeare Library.

[8] 安德烈·巴赞. 1987. 电影是什么[M]. 崔君衍，译. 北京：中国电影出版社.

[9] 陈伯吹. 1956. 谈儿童文学创作上的几个问题[J]. 文艺月报（6）.

[10] 陈学佳. 1934. 儿童文学问题[A]//童话评论[C]. 上海：新文化书社.

[11] 李伟民. 2008. 中国莎士比亚批评：现状、展望与对策[J]. 英美文学研究论丛（2）: 36-37.

[12] 茅盾. 1990. 茅盾全集[M]. 北京：人民文学出版社.

[13] 瑙曼，等，著. 1976. 社会—— 文学—— 阅读[M]. 柏林：魏玛建设出版社.

[14] 舒伟，丁素萍. 2001. 20 世纪美国精神分析学对童话文学的新阐释[J]. 外国文学研究（1）: 128.

[15] 汪流. 1995. 中国的电影改编[M]. 北京：中国广播电视出版社.
[16] 夏衍. 1979. 电影论文集[M]. 北京：中国电影出版社.
[17] 夏衍. 1980. 写电影剧本的几个问题[M]. 北京：中国电影出版社.
[18] 亚里士多德. 1996. 诗学[M]. 陈中梅，译. 北京：商务印书馆.
[19] 周仲谋. 2015. 消费文化语境下的中国电影改编[M]. 北京：中国社会科学出版社.

基金项目：厦门理工学院 2021 年全国大创课题“英语教育戏剧实践与研究”，项目编号：202011062154。指导老师：刘芭，厦门理工学院英语专业副教授，研究方向：莎士比亚戏剧、中外戏剧教育、戏剧表演。

作者简介：刘昌茂、徐圣琳、吕晟，厦门理工学院英语系，曾在省级与国家级莎剧比赛中获奖，主要从事英语教育戏剧实践与研究。

被忽略的灵魂人物
—— 莎翁喜剧中的媒人

刘艳梅

【摘　要】莎翁喜剧中的媒人们用化干戈为玉帛的本领，扭转了男女主人公的命运；用化悲为喜的力量，让结局令人难以置信。同时，他们也制造了最喜剧性的笑料，铸就了莎氏喜剧辉煌。他们是被忽略了的灵魂人物。文章以《无事生非》和《温莎的风流娘儿们》中的媒人为例，探讨他们独有的品格魅力，剖析他们承载的丰富人文内涵，以及莎士比亚本人彼时潜在的婚恋态度。

【关键词】喜剧；媒人；乐观精神；人文智慧；高尚品质

The Neglected Main Characters: The Matchmakers in Shakespeare's Comedies

Liu Yanmei

【Abstract】The matchmakers in Shakespeare's comedies are capable of turning hostility into friendship and reversing the fate of protagonists. They are capable of turning sorrow into joy and make incredible ending out of the play. They also make comic jokes, and thus make Shakespeare's comedies brilliant. The matchmakers are the soul of the play though they got little attention. Taking the matchmakers in *Much Ado about Nothing* and *The Merry Wives of Windsor* as examples, this article aims to analyze the personality charm they have, pointing out rich humanistic connotations they carry and Shakespeare's attitude towards love and marriage at the time while writing these comedies.

【Key Words】comedies; matchmakers; optimism; humanistic wisdom; lofty character

莎士比亚用他独有的智慧勾勒出了一幅又一幅美好的爱情画卷，这让他的以爱情为主题的喜剧作品为世人所赞美。剧中的男女主人公也被学界作为重点研究人物。他们爱的力量和勇气被冠以各种美名、大为夸赞。《维洛那二绅士》（1594）中的茱莉娅对她的情人普洛丢斯（Valentine，Proteus）的爱被描述成“达到了狂热的极致”（杜米丘，2011：329）；《威尼斯商人》（1597）中“愿意把一切作为牺牲”并且选择“铅匣子”的巴萨尼奥（Bassanio）被认为是“整个戏剧中最有魅力的男主角”（贝文顿，2014：52）和“最美求婚者”（刘艳梅，2017：90）；《皆大欢喜》（1599）中在摔跤场上摔倒浑身蛮力的查尔斯（Charles），在亚登森林杀死一头饥饿的狮子,而“在恋爱的情场,他却摔倒了自己”(傅光明,2017:120)的奥兰多(Orlando),被誉为情场大力士。这些人物都在剧末“有情人终成眷属”,被推崇为莎士比亚喜剧中的爱情典范。

然而,“佳偶”并非“天成”,他们能够在追求爱情的道路上闪耀光彩,双方互为吸引,他们身旁的特殊“陪衬”—— 媒人功不可没。《皆大欢喜》中,西莉亚（Celia）“不时伺机插话打趣”才“牵引出”罗瑟琳和奥兰多“一次又一次机智风趣、极富戏剧性的对谈”(2017: 122)。莎翁喜剧中的媒人不像很多其他戏剧中的媒人一样,仅昙花一现,他们贯穿始终,推动剧情,在剧中发挥着更大的作用和蕴含了更多的意义。他们用化干戈为玉帛的本领,扭转了男女主人公的命运;他们用化悲为喜的力量,让结局令人难以置信;他们制造最喜剧性的笑料,铸就了喜剧辉煌。相较于被大为夸赞的男女主人公,他们身旁的媒人才是剧中的灵魂人物。莎士比亚喜剧中的媒人们男女皆有、门第悬殊。既有地位显赫的皇室贵族,也有身份卑微的市井百姓。比如,《无事生非》(1598)中,有被好友称作“医治相思的妙手”的阿拉贡亲王彼得罗（Don Pedro）(莎士比亚,2014:27);《温莎的风流娘儿们》(1598)中,有在婚姻大事上“既想帮这个,又想帮那个”的女仆快嘴桂嫂(Mistress Quickly)。令人遗憾的是,这些身份特殊的灵魂人物却无一例外地鲜有受到关注与青睐。本文将以亲王彼得罗和快嘴桂嫂为代表,探讨莎士比亚喜剧中的媒人们独特的人格魅力,剖析他们所承载的丰富人文内涵,以及莎士比亚本人在创作喜剧时期潜在的婚恋态度。

一、化干戈为玉帛的说媒本领

戏剧作品中的媒人们通常精明能干,擅于周旋协助,能替“郎有情妾有意”的双方牵线搭桥,成人之美。而莎士比亚喜剧中的媒人更胜一筹,他们能把弄僵了的局面扭转过来,把有矛盾的双方拉拢。科尔奈留·杜米丘(Corneliu Dumitriu)(2011)称他们是撮合双方的“斡旋者”(2011:453)。在《温莎的风流娘儿们》中,落魄的封建爵士福斯泰夫(Sir John Falstaff)企图勾引富农之妻。视维护家庭荣誉为己任的富农之妻将计就计,假以约会之名“长期诱敌”(莎士比亚 2013:35),以达惩戒的目的。这场正邪相对的家庭保卫战共三个回合。其间,福斯泰夫一次比一次被捉弄得更惨,一次比一次更加不愿再与富农之妻见面。周旋于双方的快嘴桂嫂却能次次成功说服福斯泰夫重返“战场”。面对因头一次刚约会即被“丢在河里,灌满了一肚子的水”,还仍处于狼狈不堪、愤愤不平的福斯泰夫(2013:90),桂嫂游说道:是傅家仆人误会了主人的意思,才把他扔进泰晤士河里;又说傅妻就此事伤心难过,再次约他就是为了要“好好儿补报”(91)。桂嫂在说明事情“原委”的同时,打着“歉意”的旗号对他施以诱饵,使他心猿意马、重燃赴约之心。福斯泰夫当然是既没得到 “补报”,还被打得体无完肤。这给福斯泰夫对傅妻先前就有的憎恨之情,无疑是火上浇油。而福斯泰夫不再与之见面之心,更是坚定无比。尽管如此,在又一次的邀约僵局中,桂嫂仍能随机应变,用上了对应的苦肉计。当福斯泰夫说自己被打得“五颜六色”,桂嫂就说傅妻身上也被她家吃醋的汉子打得“一块青一块紫”(119)。桂嫂所言无非是让福斯泰夫觉得傅妻是与他患难与共、真情相随的“红颜”,而绝非让他只身被嘲的“祸水”。桂嫂用她的智慧和三寸不烂之舌巧妙地化解了福斯泰夫心中的怨恨,升华了他对富农之妻的情感。

中国莎士比亚研究会的李伟民教授认为：莎剧中的媒人尤其“善于操纵”（李伟民，2007：77）。面对不同的说媒对象和说媒难度，为了最终能扭转僵局，莎翁喜剧中的媒人还会故意先让局面变得“复杂”“紧张”（李伟民，2007：77），再巧妙地顺势化解矛盾。他们把“对弈的双方”掌控于股掌，让其听之任之、顺其意而行之，最终让双方变得和平而友好，甚至相互爱慕。《无事生非》中，亲王给好友培尼狄克（Benedick）和总督的侄女贝特丽丝（Beatrice）说媒的难度，相较于桂嫂，有过之而无不及。因为桂嫂需要说服的只有福斯泰夫一人，而亲王要说服的是培尼狄克和贝特丽丝两人。这两人平时一见面就唇枪舌剑，互不相让。贝特丽丝曾说培尼狄克是一个“言语无味的傻瓜”（2014：49）；培尼狄克则说贝特丽丝是“母夜叉的变相”（59）。两人之间从未显露出一丁点的友善，更谈不上爱情。并且，两人一个说自己终身不娶，一个称自己终身不嫁。用亲王的话说，一旦直接说媒，他俩必定把此事“当作一桩笑话”（85）。要撮合本是冤家对头的男女双方，如若安于常规，难以如愿。因此，亲王采用了独特的说媒方式—— 编造谎言、让人偷听，让剧情变得复杂，让人物变得紧张。

在培尼狄克这边，亲王先是掐准时间，让“谎言之箭秘密地被安排而且适时发射”（2011：460），轻松地使偷听者瞬间中计、欲罢不能。在《无事生非》的第二幕第三场，乐工刚唱完一小段，亲王立刻命其退下，并故作神秘、压低声音向奥那托（Leonato）提起“贝特丽丝在恋爱着培尼狄克”（2014：81）。这让躲在暗处的培尼狄克竖起耳朵恰好能够听得到。亲王选择在闲杂人等一离开便提起此事，凸显出说话内容的紧迫性、秘密性和重要性。这样，偷听者培尼狄克就会因他们谈论的时间点和提及的人物而瞬间神经紧绷，落入圈套。亲王抓住时机用早已编好的美丽谎言，成功走出了他的第一步。接着，亲王故意通过里奥那托之口说出贝特丽丝“爱得他（培尼狄克）像发狂一般”“一天到晚坐看出神”（83）。安排里奥那托来说出这些话，亲王有两点用意：第一，凸显真实性。里奥那托是希罗之父，而希罗又是贝特丽丝的好姐妹，那么，身份特殊的里奥那托知道贝特丽丝的真实恋情也就理所当然；第二，强调可信性。里奥那托是一个“庄严”的“白须老头”，他的总督身份让他格外德高望重。他的身份、地位和外表无不让人对其深信不疑。就在此时，亲王顺势附和，说贝特丽丝“绝世聪明”“品行也是无可疵议”（87）。这正好为他在培尼狄克这边的最后一步做好了铺垫：亲王说自己“很喜欢培尼狄克”，并且希望他能够平心静气“反省一下，看看他自己多么配不上这么一位好姑娘”（89）。这是亲王说媒的总结性话语。他是用自己亲王的身份，用略带命令的口吻，暗示偷听者培尼狄克不要因为错过一位好姑娘而失去亲王一直以来对他的厚爱。亲王环环紧扣再加“威逼利诱”让培尼狄克自己去权衡利弊，最终做出了亲王想要的判断。

在贝特丽丝这边，亲王除了如法炮制谎言，还额外采用了激将法。他们在谎称培尼狄克对她有爱慕之情后，打着避免培尼狄克因得不到所爱而深受打击和要让培尼狄克死心的旗号，说要诽谤贝特丽丝。贝特丽丝本人高傲、自命不凡，非常看重自己的名誉，决不允许自己的名誉受到一丁点的毁损，更不想因此而受到一众凡人的鄙视和嘲笑。基于此，媒人们故意提到要捏造谣言，并强调谣言“对她的名誉没有什么损害”（101）。他们非常清楚，此话一出，贝特丽丝立刻被击中要害，受到如人所料的刺激。紧接着，媒人们提及培尼狄克各方面“都可以在意大利首屈一指”（103）。这看似赞美的话语，实则增加了贝特丽丝内心的焦虑、紧张和不安。她非常清楚，一旦造谣必定生事：除了名誉受损，还会错失佳人。所以，这一步让贝特丽丝妥妥落入圈套，用媒人们自己的话说，赞美只是“诱人的美饵”（97）。最后，媒人们转而夸赞贝特丽丝“心窍玲珑”（103）。这是完全掌握贝特丽丝心理活动的媒人们再次暗示她一定要想明白了，怎样做才理智又划算。在亲王等人的引导下，贝特丽丝最终丢掉了狂妄、抛弃了骄傲，喃喃自语："培尼狄克，爱下去吧，我一定会报答你。"（103）媒人们利用了贝特丽丝的自尊心，以刺激为主的方式，激起了她想维护自己正面形象的强烈欲望以及她恋爱的潜能，得到不同寻常的说服效果，最终成全了一对偷听的"仇人"。

亲王曾称培尼狄克为"野牛"，可见培尼狄克的倔强早已让人领略。但亲王同时说"总有一天，野牛也会俯首就轭"（23）。亲王能有如此乐观而肯定的预见，完全来自他对自己说媒智慧和掌控全局的信心。莎士比亚喜剧中"精明机智、善于揣摩人物心理、娴于辞令"的媒人形象被亲王和桂嫂活画了出来。他们"说媒过程逻辑严密、层次分明"（梅东伟，2012：59），他们化干戈为玉帛的说媒技巧代表着莎剧媒人独特的人文智慧。

二、化悲为喜的力量

1588 年，英国在打败西班牙"无敌舰队"后，国势大振。这之后的十余年，伊丽莎白一世的中央主权尚属巩固，王室跟工商业者及新贵族的暂时联盟也尚在发展。经济繁荣、世态稳固使莎士比亚对生活充满乐观主义情绪，相信人文主义理想可以实现。这十年也成了莎士比亚创作喜剧的巅峰阶段，而乐观主义也成了莎士比亚喜剧创作的基调。莎士比亚剧作中的媒人便是这种基调的传播者。这里包括三层意思。

首先，他们一身喜气、充满乐趣，为人处世总是抱着乐观的态度，凡事往好处想。表现在：第一，对人。他们怀揣一颗欣赏之心，擅于说人好话。《无事生非》中，梅西那总督里奥那托因为觉得侄女贝特丽丝说话太过尖利刻薄，告诫她这样会"一辈子也嫁不出去"（41）。但在剧中媒人亲王的眼里，贝特丽丝的牙尖嘴利恰好是她的"风趣本色"，说她"真是一个快乐的小姐"（65）。第二，对事。亲王遇事非但不烦恼、不忧愁，还满脑子充满促成喜事的快乐遐想。迫不及待要和希罗成婚的克劳狄奥在得知婚礼要在一周后才能举行，摇头长叹事情的不尽如人意。作为他好友的亲王却说要把这几天"过得一点也不沉闷"，说自己是"爱神"，要让"培尼狄克先生和贝特丽丝小姐彼此热恋起来"（67）。再者，亲王观察力敏锐，擅于发现他人的快乐，尤其能看出陷入恋爱的人热爱生活、乐观阳光的蛛丝马迹。闻出了培尼狄克"用麝香擦他的身子"的是亲王、看出了"他在搽粉"的也是亲王。这让曾经认为恋爱浅薄且无聊的培尼狄克也不得不承认"我已经不再是从前的我啦。"（107-109）亲王就是这么一个自己快乐，又能发现他人快乐的欢喜媒人。

除了《无事生非》中位高权重的亲王这样的媒人，《温莎的风流娘儿们》中小人物快嘴桂嫂也十足乐观。这通过桂嫂的"傻人"形象表现。剧中，每次富农之妻想捉弄福斯泰夫，她们都让口中的"傻女人"（2013：79）桂嫂替之前往邀约。原因有二：第一，喊得动。桂嫂同时帮助自己的主人凯易斯大夫、法官的侄儿史量德和少年绅士范通三人追求裴安痕。这给人一种不知孰轻孰重、见人就帮、见事就做、瞎忙活的"傻人"形象。但她的这种"傻相"恰恰体现了她不随意扫人兴致、乐此不疲替人做媒、快活而积极的媒人特质。她被称为温莎小镇上的"大红人"。正是由于这一点，富农之妻每次想"私会"福斯泰夫，都会让来者不拒的"傻"桂嫂代为牵线。第二，会成事。腹怀美意气自喜的桂嫂给人快乐、阳光的感觉，是一位不折不扣的乐观主义者。乐观主义者不管在顺境还是逆境中都通常抱有积极心态，这推动他们向目标前进，进而取得成功。自带喜感正能量的桂嫂在邀约福斯泰夫这件事情上总能给人带来喜讯。这正应了那句俗话——“爱笑的人运气都不会太差”。因此，富农之妻口中的“傻”实为“喜”的代名词。张泗洋先生就曾指出，包括快嘴桂嫂在内的温莎的风流娘儿们中“风流”一词，实为“快乐”的误植。（张泗洋，2001：693-694）

其次，媒人们能够制造笑料、成就喜剧。莎剧中，喜剧性的笑料“来源于某些看似不可更改的情形的逆转”（2012：461）。《温莎的风流娘儿们》中，品性邪恶的福斯泰夫多次受惩，还胆敢一再与他人之妻“私会”，但最终却在橡树之下转而知错悔改，成功“逆袭”。《无事生非》中，原本个性强烈的贝特丽丝对男性异常冷漠，却“成为真实感情的俘虏”，最终和曾经对女性失去信心的单身主义者培尼狄克逆袭成婚。科尔奈留·杜米丘称，这是“难以置信的结局”（89）。这些难以置信的、逆转性的结局制造了喜剧性的笑料，而这些“笑料”的推手无疑就是剧中的媒人。《无事生非》中，贝特丽丝与培尼狄克的爱情进行过程被称为“全剧的精华所在”（张丽，2009：91）。两人的恋爱过程实则就是亲王做媒的过程，因为媒一做完，偷听的两人随即步入婚姻殿堂。因此，该喜剧的精华实则就是说媒过程，而这一过程也被称为“莎士比亚创造的最富有喜剧性的喜剧情节”（91）。综上，莎剧中的媒人们成功扭转了剧中男女主人公的命运，这成为“喜剧性的笑料”，也成为“喜剧的精华”。因此，媒人们为推动莎翁喜剧走向辉煌，立下的是赫赫之功。

最后，媒人们把自身的喜感发挥到极致的表现是他们能够化悲为喜。他们搭桥牵线，建立了人物间的联系，这种联系有时候聚合人物命运，有时候却分离人物命运，但即便如此，它们仍然能推进剧情朝好的、喜的方向发展。（梅东伟，2012：56）亲王主动替克劳狄奥向总督提亲，让克劳狄奥与之暗恋的总督之女希罗关联起来；桂嫂给福斯泰夫捎信，成为富农之妻与福斯泰夫间的纽带。桂嫂和亲王都帮助建立了人物间的联系，但在这一过程当中，他们又或无意或有意地分离了人物的命运，推动故事情节的发展。（2012：460）《无事生非》中，少年贵族克劳狄奥立下战功、深得亲王的信任和器重。亲王同父异母的弟弟约翰因此心生妒忌。约翰借假面舞会故意向克劳狄奥谎称亲王替之提亲的是亲王自己，以此打击和报复克劳狄奥。听到此消息的克劳狄奥伤心欲绝，因为“情敌”既是自己好友又是亲王，他发出了“永别了，希罗”和“希望他姻缘美满”的心碎而绝望的呐喊（2014：53-55）。因亲王的热情和善行招来的嫉妒浇灭了克劳狄奥对爱情的美好期待，造成了克劳狄奥和他所爱之人命运的暂时分离。但正是有了无意的拆散，才能迎来风雨之后的彩虹。当克劳狄奥后来得知真相，喜悦之情溢于言表，称“静默是表示快乐的最好方法”，并说要把希罗“当作镶宝一样珍爱。”（63）源于亲王的爱情挫折让克劳狄奥体会到爱情的来之不易，也让克劳狄奥更加珍惜对方。这未尝不是一件好事、喜事。

无独有偶，《温莎的风流娘儿们》中的桂嫂也让分离最终成为喜事。福斯泰夫是一个对他人之妻有非分之想的负面人物。一次次偷情未遂又惨遭捉弄的他早想洗手不干，但桂嫂“引领”有方，终于在第三次的“森林约会”中让他主动招供，承认自己“做了坏事”（2013：137）。所以，桂嫂的多次邀约和拉拢看似拆散了福斯泰夫和他“中意”的富农之妻，实则给了福斯泰夫一个获得救赎、重新做人的机会。与此同时，富农傅德也对自己的妻子有了全新的认识和信任。傅德是个向来爱猜疑的“吃醋的汉子”（53）。他装扮成名叫白罗克的绅士去见福斯泰夫，不惜用自己“全部的钱”想要从福斯泰夫那里套取妻子出轨的信息；不知实情的傅德被福斯泰夫龌龊的语言几乎气破肚皮，还大骂自己的妻子是“不要脸的东西”（104）。庆幸的是，傅德在深林中看到福斯泰夫的真面目和“名节无亏”又“问心无愧”（108）的妻子之时，他表示“以后再不疑心”（137）。此番波折不仅维护了傅妻的名誉，还除掉了傅德的嫉妒之心，也增强了其家庭凝固力。而福斯泰夫在三次的“约会”进程当中，也只是成为一个“无伤大雅的好玩人物”（2015：57）。没有桂嫂的邀约、拉拢，也就没有福斯泰夫最终的低头认错，更没有傅德对自己妻子的全新认识和信任。桂嫂的这根红线牵出的可是双喜临门。无论是无心之失还是有意为之，莎剧媒人们都成功推动了剧中人物化悲为喜的转变。

三、正直高尚的品格境界

婚姻向来被视为人生大事，它是爱情的象征，是责任的代名词，它被设计成“人类最接近最亲密的相互关系”，它决定了人们生活中最亲近而频繁接触的人。在婚姻中，“夫妻的结合不仅仅是性需要，而应是人生目标和心灵的结合”（于文杰，2006：125）。只有两人目标一致、心灵相通才有可能创建美好的婚姻，才有可能让家庭和谐、事业顺利。《温莎的风流娘儿们》中的桂嫂深知婚姻的意义和重要性，在裴家小姐安痕的个人问题上，虽然媒人的身份让她对安痕（Anne Page）的追求者们个个都施予帮助，但她最终的决定显示了她高尚的人文主义品格。

安痕的第一位求婚者史量德（Slender），是一个说得出“以前的子孙”和“以后的祖先”，连求婚都不会的傻子。对于自己的婚姻，只要法官叔父点头，他也就毫无微词。（莎士比亚，2013：4）这样的人何来人生目标？又怎能与安痕产生共鸣？第二位求婚者凯易斯大夫（Doctor Caius），他精通医学，也擅长剑术，可谓文武双全，可为人遇事就暴跳如雷，这样的性格也没有可能与安痕心灵相通。反而范通（Fenton），知书达理，会说漂亮话，与众人为善的同时，又懂得知恩图报。经常在桂嫂帮忙之后，他都会给予对方赏钱表达谢意。（89）桂嫂深谙此道。所以，虽然史量德有当法官的叔父，虽然凯易斯大夫正是桂嫂作为仆人身份所伺候的主人，虽然范通毫无家世背景，虽然桂嫂本人也愿意替他们三人“同样出力”，但用桂嫂自己的话说，还是要替范通“更加出力”（88）。与此同时，孝顺的安痕既“答应”了父亲让她嫁给史量德的安排，也“服从”了母亲让她嫁给凯易斯大夫的旨意。但作为安痕好友的桂嫂发现安痕对于范通眼皮上的一颗小疙瘩都能够“足足讲上一点钟”，因此她非常清楚，安痕的心“既不在这儿也不在那儿”。（27-29）桂嫂最终帮助安痕和范通打造了属于他俩的幸福婚姻。帮助范通，体现了桂嫂不畏权贵、不被利诱、拥有媒人当以“门当户对”，尤其在思想境界上“门当户对”为准绳做媒的职业操守和高尚品格；而帮助安痕，体现了桂嫂避免处成强迫婚姻和崇尚婚姻自由的人文主义品格。（马成俊，1991：114）

《无事生非》中的亲王对于希罗“幽会他人”一事的反应也充分体现了他为人的高尚。心生妒忌的约翰无中生有，说克劳狄奥的未婚妻希罗私下与他人幽会。听到这个消息的亲王，像天下所有劝和不劝散的媒人一样，直接反驳：“我想不会。”（2014：115）但当他亲耳听到、亲眼见到希罗的“下贱之举”时，毅然决然地反对婚礼的继续举行，并打算帮着克劳狄奥羞辱希罗。在即将举办婚礼的教堂里，当希罗不承认此事时，亲王当着众人的面向“不诚实”的希罗吼道：“哼，你还要抵赖！”（151）亲王不忍坐视婚姻中的男主人公将要娶到一个不贞洁的女子而受人之愚，所以，哪怕希罗的父亲是权高位重的总督，哪怕希罗和克劳狄奥的婚姻是自己一手促成，哪怕结婚仪式举行在即，亲王也一点没有因要顾及希罗的总督父亲的情面和自己一言九鼎的尊颜而对希罗“幽会他人”一事听之任之。与此同时，虽然培尼狄克和神父一样，都觉得亲王如此发怒，一定事有蹊跷、有误会，但也仍肯定地坚持认为亲王是一位“正人君子”（159）。在亲王知道“幽会”的真相后，他用自己的灵魂起誓，表示愿意领受希罗父亲的“任何重罚”（201）。亲王在此事中确实受到约翰的蒙蔽，但他对此事的一系列反应却真切体现出他对事不对人的正派作风；同时，“迷途知悔”又展现出亲王敢作敢当、毫不推卸的高风亮节。正是亲王犯下了这一“无心的错误”（201），才更证明了他是“一个好心的媒人”（2012：189）。劳伦斯·斯通（Lawrence Stone）说莎士比亚的喜剧就是绕着“忠于婚姻的爱”的主题打转。（斯通，2014：191-192）那么，亲王的所作所为正好替希罗和克劳狄奥打响了他们忠于婚姻保卫战的第一枪。

人文主义婚恋观认为幸福的婚姻必须建立在平等和相互尊重的爱情基础上（赵淑萍，2010：124）。亲王不希望见到任何一方有不尊重对方的行为出现。桂嫂也觉得其他人和安痕不匹配、不平等。“英国小说之父” 丹尼尔·笛福（Daniel Defoe）认为：“婚姻是一至关幸福的生活状态……世界上最合理的事是婚姻中的当事人应被赋予婚事的最后决定权。”（2014：187）亲王和桂嫂都秉持良心，支持并帮助了他们的婚姻当事人行使了最合理的决定权。无可否认，这是莎剧中的媒人们成全他人幸福婚姻的人文主义高尚之举。

结　语

如果因为在先前的莎翁喜剧人物研究中，唯爱情中的男女主人公备受关注，我们可以用“只羡鸳鸯”来解读的话，那么，剧中的媒人恰巧更像不被艳羡的“仙”。因为，如上所述，他们的说媒本领，如“仙”腾云驾雾般潇洒娴熟；他们的生活态度，如“仙”般自在快活。他们的品格境界，亦如“仙”般正直高尚。他们是剧中被忽略了的灵魂人物。

有意思的是，莎剧中的媒人们大多都是单身，这和喜剧集中创作时期（1590—1600）的莎士比亚本人很是相似。喜剧《无事生非》和《温莎的风流娘儿们》皆写于 1598 年，其中《温莎的风流娘儿们》更是“以英国为背景，与当时现实生活紧密相连”（韦尔斯，1986：65）。而当时现实生活中的莎士比亚正处于独自生活、剧作创作的前期。1583 到 1585 年间，莎士比亚和其妻安妮·海瑟薇接连生了苏珊娜、哈姆内特和朱迪斯三个小孩。在人们“的确倾向于组建大家庭”的当时，莎士比亚不仅再没有其他小孩出生，更是在 1592 年只身前往伦敦工作。一去二十载。贝文顿（David Bevington）（2014）在他的著作《莎士比亚：人生经历的七个阶段》中提到：有迹象表明，莎士比亚与安妮在生完双胞胎（哈姆内特和朱迪斯）之后“并没有继续同床”（2014：5）。格林布拉特（Stephen Greenblatt）也曾说：“没有任何迹象”体现或反映莎士比亚“夫妻间快乐和悲苦的分享”。（霍德尼斯，2018：107）并且，如霍德尼斯（Graham Holderness）（2018）所描述，在历史记录中，“‘爱’这个词从来没有存在于他们夫妻之间”。（同上）这都意味着莎士比亚婚姻的名存实亡。长期分居的莎士比亚过着犹如单身的生活。在《无事生非》剧末，培尼狄克呼唤亲王：“娶个妻子吧，娶个妻子吧。”（2014：231）这似乎是莎翁借之调侃自己当时生活寂寞的肺腑之言。不过，这也恰巧反映了莎翁犹如剧中媒人一样，虽是“孤家寡人”，但也还具有乐观积极的婚恋生活态度。

参考文献

[1] 大卫·贝文顿. 2014. 莎士比亚：人生经历的七个阶段（第 2 版）[M]. 聂珍钊，王松林，编. 谢群，等，译. 上海：上海外语教育出版社.

[2] 傅光明. 2017.《皆大欢喜》："欢庆"喜剧中风采各异的人物[J]. 东吴学术（6）：120-122.

[3] 格雷姆·霍德尼斯. 2018. 莎士比亚的九种人生[M]. 孟培，译. 黑龙江：黑龙江教育出版社.

[4] 科尔奈留·杜米丘. 2011. 莎士比亚戏剧辞典[M]. 宫宝荣，等，译. 上海：上海书店出版社.

[5] 劳伦斯·斯通. 2014. 英国的家庭、性与婚姻 1500—1800[M]. 刁筱华，译. 北京：商务印书馆.

[6] 刘艳梅. 2017. 雨果"美丑对照"原则下看《威尼斯商人》的正剧性[J]. 中国莎士比亚研究通讯（1）：90.

[7] 李伟民. 2007. 莎士比亚研究—— 构筑起心灵的家园—— 兼评张冲的《莎士比亚专题研究》[J]. 外语研究（2）：76-79.

[8] 李伟民. 2015. 回到话剧审美艺术本体的外国戏剧改编—— 莎士比亚喜剧《温莎的风流娘儿们》的舞台叙事[J]. 人文杂志（4）：54-60.

[9] 马成俊. 1991. 媒人琐谈[J]. 青海民族学院学报（社会科学版）（2）：110-116.

[10] 梅东伟. 2012. "三言"、"二拍"中的媒人与说媒场景[J]. 南都学坛（5）：55-61.

[11] 斯坦利·韦尔斯. 1986. 莎翁别具一格的喜剧——《温莎的风流娘儿们》[J]. 小丹，译. 理论探索（3）：65.

[12] 威廉·莎士比亚. 2013. 温莎的风流娘儿们[Z]. 朱生豪，译. 朱尚刚，审定. 北京：中国青年出版社.

[13] 威廉·莎士比亚. 2014. 无事生非[Z]. 朱生豪，译. 上海：上海世界图书出版公司.

[14] 于文杰. 2006. 现代化进程中的人文主义[M]. 重庆：重庆出版社.

[15] 张丽. 2009. 莎士比亚戏剧分类研究[M]. 北京：中国社会科学出版社.

[16] 张泗洋. 2001. 莎士比亚大辞典[Z]. 北京：商务印书馆.

[17] 赵淑萍. 2010. 女性主义视野下的中西方婚恋观[J]. 江西社会科学（12）：124.

基金项目：本文为 2020 年四川外国语言文学研究中心资助项目"历史观照下莎士比亚喜剧作品中的爱情主题研究"（项目编号：SCWY2020-14）的阶段性成果。

作者简介：刘艳梅，四川传媒学院副教授，香港中文大学英语系东西方戏剧专业硕士，主要从事英美文学和莎士比亚戏剧研究。曾在《中国莎士比亚研究通讯》《四川戏剧》等刊物发表莎士比亚戏剧相关研究性文章。

英语专业第二课堂与美育功能的构建

—— 以上海大学外国语学院莎士比亚戏剧节为例

贾小琴　梁　苗

【摘　要】美育作为教育的重要组成部分，以艺术和审美来丰富情感、陶冶人格、提升境界，实现以美育人、以美化人、以美铸魂。本着提高学生美育能力为目的，各院校都在探索适合自己的独特的第二课堂方式。莎士比亚戏剧是英美文学教学中必不可少的内容，其语言特色、思想深度等都是提高学生人文素养的有效手段。莎士比亚戏剧节通过“以演促学”模式，实现“第一课堂”和“第二课堂”的无缝对接。据此，以上海大学外国语学院莎士比亚戏剧节为例，探索上海大学外国语学院莎士比亚戏剧节对学生美育功能的作用。

【关键词】英语；第二课堂；莎士比亚戏剧；美育

The Second Class of English Major and the Construction of Aesthetic Education Function

— Take the Shakespeare Festival of School of Foreign Languages of Shanghai University as an Example

Jia Xiaoqin　　Liang Miao

【Abstract】Aesthetic education, as an important part of education, enriches emotions, cultivates personality and elevates the realm of thought with art and aesthetics, so as to achieve the goal of educating people, improving people and building soul of people with beauty. With the aim of improving the ability of aesthetic education of students, many colleges and universities are exploring their own unique second class mode. The plays of Shakespeare are an indispensable part in the teaching of English and American literature. The language features and ideological depth of the plays are effective means to improve the humanistic literacy of students. Through the mode of “promoting learning by acting”, the Shakespeare Festival realizes the seamless connection between “the first class” and “the second class”. Therefore, taking the Shakespeare Festival of School of Foreign Languages of Shanghai University as an example, this paper explores the role of the Shakespeare Festival in the aesthetic education of students.

【Key words】English; second class; Shakespeare's plays; aesthetic education

一、学院历年莎士比亚戏剧节大戏排演

上海大学外国语学院历年（2007—2021年）莎士比亚戏剧大戏排演见表1。

表1 上海大学外国语学院2007—2021年莎士比亚戏剧大戏排演

序号	年份	大戏名称	主要参与对象
1	2007	《傲慢与偏见》*Pride and Prejudice*	2004级本科生
2	2008	《来自天国的约定》	2005级本科生
3	2009	《罗密欧与朱丽叶》*Romeo and Juliet*	2006级本科生
4	2010	《最后一叶》*The Last Leaf*	2007级本科生
5	2011	《捕鼠器》*The Mousetrap*	2008级本科生
6	2012	《美杜莎》*Medusa*	2009级本科生
7	2013	《以爱之名》*Love For Love*	2010级本科生
8	2014	《风中奇缘》*If I Never Knew You*	2011级本科生
9	2015	《威尼斯商人》*The Merchant of Venice*	2012级本科生
10	2016	《无事生非》*Much Ado About Nothing*	2013级本科生
11	2018	《驯悍记》*The Taming of the Shrew*	2014级本科生
12	2019	《第十二夜》*The Twelfth Night*	2015级本科生
13	2021	《仲夏夜之梦》*A Midsummer Night's Dream*	2017级本科生、学院研究生

二、历年演出大戏简要回顾（2007—2021年）

2007年，我院学生首次尝试舞台戏剧表演，排演了简·奥斯汀的代表作品《傲慢与偏见》，同年成立上海大学Dramatime戏剧社。

2008年，学生原创剧目《来自天国的约定》顺利演出。

2009年，学生们首次表演莎士比亚著名作品《罗密欧与朱丽叶》并取得圆满成功。

2010年，学生原创剧目《最后一叶》顺利演出。

2011年9月，上海大学首届莎士比亚戏剧节于2011年9月在社区学院多功能厅正式开幕，校团委、社区学院以及外语学院的领导老师和一百多名同学参与了当晚的开幕式和专题讲座。同年10月，年度大戏英语悬疑剧《捕鼠器》被搬上舞台并成功展演。

2012年10月，第二届莎士比亚戏剧节暨2012年度大戏《美杜莎》公演在伟长楼圆满落幕。上海大学党委宣传部部长和文明办主任陈志宏、心理辅导中心主任秦伟、国际交流学院副院长杨静，以及外国语学院党政领导和1000余名广大师生一起观看了这部改编自古希腊神话的音乐剧。

2013年10月，上海大学第三届莎士比亚戏剧节之外国语学院2013年度大戏—— *Love for*

Love 在伟长楼隆重上演，学校相关部处、兄弟学院以及外国语学院的领导老师与近千名学生一起观看了这场精彩绝伦的演出。*Love for Love* 改编自莎翁喜剧《仲夏夜之梦》，本着在语言风格上忠于原创、在剧情上有所创新与突破的原则，学生们大胆地演绎了这部具有挑战性的喜剧。

2014 年 10 月，上海大学第四届莎士比亚戏剧节开幕式暨年度大戏 *If I Never Knew You* 在伟长楼隆重献演，外国语学院党政领导和来自全校各学院的千余名师生及亲友一起观看了这场精彩纷呈的演出。*If I Never Knew You* 改编自迪士尼经典电影《风中奇缘》。

2015 年 10 月，上海大学第五届莎士比亚戏剧节开幕式暨外国语学院 2015 年度大戏《威尼斯商人》在伟长楼成功上演。来自学校各部处、学院的领导老师，以及来自各学院的同学们热情高涨，前来欣赏这一场精彩纷呈、跌宕起伏的视觉盛宴。本次年度大戏改编自莎士比亚著名的讽刺性喜剧《威尼斯商人》。

2016 年 10 月，上海大学第六届莎士比亚戏剧节开幕式暨外国语学院 2016 年度大戏《无事生非》在伟长楼成功上演。出席本届戏剧节开幕式的嘉宾有上海大学党委宣传部部长李坚老师，上海大学学生工作办公室副主任王国建老师，上海大学团委书记许烁老师，上海大学国际事务处副处长吴英俊老师，上海大学对外联络处副处长、校友办副主任谭婷老师，上海大学校友会外国语学院分会理事邵丹青先生，上海戏剧学院教师、本次大戏指导教师俞建村教授，上海大学外国语学院教师、本次大戏指导教师朱洁副教授，上海大学外国语学院周平教授，上海大学外国语学院党委书记施雯老师以及学院党政班子全体成员。此外，上海大学附中、附属学校的老师和歌剧团的同学们以及全校各个学院的老师和同学们一起前来观赏了大戏。本次年度大戏改编自莎士比亚的喜剧《无事生非》，它诞生于莎士比亚喜剧写作最成熟的时期。2016 年是莎士比亚逝世 400 周年，今年的外院大戏不仅是大戏走过风雨十年的见证，也是表达对莎士比亚崇高敬意的一种方式，上海大学外国语学院以“年度大戏”的上演加入了世界范围内纪念莎翁活动。

2017 年 7 月，上海大学党委宣传部召开工作会议，会上公布并表彰了上海大学第四届校园文化建设品牌项目，外国语学院“莎士比亚戏剧节”项目获得立项，这是继 2016 年以来我院第二次获得校园文化建设品牌项目。

2018 年 5 月，上海大学第七届莎士比亚戏剧节开幕式暨外国语学院 2018 年度大戏《驯悍记》与《无尽之争》联合公演在图书馆报告厅成功举行。出席本届戏剧节开幕式的嘉宾有上海大学学工办主任孟祥栋老师，上海大学校团委书记许烁老师，上海大学附属中学实验学校党支部书记阮海东老师，大戏指导老师俞建村、董永杰、赵莹波、朱洁老师，外国语学院党委书记施雯及学院党政班子全体成员。此外，上海大学附中、上海大学附属学校和虎林中学的老师同学们以及全校数百名师生一起前来观赏了本次大戏。英语剧目改编自莎士比亚的喜剧《驯悍记》，它是莎士比亚的一部早期作品；日语剧目《无尽之争》是日语专业同学们原创的剧本。

2019 年 5 月，上海大学第八届莎士比亚戏剧节开幕式暨外国语学院 2019 年度大戏《第十二夜》在伟长楼成功举行。出席本届戏剧节开幕式的领导和嘉宾有上海大学副校长汪小帆，研究生工作部部长王国建，学生工作办公室主任、武装部部长孟祥栋，党委宣传部文明办副主任孙蕊，校发展规划处副处长周丽韵，校团委副书记陈中元，上海老年大学上海大学分校顾问姜继平，上海大学附属宝山外国语学校校长江澜，上海大学附属中学实验学校党委书记阮海东，上海外国语大学附属中学东校戏剧指导老师季尧吉，中国平安财产保险股份有限公司上海分公司涉外经纪业务一部副总监丁嗣劼，上海戏剧学院教授、大戏指导老师俞建村，外国语学院副教授、大戏指导老师朱洁，外国语学院党委（主持工作）副书记曾桂娥及学院党政班子全体成员。此外，上大附属宝山外国语学校、上外附属中学东校的数十位同学们以及全校近千名师生一起前来观赏了本次大戏的演出。

2021 年 5 月，上海大学第九届莎士比亚戏剧节开幕式暨外国语学院 2021 年度大戏《仲夏夜之梦》在伟长楼成功展演。全国政协常委、中国人民对外友好协会副会长、西安外国语大学前校长户思社，上海戏剧学院教授、大戏指导教师俞建村，上海大学文学院副教授、大戏指导教师张薇，上海理工大学外语学院党委副书记金小东，上海理工大学外语学院文学文化研究所负责人、莎剧总指导王影君，上海理工大学外语学院英语系莎士比亚戏剧编剧程雪芳，上海大学附属宝山外国语学校校长江澜，上海大学党委研究生工作部部长王国建，上海大学学生工作办公室主任、武装部部长孟祥栋，上海大学团委副书记王智君，上海大学外国语学院党委书记邓志勇，院长尚新，党委副书记贾小琴及副院长唐青叶共同出席了戏剧节开幕式，与上大附属宝山外国语学校的四十余位师生、全校近千名师生一同观看了大戏演出。《仲夏夜之梦》是英国剧作家威廉·莎士比亚创作的经典喜剧作品，是莎士比亚所有戏剧中最具有浪漫主义色彩的作品。

作者简介：贾小琴，上海大学外国语学院副院长，主要从事文学研究。
梁苗，上海大学教师工作部教师，主要从事文化研究。

“莎士比亚三重戏剧”的靓丽一笔

——记重庆市莎士比亚研究会国际学术研究会大学生莎剧演出

杨秀波

【摘　要】在中国“一带一路”倡议背景下，莎剧演出获得了新的意义。莎士比亚研究、教学与演出相结合，有效促进了研究成果的转化、促进教学、激发改编与表演的创造力。重庆莎学会议见证了全国各地大学生剧社莎剧演出的蓬勃景象。由于莎士比亚的研究属于“国际显学”，莎士比亚演出在全世界历久弥新，莎剧演出促进了“跨文化之桥”的建设，展示了中国大学生的才情与风采，也锻炼了大学生的表现能力，提升了他们对经典的熟悉程度，使他们对经典作品的认知更为深入。演出拓展了教学的领域，使一些有专长的教师与学生有了展现才华的舞台。一些学校的演出逐渐取得了一定的影响力，丰富了校园的业余文化生活。

【关键词】一带一路；莎士比亚；舞台演出

The Trinity of Performance of Shakespeare's Plays

Yang Xiubo

【Abstract】In the age of “The Belt and Road” , there is a lot of space in the performance of Shakespeare's Plays. The combination of Shakespeare's research, teaching and performance has effectively promoted the transformation of research results, promoted teaching, and stimulated the creativity of adaptation and performance. Creative ideas were shown on the university stage during the period of Chongqing Shakespeare International Conference.Shakespeare's plays are popular all over the world, therefore, it serves as a cross-cultural bridge. It is surprising that college students' performances were so fresh, energetic and brilliant. The performances enrich the campus life, enhancing college students' recognition of classics. They also provide some teachers and students with stage to show their special talent in acting and direction. They also enlarge the scope of teaching.

【Key Words】The Belt and Road; William Shakespeare; stage performance

在中国“一带一路”倡议背景下，中国要顺利实现“走出去”的目标，要获得在国际上的话语权，外语研究、教学有着不容忽视的地位。莎士比亚研究是全世界推崇的“显学”，各民族都在研究、阅读、演出莎士比亚的作品。著名莎士比亚研究专家陆谷孙教授曾指出：欣赏和阅读莎剧应该阅读与表演并重，是使书斋与舞台之间沟通、互动，借此不仅使莎剧舞台表演越来越丰富，也能为莎士比亚研究不断充实当下意义[1]。对莎士比亚的研究、演出是一座“跨文化之桥”，可借此开展与世界各地的交流、了解，并在此过程中扩大中国的国际影响。中国的莎士比亚研究、教学与演出的结合已经取得初步成果。

2019 年 4 月 20 日，重庆市莎士比亚研究会第十二届年会暨国际学术研究会在重庆师范大学举行。当天下午，在该校音乐厅里，来自全国各地 8 个院校的学生剧社进行了莎剧演出。作为业余演出群体，按通常理解，要达到较高艺术水准殊为不易，但演出刷新了人们的认知。大学生群体正处于创造力勃发时期，他们的演出比之于专业剧团，更有一种扑面而来的青春气息，演出的过程激情洋溢，迸发出创造新视界的渴望与蕴含的巨大能量。

一、莎剧改编别具匠心

由著名莎士比亚专家李伟民教授导演、指导演绎的浙江越秀外国语学院学生剧社演出的《李尔王》给人耳目一新之感，两个女儿谄媚李尔的场景设计在李尔在暴风雨中疯狂的时候出现，李尔的悲惨处境与两女儿的花言巧语并置，对比强烈鲜明。这样设计突出了李尔的悲剧与产生悲剧的原因—— 他不辨愚贤，听信两个大女儿虚妄的许诺，最后落得在暴风雨中流浪，上无片瓦遮拦，下无寸草遮身、落得追悔莫及的下场。有趣的是，在这戏演出前，重庆暴雨如注、大雨倾盆。重庆师范大学附近的地铁站窗边堆满防汛应急沙袋，阻挡进入的雨水溢出到屋内。电梯停运，站内的人们望着暴雨恣情倾泻无奈。自然界的雨水充沛地为演出暖场。在演出前的中午，天上乌云堆叠，如重峦叠嶂，开始演出时则雨水淋漓。人们自然推想，舞台上同样要演出一场暴风雨。舞台内外的暴风雨场景可谓相得益彰。正如评点人注意到的，这个创意设计别具一格，表演与苦难、欺骗与天真、悲剧的因与果在两相对照的“并置”中表现出强烈的戏剧冲突，反映了导演的匠心。人们从这里得到警示，警惕世人类似的欺骗性“表演”。两个学生演员将大女儿、二女儿的骄矜、狠辣表现得比较充分。相比 2016 年上海国际莎剧节上俄罗斯剧团出演的《李尔王》，这个短短的演出设计紧凑、冲突集中，更具有视觉冲击力。

二、融入中国传统文化元素

彭颖指导的重庆师范大学剧社演出的《暴风雨》中开场的海难设计别开生面：几根粗大的绳索被固定在舞台下面，众人在暴风雨中挣扎，场景看去颇为壮观。随剧情发展，后面还有米兰达嫁给斐迪南之后两人欢悦成婚，他们向台下撒糖，两只黄色包装的大虾糖打在坐在第二排的观众身上爆发出一阵阵欢声。发喜糖是纯粹的中国文化元素，揉进莎剧中，却也与剧情水乳交融，可谓“中西合璧”。然后，两人从舞台穿过，从左侧走向右侧，“米兰达”手捧着鼓起的大肚子，令人失笑。然后，“公爵”拿着拐杖，掐指计算日子，喊一声“baby”，之后婴儿哭声嘹亮，两人怀抱“婴儿”出场。这一连串程式化演出幻化出生活、生命和爱情的美好。大学生们独出心裁添上这一“婴儿出世”情节，补充出剧情给人新的希望，一系列与观众的互动环节，活跃了气氛，也使外国戏剧有了中国化的新体验。

三、戏剧表现，别出心裁

鲁跃峰指导的河南师范大学莎士比亚剧社的演出剧目叫 *How Do We Play with Shakespeare*，是压轴演出。这场演出并不似前面各个剧目依照版本，而是哲思般地探讨如何演出莎剧、如何表现人物及各个演员对人物塑造的不同理解。演出以“对话”“探讨”的形式展开，具体说是一个人物几种演绎法。就奥菲利娅来说，现代改编版的奥菲利娅不甘心默默无言死去，不再楚楚可怜、依附父兄：“如果我演奥菲利娅，我就不要她被哈姆雷特欺负。我想要做真正的贵族少女”；而“哈姆雷特”也渴望享受爱情：

啊，女神，我美丽的奥菲利亚，
别去尼姑庵。我们结婚吧，快快乐乐享受人生。

另一位学生演员王雨晴则说：“如果我演奥菲利娅，我要比哈姆雷特还要疯。她没有犯错，却受苦太多。太多的痛苦她无法承托，她在死之前先疯了。她一定比哈姆雷特还要疯狂。” 接下来她唱的情人节，以歌声演绎悲情。

(Sings)
To-morrow is Saint Valentine's day,
All in the morning betime,
And I a maid at your window,
To be your Valentine.
Then up he rose, and donn'd his clothes,
And dupp'd the chamber-door;
Let in the maid, that out a maid
Never departed more.

By Gis and by Saint Charity,
Alack, and fie for shame!
Young men will do't, if they come to't;
By cock, they are to blame.
Quoth she, before you tumbled me,
You promised me to wed.
So would I ha' done, by yonder sun,
And thou hadst not come to my bed.
（《哈姆雷特》第四幕第四场选段[2]）

美声唱法的虚幻、缥缈将奥菲利娅唯美的悲情恰到好处地传达出来，入乐借魂、词曲动心，使这个沉默的形象在音乐中获得了新的生命。2016 年莎剧节意大利剧团的特征就是擅唱。在歌词中有一重生命、表演中有一重魂魄，在销魂的歌声里又获一重唯美的生命之魂。一个绝佳的演员，像生命里无数美好的事物或人一样，在剧中溶化了自己。

以讨论贯穿始终，连缀各种精彩，不仅形式新颖活泼，而且演员表现出色，对同一人物的理解与表现见仁见智，对比鲜明，比较充分地体现出莎剧演出的多元与对话性，展示出莎剧理解与阐释的多种可能。

Zha Xiaoyu：Your Ophelia is great. But I would prefer to do Juliet.

Mr. Lu：Why?

Zha Xiaoyu：If I were to play the role of Juliet, I would make her a more confident, lovely, sunny and self-esteemed girl, just like me, just like myself, will do everything for my love.

以讨论贯穿始终，连缀各种精彩，不仅形式新颖活泼，而且演员表现十分出色，对同一人物的理解与表现见仁见智，对比鲜明，比较充分地体现出莎剧演出的多元与对话性，展示出莎剧理解与阐释的多种可能。

当然，虽然里面主张莎士比亚戏剧中国化、本地化，以汉语演出，但是作为外国语学院学生演出团体，他们大部分是用英文演绎莎士比亚剧情的。

四、戏剧演出对教学的促进

演出是教学的有效手段，不仅让学生学习了英语，更让学生发生了气质上的改变—— 这种“塑造”作用正是大学教育所追求的。大学时代是人格塑造的时期，大学生处于尚未定型的人生阶段，这个时期的经历势必影响到他们的形象、气质、人格及未来。演出者设计由一位演员在舞台右侧（观众视角）拉小提琴，如泣如诉的琴声配合人物演出、烘托气氛。演出奥菲利娅的演员扑倒在地、悲叹“时流的明镜、人伦的雅范、举世瞩目的中心”的凋零，悲叹心上人的疯狂。演员长发垂肩、丝裙曳地、语声清丽、柔肠寸断，表现的人物具有感人肺腑的力量。在后面鲁老师评论的时候说：“每次看演员演奥菲利娅他就在那里哭，果然是‘如泣如诉’。”如此动人心弦，不知学生与导演为此付出了多少心血。2016 年上海国际戏剧节那个在圆锥形灯光内“紧锁（象征闭锁的心理空间）”的奥菲利娅的长篇倾诉，两种场景、一样动人。这种实践教学环节是中国教育的弱项。西方教育从小即开始培养学生的演讲、表达能力，补足中国教育的缺失，戏剧表演无疑是表现的良好训练手段。以美声唱法歌唱的演员出演的麦克白夫人、 疯奥菲利亚技惊四座，令人惊叹其优美的歌喉与完美演技的惊艳。些许天籁之音将人带到超越的艺术境界中。

五、译本效果显现

河南师范大学表演的罗密欧与朱丽叶一段告别场景采用的是辜正坤的译本，“罗郎”，这种古色古香的汉语译本初看上去显得有点怪异，但是这种半古典的剧词在小演员口中却流畅婉转、富有韵律。

朱丽叶：天未曙，罗郎，何苦别意匆忙？
鸟音啼，声声亮，惊骇罗郎心房。
休听作破晓云雀歌，只是夜莺唱，
石榴树间，夜夜有它设歌场。
信我，罗郎，端的只是夜莺轻唱。
罗密欧：我巴不得栖身此地，永不他往。
来吧，死亡！倘朱丽叶愿遂此望。
如何，心肝？畅谈吧，趁夜色迷茫。
朱丽叶：不是夜，天已亮；快走，快逃！
那鸣啼嚣嚷，正是云雀跑调高腔，
如此喧声，难听刺耳，扰我胸膛。
人道，云雀多美声，荡气回肠，
这只不一样，惟使我们天各一方。
人道，云雀曾与丑蟾蜍交换双眼，
啊！我但愿它们也交换歌喉音腔，
那嗓音迫你，松开我俩缠绵拥抱，
猎猎晨歌急，促你远赴白日边疆。
啊！现在快逃吧；天越来越亮。
罗密欧：天越来越亮，我们悲哀的心却越来越黑暗。
（《罗密欧与朱丽叶》第三幕第五场选段[3]）

别意匆匆忙，今宵歌嘹亮。悲声婉，词传情。眉目秋波，跃动姿态，幽幽传心曲。曲径通处，林山夜月、云雀唱晓，催情人了却缠绵，白日却送情人入幽暗。古调声韵清，读来也，宛转流畅。阅读与演出效果存在差异，不同译本需经过舞台的检验才能显现与准确性和表现力。实践是检验译本效果的重要标准之一。

六、舞台“时差”效果

大学生剧社演出时间一般二三十分钟左右，最后一部剧因为表现人物、场景众多，用时稍长。在这样短暂的时间内，观众的感觉却是看了很久，似乎他们演出的并不是二三十分钟，而是两三个小时。短短的时间内包含了很大的戏剧容量，造成奇异的效果。当然，这与观众先知了莎剧剧情有关。在座的多是英语专业学生、教师、莎士比亚戏剧研究者，对剧情多了然于心，对于剧本的改编也较敏感。这种舞台上下的互文大概也是这种演出效果的一种辅助因素。背景、服装、道具与表演结合，达到了良好的舞台效果。

冯涛指导的东北林业大学演出的《罗密欧与朱丽叶》，在罗密欧与朱丽叶殉情场景中，用雪地中两只鲜艳的玫瑰作为背景。画面简洁、玫瑰突出，映在雪地上的影子呈蓝色。色调素雅中有鲜丽，冰雪的寒冷衬托被覆冰霜的玫瑰，象征意义显豁。令人同情其凄恻。

柏杰辰指导的四川外国语大学的《驯悍记》，两个演员能量充沛地“打斗”。女演员突出了凯瑟琳娜的彪悍，彼特鲁乔“驯悍”的辛苦，肢体冲撞中，两人的耳麦纷纷掉落，场景热闹、火爆。西南大学演出的《麦克白》剧情紧凑，一气呵成，颇有紧张感。

此外，还有长江师范学院剧团演出的《奥赛罗》，厦门理工大学演出的蒙古版《麦克白》，南昌大学演出的《威尼斯商人》。九台校园演出剧目规模空前，这是莎士比亚教学、演出的成就。虽难免有不尽如人意处，但这样的业余团体所达到的水准令人惊叹，中国的莎剧演出在舞台上呈现出的清新活力令人惊喜。舞台设计、导演者的用心令人赞佩！

方寸之间的舞台，一直是在学界边缘化、被忽视的地方，大概因为演出需要长期艰苦的训练，想要演得出色殊为不易，组织、训练难度巨大。学生平时要上课，老师要教学、科研，但是在这样艰苦的条件下，能够克服重重困难，将演员、演出达到这样的水平，在观众的眼中、心中点亮一盏灯火，值得嘉奖！莎士比亚的教学、研究、演出应该是三位一体，只有教学与研究是不够的。演出才是新鲜的、活的莎剧。这种运用灯光背景、简单的道具、美丽的服饰、精湛的表演的艺术，使校园里诞出清新的学风。

参考文献

[1] 丁骏. 2016. 书斋与舞台的沟通—— 陆谷孙谈“万世莎翁”[J]. 英美文学研究论丛(24).
[2] 莎士比亚. 2015. 哈姆雷特[M]. 辜正坤，译. 北京：外语教学与研究出版社.
[3] 莎士比亚. 2015. 罗密欧与朱丽叶[M]. 辜正坤，译. 北京：外语教学与研究出版社.

基金项目：2018 年广西哲学社会科学规划研究课题“莎士比亚戏剧人物研究”（批准号：18BWW002）阶段性成果。

作者简介：杨秀波，桂林理工大学副教授，主要从事英美文学、莎士比亚研究。

“译坛巨擘　空谷幽兰”：永远的朱生豪

—— 纪念朱生豪 110 周年诞辰一瞥

李治薪

朱生豪（1912—1944），浙江嘉兴人，著名翻译家、诗人，他翻译了莎士比亚戏剧 31 部，并将毕生才华献给了中国的翻译事业，献给了中国莎学。

2022 年 2 月 27 日，恰逢暖阳。嘉兴市政府为推广嘉兴文人文化，举办了“大师有约”第二场活动“译坛巨擘 空谷幽兰”—— 纪念朱生豪先生 110 周年诞辰，在嘉兴市党群服务中心举行。为了纪念这位天才的翻译家、莎剧翻译家，这次纪念活动由戏剧演出、人物访谈、新书发布、图片展等几大板块组成。

一、话剧的生动叙事：民族英雄朱生豪

此次纪念活动的一个重点，就是以话剧形式赶排了《朱生豪》。在话剧《朱生豪》之前，就已经拍摄有电视剧《朱生豪》、电影《朱生豪》和多部以朱生豪生平、译莎经历为主的纪实片。这部话剧《朱生豪》由嘉兴市“黑盒子”剧社演出，张波编剧、导演的《诗侣莎魂》舞台剧以朱生豪与妻子宋清如因诗结缘，成为伴侣，奋力译莎为背景，叙述了朱生豪在贫病交加之际以生命拥抱莎士比亚的全过程。朱生豪宋清如的这段旷世爱情跨越了时空，连同莎士比亚的作品中的人物也“穿越”于舞台之上，在朱生豪、宋清如与观众之间形成了一个对话的场域。朱生豪的生活和翻译莎士比亚作品中的人物一次次地在追光和不断变换颜色的舞台灯光中“穿梭”于现实和虚构的场景之中，展示了主人公那纯洁的爱情和为理想而献身的精神。翻译莎士比亚戏剧，介绍世界文学戏剧经典是为中华民族争一口气，是替百年来的中国翻译界完成了一件最艰巨的工程。在话剧中，莎士比亚的灵魂仿佛附身了因贫穷的生活和昼夜翻译而身体羸弱的朱生豪身上，笔下人物的青春、爱情、理想、书信、诗歌、译莎生动地呈现在舞台上。正是“萋萋芳草诗友情，伉俪相携译莎路”。

朱生豪在 23 岁时就接下了独自翻译莎士比亚全集的任务。对于一个刚出校门的大学生来说，任务之艰、之重是可想而知的。但朱生豪不畏艰难，以他天才的译笔，将自己的全部感情倾注于莎士比亚戏剧的翻译之中。新文化运动和“五四”运动以后，现代白话文仍然不成熟，文言文也不肯就此退出语言的舞台，这正是一个文言文与白话文的交替的时代。采用何种形式翻译莎士比亚戏剧是摆在青年翻译家面前的一个重要课题。从翻译界的实践来看，外来语种的翻译使处在文言与白话选择中的翻译家，要么使用传统文言文，要么和莎士比亚一

样不断创造出贴合的“白话散文”。在110多年后的今天，经过时间的检验和社会的不断选择，毫无疑问，朱生豪的译莎是成功的，是得到了广大读者认可的。从话剧《朱生豪》的叙事中，我们看到，在日寇法西斯的全面侵华战争面前，他始终不忘译莎，当时的生存环境极端恶劣，抗战的烽火燃遍华夏大地；在日本侵略者铁蹄的践踏之下，普通中国人的生存都成问题，但朱生豪仍然埋首于莎士比亚戏剧，矢志译莎，翻译的稿件因战乱多次被毁、丢失，但他并没有气馁，在常熟、在嘉兴，他一次次选择重新翻译莎士比亚，依靠着这股坚韧不拔的精神和民族气节，展现了我们的民族的内在精神。朱生豪的爱国思想表现为译莎是为我们民族争一口气，日本人嘲笑中国没有文化，连《莎士比亚全集》的译本都没有。我们不但有《莎士比亚全集》，而且拥有放在全世界任何优秀译本面前都不逊色的《莎士比亚全集》。朱生豪以他的生命实现了这一理想。朱生豪以他的才华将莎士比亚的现实主义与浪漫主义展现淋漓尽致地展现在读者和观众面前，历经时态的淘洗和社会的变迁，朱译《莎士比亚全集》，依旧被广大读者所欣赏、所珍爱。1944年，年仅32岁的朱生豪倒下了，但他留下了不朽的翻译作品——《莎士比亚戏剧全集》，朱生豪无愧于中国翻译界的“民族英雄”的称号。

朱生豪在《〈莎士比亚戏剧全集〉译者自序》中写道：“余译此书之宗旨，第一在求于最大可能之范围内，保持原作之神韵，逼不得已求其次，亦必以明白晓畅之字句，忠实传达原文之意趣；而于逐字逐句对照式硬译，则未敢赞同。”翻译莎士比亚的难度，在白话文还在发展的时代，是艰难重重，除了上述的客观外在因素，还有翻译莎翁作品的自身难度。据统计，莎士比亚的戏剧有三万多词汇量，中国非英语母语国家的作家，难以体会其深意；莎士比亚的戏剧写法丰富，有俚语、呓语等，其中的诙谐幽默不易被察觉；戏剧句式风格多样，散文式、诗体的对话，插科打诨的言语，选择任何一种方式翻译，都会让莎士比亚戏剧有缺憾。

罗新璋是这样评价朱生豪的：“朱生豪本身文字功夫非常好，因此能够在不拘泥于原文字词的情况下，在译文中保持原作的风采和韵味。”带有韵律的散文，使他的译文读起来有诗的味道。朱生豪翻译的是神韵，“朱生豪译文胜就胜在他不仅将原文的意思翻译出来了，更让读者感受到了文字之美。”朱生豪是个浪漫的才子，他停止了自己的创作，将自身的才气的芬芳，散发在了《莎士比亚全集》的翻译中。

二、对话天才翻译家

舞台上灯火通明，观众从朱生豪的生平中走出，主持人拿着话筒主持接下来的访谈。

台上由中国莎士比亚研究会理事、嘉兴市朱生豪故居管理所名誉所长、朱生豪之子朱尚刚，浙江文学院院长、浙江文学馆馆长程士庆，嘉兴学院中文系副教授、嘉兴市文艺评论家协会副主席汪娟三人齐坐在沙发与主持人交流。程士庆对朱生豪与宋清如的婚姻表示崇高的敬意。朱生豪夫妻二人聚少离多，在他生前，恋爱与婚姻的陪伴常处异地，在他去世后，宋清如一人独自生活了半个世纪。朱生豪对爱情，正如木心诗歌“一生只够爱一个人”。他一生只爱了宋清如一人，宋清如亦然。

1942年，因“宝塔诗”而经历了十年的爱情漫漫长路，抵达了终点，他们结婚了。婚后的生活极其简单，朱生豪“译莎”，宋清如“烧饭”。恋爱十年，结婚两年。这是朱生豪一生的爱情故事，简单，刻骨。1944年，他的一生定格在了32岁。妻子宋清如一个人带着只有

13 个月大的儿子朱尚刚，在艰难的岁月里，她成了“西风中飘零的败叶”。现场的朱尚刚为了更加立体地还原了有血有肉的父亲朱生豪。纪念活动还举行了以朱生豪的一生为线索的《朱生豪年谱长编》首发式和参观“纪念朱生豪先生诞辰 110 周年展”活动。

三、朱生豪、宋清如：生命中的挚爱

宋清如在整理二人来往的信出版后，在序中写道“朱生豪的书信，主要是他独特个性的表现，并非执着于异性的追求”。对朱生豪而言，现实是令人痛苦的地方，只有纸张上一个个的文字，才是他精神的归属。他在写给宋清如的 540 封信中，有着俏皮的各式的署名：猪八戒、丑小鸭、常山赵子龙，对宋清如的称呼也是变化不停：傻丫头、宝贝、好友。这与他日常的性格截然相反，即使是婚后面对宋清如，他也是寡言少语，甚至用信来交流。在信中的他，又恢复了俏皮的模样。这或许是朱生豪爱宋清如的方式。他的爱都寄托在信纸上，这也为他之后的翻译奠定了基础。对外，他把爱给了宋清如，对内，他将爱，放在文字里，放在了翻译中。他毫不掩饰地说，翻译是无意义的，因为这不是自己的作品。可他毅然把生命，献给了翻译事业。生活的痛苦，不只是他儿时父母的离弃，还有生活的清贫，物质的匮乏，身体的羸弱，唯有精神，能战胜一切。在翻译中，他遇到了莎士比亚，他找到了自己。

如果说朱生豪现实的归属是宋清如，那么精神的归属是对莎士比亚作品的翻译。

在生活体验的领域，朱生豪面临一系列的生存危机—— 自我生存环境而言，从小父母离世寄人篱下；社会大背景而言，朱生豪活在新旧社会交替，社会动荡不安的时代；朱生豪短暂的二年的婚姻而言，一贫如洗—— 这些都让朱生豪这个原本“古怪孤独”的性格更加沉浸在自我的精神中，这个世上，唯有宋清如能给他送去温暖，唯有莎翁，在 180 万字中与他对话，感受他的孤独。朱生豪用短暂的一生，谱写了自己悲壮而又传奇的一生。他用自己的青春、才华、汉语、用莎士比亚的作品表达了自己对生活的独特理解。

四、面向未来：永远的朱生豪

宋清如参与演出的电视剧《朱生豪》，1992 年播出上下两集，她因此获第十二届“飞天奖”的荣誉奖。这部影片是纪念朱生豪 80 周年诞辰所制作，由嘉兴电视台摄制。彼时离朱生豪去世已有 48 年。即使他离开人世间已有 48 年，但他的影响依旧，他永远活着，他的译作，他的精神，哺育了新一代的中国文学创作者。而影视的呈现，让更多人知道了莎士比亚在中国，在中国有个朱生豪这位翻译家。

时至今日，为了纪念朱生豪先生 110 周年诞辰，由嘉兴市党群服务中心、嘉兴市文学艺术界联合会、嘉兴日报报业传媒集团联合主办了一次“译坛巨擘 空谷幽兰”活动。数字化建设的嘉兴，让此次活动走到了线上，不便到现场的观众可通过线上实时参与其中，感受朱生豪在嘉兴的人文魅力。发展迅速的传播媒介—— 影像，让更多人了解了朱生豪。传统的媒介也在发挥其影响力。

“最会写情诗的翻译家”“民国最会说情话的男人”，既有网友情切的称呼，也有出版社所取贴切的称呼。不难看出，朱生豪从传统的翻译家走进了平常百姓家，年轻人无人不爱朱生豪的“情书”。尤其是当代年轻人对朱生豪情话的喜爱，一时成为网络用语。“我是宋清如至上主义者”“也许你望着月亮时，我正在想你”“我是属于你的，永远而且完全地。愿你快乐”。这些经典朱生豪语录，经时间沉淀，如今闪闪发光。而他的译作更是经久不衰，至今各出版社仍在沿用他的译作，时代文艺出版社、译林出版社、时代文艺出版社等，依旧能看到朱生豪的身影。朱生豪的信，既受到了年轻人的追捧，又有极高的学术价值，是研究莎士比亚翻译和白话文的探究都不可避绕的一道墙。正如《嘉兴日报》记者许金艳采访中国莎士比亚研究会副会长李伟民教授时，李伟民所言：“嘉兴一贯重视名人文化的建设”，“朱生豪在世界莎学领域树立了一座中华民族文化的巍巍丰碑”。

有朱生豪的地方就有莎士比亚。世界文豪莎士比亚的灵魂，与中国诗人朱生豪走在嘉兴的东米棚下，走在江南特有的窄窄的小巷和南湖畔，吟唱着莎士比亚的诗剧。

作者简介：李治薪，浙江越秀外国语学院中国语言文化学院，《浙江法制报》记者，主要从事戏剧与文学研究。

第六编

莎学书简（5）

莎学书简（5）

朱尚刚　孙福良　彭镜禧　杨林贵　曹树钧　李伟民　李伟昉

《中国莎士比亚研究》已经连续四辑出版《莎学书简》，这些“莎学书简”一经出版就得到了很多学者的好评，纷纷撰文予以肯定，强调其出版在外国文学研究界、莎学学界本身就是一个具有承前启后性质的创举。《莎学书简》的出版已经在莎学界、外国文学比较文学研究领域引起了很好的反响。

从已经出版的《莎学书简》来看，莎学学者之间的通信本身就已经构成了中国莎学史研究的一个不可或缺的有机组成部分。这些莎学学者在通信中满怀激情地讨论、展望、推动着中国莎学研究事业的发展。每当我们打开这些尘封多年的信件，我们就会发现学者们的每一封信都在探讨中国莎学的发展，从这些已经泛黄、发脆的信函里，我们可以感受到莎学研究者那一颗颗跳动着的滚烫的心，以及他们热爱祖国、热爱人民、热爱莎学研究、热爱外国文学研究事业的一腔热血。

我们非常高兴地看到这些“莎学书简”一面世，就有外国文学研究者、莎学研究者加以引用，因为这些书简恰恰是学者们真性情的流露，是学术史的真实记录。同时，我们也希望学界在利用这些“书简”时能够严格遵守学术规范，注明信件出处。

需要说明的是，这些“书简”表面上看是写给某个人的，但是联系起来全面地审视，我们认为这些“书简”的文学研究价值、莎学研究价值、史料研究价值绝不仅仅局限于此，因为从这些“书简”中我们能够清晰地感受到 20 世纪，特别是 20 世纪 80 年代以来中国莎学顽强有力地跳动着的脉搏。

如果说《傅雷家书》只是父亲与儿子之间的心曲的真情吐露的话，那么《莎学书简》则在更为广阔的社会语境中和更多学者之间架设起了学术交流的桥梁，清晰而真实地勾画出中国莎学发展的昨天、今天和明天。在当今电子信息时代，电话、短信、微信联络日益增多，而书信这种古老的通信方式也就显得日益珍贵，“莎学书简”理应得到我们的珍爱，而出版这些“莎学书简”本身就带有抢救莎学史料的意义和学术价值。需要特别说明的是，由于这些“书简”均为手写体，“书简”提供者提供的又多是“书简”的复印件，即使是原件，由于时间已经过去了10~30年，有些字迹已经很难辨认，凡是一时难以辨认的字迹均以“□”代替。信函书写各有特点，且手写体辨认困难，四川外国语大学国际商学院数学教授陈莉老师与学生助理王雅雯、周碧莹、黄雨菲承担了《莎学书简》繁难的文字录入工作，有时边录入边研究，进展较慢，在此对陈莉教授及学生助理表示衷心感谢。

同时感谢“书简”提供者无私地为莎学界提供了这些信函。本辑“书简”主要由朱尚刚、孙福良、彭镜禧、杨林贵、曹树钧、李伟民、李伟昉提供。据本书编者掌握的材料来看，还有大量的“书简”没有来得及录入，相信假以时日，我们还会陆续出版这些书信，同时也准备把这些“书简”汇编成册予以出版，为21世纪中国莎学的进一步繁荣与发展做出我们应有的贡献。

在征集书信准备出版的几年中，我们不断收到各种对“莎学书信”出版的认可、鼓励，正是这些来自学界的勉励和督促，鼓舞、鞭策着我们克服各种困难，不断勇毅前行。需要特别提到的是，在《莎学书简》出版的过程中，朱尚刚先生的鼎力支持。当我们请求朱尚刚先生，想公开朱生豪与宋清如的一些书信时，朱尚刚先生立即联系浙江工商大学档案馆，为我们调出了他已经捐赠给浙江工商大学档案馆从未发表过的书信，其中包括中国台湾莎学翻译家虞尔昌的儿子——同济大学虞润身教授与宋清如、朱尚刚等联系的信件，使得我们能够从中一窥海峡两岸莎学学者血浓于水的心心相念之情。本辑公开的“莎学书简”尤其值得关注朱尚刚先生为我们提供的1946年朱生豪的胞弟——四川大学教授朱文振先生与其大嫂宋清如讨论《莎士比亚全集》出版撰写“译者生平”的《对“译者小志”拟商数点》一信，此信件是第一次公之于世。在《对“译者小志”拟商数点》中，我们看到了朱生豪的“忠厚诚朴与与世无争”，看到了朱生豪决心为中华民族的文化建设矢志译莎，看到了朱生豪深厚的中国古典文学修养，以及朱文振对出版《莎士比亚全集》和对撰写朱生豪生平材料的增删意见。朱文振的《对“译者小志”拟商数点》全文共计“十六点”，本次仅公开一至三点和十五至十六点，以及“附”的内容。这篇《对“译者小志”拟商数点》写于 1946 年，由于是手写体，加之纸质不佳，很多字句难以辨认，故在李伟民精心录入的基础上，再由朱尚刚先生仔细订正，保证了《对“译者小志”拟商数点》文字的准确无误。我们欣慰地看到《莎学书简》已经列入了国家编辑出版图书的计划，正式出版时将以《云中锦笺——中国莎学书信》作为书名，这一书名也是李伟民与杨林贵几经讨论，最后定名的。我们相信“莎学书简”结集出版后还将会在莎学界、学术界和翻译界引起更加巨大的反响和深远的影响。

对“译者小志”拟商数点*

一、于其秉性一节之中似可增一章，以记其忠厚诚朴与世无争。

二、毕业之江为廿二年（同年弟毕业附中，故记忆甚确）。

三、“莎翁著作之价值……一洗此耻”诸语，未识果为直接引用者否？若系渲染烘托之笔，则似亦以援类其口吻者为佳，如“以莎翁著作之伟大佳妙，而吾国乃至今尚无全集之译本，宁非憾事？余决勉力成之。”（大意如此，修辞请裁决）同时亦较含蓄，然否？

……

十五、于其对国故经籍方面之所好及所得，可否亦有较着重之提述（国文系乃其主系也）。其大学时代情形，嫂当知之甚详。弟所知者彼在中学时代，对《论》《孟》《诗》《骚》等等均已相当娴熟（因文科必读），近代经儒典籍如《宋儒学案》《明儒学案》等等亦在研读之列。

十六、文中记其有关译莎者已够详尽。惟于其早年生活似嫌不足，于其一般品性似嫌笼统，上述有若干具体事例，可否请酌量选用增入。弟意此文为志其“人”，而非仅志其译莎一事，故虽云“小志”亦不妨详而略细也。

附：

一、《自序》是否可改为《译者自序》以免误会，末尾可否添书作成年月？

二、草拟《莎翁传略》一篇请酌编于《译者自序》之前或后。此文篇首不必注明出何人手。

三、另拟《附记》一篇，可否附登，请予裁夺（若用则附卷末）。

四、《自序》等文不知将刊于每单行本抑每“辑”（自序中所定之辑）抑仅刊于第一个单行本？弟意最好向书局交涉遵照译者意向分成四辑，则每辑可刊《自序》等文。史剧原定在最末，待续译完竣再排印，或亦尚不致脱节（前三辑排印恐非一年半载可毕）。

五、《莎翁传略》文笔务请削正，弟素病涩硬，此文中亦当不免，非谦套语也。《附记》若亦用，则亦请修改。

六、请人作序事，目前困难太多，如学校下月即结束准备迁京，五月启程，现均在忙乱不安定之中；又如原译均未及睹，外人作序太乏根据；等等。否则，此间系主任范存忠当可为之，老前辈楼光来老师虽不喜著述，或亦可一试。此事只好待返京安定后再说。

奉手示后 即开始嘱为各事，惟苦于琐事纷烦，每日仅一、二小时可专心于此，致迟复命，谅之。昨晚□事，合亟寄上，余不及告，待后再陈。此请大嫂安康

振弟　拜上

一九四六年三月十日

*关于朱文振先生《对“译者小志”拟商数点》书简的编辑说明：

李伟民与杨林贵在编纂《中国莎学书简》（商务印书馆）时，朱尚刚先生提供了四川大学朱文振教授，给大嫂宋清如先生这封珍贵的来信，在李伟民辨识、录入的基础上，朱尚刚先

生亲自订正了（朱文振先生的《对“译者小志”拟商数点》，原件现藏浙江工商大学档案馆）。朱文振（1914—1993），浙江嘉兴人，为朱生豪先生胞弟。1937年毕业于中央大学外文系，先后在中央大学、广西大学、重庆大学任教，并任四川大学外文系教授、系主任。主要著作有《康第达》（青年书店1944年版）、《英语简史》（四川大学出版社1994年版）、《翻译与语言环境》（四川大学出版社1987年版）。20世纪50年代初，朱文振已经采用元曲体译出多部莎氏历史剧，但因所译风格与朱生豪译莎风格不同，未被出版社接受，译稿遗失。

朱尚刚先生提到：

文振叔还特地为《全集》写了一篇《莎翁传略》和一篇《后记》，于1946年3月10日寄给母亲，同时也对母亲的《译者小志》提出了16点“拟商”的意见，其中有个别似为抄写中的笔误外，大多是认为应当增补的内容，包括父亲的秉性、经历、背景等诸多方面。现在看来，这些内容若单独来看，都是值得一提的，但若全部都加进去，这篇“小志”就会变成“大志”了。可能母亲当时也是这样考虑的，所以只采纳了其中的一小部分意见。

《莎翁传略》和父亲的《莎翁年谱》虽然体裁不同，但在《全集》中的作用是一样的，不可能两篇都用。文振叔因为远在千里之外，不知父亲已经写就了《莎翁年谱》，才有此举。

文振叔写的那篇《后记》相当长，约有八千字，主要内容是关于翻译体式的讨论。因为莎剧原本是英国古典的诗剧，文振叔一直认为用白话散文体来翻译英文的 Blank verse（无韵诗）无法表现出莎剧的原有韵味，只能算是“详解式的翻译”，而要做到“艺术性的翻译”，则一定要采用另一种和英文 Blank verse 相对应的语言形式（文振叔认为用元曲体最为适当）。这是文振叔坚持了一生并且为之付出了大量心血进行实践的观点。实际上，像这种鱼和熊掌孰取孰舍的问题，本来是可以见智见仁，放开探讨并留待实践来进行检验的，但按我现在的看法，将如此篇幅的一篇论证散文体译文之不合理想的论文作为散文体译本的附记，实在是并不合适的。不知母亲当年是否有过我的这种感觉，也许她也感到为难，因为要对文振叔花了很大的心血且倾注了极大热情写的这篇东西表示否定是很难开口的。后来母亲复信文振叔时，除了将父亲《莎翁年谱》的稿子抄了寄去请他做进一步查校外，还建议将《附记》刊在《全集》之末。这倒是一个恰到好处的建议，因为那么长的附记本来不可能每一单行本甚至四辑本的每一辑都刊登，而《全集》的最后完成则还有待于文振叔补译全其余的剧本。若那些剧本用元曲体译了，那么《附记》加在后面，正好作为前后体例不同的一个说明，倒也合适，如果文振叔也用散文体译了，那么想来他自己也会改写这篇附记的。

三月二十七日，文振叔来了回信：

手示及《莎翁年谱》稿已到数日，以仍仅能每天略抽时间对付，故至今日始克查校竣事。尊抄稿因已有多处增补移改，故另抄一份寄上。所作小增或小改，大致目的均在求清晰，大体均仍原有。其他弟意可去者未去，可增者未增（唯莎氏同时代诸家中有 T. Heywood 者，手头二文学史中均未提及，无从查得其生卒年份，暂删去）。前未知森兄有此年谱故作传略，今既底稿未失抄校付印，则传略或可免刊，以省重复，可请裁决也。云附记刊全集之末甚是。尊抄年谱稿暂存弟处，免信件过重。底稿仍寄上，请善藏之……

在信的末尾又加了一段文字：

又森兄对三李之奇才（义山之丽，长吉之鬼，太白之逸）均曾有极大喜爱，或可插入《译者小志》中否……

这样，关于《年谱》《传略》和《后记》的问题就算是处理定了。关于父亲的“义山之丽、长吉之鬼、太白之逸”那几句话，大概因为《译者小志》总体框架已定，所以也没有收入。不过那几句话确是对三李诗歌艺术风格极为精当的评价，大概也属于夏承焘先生为之“一唱三叹”的“前人未发之论”吧。母亲晚年所写介绍父亲生平的文章中经常引用这几句话。

那篇《译者小志》，后来正式出版时改称《译者介绍》。

（见朱尚刚：《诗侣莎魂——我的父母朱生豪、宋清如》，商务印书馆2016年版，第269~271页）

在此，我们先行公开了极为珍贵的朱文振先生的《对“译者小志”拟商数点》的部分内容及信件第2页的影印件，以飨读者。该信件的全部内容及信件的影印件将在商务印书馆出版的《云中锦笺——中国莎学书信》中公开。在书简录入过程中，由于年代久远，有些字迹已经很难辨识，凡是难以辨识的字迹均以“□”代替。（编者）

宋清如先生：

寄上拙稿一卷，请指正。不才也是千千万万朱生豪译本忠实读者之一。而且非朱译，不成其为莎士比亚。人文版莎翁全集出来，跟朱译对了一下，保存百分之九十五以上，才购买一部。我尤其爱读朱先生译的诗。看书累了，抽出莎集，随便叫我老婆读一首。有一次，读后，我这位朱译崇拜者，也只好说，这首译得不怎么样，过一会儿，我老婆翻到书目页，不胜欣喜地告诉我，这不是朱生豪译的。

“世界书局”版上的“译者自序”和“译者介绍”，我以前都恭录了一份。我总觉得评论界对朱先生的译笔没有给予足够的评价，可惜我不专攻英国文学。仅在拙文中引朱先生一段“自序”，表示不胜敬意。这篇“自序”，好像解放后—— 或许是我孤陋寡闻—— 在此文才第一次引用！好在朱先生的译本能传下去，一直活在读者心中！他的才能自有一代一代的赏识者！我每次读“译者介绍”，都深为感动！跟这样有才能的人生活在一起应该是很幸福的，可惜朱先生过世太早了！这就是人生！

匆匆。

祝

康健！

璋* 拜上

一九八三年八月二十二日晚

*关于罗新璋先生书信的说明：这是罗新璋先生 1983 年 8 月 22 日写给宋清如的信。罗先生在 1983 年第 7、8 两期《翻译通讯》上发表了他的论文《我国自成体系的翻译理论》(此文后来收入他所编的《翻译论丛》书中，商务印书馆，1984 年 5 月)，是在新时期中较早对朱生豪的翻译从理论高度进行评价的论述，认为“朱光潜提出的‘神似’，傅雷提出的‘传神’的翻译理论，是对严复提出的‘信达雅’的翻译原则的突破。这种‘神似神韵之说二三十年代就有人提过，但影响不大，一方面可能是表述上不够有力……更重要的，是那时的翻译实践还没有提供足够的令人信服的实例’”，认为正是朱生豪的翻译成了这一理论“令人瞩目的范例”。他对朱生豪译文的评价“朱生豪译笔流畅，文辞华赡，善于保持原作的神韵，传达莎剧的气派”也为后来的许多研究者所引用。论文发表后，罗先生将两期《翻译通讯》寄给宋清如，同时写了这一封热情洋溢的信。(李伟民)

清如学嫂：

受人之托，冒昧得很，叨在是之江先后同学，写了这封信给您。我在同济大学建筑系任教，同校有一位测量系的讲师，想知道朱生豪兄身后家属情况。上海之江校友会（筹），仅知朱兄 1933 年之江毕业，任世界书局英文编辑。1943 年逝去，是早年译莎士比亚戏剧专家。

朱兄生前好友虞尔昌亦是之江校友①，1926 年之江毕业，1947 年秋应聘台大任教，现是台湾大学西洋文学系教授，莎士比亚研究学者。我的同事讲师，所以恳请我代为了解，态度是真诚的，是尔昌的儿子，与我是 71 年时干校参加劳动时一起生活过。为人忠诚老实。言下之意，尔昌在台是在朱兄生前研究的基础上继续研究莎氏著作，并在台出版。尔昌一直在怀念朱兄家属，在与他儿子通信中一再询问。所以他的儿子要求我设法打听，我认为义不容辞，尽力架桥深盼能在不久的将来，你们双方旧世谊重述旧好启进后辈世谊。

我 1941 年毕业之江，在之江任教。之江沪地校友筹会我系责任人之一，代校友寻访旧知包括家属分内之事，亦是我校友会工作的一个方面。毛遂自荐，斗胆询问希明者谅解，特此函询赐复为盼，此致敬礼。

学弟　一清　上

一九八四年五月二十日晚上

通信处：上海溧阳路 964 弄（浙兴里）187 号。

① 编者注：写信人当时称朱生豪与虞尔昌为“好友”，是写信人并不了解朱生豪与虞尔昌为之江大学先后校友，彼此并不相识。

宋老师：

春节将临，首先问候您福寿安康，全家幸福。

今天尚刚弟来沪，带来了您赠送的一套 1978 年版的《莎士比亚全集》。我将去信告诉海外的亲人，并向您表示深切的感谢！

由于明天（14 日）我要去外地出差，忙于事务，故尚刚弟来同济，也未能招待好，并陪他多讲讲，还望尚刚弟见谅。台北家父多次来信都称颂朱生豪先生和您老人家，家父是 1947 年应聘去台湾大学任教的，大陆解放音讯隔断，故他未能知晓生豪先生翻译莎翁历史剧的情况，按世界书局 1947 年的版本，还缺少十个历史剧。有感于生豪先生译笔之优美，文理之通畅，而不幸英年早逝，故家父从 50 年代初之前后，便立志要继续生豪的工作事业，补译莎翁之历史剧。历几年到 1957 年，再由台北世界书局发印了由朱生豪先生和家父（虞尔昌）所译的《莎士比亚戏剧全集》。分五册精装，第一、二、三卷为生豪先生之原译作，第四、五卷为家父所译的历史剧及评论。近年来，老人家多次经美国转寄来信，都一再赞赏生豪先生为事业不顾贫病交加的牺牲精神，他更高兴您还健在，并赞扬您支持和继承生豪先生事业所作出的贡献，诚如不久前我给尚刚弟信中所引用的家父在 1984 年 10 月 6 日来信所讲到的："生豪对介绍一位西方最伟大的作家和诗人所作过的贡献，诚属不朽。人生之价值，不在其年寿之长短，而在其对人类社会所作之贡献。生豪如无其夫人之共患难，受尽千辛万苦何能发挥其才华有此成就。想到此，读者在欣赏生豪所译莎剧之同时，亦应对朱夫人表示敬意和谢意也。"

这一些信，尚刚弟此次来沪，我已给他看过了。并将家父第一次提到生豪先生的那封来信（1984 年 4 月）复印件交给了尚刚弟。

上个月前，接我在美国太空总署工作的胞妹来信，谓，我在台北的八十高龄的父亲，突发了肝病，病况较重，她也即将赴台去看望老人，我们在大陆的亲人都为之十分焦急，但愿能逢凶化吉，转危为安，以期有重会之日。

生豪先生与家父所合译的莎剧全集，迄至 1980 年，已由台北世界书局重版了三次，深受海内外读者之欢迎。此外，有感于那边所见莎士比亚十四行诗一些译本的粗劣，家父还花了一年时间，三易其稿，翻译了《莎士比亚十四行诗全集》，于 1961 年由台北世界书局出版。

可惜由于众所周知的原因，海峡两岸阻隔。台北所出版的《莎士比亚戏剧及诗全集》，迄今在大陆仍未见到。我想再不多久，我在美国的妹妹会把它们寄来的。

最后，再次谢谢伯母赠予的莎翁全集，并祝愿您健康长寿！

同济大学 测量系 虞润身 上

一九八五年二月十三日

宋老师，尚刚弟：

你们好！久未通信，谅全家安康。去年 12 月 25 日《嘉兴报》载文迄今，生豪先生和我的父亲更见到尚刚弟的怀念文章和宋老师的诗，我的心里也总是激荡着对慈爱的父亲的怀念。

于今，首届中国莎士比亚戏剧节刚过，听着熟悉的剧名和生动的台词，多彩多姿的表演，更使我怀念为译莎事业而倾注了毕生心血的先贤。作为台湾地区莎士比亚学者，我的父亲是朱先生译莎事业在海峡彼岸的接力人。他把自己的译作（历史剧和诗篇）当成是朱先生对莎翁译著的继续。并早在 1957 年 4 月就由台北世界书局出版了以朱译 27 部喜悲杂剧为基础，由虞补译十个历史剧的《莎士比亚戏剧全集》作为第一部完整可读的中文版莎翁戏剧全集。到 1980 年已印行了三版。不久前，这一套台北版的《莎士比亚全集》已由我在美国的妹妹寄来了。这是父亲生前准备好要寄给我的一套以志永久的纪念。全集共五卷（精装），一、二、三卷是朱译的 27 部戏剧。并有朱先生在一九四四年四月写的“译者自序”（大概就是 1947 年 4 月版本的自序）三、四卷是虞译的十部历史剧，“莎士比亚评论”，及朱先生早年写的“莎士比亚年谱”。这封信里先把这一套全集的封面，及“译者自序”的复印件寄上给你们看看。

校刊要我写一篇纪念台湾莎士比亚学者，虞尔昌教授的文章，我已作毕交上去了。用关汉卿的词句《发不同青心共热》为命题，以怀念我的父亲继续朱生豪先生的译莎事业，共同为我中华争气的事实。文中引用了父亲来信中对朱生豪先生，朱夫人的崇敬之情。父亲说：“……生豪的文章十倍于我。不幸早逝，为我国文坛之一大损失。生豪对介绍一位西方最伟大作家和诗人所作的贡献，诚属不朽！人生之价值，不在其年寿之长短，而在其对人类社会所作之贡献”，“……生豪如无夫人之共患难，受尽千辛万苦，何能发挥其才华而有所成就？想到此，读者欣赏生豪所译莎剧之同时，亦应对朱夫人表示敬意，谢意也。”

值此首届中国莎士比亚戏剧节圆满闭幕之际，我和我的爱人衷心祝愿宋老师健康长寿，愿尚刚弟工作顺利，全家幸福！

我们已迁住新居，比以前宽敞多了，新居在同济新村 513 号 402 室，尚刚弟如来沪，欢迎光临！

同济大学　虞润身

一九八六年五月十日

尚刚弟：

去年纪念朱生豪先生80诞辰，有幸在上海相见，同时也见到了您的孩子之江。可惜那次叙会所摄的照片，由于胶卷未装对，没有成功，特致歉意。

纪念会活动之后，我向在美国的母亲写了信。家父在生前对生豪先生十分敬重。他在来信中写道："……生豪的文章十倍于我，不幸早逝，为我国文坛的一大损失。生豪对介绍一位西方伟大作家和诗人所作的贡献，诚属不朽，人生之价值，不在其年寿之长短，而在其对人类社会所作之贡献。"家父对您的母亲朱夫人也深表感激和敬仰，就在他病重前的1984年春的信中，老人写道："你告诉我有关生豪的资料十分可贵，承朱夫人惠赠生豪照片，更觉珍贵，我拟著文叙述生豪一生及身后情形，在报章杂志发表……生豪如无夫人之共患难，受尽千辛万苦，何能发挥其才华，有此成就？读者在欣赏生豪所著莎剧之同时，亦应对朱夫人表示敬意，谢意也！"

我的继母在1984年12月，家父在台北逝世一年之后，去美国定居，现住在休斯顿，并任休斯顿中华老人协会的理事，热心于社会服务的工作，但近年健康不够好，行动不甚方便。两个在台湾出生的妹妹都在美国搞电脑工程。

母亲对朱夫人是十分敬仰的，她早有从台湾寄一套台北世界书局1957年4月版的朱、虞合译的《莎士比亚戏剧全集》赠给朱夫人的愿望，但她身在美国，曾两次托人从台湾经香港直邮，都未能安全到达。于是不得不再托友人将书带到美国再从美国邮到上海来。终于在上个月到达了上海。承母亲的旨意，或拟在四月上旬（初定于4月6日），将这部精装5卷的全集带到嘉兴来，并向朱夫人和您的一家人致问好。故今特来信相告。您的一家是否仍住在嘉兴，东米棚下老宅？我想从上海赶快车到嘉兴是上午9点左右，下车看到老宅也是方便的。

学校的工作很忙，我和老伴住在上海。

请代我向朱夫人问安，祝老人永远健康长寿！

4月上旬，您是否在嘉兴？盼早日回信

同济大学　虞润身

一九九三年三月二十一日

尚刚弟：

接到您的信，十分高兴。朱夫人安康，小之江学习优秀都令人欣喜。

我原想在四月六日到嘉兴来，向朱夫人和您问好，并赠台湾版的《莎士比亚戏剧全集》。但几天前又接国家测绘局的邀请，要我在 4 月 6 日参加广州的一个由国家测绘局主持的新型仪器鉴定会，我受聘为鉴定委员会成员，这样我在 4 月 4 日就从上海飞广州，约到 4 月 10 日才回上海，而 4 月中旬又有一个全国的仪器使用学习班要开课，这样我要到 4 月下旬才能到嘉兴来。届时我将打电话与您联系。

如果您在 4 月中旬有机会到上海出差，则请光临同济（届时我在校里上课）。我们也好叙谈叙谈，并把这部全集早日带到朱夫人的身边。

祝，全家安康，并代问候朱夫人。

虞润身

一九九三年四月一日

尚刚弟：

今寄上我们的合影以作留念。

父辈为翻译莎士比亚戏剧，历尽艰难。正是上海世界书局出版朱译《莎士比亚戏剧集》(二十七个剧本）十周年的那天，于海峡彼岸的台北，由台北世界书局出版了中国第一部完整的《莎士比亚戏剧全集》。它包括了朱先生原译的二十七个剧本和家父补译的十个历史剧。此为中国文坛之盛事。写入历史的那天，也就把海峡两岸的两位学者的理想和生命连在一起了。同是之江人，家父比朱先生年长，一个是学兄，一个是学弟，但生前并未谋面。只是 1947 年家父在去台湾大学任教之前夕，读到上海世界书局刚出版的朱译莎剧集。他从酷爱莎剧，熟读莎剧原著，也对比当时业已由别人译出的莎剧译本，从“有比较才有鉴别”出发，惊赞朱先生的译作，在信、达、雅这几方面高超的成功。诸多的译作“尚未有能出于其右者”。而痛惜朱先生的“英年早逝”，遂下决心在台北继续完成朱先生未竟的事业。然 50 年代台湾经济匮乏，教授的工薪微薄，不少教师只能多兼课填补生活开支。家父却不为所惑，一间陋室，一张旧书桌，上课之余，译作不辍。母亲作为他的助手也同甘共苦，膝上铺一块门板，为他抄写誊清稿件，改了誊，誊清了又改，从无怨尤。粗茶淡饭清贫度日。历十载终于中译莎剧始成完璧。

今、明两天中午，上海电视台播放电视剧“朱生豪”人们将更能从荧幕上见到朱先生和朱夫人的高尚气质和不朽的贡献。

值此电视剧播放之际，我写这封信，以表达对父辈的追忆。

祝朱夫人健康长寿！

祝您全家安康，幸福！

虞润身

一九九三年六月二日

朱尚刚先生：

您好！

上月中旬（7.11—7.15）我同敝校外语学院张奎武教授一起赴澳，在布里斯班市昆士兰大学的圣·约翰学院参加了由澳大利亚莎协与新西兰莎协联合举行的题为“莎士比亚的物质性——教学、历史和演出”的莎学学术会议。我与张奎武教授应邀做关于中国莎学的专题演讲。我们的两个题目为：“中国莎学的发展过程及其特点，兼及用中国人的眼光接受莎士比亚的审美价值”；“中国的莎士比亚翻译，兼及朱生豪译莎的贡献”。我们的发言引起与会者的浓厚兴趣，就中国莎学的翻译、演出提出了不少问题，而对令尊的贡献与精神表示致敬。澳大利亚拉特罗布大学的吉列斯教授对中国莎学很感兴趣，听了我们的发言之后提出希望能够得到嘉兴电视台为纪念令尊 80 诞辰而制作的上下两集电视剧《朱生豪》的拷贝。我觉得这是一件好事，这表明天才的年轻的诗人、翻译家朱生豪的名字已经冲出国门，开始走向世界。因此，我想我们应该帮助吉列斯，这实际上是他在宣传我们中国的莎学。此事烦您与嘉兴电视台联系一下，请他们予以关照。如果您对此事同意，嘉兴电视台也同意，然后再商量如何操作的问题。敬请赐复。

东北师大莎士比亚研究中心　孟宪强

一九九八年八月一日

孙福良同志：

您好！

“通知”收到了，现根据“通知”精神将有关材料一并寄上。

欣闻明年 4 月举行“上海国际莎剧节”，非常兴奋。我们感谢中莎会—— 特别是中莎会秘书处的同志们—— 为繁荣中国莎学，举办莎剧节所做出的巨大努力。

88 年 11 月我的研究生杨林贵去苏州迎接美国密歇根州萨基诺大学的王裕珩教授时，我曾让他去上海、杭州拜访张君川副会长和您。他见到了张君川教授，遗憾的是未能见到您，但他说通了电话。感谢中莎会领导对我们的鼓励与关照。张君川教授曾对杨林贵提出：1990 年莎剧节时，吉林省是否能够演出一台吉剧形式的莎剧？对张君川教授提出的这个问题，我们进行了研究，我们觉得还是有可能的。我省领导对发展莎学比较重视，几年来对吉林省莎士比亚协会的工作给予了许多支持。因此我想，如果中莎会正式向我们提出这个问题，我们省的领导会支持的。在我们接到中莎会的公函之后即可向省里申请经费，进行准备。希望能够尽快听到中莎会关于这个问题的意见。

我们出版的《莎士比亚的三重戏剧》已由杨林贵给您寄去，谅已收到。

因为现在已经放假，所以来信请寄我爱人处，我家距离师大中文系较远，而离我爱人上班的师大附中很近，来信请寄：吉林省长春市东北师大附中陈凌云处。

即颂

冬安！

孟宪强

一九八九年一月十八日

孙福良同志：

来信敬悉，殊为感盼。

久病住院，执笔乏力，谒简述心意如下：

一、祝贺朱生豪先生诞辰八十周年纪念大会成功，贺词已挂号寄上。

二、感谢同志们终于允许我几年申请辞去中国莎士比亚研究会会长职务。

我赞同同志们推荐方平同志继任。

请代我向全体同志问好。

曹禺*

一九九二年四月

北京医院

*关于曹禺先生1992年4月给孙福良先生来信的说明：中国莎士比亚研究会经中华人民共和国文化部批准，于1984年12月正式成立于上海。中莎会成立后先后于1986、1994和2016年举行了三届莎士比亚戏剧节和多次国际、全国性的莎学学术研讨会，极大地推动了中国莎士比亚研究、演出和翻译。但是20世纪90年代以后，很长一段时间，中国莎学研究较为沉寂，举行的学术活动不多。很多老一辈莎学研究者目睹这一局面，担忧日甚一日。但是他们仍然积极推动中国莎学研究的深入发展，并对中国莎学未来发展的趋势和中莎会组成人员以书信方式进行了多方面的探讨，通过"莎学书简"的往返，可以看到老一辈莎学学者对莎学和世界优秀文化的热爱。在电子邮箱、短信、微信、QQ如此泛滥的今天，书信已成为稀有的交流沟通方式。《莎学书简》也成为中国莎学研究史料的绝响之一，在中国莎学研究史上具有重要的文献和学术价值。

中国莎士比亚研究会是全国性的学术团体，并作为团体会员加入国际莎协组织。作为全国性文化组织，由中国戏剧家协会作为归口部门。在业务上与中国社会科学院、中国戏剧家协会建立密切联系，在行政上接受会址所在地政府机构和社会科学研究机构的协助和指导。中国莎士比亚研究会团结全国从事莎学研究，演出莎士比亚剧目的专家、艺术家，开展学术讨论，促进国际交流，借以推动我国戏剧艺术的繁荣和发展。中国莎士比亚研究会第一届理事会（1984年12月4日通过）成员主要有：

名誉会长：胡乔木；

会长：曹禺；

副会长：卞之琳、王佐良、孙家琇、李赋宁、张君川、杨周翰、陈恭敏、黄源、黄佐临；

理事：方平、孙大雨、吴富恒、陈嘉、陆谷孙、季羡林；

中国莎士比亚研究会基金委员会名誉董事长：巴金；

《莎士比亚研究》编辑部主任：余秋雨。

曹禺为中国莎士比亚研究会首任会长。1998年9月25日，中国莎士比亚学会作出关于增补领导人员的决议，中国莎士比亚研究会会长为：方平。2002年6月1日，中国莎士比亚学会作出关于增补新领导人员的决议，增补李伟民、戴晓彤为中莎会理事，并发展一批新会员。

2016年我曾与杨林贵教授商讨搜集，中国莎学学者的书信予以编辑、出版，2017年我与杨林贵又进行了进一步商讨，决定先从手头已有的书信搜集、开始。这一工作启动之后，得到了许多学者的积极回应，上海戏剧学院原副院长孙福良教授寄来了曹禺先生给中莎会的来信，曹树钧先生、朱尚刚先生也寄来了多封信件，而且许多同仁纷纷来电表示支持。我手头亦保存有诸多莎学学者、前辈的来信，从中可以看到中国莎学发展的轨迹。(李伟民)

孙福良先生：

您好！

上次在香港见面之后，黄清霞和我便着手筹办组织香港的莎士比亚学会。

我们约见了有兴趣组织和支持这学会的人士，出席初次筹备会议的有：

香港大学英文系高级讲师黄清霞教授
香港中文大学英文系系主任谭国根教授
香港中文大学英文系系主任 Andreus Partin 教授
香港浸会大学英文系系主任叶少娴教授
香港浸会大学英文系 Clayton Mactengie 副教授
香港浸会大学英文系温梁咏裳助理教授
香港浸会大学英文系翻译学教授及翻译中心主任黎翠珍

是次会议亦邀请了香港演艺学院戏剧院院长锺景辉先生，锺先生表示支持，但因排演未暇出席。

会议讨论结果决定在香港办“香港莎士比亚学会”，欢迎学术、翻译、戏剧界人士参加，以促进莎剧研究、教学、翻译和演出等活动，与世界各地进行莎剧活动的人士和机构交流。我们已获得浸会大学校方同意，借用本校翻译学研究中心为暂时会址，以便开始搜集有关莎剧研究、演出的文献。我们目前正循本港法例程序办理创会手续，待后便召开大会选举，然后便开始运作。一待开好大会，选举干事之后便与孙先生联络。

暂此报告。并问

祺安

黎翠珍

一九九六年四月二日

福良老师并方平、宪强二位先生：

上封信谈及中莎会在国际莎协执行委员会代表一事，想已收到。

最近收到澳大利亚学者 John Gillies 的来信（你们在洛杉矶见过的。宪强先生曾与他一起吃饭并讨论过中国莎剧演出），希望进行一项与中国莎剧演出有关的项目。他们在日本的同样工作已完成。根据在日本的工作经验，他们倾向于找寻一位熟悉英文及莎剧演出的个人来负责和推动这项工作。信中征询我的意见。我已回信建议他们，因为中国的情况和日本不一样，在中国办这样的事，还是通过中莎会最为方便，成功的把握也最大，所以仍是以与中莎会商议、确定为好。我建议他们直接写信给你们三位。再次，特先向你们报告。希望这个项目能尽早开始。

近年来，我们参加了不少国际交流活动，如有什么消息和发展，当再转告你们。我们一直十分热切地希望能为国内的戏剧与莎学研究出些力。

祝好！

李如茹

一九九六年九月九日

上海戏剧学院　孙福良副院长：

致国际莎协全体会员

新一届执委会选举

根据协会章程，协会的日常工作应由一个委员会执掌，委员会由一位会长、二位副会长及不多于 18 位委员构成。洛杉矶大会期间举行的协会全体会议上发出公报：新一届执委会应按时产生。现执委会已按惯例非正式地征求了会员的意见，认真考虑了新一届执委会的构成，坚持在会员认可之前进行推荐提名。与以往一样，这种做法一直被认为是最好的方式，因为如果向分散在世界各地的会员征询提名的话，那么选举的过程会拖长，而且花费也会增加。在背面的提名表上，现任执委会已充分考虑到执委会应反映协会的国际特点，包容广泛的兴趣和经验。这个推荐名单已在洛杉矶全体会议上征求意见，未遇异议。新名单中包括半数以上现任执委会成员。

当然，不管会员是否参加这次大会，都有权利有不同提名，如果这样，那就需要再进行一次邮政选举。不同提名的最后截止日期为 1997 年 4 月 30 日，寄至莎士比亚中心执行秘书长，地址：Stratford-upon-Avon CV37 6QW，UK。若到期没有收到进一步提名，那就意味着会员认同现提名，背面名单所列人员将构成新一届执委会委员，任至 2001 年。

执行秘书长及会计　苏珊·布洛克博士

一九九七年三月

孙院长：

您好！

非常感谢您向香港莎士比亚学会推荐我参加莎士比亚在香港学术会议！由于您的鼎力相助，香港莎学会会长黎翠珍教授为我发来了正式邀请函（上月 27 日收到的），内称香港莎学会将为我提供“来回吉林—香港的机票，四晚住宿（12 月 11 日星期四至 14 日）及每日提供津贴”，对此我十分兴奋，同时这对我继续从事莎士比亚研究来说也是一个极大的鼓舞。这些年来孙院长对我的帮助和提携我十分感激。我今后将尽力多为中莎会做些工作。上月底我给黎翠珍教授写了表示谢意的信函，同时寄回了“回执”和“论文提纲”，现将“论文提纲”的复印件寄上，请孙院长指正。9 月初我校已经开始为我办理申请赴港手续，我力争 10 月底完成我向大会提交的论文，不知这次香港莎学盛会“中莎会”是否还需要做些什么准备工作？如有什么需要我去做的事请孙院长示知。

杨林贵已于上月中旬去美国德克萨斯州的 A&M 大学英语系攻读英国语言文学博士学位。他每月要为低年级学生批些作业，作为《莎士比亚季刊》主编的助理，他每周都要在《季刊》工作些时间。他的功课和工作很忙，刚一开始不太适应，现在已经好多了。他让我把这些情况告诉孙院长和曹老师。

谨祝

秋安！

孟宪强

一九九七年九月十九日

亲爱的孙教授：

作为两年一度举行的第四届澳大利亚和新西兰莎士比亚协会大会的组织者，我谨向您发出正式邀请，邀请您出席本次大会。本次大会将于 1998 年 7 月 11 日（星期六）至 7 月 15 日（星期天）在澳大利亚布里斯班昆士兰大学圣约翰学院举行。

您在中国的莎士比亚方面的研究引起我们协会成员们的极大兴趣，而我们协会是由来自澳大利亚和新西兰各大学中从事莎士比亚研究的，资历或深或浅的教授及研究生们组成的。我们期待一批国际代表出席会议，其中包括您以及安德鲁·古尔教授（瑞汀大学）、简·哈沃德教授（哥伦比亚大学）、米歇尔·姆林教授（伊利诺伊大学）、海德·杜布罗（威斯康星大学）。

我希望您已经收到了我们的登记表和信息小册子的复制件。

其他的信息可以在大会网址上获得：

（网址）http: //www.of.edu.au/-enmfothe/shakes.htm

如果对大会日程或对布里斯班的旅程有什么需要询问的话，请在以后的几个月中同我们联系。我还想补充的是，格里菲斯大学的柯林·麦克拉斯教授拉特罗伯大学的约翰·盖莱斯博士特别盼望在澳新莎协大会上同您会晤。

我同样盼望在’98 会议上与您见面。

您诚挚的　洛德·戴维斯博士

一九九八年三月六日　昆士兰大学

镜禧：

“A History of Fortinbras”稿校对交出去之后，仍发现若干表达方面的缺陷，有些是 Dr. Ann Carver 所指出的。又一直想“A History of Fortinbras”虽然原来在题目上已有反讽的含义（哪儿有什么 history？），仍嫌呆板，不如直接道出其琐碎，乃改成“The Fortinbras Fragments in *Hamlet*”用上很普遍的 alliteration 并正规的点名 *Hamlet* 剧本。整体说来，与哈姆雷特的终极灵感比较，似仍以英文稿较佳，可惜已无处发表，只复印若干份，第一份送给你留纪念。或者送人（北大乐黛云教授会介绍若干位教莎剧的老师谈谈）。

师母与我暂定行程上是 8/20—31 在英国。你们何时抵达 Oxford?

（你送我的 *The Historical Renaissance* 只翻了翻两篇，似乎还能懂。论 *Measure for Measure* 那篇所想到的题目都很调皮或 shocking，如“公爵的鬼胎”，“维也纳色情专业区”，“伊莎贝会嫁给他么？”）

朱立民

一九九〇年四月二十九日

镜禧：

“Reportage in *Romeo and Juliet*”太棒了。从今以后，对 Benvolio 必得另眼相待了。你写的英文愈来愈 relaxed，or well-poised。看法娓娓道来，阅者不感到任何胁迫味道的 persuasion 而自然接受。高！用今日青少年术语“帅呆了”不知恰当否？

Joseph A. Porter 那著作不知有否用到或提到 R. V. Utterback “The Death of Mercutio”，*SQ*（1973）？

你真是独具“慧”眼；我从未觉得 Benvolio 还有这么“阴”的一手。正如 Duncan 说的 There's no art/To find the mind's construction in the face.

用 Shakespeare 的 source（s）来 appraise 他的功夫（在剧本内呈现的功夫），这是学术研究正当领域。若以它去解释或诠释剧本内容，则我持很深的保留态度（纯以读剧本者或观众立场而言），因为我们欣赏的对象是 text of the play 或 performance itself，不该涉及其他之物；所谓“其他之物”是 that/which is “not available” to the reader or viewer。（New Criticism 的后遗症？！）

因为你可以说只是顺便提了一下，不涉及关键性的重大问题，那就没什么。

在用字方面，gallant gladiator 的 alliterative effect 固然好，可是 gladiator 这个字引出的 image 必然是古罗马 arena 中那些凶狠、残暴的职业斗士；而 gallant 一字应指 kind and considerate，尤其（似乎）与女人不可分，献殷勤的味道和形象与 gladiator 不相配。我对用字有很多个人的偏见。此可能即一例。

Congratulations！

朱立民

一九九二年三月八日

彭镜禧教授大鉴：

有幸在洛杉矶与您结识，十分高兴！感谢您和裕珩兄的热情款待！您的坦诚、热忱给我留下了很深的印象。遗憾的是由于时间紧促未能来得及向您请教，也未能来得及请您介绍台湾方面莎学的情况。在洛杉矶我们度过了一段美好的时光：裕珩兄、莱维斯教授我们共进早点，在亨廷顿图书馆草坪上叙谈以及充满友情的午宴等情景都历历在目。现将拍摄下的这些记录我们珍贵回忆的照片奉上，以作纪念。

94 年以来我一直盼望着能够开展海峡两岸的莎学研讨活动，沟通情况，加强联系，进行合作，我以为这对于提高我们在国际莎学领域的地位，促进我们的莎学的发展将是一件很有意义的事情。同时，我想届时我们还可以协商海峡两岸合作出版《中国莎学年鉴》（中，英）等问题。回来后在报纸上已看到两次海峡两岸学术交流的报道，一是儿童文学研究的（有点记不清了），一是在台北举行的海峡两岸古籍研讨会。目前，海峡两岸的学术交流活动日益增多。因此，我想如由您出面组织海峡两岸的莎学交流活动，是非常有希望成功的，不知尊意如何？

我回来后即给学生上“莎士比亚研究”选修课（每周两节，共 36 个小时）。我系学生对莎剧很感兴趣，现在 95 级学生（一年级）已经组成了“莎翁剧社”，对此我感到很欣慰。下周我们将先后向校系领导汇报我们参加大会的情况。

谨颂

大安！

孟宪强　上

二〇〇六年四月二十三日

李伟民同志：

来信和您对两本拙作的评论，前几天由学院转给了我。因正患重感冒，加上引起了老心脏病，没能及时回信，请原谅。

您的“体会”我读了两遍，首先为您的热情洋溢而感动，其次是觉得您不免过奖了！我极喜爱莎剧，也在课堂上讲授过他。但是我的研究远未达到“精深”的程度。我常为此感到惭愧，只能以“毕竟尽了最大力气”的想法稍稍原谅自己。

您一连写出了《评孙家琇〈莎士比亚辞典〉》《各具风格特色，荟萃莎学精华》和《来自真善美的永恒动力》三篇文章，完全说明您对中国莎学的关心，也特别说明您对莎士比亚的热爱。对于国内莎评或有关书籍进行介绍、比较研究和评论，这在中国莎学领域中是一件十分可贵的新事。我更为此感到高兴。希望您以后能继续这方面的工作。

我那本《戏剧》的书名容易使人误会成莎士比亚对西方现代戏剧的影响。实际上，该书名是指书内两方面的内容，此外是有关于“影响”的几篇译文。您没有指出。另外，我是在吸收借鉴西方较好的莎评观点的同时，批驳其荒谬论点的，不是对西方论说一概予以否定。当然，您肯定我提供资料，就含有借鉴的意思。

不多谈了，再一次谢谢您！谨祝

夏安！

孙家琇*

一九九六年七月十一日

*关于孙家琇先生书信的说明：孙家琇先生（1915—2001）在我国著名的莎士比亚研究专家队伍中犹如耀眼的星座熠熠闪光，因为在众多的男性杰出莎学研究者中间，在以思辨见长的莎学研究领域，她以广博的学识、深刻的思想、严谨的思辨、严密的逻辑推理、深入的分析和富于文采的评析在中国莎学研究领域独树一帜，赢得了莎学界、戏剧研究界和文学界的尊重。她的一系列莎学专著、戏剧作品、散文和小说在莎学研究者中间具有广泛而深刻的影响，尤其是她的莎学论著在中国莎学史上留下了浓重的一笔，成为20世纪中国莎学研究不可多得的宝贵财富。

我国著名莎学家孟宪强先生认为，在20世纪20—30年代莎士比亚普遍不受国人重视的情况下，中国戏剧改良运动关注易卜生“社会问题剧”，文学家、戏剧家和各个文学派别虽然都承认莎士比亚的伟大，但毕竟他们还来不及对其进行深入研究，在那个时代，社会问题毕竟比人性问题要更为紧迫和直接。孙家琇是我国改革开放以来最为著名的莎学家之一，著名学者钱锺书先生说：“在我国莎学界中孙家琇先生是最有学问的老先生之一”。钱锺书在晚年已经谢绝一切题字的情况下欣然为孙家琇主编的《莎士比亚辞典》题签，并在《围城》上题字、签名后赠给孙先生，为了表示对孙先生的关怀，钱锺书和杨绛还联名给孙家琇先生写了慰问信。在老一辈莎学家中间，孙家琇先生出版了多部厚重的莎学研究论集，为中国莎学在改革开放后的迅速崛起起到了非常关键的作用。

1933 年，孙家琇考入燕京大学英国文学系，1936 年入美国加利福尼亚大学暑期莎士比亚戏剧班学习 1937 年在美国米尔斯大学获学士学位，1937 年在美国蒙特霍留克大学研究院戏剧文学系取得硕士学位，并获得该校学习成绩最高奖，成为世界上第一个获得该校最高奖的女生，并任该校实验剧场教员一年。1938 年夏在哈佛大学剧本创作班学习。1939 年回国后，先后在西南联合大学、同济大学、武汉大学、南京金陵大学、南京戏剧专科学校和中央戏剧学院任讲师、教授。孙家琇先生曾长期担任中央戏剧学院戏剧文学系主任、莎士比亚研究中心主任，并两次担任全国政协委员，1979 年被选为全国三八红旗手。

1937 年，在灾难深重的祖国召唤下，英华灿然的孙家琇和巫宝三先生怀着“忧国愤时之念，怀乡思家之情”投身于祖国的怀抱和伟大的抗日战争。从美国—意大利—越南海防到抗日大后方的昆明，在人畜共处，门窗紧闭，摇摇晃晃的闷罐车中，几经辗转才到达春城。1939 年 10 月 1 日，深感国艰家难的孙先生和巫先生就持张泽熙函到西南联大联系工作事宜。当生活窘迫到以变卖衣服度日的时候，在西南联大为躲日军飞机轰炸“跑警报”，上课跑几十里偶尔才能搭上运煤车的日子里，先生除了抱定抗战必胜的坚定信念外和最强烈的对真理与正义的吁求，始终割舍不下对莎士比亚研究的一往情深。她明白个人命运必然与国运紧紧相连。回国后，她先后在西南联大、同济大学、武汉大学、南京金陵大学、南京戏剧专科学校、中央戏剧学院任讲师、教授。

2000 年 9 月，因为我的一篇《莎士比亚与清华大学—— 兼论中国莎学研究中的“清华学派”》的长文，想请曾经在西南联合大学任教的孙家琇先生过目。担心孙先生视力的原因，我给先生寄了放大的复印件，并就写文章时存疑就教于先生。先生很快就给我回了信。蔼然仁者的她在信中谦逊地说：“我个人在西南联大清华外文系教过一年课，但由于住处分散，同清华的老师、学者接触机会少，并没有受到清华精神多少感染。当时正是日本轰炸的时期，我每次上课从乡下落索坡要走 22 里路到昆明城边的学校上课，下午课一完就忙着往回走，幸运时才可以搭上运煤车。但是，在西南联合大学却感到时代所铸就的坚毅、顽强和敬业精神。那时的清华外文系十分重视英语教学和基础知识的培养。由于我老伴儿的工作单位得从昆明搬往四川李庄，我也被迫离开了西南联大。”

针对我文章中提到的清华外文系的培养目标是“博雅之士”。先生结合在西南联大清华外文系教书时的感受谈道：“博”是学识渊博。清华，第一给学生打下了坚实的英文基础，从而使他们能有理解和深入领会莎士比亚戏剧语言的水平和能力，以致能翻译莎剧特别是翻译诗体的莎剧。第二清华外文系文学课不是孤立地讲授莎士比亚，而总是提供了文艺复兴文学，欧洲文学史之类可以作为莎剧广阔文化、文学背景的知识。这给他们以后有关莎士比亚及其戏剧的论著自然赋予了较厚的背景因素和“比较”的角度。关于“雅”的解释应该更为深刻。这些对莎士比亚有研究的学人完全是以学问和研究世界第一流的戏剧诗人莎士比亚特别是为广大中国同胞介绍，完全当作自己一生最高的志趣。他们绝非从名利出发，完全不是为了个人出名，而用莎学或莎译当作向上爬的阶梯或敲门砖。在博雅中始终贯穿了救时世、民族、国家于危亡中的深沉忧思。（李伟民）

李伟民同志：

你好！寄上拙文两篇，请看看。这连同在《中国莎学年鉴》中发表的那篇《从〈裘力斯·恺撒〉看莎士比亚的历史、政治意识》（我想你有此书），是我去年于病情间缓时陆续写就的，原因是我国莎评中，关于《裘力斯·恺撒》一剧，剧中人以及莎士比亚本身的政治倾向，有不正确的看法与解释。此外，对于此剧在莎剧发展过程中的重要作用，及其现实意义，没有明确指出过，而一般把它视为一部较好的罗马史剧而已。我自己的看法不知对否。但我强烈感到，这出莎剧最需要以历史唯物主义观点来加以理解，否则会出错误。人们容易把“共和主义”及其代表人物抽象地，超出时代与阶级地理想化，而且使罗马历史发展的来龙去脉（换句话说，仍受唯心主义残余观点的影响）。这就需要加以提出和商榷了。

我在希望，你如果有兴趣和时间的话，能够写点评论或读后感之类，来强调一下上述问题；不知这是不是我的奢望？我这样要求，是因为深感你极关心中国莎评的发展以及中国莎评特点形成发展。

即颂

教祺！

孙家琇

一九九六年十月二十七日

因缺少正规大信封，文章分两个信封寄。

李伟民同志：

来信和文章都收到了。关于这篇文章，我有点意见，简单写在下边。

1. 文章的标题不够合适或准确。莎士比亚是 400 多年前的英国诗人，他怎能和远未出现在中国的清华大学有任何联系，一看这标题人们会感到莫名其妙，其实你文章内容要点是讲清华大学对于中国莎学的贡献，或者清华大学对于中国莎学发展的功不可没。这样的标题就有文章可做了。

2. 全文的结构不很好，比较“平泛”，没有层次，不能引人入胜。而且难免会有重复。

3. 我个人虽在西南联大清华外语系教过一年课，但并没有受到清华精神多少感染。当时正是日本轰炸的时期，我每次上课从乡下落索坡要走 22 里路到昆明城边的学校上课，下午课一完就忙着往回走，幸运时才可以搭上运煤车。这样，我同清华的老师学者们接触的机会很少。除去印象上清华外语系十分重视英语教学之外，没有太多可回忆的。由于我老伴的工作单位（社科院经济研究所）得从昆明搬往四川李庄去，我也被迫离开了西南联大。

4. 关于文章结构，我觉得，首先说明解放后教学改革的结果使人产生了清华大学不是综合大学，而是理工科大学（没有文科）的印象，因此不容易联想到它对于中国莎学会有什么贡献。你在介绍清华以前曾经是综合大学之后，如果进而列举出那一系列从事中国莎学的名人们，多少都是清华大学培养出来的学者，或者曾在清华教过外国文学的人，把他们各自的莎学论著和翻译再列举出来，那就是对于“贡献”的最为有力的证明了。

我认为你举出这些人身上有清华大学所特有的“博雅”精神。这一点十分重要，但对于“博”“雅”讲得不够透彻。“博”是学识渊博，清华第一给学生打下了坚实的英文基础，从而使他们能有理解和深入领会莎士比亚戏剧语言的水平和能力，以致能翻译莎剧特别是翻译诗体的莎剧。第二清华外语系文学课不是孤立地讲授莎士比亚，而总是提供了文艺复兴文学、欧洲文学史之类可以作为莎剧广阔文化、文学背景的知识，这给他们以后有关莎士比亚及其戏剧的论著自然赋予了较深厚的背景因素和“比较”的角度。关于“雅”的解释应该更为深刻。我觉得这些对莎士比亚有研究的学人完全是以学问和研究（特别是为广大中国同胞介绍世界第一流的戏剧诗人莎士比亚）完全当作自己一生最高的志趣，他们绝非从名利出发，完全不是为了个人出名，而用莎学或莎译当作向上爬的阶梯或敲门砖。我很难过地发现，在现今中国有极个别的人竟然没有这类雅志，而只顾用“莎学”标榜自己。真正的博雅精神使得中国优良莎学工作者，能够在条件相当困苦的情况下，并且也能够长时期地坚持莎学研究或莎剧翻译。所以，清华大学对于中国莎学的一个重大贡献，是在于培养了一批高尚博雅的学者。

怎么培养出来的呢？这同清华大学课程的设置有关。首先就像你信中写的：“清华大学的莎士比亚教学在中国是开先河的，而且在 1949 年以前成就最大坚持的时间最长，延揽名师最多，为中国莎学事业的发展奠定了雄厚的基础。”你信中有不少篇幅介绍清华以前的课程，特别是外语系或西洋文学系；介绍了像王文显、温德等等的教学精神。这些都很有意思，也极重要，但是后面的文章，同前边关于“清华学派”的问题以及“以兼容会通文化创建中国现代文化为己任是清华大学外文系一向所标榜的教学目的……”似乎联系并不密切，使我感到脱节，或层次不清。

很对不起，我信笔写来，不知你明白我的感受了没有。总体来说，就是希望你在文章结构方面多下点功夫，把几种提法如“清华学派”“博雅精神”“兼容会通中西文化”之间的关系交代清楚，把相近似的问题集中起来，一层一层地谈。我怀疑以上这些提法似乎太多，反而把“博雅精神”看不明白了。

最近学校人事处送来了文化部发下的“专家情况登记表”，要我们填写，很费时间，由于我眼力不成，表格地方又小，填写得很乱，令人看不清楚。为此，我很着急，就不能更好地考虑你的文章了。

你的文章尽管我细读了两遍，以后又一再翻阅，总不易看清层次，所以冒昧提了以上的意见，完全可以不去管它。

好，祝

冬安

孙家琇*

二○○○年十月二十八日

我在考虑，以后我不会再给你的文章提意见了，因为我对于自己的意见没有信心；害怕反而搅乱你的思路。　　又及

*关于孙家琇先生书信的说明：孙家琇先生晚年曾给我多封来信，每每在信中指导我的莎学研究，对我的文章提出意见，使我受益匪浅。我曾发表有《莎士比亚与清华大学》的论文，该文发表以后引起较大的反响，中国人民大学复印报刊资料全文转载；清华大学文学院有关负责人向人索求、调阅拙文；《清华大学校友资料选编》第6辑全文转载；清华大学本科招生网站刊出这篇论文，作为招生宣传的材料。文章发表后，我给孙家琇先生寄去了放大的复印件，希望孙先生能够对我的文章给予指导，并在文章中向孙家琇教授提出了几个问题，其中之一，就是孙家琇先生在西南联大任教期间对我提出的中国莎学史上的“清华现象”的看法。因为我其时也在从事吴宓研究，吴宓曾有很长一段时间实际主持清华大学外文系的系务工作，据《吴宓日记》记载，孙家琇先生回国后，吴宓曾介绍孙家琇到清华外文系联系工作。孙家琇先生在指出我的文章不足之处的同时，谈了她对清华大学外文系培养目标“博雅之士”的理解；对国内某些利用莎学研究标榜自己，达到个人目的恶劣现象提出了批评。（李伟民）

伟民先生：

您好！大札与两袋大作复印件均收到，谢谢！在此之前我就在《外国文学评论》上拜读了大作《莎士比亚是共和派吗》。我很赞同您在该文中所表述的见解。我认为这种深入钻研作品，进行具体分析的解读方法正是“具有中国特色的莎学”理论的一个重要特点。老一辈学者及留学英美的学者在评论莎士比亚作品时往往从若干西方学者的具有权威性的批评模式出发，这样他们在评论莎氏作品时往往不是从具体的、历史的研究中得出某种结论；恰恰相反，而是对某种现成观点的论证，这就陷入了“述而不作”的境地。我以为这种莎评缺少独创性，并且是造成莎氏研究误读的重要原因之一。我以为中国莎学要跻身国际莎坛，为国际莎学作出中国学者的贡献，就一定要用“历史新时期中国人的眼光”去接受、阐释莎氏作品的审美价值。《俄苏莎学理论在中国的传播》是一篇很有分量的论文，从中可以看到您对这个问题所下的功夫，其中有很多很有价值的第一手资料。您对拙作的再次评论，令我非常感谢，同时也让我更清楚地看到了拙作的种种不足和缺陷—— 从材料到观点。它使我下决心对《简史》再做一次全面的修订，或以某种方式编写一本更令人满意的《中国莎学史》—— 只是现在尚没有时间做这件工作，估计得三五年之后进行。

北京的“莎士比亚日”的组织者先后给我寄来两份通知，现将其中的一份寄给您。前天树钧先生来电话，问我去不去？我说初步决定去，一个主要的目的是想看看英国皇家剧院的莎剧演出，他说孙建秋给他去电话约他在会上发言。我准备在去北京之前再同树钧先生通一次电话。我觉得北京的这次活动对扩大中莎会的队伍来说是一次很好的机会。中莎会应利用此有利时机多发展一些北京方面的会员。孙院长春节前患肺炎住院治疗，需二三周时间，估计现在很可能尚未痊愈。

听说您分得了那么好的新房，太为您高兴了，祝贺乔迁之喜！

谨颂

撰安！

宪强*

一九九八年二月九日

林贵来信让我帮他复印97年中国莎评论文，以便他向《莎士比亚季刊》推荐选入。不知您平时是否记载了97年莎评目录？如有目录烦请复印一份给我；如没有就不麻烦您了，我直接去图书馆查阅。　　又及

*关于孟宪强先生书信的说明：孟宪强先生作为一位杰出的莎士比亚研究者，在他的学术研究的一生中陆续著作、主编了《马克思恩格斯与莎士比亚》《莎士比亚三重戏剧》《莎士比亚在我们的时代》《中国莎士比亚评论》《中国莎学简史》《三色堇——〈哈姆莱特〉解读》。这些莎学论著为20世纪80年代以来的中国莎士比亚研究最重要的莎学基本读物之一，为人们了解、关注改革开放以来的中国莎学以及中国莎学学者的思考，中国莎学研究的走向提供了重要的理论资源。在孟宪强先生的这些莎学著述中，伴随着中国改革开放的大潮，伴随着莎士比亚重新回到中国，伴随着莎士比亚作品的翻译、演出、评论的繁荣以及莎士比亚学术

活动的开展，我们看到，其论著中对中国莎士比亚研究多有沦肌浃髓之论，因而为中国莎学界所称道，凡是研读过的人无不留下深刻印象，其学术研究成果在中国莎学界是相当引人注目的。

我作为孟宪强先生的一位忘年之交，因为莎士比亚的缘由，与他们家的两代人都建立了深厚的友谊，至今仍然通过书信、电子邮件和各种学术场合与杨林贵讨论着人生、社会、莎学研究和莎学学术活动的开展。2006 年 7 月，“全国英国文学学会 2006 年专题研讨会”在东北师范大学举行，在会议期间，我除了顺访已经没有了标志的“东北师范大学莎士比亚研究中心”以外，还两次专程去看望了孟宪强教授，向他请教有关莎学研究的问题。当时，他兴致很高，愉快地与我回忆了有关中国莎学发展中的闪光点，他还满怀信心地谋划着中国莎学研究的未来，为了不影响他的休息，在一个多小时的畅谈之后，我不得不依依不舍地向他告别；而当会议就要结束，几天以后再去看望他时，他却坐在病榻上正在治疗，医生不让他多说话，我在向他表示慰问后，让陈老师转达我和莎学同仁们对他的敬意，并预祝他的《三色堇——〈哈姆莱特〉解读》能够早日出版，在心中默默地祝福他早日康复。信中提到的杨林贵先生早已在美国获得博士学位，成为研究莎士比亚的国际知名学者，国际莎协执委，参加了很多国际重要莎学会议，为中国莎学在世界莎坛上发出中国声音作出了重要贡献；杨林贵教授还在国际和国内重要期刊上发表了众多莎学研究论文，主编出版了“中国莎士比亚论丛（第一系列）”（东北师范大学出版社 2014）、“中国莎士比亚论丛（第二系列）”（商务印书馆 2017）、《云中锦笺——中国莎学书信》（商务印书馆 2022），成为中国莎士比亚研究会副会长。我曾经撰写过回忆孟宪强教授莎学研究历程和莎学研究思想的长篇论文，在论文中披露了孟宪强教授给我的一些信件，我的文章发表后，即引起莎学研究者的关注，并在其论文中作了重点引述。由此可以看出，包括孟宪强教授在内的莎学学者信件在中国莎士比亚研究史上重要的史料和学术价值。

孟宪强教授在与我结交的十多年间，总共与我通信一百多封，其中的每一封信，除了谈工作、学习、研究和对我的学术研究给予鼓励之外，谈得最多的就是莎学研究、中国莎学事业的发展、建设以及莎学界的动态。在 2011 年成都和重庆的酷暑中，我再次翻阅了孟宪强先生给我的那一百多封有些发黄的书信。（孟宪强先生在与我十多年的交往中，我一共收到他的一百多封来信，可以说，这些信件篇篇都离不开谈莎学，堪称为一部资料丰富的“莎学书简”，2011 年的苦夏，我将这些书简再次翻阅了一遍，往事历历在目。在适当的时候，如果能将包括孟宪强、张泗洋、孙家琇、方平、王元化、李赋宁、刘炳善等先生这些“莎学书简”出版，毫无疑问，对人们了解 20 世纪 90 年代到 21 世纪初年的中国莎学历史是有重要价值的。方便起见，下文中我用括号中的年月日，表示孟宪强先生来信的日期。）

捧读这些“莎学书简”，泪水模糊了我的眼睛，往事一幕幕在我的眼前重现，可以说，先生的封封书简都在与我探讨莎学研究的问题，讨论着中国莎学的发展，关心着我的学术研究，解开我人生的困惑，计划着中国莎学研究著述的出版、学术会议的召开，憧憬着中国莎学真正走向世界莎学研究领域和世界莎士比亚大会在中国召开的美好明天。例如，他在 1999 年 9 月 12 日的来信中谈道：“前些日子我去泗洋教授家，当谈起我国目前莎学状况时，他特别称赞了您，他说您的莎学文章最多，对中国莎学的发展投入了大量的心血……”在信中他还谈道：“中国莎学继续深入发展的态势令人鼓舞，这两年莎译不仅数量多，学术水平似乎也在明显地提高……‘莎士比亚在香港学术研讨会’将于今年 12 月 12 至 16 日举行，我将充分利用这次会议的机会积极联系港台莎学学者，酝酿大陆及港台莎学的交流与合作。”他设想联合北京大学和台湾大学在北大召开“海峡两岸莎学研讨会”（1999.8.31）。后来，他还随信寄来了《吉林社科联》上刊登的《孟宪强教授在香港畅谈莎学在中国》一文，供我了解莎学研究动态。从上面的这些文字可知，宪强先生不但与我谈莎学研究，还与我谈人生，谈要正确地对待名与利，正确对待人生中的困顿与挫折。甚至，他还以自己的经验告诉我，学术研究应该是我们快乐的唯一源泉。由于科研成果丰硕，宪强教授在中国莎学界有很高的学术声望。但由于多种原因，教授的职称却迟迟没有解决，等到终于获得这一迟到的教授职称时，他淡定地写信告诉我：在学术研究上“这些年我没耽误什么”（1996.12.29），表现出一个学者视学术研究为生命的豁达和气度。对于《四川戏剧》和一些刊物对莎学如此重视，他认为“对我们的莎学研究既是一种激励，更是一种支持”（1999.4.28），不要去计较个人得失。

可以说，我是在孟宪强教授、张泗洋教授、孙家琇教授、孙福良教授、贺祥麟教授、阮珅教授、蓝仁哲教授、裘克安教授、屠岸先生、王元化先生、徐克勤教授、孙法理教授、刘炳善教授、王忠祥教授、华泉坤教授、方平先生、曹树钧教授、郑土生副研究员的鼓励提携之下一步步走向莎学研究领域并因此而改变了环境的。忘不了，是孟宪强、张泗洋先生联名推荐我加入中国莎士比亚研究会，并且给我寄来了《中华莎学》最初创刊的三期杂志。（1993.12.16，1994.1.3）每当回忆起那些尘封的往事，阅读先生给我的来信时，我都会从心底涌起对这些前辈学人的感激之情。尤为令人感动的是，作为一位知名学者，宪强先生在与我的交往中表现了平等对话和谦虚的美德，为当今的我树立了一个优秀的榜样。在 1994 年 5 月 21 日的来信中，孟宪强先生考虑我参加“’94 上海国际莎士比亚戏剧节”可能没有收到邀请函一事，表示如果我届时没有收到中国莎士比亚研究会的邀请函，他与张泗洋先生商量就由吉林莎学会挤出一个名额让我能够赴会。对我的《从文学向文化的转移》一文中关于中国出版莎士比亚戏剧连环画出版情况的论述，宪强先生谦虚地说，我了解得没有你那么全面，拜读大作时正在进行拙编的一校，我便将大作中这方面的内容补了进去，谢谢您使拙编避免了一个遗漏。（1994.5.21）拙作《莎士比亚在中国》已完稿（34 万字）……经与泗洋教授研究，该书改名为《中国莎学简史》，曹禺先生已写来书名题签，李赋宁教授、张君川教授等写来了题词。……从大作中可以看出您对中国莎学不仅关心而且积累了丰富的材料。现将拙作目录（初稿）寄上一份，望能审阅并提出意见。当我收到这封信和《简史》的目录时简直是诚惶诚恐，并不揣浅陋地提出了一些所谓的建议，没想到这些建议却受到了先生的重视，并给我分配了有关研究任务。

等到 1994 年上海国际莎士比亚戏剧节举行时，宪强先生带来了献给“1994 上海国际莎士比亚戏剧节”的装帧典雅、印刷精美、搜罗繁复、排比详尽，阐释、考证精详的莎学著作，引起了与会人员的注意、羡慕和兴趣。这就是东北师范大学莎士比亚研究中心主任孟宪强教授所著的作为“东北师范大学文库”之一的《中国莎学简史》（以下称《简史》）。这就是说，随着中国莎学事业的起起伏伏，经过多年研究的准备与实践，《简史》的出版就是顺理成章、水到渠成之事了。我迫不及待地翻阅着这本藏蕴丰厚、活色生辉的高质量著作，它不但使我们看到了莎士比亚在中国人心目中的地位和喜爱程度，也亲睹了中国人民在传播莎士比亚经典中所走过的艰难曲折的道路。在莎士比亚的名字已经传入中国一百六十多年之后的今天，莎学在中国的遗迹值得我们去追寻，莎士比亚在中国的巨大影响值得我们去描述，中国莎学家前赴后继、发人深省、可歌可泣的敬业与献身精神值得我们去纪念，中国莎学的中国特色值得我们予以总结和发扬。长期以来，宪强先生的莎学研究贯穿着一条主线，那就是突出莎士比亚在中国的研究，他多次强调，梳理、研究一百多年来莎士比亚在中国的影响是中国莎学研究者义不容辞的责任，在世界莎学研究格局中，中国学者应当慨然担当起这一任务——莎士比亚在中国的研究，对于今天中国的莎学研究来说，总结我们自己的莎学研究成果，梳理我们的实践与理论嬗变过程，不仅有着重要的历史意义，而且有着重要的现实意义。难怪众多的学者欣然为他的一系列著作的出版题词。他们是曹禺、卞之琳、李赋宁、孙家琇、张君川、方平、张泗洋、赵澧、索天章。正如孙家琇所说这是“一部关于近百年来莎士比亚在中国传播的各个方面的颇有概括性的力作”。李赋宁也对《简史》一书予以充分肯定，认为:“莎士比亚的作品是世界人民的共同财富。中国学者和翻译家对莎氏作品的研究和翻译，为世界莎学的进展做出了很大的贡献，因此很有必要总结一下我们在这方面做出的成绩”。为此，他也多次鼓励我做好莎士比亚在中国的研究，他在参加了第七届世界莎士比亚大会的各项学术活动后，在广泛接触外国莎学学者时感受到“莎士比亚在中国”这个题目越来越受到国际莎学界的关注（2001.5.10），为此，他对“莎士比亚在中国”这一课题充满了期待、信心和理论研究的自觉。

孟宪强教授为中国的莎士比亚研究事业贡献了毕生的精力，他所留下的一系列论著已经成为研究莎士比亚、研究莎士比亚在中国的重要文献。而上述这些方面，正是孟宪强先生“非常喜欢‘用中国人的眼光看莎士比亚’这一重要的文化命题，‘力图对莎士比亚的各类戏剧作品做出个人的理解，以形成具有中国特色的莎学理论体系、思维模式和独特风格’”的动力，这也是孟宪强教授莎学研究中的一个相当重要的指导思想。（李伟民）

李伟民先生：

您好！

大札、《图书馆苑》和大作复印件均收到，谢谢！我反复地读了来信，深为您执着莎学的精神所感动。前些日子我去泗洋教授家，当谈起我国目前莎学状况时，他特别称赞了您，他说您的莎学文章最多，对中国莎学的发展投入了大量的心血。您宁愿物质生活条件差些，而不愿舍弃对莎学的追求，体现了中国知识分子的传统美德，是很值得我学习的。您目前工作的环境有些令人不快的地方，但环境却为您提供了充分展示才能和实现个人愿望的良好条件，所以对那些不必介意，这些都可以被我们辛勤劳动的汗水所冲淡和洗刷。我们不断地耕耘，不断地收获所带给我们的良好感受使我们的生活感到充实，充满了喜悦，不断享受着创造与成功的快乐。我想，对我们来说，最重要的还是健康的问题，一定千方百计地保护好自己的身体，吃药、营养、休息、情绪，诸因素都很重要。因为我自己经历过身体的病情，所以对健康的问题特别在意，这比一直健康的人来说，也许是一个有利的因素，所以当我进入老年阶段的时候，长期注意显出了效果，根据我自己的经验，希望您一定要时时不忘健康问题，在任何情况下都不要过累。

关于 1995—1996 年中国莎学概述那篇大作，我仔细地拜读了两遍，感到非常好！它展示了中国莎学继续深入发展的令人鼓舞的态势。这两年莎译不仅数量多，学术水平似乎也在明显提高。您对这两年的莎评（包括莎著、翻译等）进行了分门别类的研究，逐一加以阐述；您为这篇文章所花费的功夫之多是可以想见的。这是关于中国莎学研究的力作。待过些日子去图书馆时我一定借出《四川戏剧》一读，以分享您的成功。这篇文章又鼓舞了我继续筹备出版莎学年鉴的想法。虽然不一定能成功，但我还是想尽力去争取一番。

我谈到的一系列的莎学活动，现在有一项已经落实了，即“莎士比亚在香港”学术研讨会将于今年 12 月 12 至 16 日举行，由香港莎士比亚学会、香港浸会大学英语系主办，香港艺术局，香港中文大学英文系协办，届时将有英、美、澳、加等国的学者到会，大会特邀两名内地学者，一位孙福良副院长，另一人是我，他们已于 8 月下旬分别为我们二人发来了由香港莎学会会长黎翠珍教授签署的正式邀请函，内称大会为我们提供往返机票，四天住宿和每日津贴，敝校外事办已开始为我申请赴港手续。我向大会提供的论文题为《趋真与变异的独特过程—— 中国对莎士比亚及〈哈姆莱特〉的接受》。论文提纲已寄去香港莎学会，现正全力撰写论文。我能作为“莎士比亚在香港”特邀嘉宾被邀请，感到非常荣幸、非常兴奋；同时这对我也是一个极大的鼓舞。我将充分利用这次会议的机会积极联系港台莎学学者，酝酿大陆及港台莎学的交流与合作。

林贵已于上月中旬赴美学习，入德克萨斯的 A&M 大学英语系攻读英国语言文学博士学位。世界著名的《莎士比亚季刊》（*Shakespeare Quouterly*）的编辑部就设在这个大学。林贵除上课之外，要给低年级学生批作业，作为《季刊》主编的助理，林贵每周还要在编辑部工作一些时间，功课很重工作也较忙，他来信时让我把他的情况告诉您。

拙著《三色堇〈哈〉解读》的出版问题正在联系。因为敝校出版社已先后出版了 3 本莎学著作—— 都是赔钱的书。所以经过考虑我觉得这次我不宜再向敝校出版社提出出版要求。连出三本莎学著作早已引人嫉妒了。这是难免的事情；另寻出路应是上策。我原想将此书能给明年的“莎士比亚在中国”学术会议，现在看必须调整自己的想法；除了自己学校的出版社外，其他出版社恐怕都难以很快问世。此外，我还想在出版前将该书中的一些重要却应加以整理单独发表。不过，这都是明年才能进行的事情了，因为从现在起我要全力以赴地撰写《变异与趋真的独特历程》。

谨颂

金安！

孟宪强

一九九九年九月十二日

伟民先生：

你好！

由于中莎会对拙作《中国莎学简史》的重视和宣传和同行的积极评价，特别是你的书评，扩大了拙作的影响，因此获得了我省第四届社会科学优秀成果奖著作类二等奖。这次我省评奖一、二等奖项控制很严，著作类一等奖中文学类只有二种，二等奖也只有四种。拙作能够获得这样的荣誉，首先要感谢那些曾对拙作给予过各种帮助的莎学界前辈和同行；同时我也感到这是对我莎学研究工作的一个鼓励，令我感到很欣慰。

我校今年出版基金资助申请和评审工作现已开始，今天上午我将拙作《三色堇》送到了系里。在系里我看到了通知，内称，今年学校出版社提供 60 万元，资助 12 种优秀教材和著作出版。通知说，在以往四年中曾获得过资助者不能申请，同时说，这次将改变以往只重视学术性的选择，同时也要考虑经济效益，包括博士论文的出版也要经过评选。看来，这次拙作获得资助的可能很小—— 三年前我曾获得过一次资助，也更增加了我申请的难度。原来我对申请基金资助还抱有相当的希望。现在面对这样的出版形式，再得另图良策了。

最近没和树钧先生联系，不知河北省莎士比亚协会成立没有？也不知方平教授主持翻译的《新莎士比亚全集》是否出版？关于由辜正坤教授张罗举行莎学会议的事情，我感到困难较大，怕难以落实。为了中莎会的工作，为了推动中国的莎学事业，我想河南大学刘炳善教授那里是可以考虑搞一次莎学会议的。上次我们通话时，我曾谈了我的这个想法，今天在给你写信的同时，我也给树钧先生写了信，说了我的想法。我觉得如果请刘教授张罗全国性的莎学会需要解决一个问题，就是名分问题。如果刘教授仅仅是中莎会的理事的话，他大概不会愿意承担这件事，因此我想可否将刘教授增补为中莎会副会长。我觉得刘教授具备这个条件：（1）他是博士生导师，开设莎诗研究课程；（2）出版《莎士比亚字典》；（3）翻译出版一种莎剧；（4）发表过多种关于英国文学的著述；80 年代中后期发表了不少莎学论文；（5）对莎学研究热心；（6）有项目，经费较充足；（7）在老一辈学者教授中，刘教授年龄不算太大（1927 年生），今年 72 岁（方平教授 1921 年生，今年 78 岁）。我想现任中莎会副会长中还真缺少刘炳善教授这样一位教授，我跟树钧先生说，请他方便中把我的上述想法跟孙院长说说。

我现在仍在修改、定稿我的《中国接受莎士比亚的文化价值取向》。

上次电话中已经说了，以后再来信仍请寄“东北师大附中”，详情不再赘述。

谨颂

文安！

孟宪强

一九九九年九月二十三日

随信附：《荣获吉林省第四次社会科学优秀成果奖名单》，《社科信息报》1999 年 7 月 30 日，第二版。

李伟民先生：

你好！

大札和照片收到10多天了，因为这些日子较忙，迟复了几天，望见谅。

谢谢你介绍了杭州会议的一些情况，其实这类学术会议的作用就是沟通情况，交流成果，以文会友，展开不同学术观点的争论；不过这种争论很难深入，这可能就是所说的一些学术会议的“通病”。洪忠煌教授来信说已经将“会议论文提要汇编”寄给了我（估计过二三天就可以收到了），他还说论文集将于9月开学后开始运作，拙文将全文收入。

前几天孙院长给我来了电话，谈及中莎会领导人选的增（补）情况，他说，刘炳善为中莎会顾问，你和戴晓彤以及上戏的一位教授（名字我没记住）为理事。

上周，吉林省华侨外院院长秦和约见了我，她说要聘我去该院组建莎士比亚研究中心，任专职主任，主要工作为开展莎学研究，举办莎学活动，组织学生演出莎剧。华外是我省第一所民办院校，也是办得最好的，院长秦和女士是教育博士，政协委员，三八红旗手，《吉林日报》曾以整版篇幅报道过她的事迹。她说要把学院办成全国一流的民办院校。该院新校舍耗资几千万元，已在长春旅游风景区净月潭落成（东北师大在那里也建了几个学校），设备齐全，有功能齐全的国际学术会议厅，室内游泳池等，院长说可以给中心一间专用的办公室，对中心的莎学活动学院都会给予支持。听了以后感到很兴奋，当即表示欣然同意。吉林莎协因我退休，挂靠在东北师大困难重重！华外莎士比亚中心成立之后我即将吉林莎协的办公地点移至华外，以华外为正式挂靠单位，在我退休四五年之后享有了这样的机会真是难得，这对于我晚年多为莎学做些工作提供了机会和舞台，待中心成立之后再将有关情况告诉你。

谨颂

暑安！

孟宪强

二〇〇二年八月一日

李伟民同志：

谢谢你的来信和《莎士比亚研究专辑》(2005.3)。

我是外交部离休干部，但实际从1937年以来就研究英国文学特别是莎士比亚。

1984年中莎会成立时起，我就致力于主编《莎士比亚注释丛书》(商务印书馆)，因为我感到中国人搞莎评，根本的根本是彻底了解莎氏原著，如你话云，文本研究是首要的。我主编莎注，用英汉双语，但不搞原文考据。这套丛书已出了30种，我看完的稿已达40种。商务出此书很慢，每年一、二种。最后译本由美国王裕珩承担，他却迄未交稿，连音言都不通。因此我无法说，这部丛书何时可以真正完成。但我相信，它对中国青年学子已经起了作用。(附言：专辑37页上栏注6钱兆明是我们丛书中的一种，没有写明白。)

翻译方面，我改译朱生豪译莎五种，南京译林本收我的改译四种。我认为现在研究莎译，应以“译林本”为起点。朱生豪本缺点不少，但名气在外，贻害不少。

商务承诺年底前出版我的另外两书，(1)《莎士比亚年谱》(修订版)，这是国内外莎传的最简单而实在的读本。(2)《莎士比亚评介文集》，为我的短文集。

希望你们请人写文介绍我的工作，欢迎批评意见。

如果你们登高一呼，恢复中莎会，我一定支持。

祝好！

裘克安

二〇〇五年十一月二十七日

你们是否可请孙法理参加为顾问？

伟民同志：

谢谢：（1）你的来信。

（2）你惠赠的大作《中国莎士比亚批评史》当慢慢拜读。

（3）寄来成都会议的材料。

我现在身体情况不很好。这次未能去成都，很可惜。如你以后来北京，请来会下晤谈。

我的文章请你早日予以发表，因为拖得太久，就更没有什么意义了。

你在贵校院刊上写道："力图构建新的真正具有特定中国学术价值理念的莎士比亚研究模式，并在此基础上拓宽、丰富国际莎士比亚研究的理路"，我支持这一努力。我一向避免过于用阶级斗争论去看莎士比亚，所以我编《莎士比亚年谱》，主编《莎士比亚注释丛书》，一切从文本和历史事实出发，我自问在中国莎学者中是独树一帜的。

祝

一切都好！

裘克安*

二〇〇六年十月二十五日

*关于裘克安先生书信的说明：裘克安教授主持商务印书馆"莎士比亚注释丛书"的出版，并撰写有《莎士比亚评介文集》（商务印书馆，2006）。大约是在2006年，裘克安教授在来信中惠赐给我，可能是他晚年的最后一篇莎学论文。我收到后，联系了我校的《四川外语学院》（校报），校报当即表示全文照发（当时，为了慎重起见，我将裘克安先生的原稿也交给了校报，可能现在已经无从查找裘克安先生的原稿了），裘克安先生的文稿很快在我校校报上刊登了出来。校报发行后，我给裘克安教授邮寄了两份，后来不久，就得到了裘克安先生逝世的消息。（李伟民）

伟民同志：

大札和大作都收到了，谢谢！

您的评论文写得很好，尤其是将拙编归纳出四个特点，可以说是独具慧眼，只是在最后一个特点里以拙文为例，使我感到惭愧之至。其他点评都切中肯切中肯綮。总的来看，溢美之词多了一点。过奖了，不敢当，有待努力吧。

我自告奋勇，参加了方平先生主编的《新莎士比亚全集》（诗体译本）的翻译工作，已译完《维罗纳二绅士》和《结局好万事好》。现正赶译《特洛伊罗斯与克瑞西达》。

您在莎学评论中做出了很大的成绩，盼能经常读到您的新作。

四川的比较文学研讨会曾给我寄来通知，因忙于翻译，抽不出时间写论文，只得缺席。失去了一次学习机会，甚感遗憾。

今后望多多联系！即祝

撰祺

阮珅*

一九九五年十月三十日

*关于阮珅先生书信的说明：阮珅先生为武汉大学教授，曾任武汉大学莎士比亚研究中心主任（该中心 1989 年 4 月成立）。改革开放以来，阮珅在《外国文学研究》《武汉大学学报》上发表了多篇重要的莎士比亚研究论文。主编了《莎评辑录》（武汉大学出版社 1991 年版），1993 年 5 月主办“武汉国际莎学会议”，1999 年主持翻译湖北教育出版社出版的“莎士比亚经典名著译注丛书”及《莎士比亚十四行诗集》和多部莎剧译本；主编的《莎士比亚新论》收录多篇重要莎学论文，该书出版后，我在学习的基础上，曾经撰写发表了长篇书评，对该书进行评论，并将书评寄给阮珅教授征求他的意见。阮珅还出版有《莎士比亚论稿》。（李伟民）

伟民同志：

惠寄大作《评〈中国莎学年鉴〉》复印件收到了，谢谢！文章写得很好，所论各点切中肯綮。

武汉莎士比亚中心因限于经费，今年还没有开展什么活动。目前，我们正在全力以赴编写《莎士比亚译注丛书》，先出十册，悲喜剧各五册，这是湖北教育出版社的约稿，已列入今年的选题计划，九月份需完成任务，正进入最后冲刺阶段。

寄上几份资料作为回报，也算是交流一些情况和信息，顺便说明一下：去年我是个人应邀去参加莎学大会。到了洛杉矶以后，方老等把我“拉进了”代表团，该团本不包括我。

在洛杉矶期间，写了几首打油诗，现收其中一首《踏莎行》抄呈，请雅正：

莎学怡情，波音会意，兼程昼夜穿云际。方辞海峡倒春寒，半天抵美晴光里。　　东国鸿篇，西篇钜作，专题研讨多方位。新交对饮啖咖啡，嘎啦（gala）献演高潮起。

匆此即祝

暑祺

阮珅*

一九九七年七月十一日

*关于阮珅先生书信的说明：1996年，中国首次组成了莎士比亚代表团赴美国洛杉矶参加第六届“世界莎士比亚大会”，引起了国际莎学界的关注，也向世界莎学界展示了中国莎士比亚研究所取得的成绩，向世界莎学组织赠送了一批中国莎学论著，武汉大学阮珅教授也是代表团成员之一。我曾撰写孟宪强教授的《中国莎士比亚年鉴》书评，比较详细地指出该书对莎学研究的重要价值，并把发表后的文章复印一份，寄给了阮珅先生，请他提出意见。（李伟民）

伟民同行：

《中华莎学（7）》收到之日即复函致谢，可能邮寄失误。读到尊文《世界上的莎士比亚图书馆》之时，不巧又逢搬家，从四月底到今天，天天忙，打包、处理旧家具、装修新房子、添置新东西，找着笔找不见纸，一直折腾到现在，总算初步安定下来了，才得空给您复信，请多多原谅!

中莎会自几位新副会长上任，似乎活动不太多；新年前后北京演了《第十二夜》，再也没有听说哪个地方有什么大动作。中华莎学大有“万花纷谢一时稀”的感觉。唯独您能挑起编辑《中华莎学》的重担，又负联系开会的繁忙任务，还能抽时间写莎研文章，确系难能可贵。但愿 2002 年莎学会上能在天府之国向您当面致贺。

这一年来，我光忙了房子问题（东挪西借凑集资款、排队选房号……），大房子（126 平米）总算住上了，债也负上了，唯独没抓主要东西—— 很少写东西。手边有两年前写的辅导材料，顺便寄来，请多多指教。

祝

多出成果！全家幸福！

徐克勤*

二〇〇〇年六月十五日

*关于徐克勤先生书信的说明：山东师范大学徐克勤教授著有《莎士比亚名剧创作欣赏丛书》(1~6 册)。我曾经写有介绍《世界上的莎士比亚图书馆》一文，并寄给了徐克勤教授，自上海国际莎士比亚戏剧节以来，与徐克勤教授时有书信往还。当时《中华莎学》的出版又遇到很多困难。因此，由我、方平先生出资，曹树钧教授主编，由我、史璠承担起编辑、印刷、邮寄等工作。《中华莎学》出版后，由我每期寄给中莎会会员及全国莎学、戏剧爱好者。《中华莎学》在困难境遇中坚持出版，起到了团结全国莎学爱好者和研究莎学、沟通信息的重要作用。(李伟民)

伟民先生：

《英语研究》收到。多谢！拙文能与洋博士大作同登显著版面，深感您的大力相助。杂志寄到之日，即被同行拿走。文学院一级学科已正式批下，我学位点几个博导正准备招博士生，日夜忙于著书立论，希望您这位大主编能帮大忙。《英研》如有富余，请代买几本，费用即时寄到。

飞京公干，可折道来济一游，我们会尽力接待。

致

诚心敬意

徐克勤

二〇〇七年八月十四日

李伟民同志：

大函收悉。关于拙编莎氏词典出版一事，奉答如下：该书内芯（词典正文）早于年前排好，出版社也计划于去年底出书。但因该书已列入国家重点出版项目，领导为精益求精，增加校次，拟出豪华版，延请著名美术家设计。以此时间拖延。但估计面世之期不远（六七月间），请稍待。届时当由出版社与你直接联系征订。

因出版日期拖延，各方读者有关此事来函询问，无法确答。另外，词典的编纂、校对，诸事纷繁，不得不集中一切时间精力于工作。各方亲友，疏于联系。今后工作仍多，来信恕不能一一回复。此亦无可如何，想荷鉴原。专此祝

文安

刘炳善*

二〇〇〇年六月十七日

*刘炳善先生书信的说明：河南大学刘炳善教授编撰的《英汉双解莎士比亚大辞典》引起了学界特别是莎学界的关注，为此，我曾给刘炳善教授去信，询问《英汉双解莎士比亚大辞典》出版的情况，因为，当时我已经在《外语教学与研究》等期刊上发表了评孙家琇教授主编的《莎士比亚辞典》以及朱雯等编辑的《莎士比亚辞典》，以及在《外国文学》上发表的评《莎士比亚辞典》的文章，故写信给刘炳善先生，以便对这本《英汉双解莎士比亚大辞典》在学习的基础上进行评论；后来还在《辞书研究》2003 年第 1 期上发表了《莎学灵魂的聚焦与重铸：评张泗洋主编的〈莎士比亚大辞典〉》，在《辞书研究》2004 年第 6 期发表了《普及推广莎士比亚研究的基本建设：评〈英汉双解莎士比亚大词典〉》。（李伟民）

李伟民先生：

大函谨悉。承为贵刊约稿，盛意可感。遗憾的是我在近期内必须为拙编莎氏词典进行修订工作。其繁重程度如负大石攀登高山，且每日不能停下，计日程功，铢积寸累，届时才能完成任务。因此，实无力他顾，并各方亲友来信，亦往往不能及时答复。

编词典一事，任重而道远，烦苦万状，可于陆谷孙教授为《英汉大词典》缩写序言中见之。实情如此，谅荷鉴原。

专此顺祝

编安

刘炳善

二〇〇三年九月三十日

李伟民同志：

寄来的信、文章和《读书人报》都收到，太谢谢了！评《时代》的文章，写得很好，发表后请寄我一份为盼。

看来，您对莎士比亚很有感情，堪称老莎的知己，你希望多多掌握有关研究他的资料，这一心情我很理解，所以也很愿意为您尽力。您要的《莎士比亚引论》，我不是说没有吗？我是没有了，早都送人送光了，但我的儿子张晓阳有几部存放在我这儿，他在英国读莎士比亚博士学位，一时回不来，我就挪用他一部，先给您寄去再说。“引论”和“研究”都是我给研究生讲课用的讲稿，一些问题考虑得很不成熟，错误也不少，希你批评指正。

祝夏安！

张泗洋

一九九二年七月二十八日

伟民先生：

您好！

10 月 10 日来信，两个复印件都收到了，非常感谢。《莎士比亚戏剧故事全集》将于下个月初全部发稿。故事前面将有 20 多篇由我国莎学界老前辈撰写的导读文章。您是我国莎学界的中青年优秀学者之一，很有代表性。您是否愿意写点学习莎士比亚的体会（三千字之内）尽快寄给我。如果过去发表过类似的小文章，寄给我一个复印件也可以。如果没有时间写，也没有类似的体会，也可以自选您过去发表过莎评文章（不超过四千字）。总之，我希望“导读文章”中有您一篇，它对青年读者会有帮助的。莎士比亚本人也是在艰难困苦中自学成才的！

同行　郑土生

一九九五年十月二十七日

李伟民先生：

您好！我七八月暑假期间去了英国。八月下旬回校，收到了您 7 月 25 日的来函，十分高兴、十分感谢。冀望您能拨冗为《蒋春霖》作书评，记得年前我看到您为拙书写的《朱淑真研究》书评，欣喜非常。尝试将《蒋春霖评传》寄往书报社转呈给您。能够取得联络，实为高兴。

我已开课，加上行政会议的繁杂之务，工作又再忙碌起来。大函说及您对朱淑真有关材料搜集了一些，我刻下正为河北一出版社撰写约二十万字的《朱淑真传》，恳切希望您可给我提供宝贵的资料和意见，谢谢!

我除了研究的论文之外，也在课余为报纸杂志撰写小品及散文等，我的散文集因手头只有自己的藏本未能寄给您，很抱歉。我已致电出版社，若他们仍有书可给我的（出版社现正计划再版拙书），我收到后当即奉寄。

专此敬祝

教安

黄嫣梨*

一九九八年九月十日

*关于黄嫣梨先生来信的说明：黄嫣梨女士为香港浸会大学教授，主要研究中国古代文学，著有《朱淑真研究》《蒋春霖评传》等著作多部。我在研究莎士比亚的同时，对宋代女词人朱淑真研究也很着迷，曾在《历史大观园》上撰写有《朱淑真与酒》，在《史学史研究》上撰写了比较全面的《朱淑真研究六十年综述》，在《中国文化研究》上撰写有评黄嫣梨教授的《朱淑真研究》等论文。文章发表后，寄给黄嫣梨先生请教。黄嫣梨先生后来给我寄来多本她的著作。（李伟民）

伟民先生：

去岁十二月二十九日惠寄大作复制件并附言均已奉悉。十分高兴读到您对我们拙著的评价。五六十年代我们从事莎剧译述时，一直在孤独中工作，现在我们两人一个病残一个从事他项研究，遇到一位同样热爱莎翁的朋友，真是说不出的高兴。新春就到了，祝健康幸福。

附上近作复制二件。

通讯处：上海衡山路衡山宾馆 1031 房，邮编 200030。

王元化*

二〇〇一年一月二十日

*关于王元化先生书信的说明：王元化先生曾任中共上海市委宣传部部长。王元化先生为莎评翻译曾经倾注过很多心血。我曾经撰写有研究王元化先生莎学思想的文章在《四川戏剧》发表。这是国内最早研究王元化莎学思想的文章。文章发表后引起一些反响。近二三年国内又陆续发表了几篇王元化莎学思想的论文。文章发表后，我给王元化先生复印寄去，希望能够得到他的指教。由华东师范大学陆晓光教授主持的“王元化研究中心”及其网站将我的这篇文章列为该中心重点介绍的文章。（李伟民）

伟民同志：

3月27日来信收到。以前惠寄的《中华莎学》，尤其是《光荣与梦想》都收到，谢谢！

这些年来你在莎学研究上做了那么多工作，写了那么多文章，真是个刻苦的人，值得称道。

南京师大来函要我推荐一批学者写讨论莎士比亚历史剧的论文，我推荐了你、史璠、台北的彭镜禧和开封的刘炳善。

我从1998年出版译林社莎集里的十多部译作之后，虽也写点论莎的东西，却不由自主地做着别的工作。不知道为什么莎学会开会也不大通知我了。你们的杭州会议我就不知道。唯一的解释似乎是我搬家后没有通知莎学会新地址。寄到老地方，丢了。但我也不知道莎学会有没有大本营，在什么地址，无法通知。所以很被动。但寄到外语系（现在叫院了）的则没有丢失。

这一次接到信没有回，心里有个想法，4月4日要开重庆翻译学会，你既到了川外，很可能在会上碰到。没想到你竟没有来。你来重庆没有？

我的电话是：6886××××。

此致

敬礼

孙法理

二○○三年四月十一日

李伟民同志：

您好，谨致诚挚问候。

《中国莎士比亚研究》征稿函，已收悉，谢谢。拟撰写《选择·综合·超越·创新—— 讲授“莎士比亚研究”课程的感悟》一文，当遵嘱届时寄交文稿。

耑此布复

近祺

王忠祥*

二〇〇六年元月十日

*四川外国语大学一贯重视莎士比亚研究，我曾经征得学校的同意，计划由我校主编、出版刊物《中国莎士比亚研究》，但由于多方面的原因，该刊的出版一直没能实现。(李伟民)

李伟民老师：

如晤！

感谢您2005年12月20日给我寄来《中国莎学研究》征稿函。

贵院编辑出版《中国莎学研究》大型学术文集，必将推动我国莎士比亚研究的进一步发展。对您的创意和工作，甚表钦佩！

作为莎士比亚研究的爱好者，理应支持。现将《从巴赫金的对话理论看〈麦克白〉的自我意识》一文的文字稿和软件寄给您。是否刊用，请您定夺。

另外，我有拙作《藏在柜子里的叙述者？——浅析E. M. 福斯特的〈霍华兹别墅〉》一文投贵校学报。一并寄上，能否刊用，亦请定夺。

欢迎您拨冗来安徽大学学报编辑部和外语学院指导工作。

望保持联系。

祝

春安！

华泉坤* 敬上

二〇〇六年三月十六日

*关于华泉坤先生来信的说明：安徽大学副校长华泉坤教授在得知四川外国语大学即将出版《中国莎士比亚研究》期刊后，表示支持，并很快惠赐了他的最新力作。但由于《中国莎士比亚研究》刊物出版搁浅，后来华泉坤教授的稿件刊载于《四川外语学院学报》。（李伟民）

尊敬的李伟民教授：

您好！自 2009 年 11 月于重庆分别以来已一年半有余，不知您工作生活如何？

华泉坤老师和我经常谈起在重庆期间您对我们的热情接待，正是您细致周到的安排和亲自陪同使得我们倍感温馨，在领略重庆优美风光的同时，更感受到您的好客与豪爽。再次衷心表达我们诚挚的谢意！

您寄送我的三本专著我一直在研读。您数十年如一日坚持研究莎士比亚，不畏艰辛，笔耕不辍，从而在莎研领域有了自己的一席之地，并得到了众多大家的首肯。华老师一直告诫我要向您学习。

在参加"第七届中国戏剧学术研讨会暨中外戏剧与莎士比亚研究论坛"回来后，我将在会议上宣读的论文《〈特洛伊罗斯与克瑞西达〉和〈伊利亚特〉之比较》重新整理、修改润色。鉴于贵校学报《外国语文》的权威性和广泛影响，华老师建议我将论文投给贵刊。目前我申评副教授职称，急需论文，我们学校认可贵刊的文章，所以请您对我的论文给予指教，如能在贵刊刊发，则不胜感激！

李教授如有机会，欢迎到安徽做客。

祝您工作顺利，生活幸福！

田朝绪　敬上

二〇一二年六月二十一日于合肥

李伟民同志：

来信前天始转到我手，回信迟了，乞谅。

你要的《莎士比亚—— 他的作品及其时代》一书，很抱歉，我也没有了。我原来有四十几本，都被人要光了，现在我自己只有一本，实在对不起。

出版社早就说要再版，可是至今没有消息。我希望他们能够不怕赔本，早日出书以满足莎士比亚爱好者的要求。

专此奉覆，祝

新年快乐！

索天章*

十二月七日

*关于索天章先生书信的说明：索天章先生的这封来信写于 1993 年 12 月 7 日，其时中国出版的莎学论著不多，索天章教授的《莎士比亚—— 他的作品及其时代》是一部重要的莎学研究著作，但是已经很难买到，因此，我写信向索天章先生购买。（李伟民）

伟民教授：

赠书收到，非常感谢。记得我们曾通过信，在北大见面时却忘记了。通信时你似乎不在川外，我去川外讲学时没见到你，只记得川外招待特别好，法文系黄新成教授还送了我两本《法汉大词典》，编得非常好。不知道他还在川外吗？见到请代致谢。

专此祝好！

许渊冲

二〇一三年十二月十日

戏剧学院转中国莎士比亚研究会并首届中国莎士比亚戏剧节：

当此由中国莎士比亚研究会发起、上海戏剧学院、上海市文化局、剧协上海分会联合主办的首届中国莎士比亚戏剧节即将在上海正式举行时，承蒙你们盛情邀请参加开幕式，至为感激！

今年我国举行首届中莎士比亚戏剧节，并在全国各地用各种剧种演出莎士比亚戏剧作品，这在我国的戏剧运动史上，同时在世界各国演出莎翁的戏剧史上，都是一次具有重大历史意义的空前创举。我因工作关系，不拟前来上海参加你们的盛会，谨在此向你们表示热烈的祝贺！祝首届中国莎士比亚戏剧节胜利举行，并祝愿，通过这次戏剧节，在开展我国莎士比亚的研究和演出莎翁的戏剧作品方面，都能取得更新的成就和作出更大的贡献！

此致

敬礼！

戈宝权①

一九八六年十月五日于北京

① 戈宝权先生为著名学者、翻译家，中国社会科学院外国文学研究所研究员。为纪念莎士比亚400周年诞辰撰写有《莎士比亚作品在中国》，该文用了较大篇幅详实评注了莎士比亚作品最早传入中国的情况。

李伟民老师：

你好！我是戈宝权先生的夫人。年前友人转告你在北大的《中国比较文学通讯》上写的文章。首先谢谢你对戈宝权先生的关心。从文章中可看出你是位治学严谨，学识渊博的学者。因此我请北京友人帮助得知你的地址。写信向你表示感谢!

在此谈谈戈先生近况。他住在南京富贵山医院，边休养边治疗，他患有帕金森综合征。因用脑过度得了严重的脑萎缩，不能行走已近五年了，近两年记忆力特别差，他没有任何痛苦。对我来说是个最大的安慰。

所里的同志提出为戈先生出一本纪念文集，稿子已收了不少。我现着手给他编都不能很完整的年谱及著作目录，但我尽力编好些，再就是编他的文集。目前正在整理收集文章，争取明年编完。我在编写画册中，写了两篇小文，请你指教，看看在四川地方能否转发，但不必为难。

现想请教你，我想在纪念文集中用的那篇文章，或请你再改写也行，字数不限，时间年底前寄到。信纸上的地址交林鸿亮先生收。他是波兰文学专家，获“十字”勋章的，由他来编。你能否改写或就用那篇文章都可以。我希望能有你的文章为本书增光。请你往南京家中写一封信告知。

地址：南京，后半山园五号×—×幢

邮编：210016

电话：025-482××××

我于 11 月 10 日前回南京家中，今后信件请寄往南京。

祝你全家人

安好!

梁培兰* 敬上

一九九八年十月二十八日

*关于梁培兰先生书信的说明：梁培兰先生是戈宝权先生的妻子。戈宝权先生是我国重要的莎士比亚研究、比较文学研究和俄罗斯文学研究权威。戈宝权先生撰写有《戈宝权比较文学论文集》一厚册，是中国比较文学研究和莎士比亚研究的重要文献。该书出版后，我通过认真研读，撰写了一篇书评，发表在《中国比较文学研究通讯》上。梁培兰女士读到后，专门给我写了一封信对我表示感谢，并随信寄来了两篇文章，后来发表在我主编的《教育与实践》上。中国社会科学院外国文学研究所编辑《戈宝权先生纪念文集》约我撰写了“纪念研究戈宝权先生比较文学研究思想”的文章，该书由江苏人民出版社出版。(李伟民)

林贵先生：

您好！

承蒙赐寄 1996 *SQ* Bibliography，对您的厚意，十分感谢！拙文《驯悍记》，介绍简要，概况了中心思想，足见功力。由于我粗枝大叶，上次寄信时未在信封左上角写明舍间地址，*SQ* 寄往“上海译文”，我已退休，出版社看望老同事，才收到您的赐赠，但已隔了一段时间。

我因左眼患高度近视，在医院动了摘除白内障手术（超声、乳化），反应较大，一个多月，读、写不便。眼力逐渐恢复时，又接连收到复旦大学英文系博士论文一厚册、外国语大学硕士论文二篇，都要写详细评阅意见，并参加答辩，很花时间，无暇旁及。到这个月 22 日最后一场答辩结束，才算松了一口气。积下来许多事情得赶紧处理，因此没能赶上新年来到之前向海外好友们致以千禧年的祝贺，实深歉意，还请见谅！

《外国文学研究》1999 年 1 月发表拙文《马歇斯的双重放逐：论科里奥兰纳斯》，您如有兴趣一读，当复印寄奉。去年 8 月访英，在新“环球剧场”欣赏了 *Merchant of Venice* 的演出，写了《泰晤士河畔的新“环球剧场”》一文，将于明春发表，当一起寄奉请正。

“河北教育”来信告知，已在深圳付印《新莎士比亚全集》，明年元月见书。定价多少还不知道，以后当写一英文简介寄您。

又，出版社告知，《新全集》已和台湾出版社签约，由他们引进《新全集》繁体字版权。我为全集写“译后记”已发表于台湾大学主办的《中外文学》1999 年 7 月号。在新千年即将来临之际遥祝身健笔健，万事如意！

请赐寄“200031 上海太原路 63 弄 2 号”。

方平

一九九九年十二月二十九日

林贵：

近日从 Prof. Levith 来信看，你是去西班牙开了会议，究竟如何？如去了，请告诉我一些会议的情况。不然，可否寄我一本 *Shakespeare Quarterly* 杂志，内容是有关的。这种杂志我在此买不到。

钱兆明注 *Venus and Adonis* 与 *The Rape of Lucrece*，稿就，我已给他修改了。你对 *Merry Wives* 的注释工作紧张如何了？希望你在暑假抓紧进行。

我自己动手注 *Henry VI*，由于在此工具书不全，此项工作要带到北京去才能完成。

最近又买了一些书，如 *Cambridge Companion* 新版，Goddard 的 *The Meaning of Shakespeare*，但未读多少。我闲时看些现代小说，比较喜欢英国人的作品。

张泗洋和晓阳近况如何？孟宪强过去学历怎样？他的英文程度如何？长春现在莎研工作怎样？有无在哈尔滨开莎学会议的消息？

祝

身体健康，工作顺利！

裘克安

二〇〇一年八月十三日

另，我约于 10 月上旬回国。

杨林贵教授钧鉴：

寄来中国莎士比亚论丛（第一系列共 8 册）已经收到。谢谢，迟复为歉。

你们主编的这套丛书质量太高，花了不少心血，代表了中国学者研究莎士比亚的水平，值得赞赏。也收录了我的论文《情趣无穷的〈驯悍记〉》，十分感激！

其中不少老同志均是我的老朋友。其中贺翔麟教授久无消息，不知他还健在否？请通告。此兄十分活跃，我多次去信均无回音，不知怎么回事？

早年你来访时，在我家吃过东坡肉，你十分赞赏，这是我老伴做的，她已故世数年，今我成了失独老人，十分孤寂。少年夫妻老来伴，这是真理。你还年轻，正当盛年，也请好好保护你的贤妻。

我无以为报，今寄上我最后一部著作《求真斋文存》，请你指教。如今我已 94 岁，记忆力严重衰退，已难以为文。这是自然规律，我一生平庸，无怨无悔，随时等得上苍的召唤，一旦召唤，我即离世，进入天国，和先我而去的亲友相聚，这也是一种幸福。

孟宪强兄是我的好友，比我年轻，怎么会先我而去，惜哉，大概他为莎士比亚研究太辛劳了吧！由此看来，凡事都需适可而止，不少老专家因笔耕太勤而离世了，这是重大的损失。而今我已封笔，以文化养生度过我的余生。平时阅读书报，约见朋友，有时练练书法，不再为文章。祝羊年大吉，创作丰收！

附上一些书法，请正学。

收到后请电复或函复，谢谢。

垂暮老人　任明耀

二〇一五年十一月六日

杨老师、李老师：

新年好！谢谢您的热情祝福！也祝您新年健康快乐，一切顺利！

您说的原信扫描件，我这里都是有的，但一些较有代表性的信件，往往版面效果不大好，有的字迹不清，有的写在其他纸张的反面，背面的字迹也透出来了，还有两封信原先有点破了，我也没有经验，用透明胶带补了一下，结果时间久了以后，留下了很深的黑色痕迹。也许你们有技术手段能多少改善一些吧？

从内容方面，我选了以下几封信的扫描件（主要考虑其代表性），供你们考虑选用：

1. 关于“你崇拜不崇拜民族英雄”的信，此信从一个侧面显示了他以整个生命之力从事译莎事业的动力所在，可惜信的下面贴过胶带纸，把画面毁了。我在《诗侣莎魂》中用作插图时，只用了这一部分，没有用全信。

2. 关于“蚊子臭虫变少”的信，展现的是他刚投入译莎工作时投入的精神状态（此前一度感到彷徨苦闷），连蚊子也“没有功夫理它们”了。这封信的画面效果比较可以。

3. 关于翻译计划的信，这封信全面地向我母亲叙述了他的总体翻译计划，其中也有他对许多莎剧的评论分析，我觉得在学术上较有价值，版面质量也还可以，就是长了一点，共有 8 页。

4. 关于翻译“双关语”的信，这是在他在经过创造性的劳动，解决了 approach 和 repproach 双关语翻译的难题后在我母亲面前“自鸣得意”的一封信，也较有典型意义。只是背面有字迹透出来，不知有没有办法处理？

5. 有关他在翻译《威尼斯商人》时开始曾参考梁实秋的译文，后来发现“反受其累”的信。可以反映出他进行翻译时的严谨态度。但此信字迹比较模糊。

6. 关于我母亲帮助誊抄时，把“我要如今”改成“我如今要”，被他“打手心”的信，显示了他在翻译中对“音韵和谐”的讲究，也较有代表性。不过这封信也有一块因贴过胶带留下的黑影。

在《诗侣莎魂》出版时，有几封信我用软件简单处理过，当然水平是很低的，也发给您看一看。相信你们能做得更好。

我母亲的信都没有能留存下来，只能遗憾了。

祝你们的辛劳成果顺利问世，为我国莎学事业再立一功！

朱尚刚

二〇二二年一月六日

树钧同志：

你好！

北京之行如何？想你们业已返校，忙于课程了，辛苦了！

拙序原信笔写来，尤其看到你们的大作，材料丰富，见解明晰当时非常兴奋，写下来就不能停笔，想不到有二万字以上，我正想整理删减，想不到你们来信那么早，催稿那么急，只能麻烦你了！非常抱歉而且感谢！

你信上说四月将举行莎士比亚纪念会，你们这篇文章正可扼要报告，大家在筹备国际莎剧节及二届莎剧节时正需要这种材料，必然深感兴趣，也可预先介绍。

请代问福良、俊峰好。问小俞好！ 附函请代转！想不久可以见面，实当面谢！

祝新的一年万事如意，成绩斐然！

全家好！

君川

一九八九年二月十七日

曹老师：

您好！

3 月 12 日信悉，谢谢您的关心和精心安排。

关于 4 月 23 日的活动，我母亲自当尽力参加，不过情况并不很乐观。因为她自从前年因癌症开刀以后，身体情况确实相当弱。从最近一个月的情况看，稍一走动就感体力不支，因此相当时间均以卧床为主，直到最近三四天才略微好转。这样的情况终难赴会，即使勉强去了，如果消耗太大的话，怕要得不偿失。当然，如果今后一段时间能有明显好转，还是准备争取去的。经了解，嘉兴上午 8 时有一班长途汽车到上海西站（徐家汇附近漕溪北路上）。因嘉兴长途汽车站到我家较近，还算方便，上海西站到戏剧学院也较近，且停车问题较好解决，因此你们不必派小车长途来嘉兴了，只要 22 日下午 2 点左右到徐家汇接一下就行。如果我母亲不能去，我就 23 日晨自己去，就不必接了。到时我会告诉你们的。

关于我父亲的书信，这和译稿的性质还是有所不同的。译稿是为了公开发表的，而这些书信毕竟是私人的东西。在一定意义上可以说是“情书”，过去我母亲是根本没有考虑要公之于世的，近几年来受到周围许多同志的启发，也认识到了这批书信具有重大的史料价值，因此现在正在考虑整理。这个工作量很大要进行挑选、归类，对原来比较潦草的字体要比较工整地抄写一遍，抄写时对一些她认为纯属私生活，不准备公开的内容还要做些删节（这也是她的权利），有的要对当时的时间、背景进行回忆，并作注释和说明。这些工作也只有她才能进行。鉴于她目前健康状况不好，只能慢慢地干，如果在有生之年能完成这一工作已经是比较乐观的估计了。在这一工作完成之前，我们还不准备把这些书信交出去。（实际上，对我父亲事迹的研究恐怕未必有其他人能比我母亲更有效，更有价值了。）当然，如果有“中莎会”的学者准备进行研究的话，我们愿意根据他们的课题，提供一切可能的帮助（比如说书信的复印件）。我上次信中说的“容后考虑”以及“准备提供复印件”就是这个意见。作为学术研究之用，应该说复印件和原件是无关紧要的。而原件则主要在于作为文物的收藏价值。对此，“中莎会”作为全国性的莎士比亚研究组织，提出要求进行收藏，当然是合理的。但是嘉兴市作为我父亲出生、成长和主要工作的地方，且已有过建立纪念馆或纪念室的考虑，杭州大学作为我父亲的母校，又是现在对我父亲的研究工作进行得最深入的单位。他们要求收藏我父亲的手迹也都有充足的理由。前不久黄源同志还曾提起过是否交给中国（现代）文学馆的问题。对这些，我的意见还是“容后再议”！一是我母亲整理工作还刚开了个头，二是到时我还要考察一下各单位的保存条件，并考虑哪个单位保存能达到最大社会效益，然后再作决定。所以这次的“赠送仪式”是否就请免了，不知行不行。这件事，确实非常抱歉，只能请您原谅了。

顺颂

敬安

朱尚刚*

一九八九年三月二十

*关于朱尚刚先生书信的说明：朱尚刚为朱生豪和宋清如独子。中莎会会员，多次参加中莎会学术研讨活动，曾多次组织、参与纪念朱生豪先生的学术会议，出版编辑多部著作，如《诗侣莎魂——我的父母朱生豪、宋清如》《朱生豪小言集》《朱生豪情书》，参与编辑《秋风和萧萧叶的歌》《寄在信封里的灵魂》，晚年致力于朱生豪、宋清如著述的整理、编辑，编辑有《朱生豪译莎士比亚戏剧手稿》，在《中国莎士比亚研究通讯》《新文学史料》《英语研究》等刊物上发表多篇论文。（李伟民）

树钧同志：

春节好！前一阵收到来信和《论黄佐临和莎士比亚的戏剧创作》；昨天又收到《“莎剧节”引起的艺术争议》，确实高兴和振奋。我虽然“过年”比较忙乱加上有些犯病，得吸氧帮助呼吸，也想写信道谢并说说我的心情。

关于佐临的文章引起我不少的回忆和思索。首先，由于早年间我们都居住在天津，我同他的妹妹黄琼玖在中西“中学”同班。我常到他们家去，因此称他为“黄大哥”。他到中西导演金润芝等演出《皆大欢喜》，我记得一清二楚。金润芝是我姐的同班同学，大家不但极为熟悉而且特别为他们的姻缘感到庆幸。解放后，见面少了，我却愈来愈从戏剧业务方面敬佩佐临大哥。他真是导演和戏剧理论大家，称得起是中国剧坛上的一面旗帜。他熟悉莎士比亚，要把莎剧和中国戏曲创造性地结合起来的心愿和努力，更令我钦佩。可惜他协助改编的《血手记》，我只看过一遍，印象浅了。这次阅读你人物介绍和分析不但加强了印象，而且进一步感到他认为“在艺术表现手法上，戏曲比莎剧更为高明”的见解本身实在高明。这就是说，我们不但可以用莎剧内容丰富我们的戏曲，而且可以用戏曲艺术为莎剧增添生命力和表现力。我觉得在这一点上，曹树钧同志，你可以大书特书之。

正好，你这次的《争议》一文对于“越剧能演《哈姆雷特》吗？”回答得很好。我没能观看赵志刚的表演而你前后看了三遍。我十分相信你所说的，《王子复仇记》不仅成功地改编了《哈姆雷特》而且在“越味”与“莎味”的结合上出现了可喜的新突破。这真是太难得了，这也是实现黄大哥历来心愿的一次努力。

文中关于对女导演雷国华对伊阿古的解释的批评，我完全同意。伊阿古是个突出的典型，我自己觉得随着西方文明的发展，像他那种把机智聪明和人伦道德完全割裂的坏蛋、阴谋家，把“真美善”彻底置于“假丑恶”之下的怀疑主义者屡见不鲜。他的形象具有超出资本原始积累时期的现实意义。导演岂不是应该挖掘这种内涵吗，怎么倒把他“美化”了一番？屠岸先生给我来信，也不同意剧中对伊阿古的解释。

我认为你对于“今天演莎剧还有没有观众？”的回答和批驳太重要了！必须加以批评和引导！你的文章既有针对性又有说服力，我祝贺你，也向你道谢（因为说出了我要讲的话）。

好，再祝猪年吉祥顺利！

孙家琇

一九九五年一月三十一日

树钧先生

您好！

今天下午我将乘班机去石家庄，四年多来译成莎剧可以全部交稿了。也许将在河北教育出版社耽搁一二星期，规划出版事宜。

恰好今天上午收到国际莎协来信，是担任执行委员会正式成员的通知。承蒙孙福良秘书长和您一直关心此事，特地把莎协来函译出，随函附上，以便了解情况。

请转告孙先生，并代为问好。待回沪后当再和您联系。祝

文安！

方平　匆上

一九九七年九月九日

回沪后我将把国际莎协来函复印一份交“中莎会”，也许可供存档之用。　平又及

亲爱的方平教授：

我以欢悦的心情欢迎你担任国际莎士比亚协会的执行委员会的正式成员，任期为1996—2001年。你的提名曾于1997年2月传达给委员会全体成员，一致通过。兹附上1996年8月上届执行委员会的会议纪要。执行委员会定于1998年8月23—28日在莎士比亚研究院召开。届时自当告知确切的会议地点和时间。

谨此问候。

苏珊·布洛克博士 执行秘书

一九九七年八月二十九日

曹树钧老师：

来信已收到。

关于向国外投寄《中华莎学》之事，按规定最好由你院科研处盖一公章，证明此刊物没有泄密情况。这样可以保险一些，如没有证明有时也会寄到对方手中的。……

你们办刊的艰辛，那是可想而知的。我正在托一些朋友，为《中华莎学》免费设计些封面，以后搞好再寄给你们审处。

至于赞助问题，目前很难办到。因为我跟企业家没有多少联系。知识分子去搞钱历来比较困难。

新疆大学中文系续枫林老师有可能联系你。她也在教莎士比亚。《中华莎学》是否可以按期寄她一份，对这些边远省份应予特别照顾。你寄来的三份通讯已收到。我将分别寄送国内外友人。以后是否可寄我 5 份？那份材料你已托经办的同志在翻译很好，这类信息是很受大家欢迎的。

向老孙同志问好，他很能干，我跟他见过几次面，比较熟，你们辛苦了，以后来信望能寄我家中较好。《中华莎学》第二期尚未收到，第一期可否再寄三本，我将分别寄往美国、加拿大、日本有关莎学专家。

祝

文安！

明耀*

一九九九年四月二十六日；五月一日

*关于任明耀教授书信的说明：任明耀为杭州大学中文系教授，1986 年应邀参加了在西柏林召开的第四届世界莎士比亚大会，提交论文《〈李尔王〉研究在中国》 发表多篇莎学论文，主要莎学著作有：《说不尽的莎士比亚—— 外国文学评论集》《求真斋文存》。任明耀先生现以 95 岁高龄，琴棋书画都有所涉猎，曾经出版了《博马舍》《京剧奇葩四大名旦》，《求真斋文存》为其论文及会议文章结集。内容包括第一辑外国文学研究、第二辑弘扬国粹京剧艺术、第三辑怀念师友、第四辑童话寓言创作、第五辑童话小品翻译、第六辑欧旅散记、第七辑读书和生活、第八辑暨南情深、第九辑国际友人、第十辑亲情可贵、第十一辑名家书信、第十二辑师生情谊等。任明耀先生晚年仍然十分关心中国莎学的发展，每期中莎会会刊《中国莎士比亚研究通讯》出版后，都由编辑部寄给先生，他拿到后都会放在书桌显要位置仔细阅读，了解中国莎学研究的最新发展。（李伟民）

树钧兄：

您好！

上月中旬给兄的信谅早已收到。由于中莎会对《中国莎学简史》的重视宣传以及李伟民等先生对拙作的积极评价，特别是你的大力帮助，为《简史》造成了一定的影响。因此拙作在推荐第四届社会科学优秀成果评奖中被评为著作类二等奖。此次译审很严格，一二等奖很少，著作类一等奖中的文学类著作只有二种，二等奖中文学著作也只有四种。拙作能够获得这样的荣誉，首先要感谢对拙作给予过各种帮助的莎学前辈和同行；同时我觉得这也是对我莎学研究工作的一个肯定，一个鼓励，令我深感欣慰。

我校今年出版著作基金资助申请评审工作已经开始。今天上午我将拙作《三色堇》送到了系里，在系里我看到了“通知”。“通知”说，这次学校出版社将出资 60 万元资助 12 种优秀教材和著作的出版。又说“在过往四年内曾获得过资助的，此次不得申请”；还说，今年将改变以往的原则，不仅重视学术性，同时也考虑经济效益；博士论文也要经过评审才能出版。由此看来，此次我获得资助的可能性很小，特别是四年前我曾获得过一次资助，这就增加了申请的难度。面对这种形势真得另寻出路了。原来我对申请基金资助还有不小的希望，现在看来这个希望太小了。

不知河北莎协成立没有？方平教授主持翻译的《新莎士比亚全集》出版没有？北京大学辜正坤那里举办莎学会议的事不知有什么进展没有？我觉得希望不大。为了中莎会的进一步发展，我想河南大学刘炳善教授那里可能考虑搞一次莎学会议。但这里涉及一个问题：就是如果刘炳善教授仅仅是中莎会理事，出于对他本人学术身份的考虑，他大概不会愿意张罗这个会议。因此，我想是否可以将他增补为副会长？从年岁较大的老一代来说，刘炳善教授占了好几个有利条件：（1）博士生导师，开设有莎诗研究课程；（2）出版过多种英国文学方面的著作，80 年代末以来发表了不少有关莎士比亚的论文；（3）出版《莎士比亚大词典》；（4）翻译出版过莎士比亚戏剧作品；（5）对莎学活动十分热心；（6）他有项目，经费较多；（7）年龄不会太大（1927 年生），今年 72 岁。上述想法我考虑了好久，不知是否妥当，希望兄与孙院长说一下我的想法。

我现在仍在修改我的《中国接受莎士比亚的文化价值取向》，估计要到 11 月底可以完成。

代向孙院长问好！

谨颂

文安！

孟宪强

一九九九年九月二十二日

树钧教授：

您好！

8.26 来信早已拜读，李伟民先生寄来的《中华莎学》也已收到。因为自 9 月中旬以来家母病重逝世，我两次回辽宁老家，心力交瘁，很长一段时间心情难以摆脱悲痛，加上家务繁杂，致使回信晚了太长的时间，实在太抱歉了，万望鉴宥。

谢谢您将拙文推荐给《中国戏剧》，他们给发的消息的复印件也收到了。遗憾的是该消息中有不确之处：中国学者此次会议期间主持会议者只张冲、沈林二人，东北师大三人并未主持会议。消息中却说 5 人都主持了会议，这与原文不符，会产生不良影响的，可又无法更改，此事也就只好如此了。信中可向该刊提一下此事，以后压缩文字时千万不要出错误。

第 8 辑《中华莎学》编辑得很有分量，容量很大，也很有特色。其中融入了您的许多心血。李伟民先生为中莎会做了不少实事，而您则为中莎会做出了很大的贡献；如果没有您的努力，《中华莎学》的编辑、印刷都是难以完成的。

关于增补戴晓彤和李伟民为中莎会副会长和理事一事，希望能尽快地通过公布。不能等到下期《中华莎学》出版时再公布决定，此事应以中莎会文件形式公布，发给每位会员。这样不仅可以显示中莎会的活力，同时也有利于中莎会的工作。中莎会差不多三四年没什么大活动了。我觉得戴晓彤那里排演梆子戏《忧郁王子》是个契机。中莎会可与河北莎协联系，利用此机会办一次较大规模的莎学活动。戴晓彤担任了中莎会副会长，此事办起来就方便有利多了，此事望与孙院长商定。

《人民日报》记者在我参与莎学大会回来之后采访了我，发表了一篇文章，现寄上复印件 1 份，供参阅并请指教。

谨颂

秋安！

孟宪强　上

二〇〇一年十月二十八日

宪强先生道鉴：

两封贺卡及信件均悉，多承关心，先谢。

出书乃传世之工作，先生能在艰困环境下勉力完成著作、公之于世，诚可喜可贺之事也。遵嘱代办入台一事，经与黄美序教授奔走了两周，至少在我们来说希望不大，其原因奉告如下：

邀请函必须由对等之民间团体发出，此间唯一相关之团体为中华戏剧协会，该会仅为空架子，赖承接个案向政府机关申请经费，此事经昨天理事会讨论结果，认为发邀请函没有问题，但迄后之一切代办入台手续也必须由邀请单位出面，据云：须盖二十多个章，该单位缺乏人手承办，故兴趣不大。

来函中虽言明一切费用自理，但行政开支，基本接待仍需经费支应，该学会并无能力承接此案、且此案无法申请到相关单位之财力支应。

去年邀请孙福良先生之“台北话剧协会”面临同样之困境经询此理事长也乏兴趣。

据云，来台手续须时两个月以上，为恐有碍行程，特函告如上，请循其他管道进行或有可能。黄美序教授已退休。弟能力有限，特此致歉。

敬祝

新春如意

弟　洪哲　敬上

一九九六年一月十七日

孟兄：

大函在校寒休前一天收到。关于由大学邀请，我在事先也考虑过，都认为时间仓促，活动难以具体落实，因而作罢。今终提起，我倒想建议你用团体之名义发信给以下几个学校，他们都是近年两岸文化交流有兴趣的。

台湾地区各大学莎士比亚均开课在英文系，故来函也请直接寄到各学校英文系，由他们再逐级签办。

1）高雄市，中山大学英文系

2）台南市，成功大学英文系

3）台中市，东海大学英文系

4）台北、士林，东吴大学英文系

淡江大学仍可来函，但英文系属外语学院。直接寄到英文系即可。函中勿单独提及黄美序及我本人，因为黄已于今年退休，我不由英文系发聘。不过，接信后，英文系主任会找我及黄商量（黄虽退休），仍有人望。

我能尽力的仅止于此了，希望把握时效，在 2 月 18 日开学后，能收到来函。

祝成功，顺便拜年。

弟　洪哲

一九九六年二月四日

孟教授：

上星期收到您寄来的两本书，至今已看完了年鉴的部分。书中对莎士比亚的介绍及有关莎士比亚研究活动均有详细记载，非常佩服。

台湾的莎士比亚教学一向由朱立民教授提倡。近两年因朱老师生病过世，一时还无法预测哪一位学者可以整合莎士比亚研究。希望不久的将来可以有两岸互相交换研究成果的机会。

祝

夏安

王仪君

一九九六年六月十日

宪强教授：

赐寄《中国莎学简史》及《中国莎学年鉴》二书，均已收到，特此致谢。

暑期我将至美国纽约参加一个戏剧会议，顺便看些演出，8月底在北京开的戏剧会议我会去，届时将向你请教。

暂此搁笔。

即颂

暑祺

黄美序

一九九六年六月二十三日

孟教授：

非常感谢您赐赠大作《中国莎学年鉴》及《中国莎学简史》两本巨著。虽未得空拜读大作，但以先生文学修养之好一定是精彩万分。

本系专攻莎剧的有四位教授。如果可能，也许可以考虑和贵研究中心做学术交流活动，希望以后有此机会。

再次谢谢您的大作。并祝

夏安

陈慧美　敬上

一九九六年六月二十六日

孟教授：

您好！因外出休养，照片寄退了，请谅。

最近李如茹来过信和传真，谈及澳大利亚朋友希望和我中莎会搞学术合作等，同时又接到香港莎学界朋友的来信。现将黎翠珍教授的信寄去，供您参考，并希望12月中旬在沪一起见面，共商合作和筹备事宜。

我已上班，身体恢复尚好，谢谢关心。

代问林贵好！

祝好！

孙福良

一九九六年十月十八日

（附信）

孙福良先生：

您好。

上次黄清霞到上海的时候，我托他带了个信息给您，报告我们在香港创办莎士比亚学会的工作已经开始。要等手续办好才可以运作。可惜的是我中间有一段时间事忙，没有跟进。到最近才继续进行。看来应该没有什么问题了。

最近接到澳洲朋友的信准备在1998年开一个“莎剧在中国演出”的国际研讨会。他们会在1996年12月到上海跟中国莎士比亚学会联络，研究筹办这个会。我们香港的好朋友也有兴趣参与，黄清霞跟我希望12月15—19日到上海跟你们一块儿计划。详细安排，黄清霞会打电话跟您商量。要是一切顺利希望在上海会面。

祝

安好

黎翠珍

一九九六年十月十三日

宪强教授：

大函敬悉。

明年九月的“莎士比亚在中国”研讨会，台湾方想必会有学者有兴趣参加。吾兄所提建议，经考虑后，弟建议由吾兄或适当人士遥洽此地英美文学学会（理事长：师范大学英语系 滕以鲁教授）或/及戏剧学会（理事长：师范大学英语系 马杨万运教授），以便安排协调。弟当尽力促成。

耑此顺颂

研安

弟 镜禧 拜启

一九九七年一月二十八日

张英先生：

您好！

闻贵会将于今日聚会，我代表中莎会向贵会的全体同仁致以诚挚的祝贺！

我会曾于今年四月初派出十二人组成莎学代表团参加在美国洛杉矶举办的第六届世界莎士比亚大会，与来自世界各国及地区的代表进行广泛的接触，取得很大的收获。国际莎学主席和秘书长对我会所取得的莎学研究、莎剧演出给予高度的评价。另外，我们也介绍了台湾地区酝酿成立莎学会和举办莎剧节的事宜，他们表示赞赏和支持。

鉴于'94 上海国际莎剧节贵会与我们的愉快合作，我们期待双方的合作能进一步加强与密切。为此提出以下建议：

一、酝酿筹备多时的台湾莎学会建议在近期内尽快宣告成立，我会期望听到贵会负责人、台湾莎学会发起人张英先生能成为首任会长的佳音。

二、台湾地区将举办莎剧节定为海内外人士所关注，建议 97 年下半年举行，我会将全力协助。

三、应美国之邀，我会将组织一台“中华舞台一绝”的精品演出，约一个半小时，每个节目三至五分钟，是从全国各地精选出来的，属“国粹精品”。由演艺界名流约三十人组成。若贵会有兴趣，演出团体将乐于赴台湾地区作商业性演出。

'94 上海国际莎剧节论文集已给贵会寄发，是否收到。

随信发出香港莎学会（筹）给我会的来信，及参加世界莎学会的有关简报以供参考。

恭祝

安康！

中国莎士比亚研究会秘书长　孙福良

一九九六年七月十八日

接传真后请给我回电。来电或传真请拨打：6248××××。

李伟昉先生：

您好！

接到您的电话以后我就想怎能弄到一本拙编《中国莎士比亚批评（评论）》呢？原想从已赠出的书中要回一本转赠给您，但想来想去总觉不妥。于是去出版社，请他们帮忙。他们说书早已售完，社里存书不能出售。他们还说可到出版社的书店去看看，请他们翻一下看看是否能找到一本。说来真巧，他们从书架下面的书柜中找到了一本下架的，虽破了一些，但终究找到了。现随信寄上，请批评指正。因为书已破旧，我折价买入，没花多少钱，这本书就送给您了，作为我们初识的礼物，请笑纳！

谨颂

夏安！

以后有事来信请寄我爱人处，即130021长春市东北师大附中陈凌云。　又及

孟宪强

一九九六年七月二十四日

注："感激与怀念"，1996年因为准备为大四学生开设莎士比亚研究选修课，发现孟宪强老师1991年编有《中国莎士比亚评论》一书，到处寻找未果，便从一个老师那里要到孟老师电话并冒昧联系孟老师。没有想到孟老师竟把这件事记在心上，非常热心、主动帮我找书，居然在出版社书店找到一本，买下后寄给我。这件事让我非常感动。虽然时隔26年，但每念及此，依然令我记忆犹新，充满感激与怀念。这件事充分体现了老一辈学者对年轻学子从事莎士比亚教学与研究的殷殷关切和大力支持。

2011年搬家后一直没有找到这本书，一直心存遗憾。这次搬家在地下室发现一包未打开的书，才看到《中国莎士比亚评论》一书就在其中。当年这包书应该是被遗漏错放在了地下室。我简直喜出望外，小心擦拭后精心收藏。夹在书中的孟老师的短信，把为我找书买书的情形细节记录得很清楚，弥足珍贵！（河南大学　李伟昉）

华泉坤先生：

您好！

暑假期间收到大著，但由于我不在校，这两日才获展读。阅读《莎士比亚新论》收获很多，也感到很亲切，因为原来很多章节以论文形式发表时，我就学习过，此次又进行了新的修订，就更使我获益了。大著的特点在于对流派的梳理、现代视角的阐释及语言艺术的解读。大著不同于以往中国莎学史上的其他书，可谓独树一帜，将在莎学史上占据重要地位。

近日我将给安大学报投去《旋转的舞台：互文在京剧与莎剧之间—— 论根据莎士比亚戏剧改编的京剧〈歧王梦〉》一文，敬请批评，感谢您的大力支持！

李伟民　顿首*

二〇〇七年八月二十九日

*华泉坤教授给李伟民先生的这封信录自“孔夫子旧书网”。

莎学书简提供者简介：

朱尚刚，浙江嘉兴朱生豪纪念馆名誉馆长，主要从事朱生豪研究与译作整理。

孙福良，上海戏剧学院教授，中国莎士比亚研究会副会长，主要从事中国莎士比亚研究与莎学活动组织工作。

彭镜禧，台湾大学外国语言文学系教授，主要从事莎士比亚翻译与研究。

杨林贵，东华大学外语学院教授，中国外国文学学会莎士比亚研究会副会长，主要从事莎士比亚研究。

李伟民，四川外国语大学研究生院教授，中国外国文学学会莎士比亚研究会副会长，主要从事莎士比亚研究。

曹树钧，上海戏剧学院教授，中国莎士比亚研究会副会长，主要从事莎士比亚与曹禺研究。

李伟昉，《河南大学学报》（哲学社会科学版）主编，中国外国文学学会莎士比亚研究会常务理事，主要从事莎士比亚研究。

第七编

莎学信息

中英合拍电影《暴风雨与仲夏夜》

由中国聚本影业和英国欣纳影业（Sinner Films）联合出品制作的电影《暴风雨与仲夏夜》近日在英格兰德比郡的哈登庄园（Hadden Hall）顺利完成英国部分拍摄。该片是新冠肺炎疫情暴发以来首部开机的中英合拍电影。

2021 年 10 月 22 日，中国驻伦敦旅游办事处携手聚本影业共同举办线上发布会。驻英国使馆文化处于芃公参、驻伦敦旅游办事处薛伶主任、聚本影业董事长王强、聚本影业联合创始人王鲁娜、聚本影业联合创始人、本片制片人朱力、本片英方导演贾斯汀·查德维克（Justin Chadwick）、英方制片人兼编剧大卫·默多克（David Murdoch）、哈登庄园女主人爱德华·迈纳斯爵士夫人（Lady Edward Manners）、莎士比亚故乡斯特拉福德市前议会主席克里斯托弗·凯托（Christopher Kettle）、英方编剧波莉·考特妮（Polly Courtney）、英方摄影指导菲利克斯·克莱默（Felix Cramer）、电影主要演员等中英嘉宾在发布会上致辞，新华社、环球时报、人民网约 40 人出席活动。

《暴风雨与仲夏夜》通过莎士比亚的经典喜剧名作《驯悍记》巧妙地串联起 16 世纪英格兰，20 世纪 30 年代上海，21 世纪当代中国三个时空，讲述了三个年轻人为坚持理想拼搏、不畏困难的奋斗故事。为突出主人公、中国翻译莎翁全集第一人——朱生豪先生的卓越贡献，编剧在三段故事中浓墨重彩地描绘了艰苦的战争年代下，朱生豪翻译莎士比亚剧作的事迹。影片通过朱生豪的事迹，歌颂了中国文学家们在国难当头时的民族气节和爱国情怀，弘扬不畏艰难、精益求精的伟大时代工匠精神。

制片人朱力向观众详细介绍了本片缘起、中英合作情况以及拍摄和制作计划。英方编剧默多克表示，他在多年前第一次听到朱生豪的故事便被深深打动，这个充满勇气与毅力的故事必须被讲述出来，让英国和全世界的人们知道。这个故事讲述的是连接：莎士比亚与朱生豪的连接，英国与中国连接、世界各地人们的连接。这部电影是对中英友谊和中英文化交流的礼赞。皇家莎士比亚剧团知名演员、莎士比亚研究专家亚历珊德拉·吉尔布莱斯（Alexandra Gilbreath）动情地表示，她多次在话剧舞台上演出《驯悍记》，对这部戏有着深厚的感情。朱生豪的故事让她意识到莎翁的创作影响之深远，即便跨越时代和语言，仍然能引起情感共鸣。

本片取景地在具有千年历史的哈登庄园，这是英国现存最完整的都铎建筑风格的庄园，《简·爱》《伊丽莎白》《傲慢与偏见》等多部电影在此取景。庄园女主人迈纳斯爵士夫人表示，自己曾经在中国工作多年，对中国充满感情，当她听到这个关于中英文化交流的故事后，便立刻决定要为拍摄这部电影贡献力量。希望这部电影能够激励中英两国更多的人投身文化交流，促进两国人民的相互了解。曾推动莎士比亚故乡斯特拉福德与汤显祖故乡江西抚州开展一系列合作的凯托先生表示，自己曾经在抚州观看《牡丹亭》演出，这个讲述青年男女冲破重重阻力在一起的故事很容易让人想起《罗密欧与朱丽叶》，这充分说明人类的情感是互通的。感谢朱生豪先生的努力，让中国人民都能了解莎翁的作品。他很高兴看到在两年前，汤显祖的所有作品也被翻译成了英文。

本片拍摄同时也得到了朱生豪故乡嘉兴市以及朱生豪家人的大力支持，朱生豪之子朱尚刚特意为发布会录制了视频。他表示，中英两国艺术家选择莎士比亚和朱生豪这一穿越世纪、跨越东西的题材进行创作，体现了两国人民积极促进文化交流的强烈愿望。80 年前父亲作为莎翁作品的翻译家，为中国人民了解英国文学建立了桥梁。80 年后恰逢父亲 110 周年诞辰，这部电影又将通过影像向英国观众介绍中国文化和中国人的精神，让两国人民对彼此有更加深入的了解和认知。

于芃公参在总结发言中表示，朱生豪先生以一生精力，将其全部作品翻译成中文，使莎翁成为中国家喻户晓的名字。这是东西文明交融互鉴的伟大故事，值得被中英人民、世界人民知晓和铭记。正如郑泽光大使在 2021“天涯共此时”项目启动致辞中所说，中英两国是东西方文明的代表国家，文明因交流而多彩，因互鉴而丰富。“天涯共此时”项目将进一步拓展中英人文交流的前景，进一步促进民心相通，为中英关系改善和发展贡献力量。他表示，《暴风雨与仲夏夜》充分体现了中英文明交流互鉴的精神，也一定能不负拉近中英民心，提升中英关系的使命。新冠肺炎疫情暴发以来，中英两国许多优质文化合作项目都被迫延期或取消。本片顺利完成拍摄，为新常态下两国文化艺术领域继续开展务实合作提供了一个范例。

聚本影业　中莎

《中国莎士比亚研究》征稿启事

莎士比亚研究在世界领域具有广泛而重要的影响。一个多世纪里，几代中国学者为莎士比亚在中国传播付出了毕生的心血。前国际莎协主席菲利浦·勃劳克班克满怀激情地说："莎士比亚的春天在中国。"为了进一步推动中国莎士比亚研究的发展，四川外国语大学决定编辑出版《中国莎士比亚研究》，以全面深入地反映莎士比亚研究的最新成果。现特面向海内外莎士比亚研究专家、莎学爱好者征求莎士比亚及英国文艺复兴时代文学艺术相关原创性研究稿件。

《中国莎士比亚研究》主要集中于以下研究方向：世界莎学研究、马克思主义莎学研究、莎士比亚总体研究、莎士比亚戏剧研究、莎士比亚悲剧研究、莎士比亚喜剧研究、莎士比亚历史剧研究、莎士比亚传奇剧研究、莎士比亚十四行诗及长诗研究、莎士比亚与世界文学研究、莎士比亚戏剧改编研究、莎士比亚舞台、银幕研究、莎士比亚翻译研究、文艺复兴时期戏剧研究、莎士比亚与同时代作家研究、新古典主义莎评研究、浪漫主义莎评研究、维多利亚时代莎评研究、莎士比亚与文学思潮研究、现实主义莎评研究、心理分析莎评研究、意象研究与莎评、新批评与莎评、历史批评与莎评、神话批评与莎评、解构主义与莎评、新历史主义与莎评、女权主义与莎评、莎士比亚与现代主义与后现代主义研究、莎士比亚宗教研究、莎士比亚教学研究、中国莎学家研究、莎士比亚与"一带一路"文化艺术研究、世界著名莎剧演员和导演研究、台湾莎学研究、香港莎学研究、澳门莎学研究、莎学书评等。除上述议题外，研究者也可就自己感兴趣的其他莎学论题撰写论文。

为了保证本学术集刊的学术性、前沿性、前瞻性，《中国莎士比亚研究》本着"宁缺毋滥"的原则，以学术质量为第一前提，请勿一稿多投。

为了保证《中国莎士比亚研究》的学术质量、编辑质量和及时出版，来稿格式请参照本书"注引格式"撰写，并请作者仔细校对，尤其是对文中的"参考文献"和"注释"（应区别"参考文献"和"注释"，并在页脚和文尾分别显示）。

文稿包括中英文标题、中英文内容提要、中英文关键词、正文及参考文献。来稿请附作者信息，包括：姓名、性别、籍贯、单位、职称、学历、主要研究方向和主要成果，以及联系方式，包括：详细通信地址、邮政编码、电话、手机、电子邮箱，以便在编辑文稿时随时联系。来稿可控制在 15000 字左右。

本书不向作者收取任何费用，文稿一经发表即向作者赠送两本样书。

联系方式：

文稿撰写完成后，请以"姓名+文章标题"为题（投稿后收到自动回复，需要对稿件再次进行修改者，请以"姓名+文章标题+修订稿"为题，重新发送），发送电子邮件（用附件形式）到：zgssbyyj@163.com；同时从邮局用挂号寄送一份打印稿到：重庆市沙坪坝区壮志路 33 号，四川外国语大学莎士比亚研究中心《中国莎士比亚研究》编辑部（邮政编码：400031）。

《中国莎士比亚研究》编辑部

附《中国莎士比亚研究》格式

1. 稿件构成

中英文标题；中英文摘要（200 字左右，内容要求严格对等）；中英文关键词 3 ~ 5 个；正文；参考文献；附录（如果有）；基金资助文章应注明基金项目名称与编号；作者简介。

2. 正文格式

二级标题单独占一行，各标题层次序号一律使用阿拉伯数字表示为：1、1.1、1.2……2、2.1、2.2……

3. 文内引用文献和文末参考文献格式要求

（1）文内夹注。

正文的引文和述评所依据的文献，以夹注的形式随文在括号内注明作者姓名、出版年和引文页码，例如“(王佐良，1982：36)”。如引用多项，则按照出版年顺序排列。同一作者的参引之间用逗号分开。文献作者如果是两个人，参引时引两个人的名字。中文的格式如“(刘润清，吴一安，2000)”，英文格式在两位作者之间加“&”号。

（2）文末参考文献格式。

中外文参考文献分别以字母顺序排列，外文在前，中文在后。格式如下：

① 期刊类：作者名（姓前名后，列前两名，后加“等”）. 出版年. 文献名[J]. 刊名，卷（期）：页码.

② 普通图书类：作者名. 出版年. 书名[M]. 版本（第一版不写）. 出版地：出版者.

③ 会议论文集：引文作者名. 出版年. 引文题目[C]//论文集编者名. 会议论文集名. 出版地（会址）：出版者.

④ 文献汇编：引文作者名. 出版年. 引文题目[G]//汇编论文编者. 论文集名. 出版地：出版者.

⑤ 学位论文类：作者名. 出版年. 题目[D]. 保存地点：保存单位.

⑥ 报纸文章：作者名. 出版年. 文章名[N]. 报纸名，出版日期（版次）.

⑦ 电子文献类：作者名. 出版年. 电子文献名[文献类型标志/文献载体标志].（更新或修改日期）[引用日期]. 获取和访问路径.

另外，所列文献必须与正文中的夹注一致。如果正文中没有夹注，参考文献中不得列出。